STORIES THAT SCARED EVEN STALIN

STORIES THAT SCARED EVEN STALIN

Edited By

BRIAN FORBES
YANA YAKUBSFELD

McNae, Marlin & Mackenzie, Ltd.
Publishers, by Special Appointment
Glasgow • New York • Los Angeles
Queens Road, Glasgow, Lanarkshire G42 800 Scotland

Stories That Scared Even Stalin Copyright © 2025 by McNae, Marlin and MacKenzie Publishers, Ltd., all rights reserved. Printed in the United States of America and in the United Kingdom. Let it be known that copyright shall be protected and defended against infringement by the Publisher.

Except as permitted by the United States Copyright Act of 1976, and the UK Copyright, Designs and Patents Act of 1988, no part of this publication may be reproduced, stored in a retrieval system or transmitted, in any form or by any means, electronic, mechanical, photocopying, recording, or otherwise without the prior written permission of the Author or the Publisher.
www.m3publishers.com

ISBN-979-8-89940-927-1

Book Design by Yana Yakubsfeld

Third Printing 2025

Introduction

Iosif Vissarionovich Dzhugashvili was born in Georgia in 1878. His mother was a serf and his father was a cobbler who frequently drank and beat his wife and son mercilessly. Iosif helped his mother with laundry and cleaning, and presumably met one of her employers, a Jewish businessman named David Papismedov, who gave the young boy money and books to read as well as the encouragement to better himself. He adopted the name "Stalin" (a Russian word, the most accurate English translation of which is 'of steel') in 1913 after receiving a position on the Central Committee of the Bolshevik Party. From 1922 when he became the General Secretary of the Soviet Communist Party until his death in 1953, he ruled through cult of personality, which also involved political repression, state terror, mass deportations, persecution and killings that are well into the millions. He also transformed the Soviet Union from predominantly a peasant society to a major world industrial power in less than two decades and the Soviet Union under Josef Stalin greatly contributed to the defeat of Nazi Germany in WWII.

The title of this anthology came about as a humorous remark. But then we got to thinking, one of the most feared men in recent history also had fearful influences of his own. Josef Stalin (1878 - 1953) certainly read some if not all of the stories you will find in this volume. Though we admit, it's unlikely they contributed much to what made him so fearsome, it is curious all the same to wonder what Stalin may have enjoyed reading for 'kicks' in between stamping out villages, disobedient farmers, and political dissidents, or at least in the formative years back in Georgia when he was in school. While we're speculating, we can't also but wonder what history may have been like had Stalin's father touched the bottle a little less frequently and put more of his physical energy into tanning shoe leather instead of the hides of his wife and son.

The world of Russian literature has never really known a specific genre of 'horror' or 'suspense'. It may have to do with the fact that horror was an actual reality of life in many of the lives of Russians. But also there were strong efforts by Czar Peter the Great and later Empress Catherine II The Great to embrace European romanticism and philosophy through westernization and enlightenment of Russia and Russian culture. The literary Russians emanating from this era were more interested in politics, poetry, drama, psychology, social psychology, romance, satire and of course, historical influences in fiction.

The fact is however that the Russian country has always had a rich history of folklore, spiritualism and superstition that to this day can not be dimmed by even the most fervent efforts at enlightenment. And many of the great writers of Russian, while educated at the finest Russian or Western European academies and Universities, were first told or listened to stories in their formative years by surfs, priests, or even collective farmers who were charged with the care of these imaginative youths. It was during these fertile times that writers such as Tolstoy, Gogol, Sologub, Pushkin and Turgenev got their first visits from the Devil and visions of ghosts, possessed animals and even vampires. These encounters would return to them later in life, many times after they had already established themselves in the critical communities and had both worked out their angst through earlier expression, as well as the luxury of fantasy.

Writers such as Dostoevsky and Chekhov had difficult enough personal lives and as a result, few demons or devils appeared in their works. Psychology and the inner workings of the tortured mind provided ample inspiration for literary vehicles and character studies.

Of all of the great Russian authors, the one who would be most expected to have entries in an anthology of horror stories would be Nikolai Gogol (1809 – 1852). Gogol was born in Ukraine and had a lot of exposure early on to the great folklore of this land. His works in "Evenings on a Farm Near Dikanka" are considered to be his greatest early works and those which brought him notoriety in the literary world. A selection from "Dikanka", "Christmas Eve" is included in this volume. Gogol became known for his dark views of society and he became known for his mix of the macabre with fantasy in both drama and satire. Also here is Gogol's "Viy" which was filmed as "Black Sabbath", and "The Overcoat", considered by many to be the finest piece of Russian short fiction ever written.

Here in this volume we have also selected "The Queen of Spades" by Alexander Pushkin (1799 – 1837). While Pushkin was better known as a poet, toward the end of his young life (he was mortally wounded in a duel, attempting to defend the honor of his wife) his works were becoming more narrative and paralleled some of the more sensitive aspects of his own life.

Ivan Turgenev (1818 – 1883) is represented here with "The Adventure of Second Lieutenant Bubnov", and "The Dog". Turgenev was best known for realistic portrayal of sociology, while his contemporaries, Dostoevsky and Tolstoy had more religious and spiritual interests. What is unusual is that "The Adventure of Second Lieutenant Bubnov" is a story more of a style one would have expected Tolstoy to have written, and Tolstoy's "The Death of Ivan Ilyich" seems on the surface at least, to be more in the realistic style of Turgenev. While Turgenev had a close personal relationship with Leo Tolstoy, it was tense and the two did not agree philosophically or theologically.

Leo Tolstoy (1828 – 1910) is also represented in this volume with a lighter, delightful tale called, "How Much Land Does A Man Need?" The tale, as moralistic as it is entertaining, was written in 1886 at a time when Tolstoy was feeling tremendous feelings of guilt over the large amount of land he owned. He gave up his property in 1910 in order to fulfill a simpler life, but died shortly thereafter.

Fyodor Sologub (1863 – 1927) had a very sardonic attitude toward life and its values and was one of the leaders of the symbolist movement in culture. He would often employ sadistic and perverse ideas to underlie the themes in his work.

Although Anton Chekhov (1860 – 1904) is known best for his character studies in his drama and short fiction, he occasionally wrote fantasy into his work, if for no other reason than to emphasize a character trait. We have chosen several short pieces to include in this volume from his early writings.

We have included two selections from the pen of Fyodor Dostoevsky (1821 – 1881). A piece of social satire called, "Bobok", presented as a conversation in a graveyard with deceased members of Russian society, and one of his early works, "The Double" which is a short novel concerning a man losing his will and sanity to his alter ego.

The editors would like to gratefully acknowledge the incomparable translations of Constance Garnett and the late dramatist and translator Arnold Hinchliffe who have made it possible to enjoy the great works of Russian literature in the English language while preserving the integrity of the authors' ideals and original works.

Первая страница рукописи рассказа А. П. Чехова
«Кривое зеркало» стр. 11

First page of Anton Chekhov's original manuscript of
"The Crooked Mirror" - Courtesy Arnold Hinchliffe

Table of Contents

Viy	*Nikolai Gogol*	1
How Much Land Does a Man Need?	*Leo Tolstoy*	37
The Queen of Spades	*Alexander Pushkin*	53
The Crooked Mirror	*Anton Chekhov*	79
The Death of Ivan Ilyich	*Leo Tolstoy*	83
The Adventure of Second Lieutenant Bubnov	*Ivan Turgenev*	137
A Terrible Night	*Anton Chekhov*	145
The Dog	*Ivan Turgenev*	151
A Dead Body	*Anton Chekhov*	165
The Overcoat	*Nikolai Gogol*	171
Christmas Eve	*Nikolai Gogol*	199
Bobok	*Fyodor Dostoevsky*	243
Invoker of the Beast	*Fyodor Sologub*	261
A Night in the Graveyard	*Anton Chekhov*	269
The Double	*Fyodor Dostoevsky*	273

Viy

Nikolai Gogol

As soon as the rather musical seminary bell which hung at the gate of the Bratsky Monastery rang out every morning in Kiev, schoolboys and students hurried thither in crowds from all parts of the town. Students of grammar, rhetoric, philosophy and theology trudged to their class-rooms with exercise-books under their arms. The grammarians were quite small boys: they shoved each other as they went along and quarrelled in a shrill alto; they almost all wore muddy or tattered clothes, and their pockets were full of all manner of rubbish, such as knuckle-bones, whistles made of feathers, or a half-eaten pie, sometimes even little sparrows, one of whom suddenly chirruping at an exceptionally quiet moment in the class-room would cost its owner some sound whacks on both hands and sometimes a thrashing. The rhetoricians walked with more dignity; their clothes were often quite free from holes; on the other hand, their countenances almost all bore some decoration, after the style of a figure of rhetoric; either one eye had sunk right under the forehead, or there was a monstrous swelling in place of a lip, or some other disfigurement. They talked and swore among themselves in tenor voices. The philosophers conversed an octave lower in the scale; they had nothing in their pockets but strong, cheap tobacco. They laid in no stores of any sort, but ate on the spot anything they came across; they smelt of pipes and vodka to such a distance that a passing workman would sometimes stop a long way off and sniff the air like a setter dog.

As a rule the market was just beginning to stir at that hour, and the women with bread-rings, rolls, melon seeds, and poppy cakes would tug at the skirts of those whose coats were of fine cloth or some cotton material.

"This way, young gentlemen, this way!" they kept saying from all sides: "here are bread-rings, poppy cakes, twists, good white rolls; they are really good! Made with honey! I baked them myself."

Another woman lifting up a sort of long twist made of dough would cry: "Here's a bread-stick! Buy my bread-stick, young gentlemen!"

"Don't buy anything off her; see what a horrid woman she is, her nose is nasty and her hands are dirty...."

But the women were afraid to worry the philosophers and the theologians, for the latter were fond of taking things to taste and always a good handful.

On reaching the seminary, the crowd dispersed to their various classes, which were held in low-pitched but fairly large rooms, with little windows, wide doorways, and dirty benches. The class-room was at once filled with all sorts of buzzing sounds: the "auditors" heard their pupils repeat their lessons; the shrill alto of a grammarian rang out, and the windowpane responded with almost the same note; in a corner a rhetorician, whose mouth and thick lips should have belonged at least to a student of philosophy, was droning something in a bass voice, and all that could be heard at a distance was "Boo, boo, boo ... " The "auditors," as they heard the lesson, kept glancing with one eye under the bench, where a roll or a cheese-cake or some pumpkin seeds were peeping out of a scholar's pocket.

When this learned crowd managed to arrive a little too early, or when they knew that the professors would be later than usual, then by general consent they got up a fight, and everyone had to take part in it, even the monitors whose duty it was to maintain discipline and look after the morals of all the students. Two theologians usually settled the arrangements for the battle: whether each class was to defend itself individually, or whether all were to be divided into two parties, the bursars and the seminarists. In any case the grammarians first began the attack, and, as soon as the rhetoricians entered the fray, they ran away and stood at points of vantage to watch the contest. Then the devotees of philosophy, with long black moustaches, joined in, and finally those of theology, very thick in the neck and attired in shocking trousers, took part. It commonly ended in theology beating all the rest, and the philosophers, rubbing their ribs, would be forced into the class-room and sat down on the benches to rest. The professor, who had himself at one time taken part in such battles, could, on entering the class, see in a minute from the flushed faces of his audience that the battle had been a good one and, while he was caning a rhetorician on the fingers, in another class-room another professor would be smacking philosophy's hands with a wooden bat. The theologians were dealt with in quite a different way: they received, to use the expression of a professor of theology, "a peck of peas apiece," in other words, a liberal drubbing with short leather thongs.

On holidays and ceremonial occasions the bursars and the seminarists went from house to house as mummers. Sometimes they acted a play, and then the most distinguished figure was always some theologian, almost as tall as the belfry of Kiev, who took the part of Herodias or Potiphar's wife. They received in payment a piece of linen, or a sack of millet or half a boiled goose, or something of the sort. All this crowd of students —the seminarists as well as the bursars, with whom they maintain an hereditary feud—were exceedingly badly off for means of subsistence, and at the same time had extraordinary appetites, so that to reckon how many dumplings each of them tucked away at supper would be utterly impossible, and therefore the voluntary offerings of prosperous citizens could not be sufficient for them. Then the "senate" of the philosophers and theologians despatched the grammarians and rhetoricians, under the supervision of a philosopher (who sometimes took part in the raid himself), with sacks on their shoulders to plunder the kitchen gardens—and pumpkin porridge was made in the bursars' quarters. The members of the "senate" ate such masses of melons that next day their "auditors" heard two lessons from them instead of one, one coming from their lips, another muttering in their stomachs. Both the bursars and the seminarists wore long garments resembling frock coats, "prolonged to the utmost limit," a technical expression signifying below their heels.

The most important event for the seminarists was the coming of the vacation: it began in June, when they usually dispersed to their homes. Then the whole high-road was dotted with philosophers, grammarians and theologians. Those who had nowhere to go went to stay with some comrade. The philosophers and theologians took a situation, that is, undertook the tuition of the children in some prosperous family, and received in payment a pair of new boots or sometimes even a coat. The whole crowd trailed along together like a gipsy encampment, boiled their porridge, and slept in the fields. Everyone hauled along a sack in which he had a shirt and a pair of leg-wrappers. The theologians were particularly careful and precise: to avoid wearing out their boots, they took them off, hung them on sticks' and carried them on their shoulders, particularly if it was muddy; then, tucking their trousers up above their knees, they splashed fearlessly through the puddles. When they saw a village they turned off the high-road and, going up to any house which seemed a little better looking than the rest, stood in a row before the windows and began singing a chant at the top of their voices. The master of the house, some old Cossack villager, would listen to them for a long time, his head propped on his hands, then he would sob bitterly and say, turning to his wife: "Wife! What the scholars are singing must be very deep; bring them fat bacon and anything else that we have." And a whole bowl of dumplings was emptied into the sack, a good-sized piece of bacon, several flat loaves, and sometimes a trussed hen would go into it too. Fortified with such stores, the grammarians, rhetoricians, philosophers and theologians went on their way again. Their numbers lessened, however, the further they went. Almost all wandered off to-wards their homes, and only those were left whose parental abodes were further away.

Once, at the time of such a migration, three students turned off the high-road in order to replenish their store of provisions at the first home-stead they could find, for their sacks had long been empty. They were the theologian, Halyava; the philosopher, Homa Brut; and the rhetorician, Tibery Gorobets.

The theologian was a well grown broad-shouldered fellow; he had an extremely odd habit—anything that lay within his reach he invariably stole. In other circumstances, he was of an excessively gloomy temper, and when he was drunk he used to hide in the rank grass, and the seminarists had a lot of trouble to find him there.

The philosopher, Homa Brut, was of a cheerful temper, he was very fond of lying on his back, smoking a pipe; when he was drinking he always engaged musicians and danced the trepak. He often had a taste of the "peck of peas," but took it with perfect philosophical indifference, saying that there is no escaping what has to be. The rhetorician, Tibery Gorobets, had not yet the right to wear a moustache, to drink vodka, and to smoke a pipe. He only wore a curl round his ear, and so his character was as yet hardly formed; but, judging from the big bumps on the forehead, with which he often appeared in class, it might be presumed that he would make a good fighter. The theologian, Halyava, and the philosopher, Homa, often pulled him by the forelock as a sign of their savour, and employed him as their messenger.

It was evening when they turned off the high-road; the sun had only just set and the warmth of the day still lingered in the air. The theologian and the philosopher walked along in silence smoking their pipes; the rhetorician, Tibery Gorobets, kept knocking off the heads of the wayside thistles with his stick. The road ran between scattered groups of oak and nut trees standing here and there in the meadows. Sloping uplands and little hills, green and round as cupolas, were interspersed here and there about the plain. The cornfields of ripening wheat, which came into view in two places, showed that some village must soon be seen. It was more than an hour, however, since they had passed the cornfields, yet they had come upon no dwelling. The sky was now completely wrapped in darkness, and only in the west there was a pale streak left of the glow of sunset.

"What the devil does it mean?" said the philosopher, Homa Brut. "It looked as though there must be a village in a minute."

The theologian did not speak, he gazed at the surrounding country, then put his pipe back in his mouth, and they continued on their way.

"Upon my soul!" the philosopher said, stopping again, "not a devil's fist to be seen."

"Maybe some village will turn up further on," said the theologian, not removing his pipe.

But meantime night had come on, and a rather dark night. Small storm clouds increased the gloom, and by every token they could expect neither stars nor moon. The students noticed that they had lost their way and for a long time had been walking off the road.

The philosopher, after feeling about with his feet in all directions, said at last, abruptly: "I say, where's the road?"

The theologian did not speak for a while, then after pondering, he brought out: "Yes, it is a dark night."

The rhetorician walked off to one side and tried on his hands and knees to feel for the road, but his hands came upon nothing but foxes' holes. On all sides of them there was the steppe, which, it seemed, no one had ever crossed.

The travellers made another effort to press on a little, but there was the same wilderness in all directions. The philosopher tried shouting, but his voice seemed completely lost on the steppe, and met with no reply. All they heard was, a little afterwards, a faint moaning like the howl of a wolf.

"I say, what's to be done?" said the philosopher.

"Why, halt and sleep in the open!" said the theologian, and he felt in his pocket for flint and tinder to light his pipe again. But the philosopher could not agree to this: it was always his habit at night to put away a quarter loaf of bread and four pounds of fat bacon, and he was conscious on this occasion of an insufferable sense of loneliness in his stomach. Besides, in spite of his cheerful temper, the philosopher was rather afraid of wolves.

"No, Halyava, we can't," he said. "What, stretch out and lie down like a dog, without a bite or a sup of anything? Let's make another try for it; maybe we shall stumble on some dwelling-place and get at least a drink of vodka for supper."

At the word "vodka" the theologian spat to one side and brought out: "Well, of course, it's no use staying in the open."

The students walked on, and to their intense delight caught the sound of barking in the distance. Listening which way it came from, they walked on more boldly and a little later saw a light.

"A village! It really is a village!" said the philosopher.

He was not mistaken in his supposition; in a little while they actually saw a little homestead consisting of only two cottages looking into the same farmyard. There was a light in the windows; a dozen plum trees stood up by the fence. Looking through the cracks in the paling-gate the students saw a yard filled with carriers' waggons. Stars peeped out here and there in the sky at the moment.

"Look, mates, don't let's be put off! We must get a night's lodging somehow!"

The three learned gentlemen banged on the gates with one accord and shouted, "Open!"

The door of one of the cottages creaked, and a minute later they saw before them an old woman in sheepskin.

"Who is there?" she cried, with a hollow cough.

"Give us a night's lodging, granny; we have lost our way; a night in the open is as bad as a hungry belly."

"What manner of folks may you be?"

"Oh, harmless folks: Halyava, a theologian; Brut, a philosopher; and Gorobets, a rhetorician."

"I can't," grumbled the old woman. "The yard is crowded with folk and every corner in the cottage is full. Where am I to put you? And such great hulking fellows, too! Why, it would knock my cottage to pieces if I put such fellows in it. I know these philosophers and theologians; if one began taking in these drunken fellows, there'd soon be no home left. Be off, be off! There's no place for you here!"

"Have pity on us, granny! How can you let Christian souls perish for no rhyme or reason ? Put us where you please; and if we do aught amiss or anything else, may our arms be withered, and God only knows what befall us—so there!"

"Very well," she said, as though reconsidering, "I'll let you in, but I'll put you all in different places; for my mind won't be at rest if you are all together."

"That's as you please; we'll make no objection," answered the students. The gate creaked and they went into the yard.

"Well, granny," said the philosopher, following the old woman, "how would it be, as they say ... upon my soul I feel as though somebody were driving a cart in my stomach: not a morsel has passed my lips all day."

"What next will he want!" said the old woman. "No, I've nothing to give you, and the oven's not been heated to-day."

"But we'd pay for it all," the philosopher went on, "to-morrow morning, in hard cash. Yes!" he added in an undertone, "the devil a bit you'll get!"

"Go in, go in! and you must be satisfied with what you're given. Fine young gentlemen the devil has brought us!"

Homa the philosopher was thrown into utter dejection by these words, but his nose was suddenly aware of the odour of dried fish; he glanced towards the trousers of the theologian who was walking at his side, and saw a huge fish-tail sticking out of his pocket. The theologian had already succeeded in filching a whole carp from a waggon. And as he had done this from no interested motive but simply from habit, and, quite forgetting his carp, was already looking about for anything else he could carry off, having no mind to miss even a broken wheel, the philosopher slipped his hand into his friend's pocket, as though it were his own, and pulled out the carp.

The old woman put the students in their several places: the rhetorician she kept in the cottage, the theologian she locked in an empty closet, the philosopher she assigned a sheep's pen, also empty.

The latter, on finding himself alone, instantly devoured the carp, examined the hurdle-walls of the pen, kicked an inquisitive pig that woke up and thrust its snout in from the next pen, and turned over on his right side to fall into a sound sleep. All at once the low door opened, and the old woman bending down stepped into the pen.

"What is it, granny, what do you want?" said the philosopher. But the old woman came towards him with outstretched arms.

"Aha, ha!" thought the philosopher. "No, my dear, you are too old!" He turned a little away, but the old woman unceremoniously approached him again.

"Listen, granny!" said the philosopher. "It's a fast time now; and I am a man who wouldn't sin in a fast for a thousand golden pieces."

But the old woman opened her arms and tried to catch him without saying a word.

The philosopher was frightened, especially when he noticed a strange glitter in her eyes. "Granny, what is it? Go—go away—God bless you!" he cried.

The old woman said not a word, but tried to clutch him in her arms.

He leapt on to his feet, intending to escape; but the old woman stood in the doorway, fixed her glittering eyes on him and again began approaching him.

The philosopher tried to push her back with his hands, but to his surprise found that his arms would not rise, his legs would not move, and he perceived with horror that even his voice would not obey him; words hovered on his lips without a sound. He heard nothing but the beating of his heart. He saw the old woman approach him. She folded his arms, bent his head down, leapt with the swiftness of a cat upon his back, and struck him with a broom on the side; and he, prancing like a horse, carried her on his shoulders. All this happened so quickly that the philosopher scarcely knew what he was doing. He clutched his knees in both hands, trying to stop his legs from moving, but to his extreme amazement they were lifted against his will and executed capers more swiftly than a Circassian racer. Only when they had left the farm, and the wide plain lay stretched before them with a forest black as coal on one side, he said to himself: "Aha! she's a witch!"

The waning crescent of the moon was shining in the sky. The timid radiance of midnight lay mistily over the earth, light as a transparent veil. The forests, the meadows, the sky, the dales, all seemed as though slumbering with open eyes; not a breeze fluttered anywhere; there was a damp warmth in the freshness of the night; the shadows of the trees and bushes fell on the sloping plain in pointed wedge shapes like comets. Such was the night when Homa Brut, the philosopher, set off galloping with a mysterious rider on his back. He was aware of an exhausting, unpleasant, and at the same time, voluptuous sensation assailing his heart. He bent his head and saw that the grass which had been almost under his feet seemed growing at a depth far away, and that above it there lay water, transparent as a mountain stream, and the grass seemed to be at the bottom of a clear sea, limpid to its very depths; anyway, he saw clearly in it his own reflection with the old woman sitting on his back. He saw shining there a sun instead of the moon; he heard the bluebells ringing as they bent their little heads; he saw a water-nymph float out from behind the reeds, there was the gleam of her leg and back, rounded and supple, all brightness and shimmering. She turned towards him and now her face came nearer, with eyes clear, sparkling, keen, with singing that pierced to the heart; now it was on the surface, and shaking with sparkling laughter it moved away; and now she turned on her back, and her cloud-like breasts, dead-white like unglazed china, gleamed in the sun at the edges of their white, soft and supple roundness. Little bubbles of water like beads bedewed them. She was all quivering and laughing in the water. . . .

Did he see this or did he not? Was he awake or dreaming? But what was that? The wind or music? It is ringing and ringing and eddying and coming closer and piercing to his heart with an insufferable thrill. . . .

"What does it mean?" the philosopher wondered, looking down as he flew along, full speed. The sweat was streaming from him. He was aware of a fiendishly voluptuous feeling, he felt a stabbing, exhaustingly terrible delight. It often seemed to him as though his heart had melted away, and with terror he clutched at it. Worn out, desperate, he began trying to recall all the prayers he knew. He went through all the exorcisms against evil spirits, and all at once felt somewhat refreshed; he felt that his step was growing slower, the witch's hold upon his back seemed feebler, thick grass touched him, and now he saw nothing extraordinary in it. The clear, crescent moon was shining in the sky.

"Good!" the philosopher Homa thought to himself, and he began repeating the exorcisms almost aloud. At last, quick as lightning, he sprang from under the old woman and in his turn leapt on her back. The old woman, with a tiny tripping step, ran so fast that her rider could scarcely breathe. The earth flashed by under him; everything was clear in the moonlight, though the moon was not full; the ground was smooth, but everything flashed by so rapidly that it was confused and indistinct. He snatched up a piece of wood that lay on the road and began whacking the old woman with all his might. She uttered wild howls; at first they were angry and menacing, then they grew fainter, sweeter, clearer, then rang out gently like delicate silver bells that stabbed him to the heart; and the thought flashed through his mind: was it really an old woman?

"Oh, I can do no more!" she murmured, and sank exhausted on the ground.

He stood up and looked into her face (there was the glow of sunrise, and the golden domes of the Kiev churches were gleaming in the distance): before him lay a lovely creature with luxuriant tresses all in disorder and eyelashes as long as arrows. Senseless she tossed her bare white arms and moaned, looking upwards with eyes full of tears.

Homa trembled like a leaf on a tree; he was overcome by pity and a strange emotion and timidity, feelings he could not himself explain. He set off running, full speed. His heart throbbed uneasily as he went, and he could not account for the strange new feeling that had taken possession of it. He did not want to go back to the farm; he hastened to Kiev, pondering all the way on this incomprehensible adventure.

There was scarcely a student left in the town. All had dispersed about the countryside, either to situations, or simply without them; because in the villages of Little Russia they could get dumplings, cheese, sour cream, and puddings as big as a hat without paying a kopeck for them. The big rambling house in which the students were lodged was absolutely empty, and although the philosopher rummaged in every corner, and even felt in all the holes and cracks in the roof, he could not find a bit of bacon or even a stale roll such as were commonly hidden there by the students.

The philosopher, however, soon found means to improve his lot: he walked whistling three times through the market, finally winked at a young widow in a yellow bonnet who was selling ribbons, shot and wheels—and was that very day regaled with wheat dumplings, a chicken. . . in short, there is no telling what was on the table laid for him in a little mud house in the middle of a cherry orchard.

That same evening the philosopher was seen in a tavern: he was lying on the bench, smoking a pipe as his habit was, and in the sight of all he flung the Jew who kept the house a gold coin. A mug stood before him. He looked at all that came in and went out with eyes full of cool satisfaction, and thought no more of his extraordinary adventure.

Meanwhile rumours were circulating everywhere that the daughter of one of the richest Cossack sotniks,* who lived nearly forty miles from Kiev, had returned one day from a walk, terribly injured, hardly able to crawl home to her father's house, was lying at the point of death, and had expressed a wish that one of the Kiev seminarists, Homa Brut, should read the prayers over her and the psalms for three days after her death. The philosopher heard of this from the rector himself, who summoned him to his room and informed him that he was to set of on the journey without any delay, that the noble sotnik had sent servants and a carriage to fetch him.

The philosopher shuddered from an unaccountable feeling which he could not have explained to himself. A dark presentiment told him that something evil was awaiting him. Without knowing why, he bluntly declared that he would not go.

"Listen, Domine Homa!" said the rector. (On some occasions he expressed himself very courteously with those under his authority.) "Who the devil is asking you whether you want to go or not? All I have to tell you is that if you go on jibbing and making difficulties, I'll order you such a wracking with a young birch tree, on your back and the rest of you, that there will be no need for you to go to the bath after."

The philosopher, scratching behind his ear, went out without uttering a word, proposing at the first suitable opportunity to put his trust in his heels.

---

* An officer in command of a company of Cossacks, consisting originally of a hundred, but in later times of a larger number.—(Translator's Note.)

Plunged in thought he went down the steep staircase that led into a yard shut in by poplars, and stood still for a minute, hearing quite distinctly the voice of the rector giving orders to his butler and some one else—probably one of the servants sent to fetch him by the sotnik.

"Thank his honour for the grain and the eggs," the rector was saying: "and tell him that as soon as the books about which he writes are ready I will send them at once, I have already given them to a scribe to be copied, and don't forget, my good man, to mention to his honour that I know there are excellent fish at his place, especially sturgeon, and he might on occasion send some; here in the market it's bad and dear. And you, Yavtuh, give the young fellows a cup of vodka each, and bind the philosopher or he'll be off directly."

"There, the devil's son!" the philosopher thought to himself. "He scented it out, the wily long-legs!" He went down and saw a covered chaise, which he almost took at first for a baker's oven on wheels. It was, indeed, as deep as the oven in which bricks are baked. It was only the ordinary Cracow carriage in which Jews travel fifty together with their wares to all the towns where they smell out a fair. Six healthy and stalwart Cossacks, no longer young, were waiting for him. Their tunics of fine cloth, with tassels, showed that they belonged to a rather important and wealthy master; some small scars proved that they had at some time been in battle, not ingloriously.

"What's to be done? What is to be must be!" the philosopher thought to himself and, turning to the Cossacks, he said aloud: "Good day to you, comrades!"-

"Good health to you, master philosopher," some of the Cossacks replied.

"So I am to get in with you? It's a goodly chaise!" he went on, as he clambered in, "we need only hire some musicians and we might dance here."

"Yes, it's a carriage of ample proportions," said one of the Cossacks, seating himself on the box beside the coachman, who had tied a rag over his head to replace the cap which he had managed to leave behind at a pot-house. The other five and the philosopher crawled into the recesses of the chaise and settled themselves on sacks filled with various purchases they had made in the town. "It would be interesting to know," said the philosopher, "if this chaise were loaded up with goods of some sort, salt for instance, or iron wedges, how many horses would be needed then?"

"Yes," the Cossack, sitting on the box, said after a pause, "it would need a sufficient number of horses."

After this satisfactory reply the Cossack thought himself entitled to hold his tongue for the remainder of the journey.

The philosopher was extremely desirous of learning more in detail, who this sotnik was, what he was like, what had been heard about his daughter who in such a strange way returned home and was found on the point of death, and whose story was now connected with his own, what was being done in the house, and how things were there. He addressed the Cossacks with inquiries, but no doubt they too were philosophers, for by way of a reply. they remained silent, smoking their pipes and lying on their backs. Only one of them turned to the driver on the box with a brief order. "Mind, Overko, you old booby, when you are near the tavern on the Tchuhraylovo road, don't forget to stop and wake me and the other chaps, if any should chance to drop asleep."

After this he fell asleep rather audibly. These instructions were, how-ever, quite unnecessary for, as soon as the gigantic chaise drew near the pot-house, all the Cossacks with one voice shouted: "Stop!" Moreover, Overko's horses were already trained to stop of themselves at every pot-house.

In spite of the hot July day, they all got out of the chaise and went into the low-pitched dirty room, where the Jew who kept the house hastened to receive his old friends with every sign of delight. The Jew brought from under the skirt of his coat some ham sausages, and, putting them on the table, turned his back at once on this food forbidden by the Talmud. All the Cossacks sat down round the table; earthenware mugs were set for each of the guests. Homa had to take part in the general festivity, and, as Little Russians infallibly begin kissing each other or weeping when they are drunk, soon the whole room resounded with smacks. "I say, Spirid, a kiss." "Come here, Dorosh, I want to embrace you!"

One Cossack with grey moustaches, a little older than the rest, propped his cheek on his hand and began sobbing bitterly at the thought that he had no father nor mother and was all alone in the world. Another one, much given to moralising, persisted in consoling him, saying: "Don't cry; upon my soul, don't cry! What is there in it . . . ? The Lord knows best, you know."

The one whose name was Dorosh became extremely inquisitive, and, turning to the philosopher Homa, kept asking him: "I should like to know what they teach you in the college. Is it the same as what the deacon reads in church, or something different?"

"Don't ask!" the sermonising Cossack said emphatically: "let it be as it is, God knows what is wanted, God knows everything."

"No, I want to know," said Dorosh, "what is written there in those books? Maybe it is quite different from what the deacon reads." "Oh, my goodness, my goodness!" said the sermonizing worthy, "and the outside of the sotnik's house; but, though he stared his hardest, nothing could be seen distinctly; the house looked to him like a bear; the chimney turned into the rector. The philosopher gave it up and went to sleep.

When he woke up, the whole house was in commotion: the sotnik's daughter had died in the night. Servants were running hurriedly to and fro; some old women were crying; an inquisitive crowd was looking through the fence at the house, as though something might be seen there. The philosopher began examining at his leisure the objects he could not make out in the night. The sotnik's house was a little, low-pitched building, such as was usual in Little Russia in old days; its roof was of thatch; a small, high, pointed gable with a little window that looked like an eye turned upwards, was painted in blue and yellow flowers and red crescents; it was supported on oak posts, rounded above and hexagonal below, with carving at the top. Under the gable was a little porch with seats on each side. There were verandahs round the house resting on similar posts, some of them carved in spirals. A tall pyramidal pear-tree, with trembling leaves, made a patch of green in front of the house. Two rows of barns for storing grain stood in the middle of the yard, forming a sort of wide street leading to the house. Beyond the barns, close to the gate, stood facing each other two three-cornered store-houses, also thatched. Each triangular wall was painted in various designs and had a little door in it. On one of them was depicted a Cossack sitting on a barrel, holding a mug above his head with the inscription: "I'll drink it all!" On the other, there was a bottle, flagons, and at the sides, by way of ornament, a horse upside down, a pipe, a tambourine, and the inscription: "Wine is the Cossack's comfort!" A drum and brass trumpets could be seen through the huge window in the loft of one of the barns. At the gates stood two cannons. Everything showed that the master of the house was fond of merrymaking, and that the yard often resounded with the shouts of revellers. There were two windmills outside the gate.

Behind the house stretched gardens, and through the tree-tops the dark caps of chimneys were all that could be seen of cottages smothered in green bushes. The whole village lay on the broad sloping side of a hill. The steep side, at the very foot of which lay the courtyard, made a screen from the north. Looked at from below, it seemed even steeper, and here and there on its tall top uneven stalks of rough grass stood up black against the clear sky; its bare aspect was somehow depressing; its clay soil was hollowed out by the fall and trickle of rain. Two cottages stood at some distance from each other on its steep slope; one of them was over-shadowed by the branches of a spreading apple-tree, banked up with soil and supported by short stakes near the root. The apples, knocked down by the wind, were falling right into the master's courtyard. The road, coiling about the hill from the very top, ran down beside the courtyard to the village. When the philosopher scanned its terrific steepness and recalled their journey down it the previous night, he came to the conclusion that either the sotnik had very clever horses or that the Cossacks had very strong heads to have managed, even when drunk, to escape flying head over heels with the immense chaise and baggage. The philosopher was standing on the very highest point in the yard. When he turned and looked in the opposite direction he saw quite a different view. The village sloped away into a plain. Meadows stretched as far as the eye could see; their brilliant verdure was deeper in the distance, and whole rows of villages looked like dark patches in it, though they must have been more than fifteen miles away. On the right of the meadowlands was a line of hills, and a hardly perceptible streak of flashing light and darkness showed where the Dnieper ran.

"Ah, a splendid spot!" said the philosopher, "this would be the place to live, fishing in the Dnieper and the ponds, bird-catching with nets, or shooting king-snipe and little bustard. Though I do believe there would be a few great bustards too in those meadows! One could dry lots of fruit, too, and sell it in the town, or, better still, make vodka of it, for there's no drink to compare with fruit-vodka. But it would be just as well to consider how to slip away from here."

He noticed outside the fence a little path completely overgrown with weeds; he was mechanically setting his foot on it with the idea of simply going first out for a walk, and then stealthily passing between the cottages and dashing out into the open country, when he suddenly felt a rather strong hand on his shoulder.

15

Behind him stood the old Cossack who had on the previous evening so bitterly bewailed the death of his father and mother and his own solitary state.

"It's no good your thinking of making off, Mr. Philosopher!" he said: "this isn't the sort of establishment you can run away from; and the roads are bad, too, for anyone on foot; you had better come to the master: he's been expecting you this long time in the parlour."

"Let us go! To be sure . . . I'm delighted," said the philosopher, and he followed the Cossack.

The sotnik, an elderly man with grey moustaches and an expression of gloomy sadness, was sitting at a table in the parlour, his head propped on his hands. He was about fifty; but the deep despondency on his face and its wan pallor showed that his soul had been crushed and shattered at one blow, and all his old gaiety and noisy merrymaking had gone for ever. When Homa went in with the old Cossack, he removed one hand from his face and gave a slight nod in response to their low bows.

Homa and the Cossack stood respectfully at the door.

"Who are you, where do you come from, and what is your calling, good man?" said the sotnik, in a voice neither friendly nor ill-humoured. "A bursar, student in philosophy, Homa Brut ..."

"Who was your father?"

"I don't know, honoured sir."

"Your mother?"

"I don't know my mother either. It is reasonable to suppose, of course, that I had a mother; but who she was and where she came from, and when she lived—upon my soul, good sir, I don't know."

The old man paused and seemed to sink into a reverie for a minute. "How did you come to know my daughter?"

"I didn't know her, honoured sir, upon my word, I didn't. I have never had anything to do with young ladies, never in my life. Bless them, saving your presence!"

"Why did she fix on you and no other to read the psalms over her?" The philosopher shrugged his shoulders. "God knows how to make that out. It's a well-known thing, the gentry are for ever taking fancies that the most learned man couldn't explain, and the proverb says: 'The devil himself must dance at the master's bidding.' "

"Are you telling the truth, philosopher?"

"May I be struck down by thunder on the spot if I'm not."

"If she had but lived one brief moment longer," the sotnik said to himself mournfully, "I should have learned all about it. 'Let no one else read over me, but send, father, at once to the Kiev Seminary and fetch the bursar, Homa Brut; let him pray three nights for my sinful soul. He knows . . . !' But what he knows, I did not hear: she, poor darling, could say no more before she died. You, good man, are no doubt well known for your holy life and pious works, and she, maybe, heard tell of you."

"Who? I?" said the philosopher, stepping back in amazement. "I—holy life!" he articulated, looking straight in the sotnik's face. "God be with you, sir! What are you talking about! Why—though it's not a seemly thing to speak of—I paid the baker's wife a visit on Maundy Thursday."

"Well . . . I suppose there must be some reason for fixing on you. You must begin your duties this very day."

"As to that, I would tell your honour . . . Of course, any man versed in holy scripture may, as far as in him lies . . . but a deacon or a sacristan would be better fitted for it. They are men of understanding, and know how it is all done; while I . . . Besides I haven't the right voice for it, and I myself am good for nothing. I'm not the figure for it."

"Well, say what you like, I shall carry out all my darling's wishes, I will spare nothing. And if for three nights from to-day you duly recite the prayers over her, I will reward you, if not . . . I don't advise the devil himself to anger me."

The last words were uttered by the sotnik so vigorously that the philosopher fully grasped their significance.

"Follow me!" said the sotnik.

They went out into the hall. The sotnik opened the door into another room, opposite the first. The philosopher paused a minute in the hall to blow his nose and crossed the threshold with unaccountable apprehension.

The whole floor was covered with red cotton stuff. On a high table in the corner under the holy images lay the body of the dead girl on a coverlet of dark blue velvet adorned with gold fringe and tassels. Tall wax candles, entwined with sprigs of guelder rose, stood at her feet and head, shedding a dim light that was lost in the brightness of daylight. The dead girl's face was hidden from him by the inconsolable father, who sat down facing her with his back to the door. The philosopher was impressed by the words he heard:

"I am grieving, my dearly beloved daughter, not that in the flower of your age you have left the earth, to my sorrow and mourning, without living your allotted span; I grieve, my darling, that I know not him, my bitter foe, who was the cause of your death. And if I knew the man who could but dream of hurting you, or even saying anything unkind of you, I swear to God he should not see his children again, if he be old as I, nor his father and mother, if he be of that time of life, and his body should be cast out to be devoured by the birds and beasts of the steppe! But my grief it is, my wild marigold, my birdie, light of my eyes, that I must live out my days without comfort, wiping with the skirt of my coat the trickling tears that flow from my old eyes, while my enemy will be making merry and secretly mocking at the feeble old man...."

He came to a standstill, due to an outburst of sorrow, which found vent in a flood of tears.

The philosopher was touched by such inconsolable sadness; he coughed, uttering a hollow sound in the effort to clear his throat. The sotnik turned round and pointed him to a place at the dead girl's head, before a small lectern with books on it.

"I shall get through three nights somehow," thought the philosopher: "and the old man will stuff both my pockets with gold pieces for it."

He drew near, and clearing his throat once more, began reading, paying no attention to anything else and not venturing to glance at the face of the dead girl. A profound stillness reigned in the apartment. He noticed that the sotnik had withdrawn. Slowly he turned his head to look at the dead, and ...

A shudder ran through his veins: before him lay a beauty whose like had surely never been on earth before. Never, it seemed, could features have been formed in such striking yet harmonious beauty. She lay as though living: the lovely forehead, fair as snow, as silver, looked deep in thought; the even brows— dark as night in the midst of sunshine—rose proudly above the closed eyes; the eye-lashes, that fell like arrows on the cheeks, glowed with the warmth of secret desires; the lips were rubies, ready to break into the laugh of bliss, the flood of joy. . . . But in them, in those very features, he saw something terrible and poignant. He felt a sickening ache stirring in his heart, as though, in the midst of a whirl of gaiety and dancing crowds, someone had begun singing a funeral dirge. The rubies of her lips looked like blood surging up from her heart. All at once he was aware of something dreadfully familiar in her face. "The witch!" he cried in a voice not his own, as, turning pale, he looked away and fell to repeating his prayers. It was the witch that he had killed!

When the sun was setting, they carried the corpse to the church. The philosopher supported the coffin swathed in black on his shoulder, and felt something cold as ice on it. The sotnik walked in front, with his hand on the right side of the dead girl's narrow resting home. The wooden church, blackened by age and overgrown with green lichen, stood disconsolately, with its three cone-shaped domes, at the very end of the village. It was evident that no service had been performed in it for a long time. Candles had been lighted before almost every image. The coffin was set down in the centre opposite the altar. The old sotnik kissed the dead girl once more, bowed down to the ground, and went out together with the coffin-bearers, giving orders that the philosopher should have a good supper and then be taken to the church. On reaching the kitchen all the men who had carried the coffin began putting their hands on the stove, as the custom is with Little Russians, after seeing a dead body.

The hunger, of which the philosopher began at that moment to be conscious, made him for some minutes entirely oblivious of the dead girl. Soon all the servants began gradually assembling in the kitchen, which in the sotnik's house was something like a club, where all the inhabitants of the yard gathered together, including even the dogs, who wagging their tails, came to the door for bones and slops. Wherever anybody might be sent, and with whatever duty he might be charged, he always went first to the kitchen to rest for at least a minute on the bench and smoke a pipe. All the unmarried men in their smart Cossack tunics lay there almost all day long, on the bench, under the bench, or on the stove—anywhere, in fact, where a comfortable place could be found to lie on. Then everybody invariably left behind in the kitchen either his cap or a whip to keep stray dogs off or some such thing. But the biggest crowd always gathered at suppertime, when the drover who had taken the horses to the paddock, and the herdsman who had brought the cows in to be milked, and all the others who were not to be seen during the day, came in. At supper, even the most taciturn tongues were moved to loquacity. It was then that all the news was talked over: who had got himself new breeches, and what was hidden in the bowels of the earth, and who had seen a wolf. There were witty talkers among them; indeed, there is no lack of them anywhere among the Little Russians.

The philosopher sat down with the rest in a big circle in the open air before the kitchen door. Soon a peasant-woman in a red bonnet popped out, holding in both hands a steaming bowl of dumplings, which she set down in their midst. Each pulled out a wooden spoon from his pocket, or, for lack of a spoon, a wooden stick. As soon as their jaws began moving more slowly, and the wolfish hunger of the whole party was some-what assuaged, many of them began talking. The conversation naturally turned on the dead maiden.

"Is it true," said a young shepherd who had put so many buttons and copper discs on the leather strap on which his pipe hung that he looked like a small haberdasher's shop, "is it true that the young lady, saving your presence, was on friendly terms with the Evil One?"

"Who? The young mistress?" said Dorosh, a man our philosopher already knew, "why, she was a regular witch! I'll take my oath she was a witch!"

"Hush, hush, Dorosh," said another man, who had shown a great disposition to soothe the others on the journey, "that's no business of ours, God bless it! It's no good talking about it."

But Dorosh was not at all inclined to hold his tongue; he had just been to the cellar on some job with the butler, and, having applied his lips to two or three barrels, he had come out extremely merry and talked away without ceasing.

"What do you want? Me to be quiet?" he said, "why, I've been ridden by her myself! Upon my soul, I have!"

"Tell us, uncle," said the young shepherd with the buttons, "are there signs by which you can tell a witch?"

"No, you can't," answered Dorosh, "there's no way of telling: you might read through all the psalm-books and you couldn't tell."

"Yes, you can, Dorosh, you can; don't say that," the former comforter objected; "it's with good purpose God has given every creature its peculiar habit; folks that have studied say that a witch has a little tail."

"When a woman's old, she's a witch," the grey-headed Cossack said coolly.

"Oh! you're a nice set!" retorted the peasant woman, who was at that instant pouring a fresh lot of dumplings into the empty pot; "regular fat hogs!"

The old Cossack, whose name was Yavtuh and nickname Kovtun, gave a smile of satisfaction seeing that his words had cut the old woman to the quick; while the herdsman gave vent to a guffaw, like the bellowing of two bulls as they stand facing each other.

The beginning of the conversation had aroused the philosopher's curiosity and made him intensely anxious to learn more details about the sotnik's daughter, and so, wishing to bring the talk back to that subject, he turned to his neighbour with the words: "I should like to ask why all the folk sitting at supper here look upon the young mistress as a witch? Did she do a mischief to anybody or bring anybody to harm?"

"There were all sorts of doings," answered one of the company, a man with a flat face strikingly resembling a spade. "Everybody remembers the dog-boy Mikita and the ..."

"What about the dog-boy Mikita?" said the philosopher.

"Stop! I'll tell about the dog-boy Mikita," said Dorosh.

"I'll tell about him," said the drover, "for he was a great crony of mine." "I'll tell about Mikita," said Spirid.

"Let him, let Spirid tell it!" shouted the company.

Spirid began: "You didn't know Mikita, Mr. Philosopher Homa. Ah, he was a man! He knew every dog as well as he knew his own father. The dog-boy we've got now, Mikola, who's sitting next but one from me, isn't worth the sole of his shoe. Though he knows his job, too, but beside the other he's trash, slops."

"You tell the story well, very well!" said Dorosh, nodding his head approvingly.

Spirid went on: "He'd see a hare quicker than you'd wipe the snuff from your nose. He'd whistle: `Here, Breaker! here Swift-foot!' and he in full gallop on his horse; and there was no saying which would outrace the other, he the dog, or the dog him. He'd toss off a mug of vodka with-out winking. He was a fine dog boy! Only a little time back he began to be always staring at the young mistress. Whether he had fallen in love with her, or whether she had simply bewitched him, anyway the man was done for, he went fairly silly; the devil only knows what he turned into. . . pfoo! No decent word for it. . . ."

"That's good," said Dorosh.

"As soon as the young mistress looks at him, he drops the bridle out of his hand, calls Breaker Bushy-brow, is all of a fluster and doesn't know what he's doing. One day the young mistress comes into the stable where he is rubbing down a horse.

" 'I say, Mikita,' says she, 'let me put my foot on you.' And he, silly fellow, is pleased at that. 'Not your foot only,' says he, 'you may sit on me altogether.' The young mistress lifted her foot, and, as soon as he saw her bare, plump, white leg, he went fairly crazy, so he said. He bent his back, silly fellow, and, clasping her bare legs in his hands, ran galloping like a horse all over the countryside. And he couldn't say where he was driven, but he came back more dead than alive, and from that time he withered up like a chip of wood; and one day when they went into the stable, in-stead of him they found a heap of ashes lying there and an empty pail; he had burnt up entirely, burnt up of himself. And he was a dog-boy such as you couldn't find another all the world over."

When Spirid had finished his story, reflections upon the rare qualities of the deceased dog-boy followed from all sides.

"And haven't you heard tell of Sheptun's wife?" said Dorosh, addressing Homa.

"No."

"Well, well! You are not taught with too much sense, it seems, in the seminary. Listen, then. There's a Cossack called Sheptun in our village —a good Cossack! He is given to stealing at times, and telling lies when there's no occasion, but . . . he's a good Cossack. His cottage is not so far from here. Just about the very hour that we sat down this evening to table, Sheptun and his wife finished their supper and lay down to sleep, and, as it was fine weather, his wife lay down in the yard, and Sheptun in the cottage on the bench; or no . . . it was the wife lay indoors on the bench and Sheptun in the yard. . . ."

"Not on the bench, she was lying on the floor," put in a peasant woman who stood in the doorway with her cheek propped in her hand.

Dorosh looked at her, then looked down, then looked at her again, and after a brief pause, said: "When I strip off your petticoat before every-body, you won't be pleased."

This warning had its effect; the old woman held her tongue and did not interrupt the story again.

Dorosh went on: "And in the cradle hanging in the middle of the cottage lay a baby a year old—whether of the male or female sex I can't say. Sheptun's wife was lying there when she heard a dog scratching at the door and howling fit to make you run out of the cottage. She was scared, for women are such foolish creatures that, if towards evening you put your tongue out at one from behind a door, her heart's in her mouth. However, she thought: 'Well, I'll go and give that damned dog a whack on its nose, and maybe it will stop howling,' and taking the oven-fork she went to open the door. She had hardly opened it when a dog dashed in between her legs and straight to the baby's cradle. She saw that it was no longer a dog, but the young mistress, and, if it had been the young lady in her own shape as she knew her, it would not have been so bad. But the peculiar thing is that she was all blue and her eyes glowing like coals. She snatched up the child, bit its throat, and began sucking its blood. Sheptun's wife could only scream: 'Oh, horror!' and rushed towards the door. But she sees the door's locked in the passage; she flies up to the loft and there she sits all of a shake, silly woman; and then she sees the young mistress coming up to her in the loft; she pounced on her, and began biting the silly woman. When Sheptun pulled his wife down from the loft in the morning she was bitten all over and had turned black and blue; and next day the silly woman died. So you see what uncanny and wicked doings happen in the world! Though it is of the gentry's breed, a witch is a witch."

After telling the story, Dorosh looked about him complacently and thrust his finger into his pipe, preparing to fill it with tobacco. The subject of the witch seemed inexhaustible. Each in turn hastened to tell some tale of her. One had seen the witch in the form of a haystack come right up to the door of his cottage; another had had his cap or his pipe stolen by her; many of the girls in the village had had their hair cut off by her, others had lost several quarts of blood sucked by her.

At last the company pulled themselves together and saw that they had been chattering too long, for it was quite dark in the yard. They all began wandering off to their several sleeping places, which were either in the kitchen, or the barns, or the middle of the courtyard.

"Well, Mr. Homa! now it's time for us to go to the deceased lady," said the grey-headed Cossack, addressing the philosopher; and together with Spirid and Dorosh they set off to the church, lashing with their whips at the dogs, of which there were a great number in the road, and which gnawed their sticks angrily.

Though the philosopher had managed to fortify himself with a good mugful of vodka, he felt a fearfulness creeping stealthily over him as they approached the lighted church. The stories and strange tales he had heard helped to work upon his imagination. The darkness under the fence and trees grew less thick as they came into the more open place. At last they went into the church enclosure and found a little yard, beyond which there was not a tree to be seen, nothing but open country and meadows swallowed up in the darkness of night. The three Cossacks and Homa mounted the steep steps to the porch and went into the church. Here they left the philosopher with the best wishes that he might carry out his duties satisfactorily, and locked the door after them, as their master had bidden them.

The philosopher was left alone. First he yawned, then he stretched, then he blew into both hands, and at last he looked about him. In the middle of the church stood the black coffin; candles were gleaming under the dark images; the light from them only lit up the ikon-stand and shed a faint glimmer in the middle of the church; the distant corners were wrapped in darkness. The tall, old-fashioned ikon-stand showed traces of great antiquity; its carved fretwork, once gilt, only glistened here and there with splashes of gold; the gilt had peeled off in one place, and was completely tarnished in another; the faces of the saints, blackened by age, had a gloomy look. The philosopher looked round him again. "Well," he said, "what is there to be afraid of here? No living man can come in here, and to guard me from the dead and ghosts from the other world I have prayers that I have but to read aloud to keep them from laying a finger on me. It's all right!" he repeated with a wave of his hand, "let's read." Going up to the lectern he saw some bundles of candles. "That's good," thought the philosopher; "I must light up the whole church so that it may be as bright as by daylight. Oh, it is a pity that one must not smoke a pipe in the temple of God!"

And he proceeded to stick up wax candles at all the cornices, lecterns and images, not stinting them at all, and soon the whole church was flooded with light. Only overhead the darkness seemed somehow more profound, and the gloomy ikons looked even more sullenly out of their antique carved frames, which glistened here and there with specks of gilt. He went up to the coffin, looked timidly at the face of the dead—and could not help closing his eyelids with a faint shudder: such terrible, brilliant beauty!

He turned and tried to move away; but with the strange curiosity, the self-contradictory feeling, which dogs a man especially in times of terror, he could not, as he withdrew, resist taking another look. And then, after the same shudder, he looked again. The striking beauty of the dead maiden certainly seemed terrible. Possibly, indeed, she would not have overwhelmed him with such panic fear if she had been a little less lovely. But there was in her features nothing faded, tarnished, dead; her face was living, and it seemed to the philosopher that she was looking at him with closed eyes. He even fancied that a tear was oozing from under her right eyelid, and, when it rested on her cheek, he saw distinctly that it was a drop of blood.

He walked hastily away to the lectern, opened the book, and to give himself more confidence began reading in a very loud voice. His voice smote upon the wooden church walls, which had so long been deaf and silent; it rang out, forlorn, unechoed, in a deep bass in the absolutely dead stillness, and seemed somehow uncanny even to the reader himself. "What is there to be afraid of?" he was saying meanwhile to himself. "She won't rise up out of her coffin, for she will fear the word of God. Let her lie there! And a fine Cossack I am, if I should be scared. Well, I've drunk a drop too much—that's why it seems dreadful. I'll have a pinch of snuff. Ah, the good snuff! Fine snuff, good snuff!" However, as he turned over the pages, he kept taking sidelong glances at the coffin, and an involuntary feeling seemed whispering to him: "Look, look, she is going to get up! See, she'll sit up, she'll look out from the coffin!"

But the silence was deathlike; the coffin stood motionless; the candles shed a perfect flood of light. A church lighted up at night with a dead body in it and no living soul near is full of terror!

Raising his voice, he began singing in various keys, trying to drown the fears that still lurked in him, but every minute he turned his eyes to the coffin, as though asking, in spite of himself: "What if she does sit up, if she gets up?"

But the coffin did not stir. If there had but been some sound! some living creature! There was not so much as a cricket churring in the corner There was nothing but the faint splutter of a faraway candle, the light tap of a drop of wax falling on the floor.

"What if she were to get up . . . ?"

She was raising her head. . . .

He looked at her wildly and rubbed his eyes. She was, indeed, not lying down now, but sitting up in the coffin. He looked away, and again turned his eyes with horror on the coffin. She stood up. . . . she was walking about the church with her eyes shut, moving her arms to and fro as though trying to catch someone.

She was coming straight towards him. In terror he drew a circle round him; with an effort he began reading the prayers and pronouncing the exorcisms which had been taught him by a monk who had all his life seen witches and evil spirits.

She stood almost on the very line; but it was clear that she had not the power to cross it, and she turned livid all over like one who has been dead for several days. Hama had not the courage to look at her; she was terrifying. She ground her teeth and opened her dead eyes; but, seeing nothing, turned with fury-- that was apparent in her quivering face—in another direction, and, flinging her arms, clutched in them each column and corner, trying to catch Homa. At last she stood still, holding up a menacing finger, and lay down again in her coffin.

The philosopher could not recover his self-possession, but kept gazing at the narrow dwelling-place of the witch. At last the coffin suddenly sprang up from its place and with a hissing sound began flying all over the church, zigzagging through the air in all directions.

The philosopher saw it almost over his head, but at the same time he saw that it could not cross the circle he had drawn, and he redoubled his exorcisms. The coffin dropped down in the middle of the church and stayed there without moving. The corpse got up out of it, livid and greenish. But at that instant the crow of the cock was heard in the distance; the corpse sank back in the coffin and closed the lid.

The philosopher's heart was throbbing and the sweat was streaming down him; but, emboldened by the cock's crowing, he read on more rapidly the pages he ought to have read through before. At the first streak of dawn the sacristan came to relieve him, together with old Yavtuh, who was at that time performing the duties of a beadle.

On reaching his distant sleeping-place, the philosopher could not for a long time get to sleep; but weariness gained the upper hand at last and he slept on till dinner-time. When he woke up, all the events of the night seemed to him to have happened in a dream. To keep up his strength he was given at dinner a mug of vodka.

Over dinner he soon grew lively, made a remark or two, and devoured a rather large sucking pig almost unaided; but some feeling he could not have explained made him unable to bring himself to speak of his adventures in the church, and to the inquiries of the inquisitive he re-plied: "Yes, all sorts of strange things happened." The philosopher was one of those people who, if they are well fed, are moved to extraordinary benevolence. Lying down with his pipe in his teeth he watched them all with a honied look in his eyes and kept spitting to one side.

After dinner the philosopher was in excellent spirits. He went round the whole village and made friends with almost everybody; he was kicked out of two cottages, indeed; one good-looking young woman caught him a good smack on the back with a spade when he took it into his head to try her shift and skirt, and inquire what stuff they were made of. But as evening approached the philosopher grew more pensive. An hour before supper almost all the servants gathered together to play kragli —a sort of skittles in which long sticks are used instead of balls, and the winner has the right to ride on the loser's back. This game became very entertaining for the spectators; often the drover, a man as broad as a pan-cake, was mounted on the swineherd, a feeble little man, who was nothing but wrinkles. Another time it was the drover who had to bow his back, and Dorosh, leaping on it, always said: "What a fine bull!" The more dignified of the company sat in the kitchen doorway. They looked on very gravely, smoking their pipes, even when the young people roared with laughter at some witty remark from the drover or Spirid. Homa tried in vain to give himself up to this game; some gloomy thought stuck in his head like a nail. At supper, in spite of his efforts to be merry, terror grew within him as the darkness spread over the sky.

"Come, it's time to set off, Mr. Seminarist!" said his friend, the grey-headed Cossack, getting up from the table, together with Dorosh; "let us go to our task."

Homa was taken to the church again in the same way; again he was left there alone and the door was locked upon him. As soon as he was alone, fear began to take possession of him again. Again he saw the dark ikons, the gleaming frames, and the familiar black coffin standing in menacing stillness and immobility in the middle of the church.

"Well," he said to himself, "now there's nothing marvellous to me in this marvel. It was only alarming the first time. Yes, it was only rather alarming the first time, and even then it wasn't so alarming; now it's not alarming at all."

Stories That Scared Even Stalin

He made haste to take his stand at the lectern, drew a circle around him, pronounced some exorcisms, and began reading aloud, resolving not to raise his eyes from the book and not to pay attention to anything. He had been reading for about an hour and was beginning to cough and feel rather tired; he took his horn out of his pocket and, before putting the snuff to his nose, stole a timid look at the coffin. His heart turned cold; the corpse was already standing before him on the very edge of the circle, and her dead, greenish eyes were fixed upon him. The philosopher shuddered, and a cold 'chill ran through his veins. Dropping his eyes to the book, he began reading the prayers and exorcisms more loudly, and heard the corpse again grinding her teeth and waving her arms trying to catch him. But, with a sidelong glance out of one eye, he saw that the corpse was feeling for him where he was not standing, and that she evidently could not see him. He heard a hollow mutter, and she began pronouncing terrible words with her dead lips; they gurgled hoarsely like the bubbling of boiling pitch. He could not have said what they meant; but there was something fearful in them. The philosopher understood with horror that she was making an incantation.

A wind blew through the church at her words, and there was a sound as of multitudes of flying wings. He heard the beating of wings on the panes of the church windows and on the iron window-frames, the dull scratching of claws upon the iron, and an immense troop thundering on the doors and trying to break in. His heart was throbbing violently all this time; closing his eyes, he kept reading prayers and exorcisms. At last there was a sudden shrill sound in the distance; it was a distant cock crowing. The philosopher, utterly spent, stopped and took breath.

When they came in to fetch him, they found him more dead-than alive; he was leaning with his back against the wall while, with his eyes almost starting out of his head, he stared at the Cossacks as they came in. They could scarcely get him along and had to support him all the way back. On reaching the courtyard, he pulled himself together and bade them give him a mug of vodka. When he had drunk it, he stroked down the hair on his head and said: "There are lots of foul things of all sorts in the world! And the panics they give one, there . . ." With that the philosopher waved his hand in despair.

The company sitting round him bowed their heads, hearing such sayings. Even a small boy, whom everybody in the servants' quarters felt himself entitled to depute in his place when it was a question of cleaning the stables or fetching water, even this poor youngster stared open- mouthed at the philosopher.

At that moment the old cook's assistant, a peasant woman, not yet past middle age, a terrible coquette, who always found something to pin to her cap—a bit of ribbon, a pink, or even a scrap of coloured paper, if she had nothing better—passed by, in a tightly girt apron, which displayed her round, sturdy figure.

"Good day, Homa!" she said, seeing the philosopher. "Aie, aie, aie! What's the matter with you?" she shrieked, clasping her hands. "Why, what is it, silly woman?"

"Oh, my goodness! Why, you've gone quite grey!"

"Aha! why, she's right!" Spirid pronounced, looking attentively at the philosopher. "Why, you have really gone as grey as our old Yavtuh."

The philosopher, hearing this, ran headlong to the kitchen, where he had noticed on the wall a fly-blown triangular bit of looking-glass before which were stuck forget-me-nots, periwinkles and even wreaths of marigolds, testifying to its importance for the toilet of the finery-loving coquette. With horror he saw the truth of their words: half of his hair had in fact turned white.

Homa Brut hung his head and abandoned himself to reflection. "I will go to the master," he said at last. "I'll tell him all about it and explain that I cannot go on reading. Let him send me back to Kiev straight away."

With these thoughts in his mind he bent his steps towards the porch of the house.

The sotnik was sitting almost motionless in his parlour. The same hopeless grief which the philosopher had seen in his face before was still apparent. Only his cheeks were more sunken. It was evident that he had taken very little food, or perhaps had not eaten at all. The extraordinary pallor of his face gave it a look of stony immobility.

"Good day!" he pronounced on seeing Homa, who stood, cap in hand, at the door. "Well, how goes it with you? All satisfactory?"

"It's satisfactory, all right; such devilish doings, that one can but pick up one's cap and take to one's heels."

"How's that?"

"Why, your daughter, your honour . . . Looking at it reasonably, she is, to be sure, of noble birth, nobody is going to gainsay it; only, saving your presence, God rest her soul. . . ."

"What of my daughter?"

"She had dealings with Satan. She gives one such horrors that there's no reading scripture at all."

"Read away! read away! She did well to send for you; she took much care, poor darling, about her soul and tried to drive away all evil thoughts with prayers."

"That's as you like to say, your honour; upon my soul, I cannot go on with it!"

"Read away!" the sotnik persisted in the same persuasive voice, "you have only one night left; you will do a Christian deed and I will reward you."

"But whatever rewards ... Do as you please, your honour, but I will not read!" Homa declared resolutely.

"Listen, philosopher!" said the sotnik, and his voice grew firm and menacing. "I don't like these pranks. You can behave like that in your seminary; but with me it is different. When I flog, it's not the same as your rector's flogging. Do you know what good leather whips are like?"

"I should think I do!" said the philosopher, dropping his voice; "everybody knows what leather whips are like: in a large dose, it's quite unendurable."

"Yes, but you don't know yet how my lads can lay them on!" said the sotnik, menacingly, rising to his feet, and his face assumed an imperious and ferocious expression that betrayed the unbridled violence of his character, only subdued for the time by sorrow.

"Here they first give a sound flogging, then sprinkle with vodka, and begin over again. Go along, go along, finish your task! If you don't—you'll never get up again. If you do—a thousand gold pieces!"

"Oho, ho! He's a stiff one!" thought the philosopher as he went out: "he's not to be trifled with. Wait a bit, friend; I'll cut and run, so that you and your hounds will never catch me."

And Homa made up his mind to run away. He only waited for the hour after dinner when all the servants were accustomed to lie about in the hay in the barns and to give vent to such snores and wheezing that the backyard sounded like a factory.

The time came at last. Even Yavtuh closed his eyes as he lay stretched out in the sun. With fear and trembling, the philosopher stealthily made his way into the pleasure garden, from which he fancied he could more easily escape into the open country without being observed. As is usual with such gardens, it was dreadfully neglected and overgrown, and so made an extremely suitable setting for any secret enterprise. Except for one little path, trodden by the servants on their tasks, it was entirely hidden in a dense thicket of cherry-trees, elders and burdock, which thrust up their tall stems covered with clinging pinkish burs. A net-work of wild hop was flung over this medley of trees and bushes of varied hues, forming a roof over them, clinging to the fence and falling, mingled with wild bell-flowers, from it in coiling snakes. Beyond the fence, which formed the boundary of the garden, there came a perfect forest of rank grass and weeds, which looked as though no one cared to peep enviously into it, and as though any scythe would be broken to bits trying to mow down the stout stubbly stalks.

When the philosopher tried to get over the fence, his teeth chattered and his heart beat so violently that he was frightened at it. The skirts of his long coat seemed to stick to the ground as though someone had nailed them down. As he climbed over, he fancied he heard a voice shout in his ears with a deafening hiss: "Where are you off to?" The philosopher dived into the long grass and fell to running, frequently stumbling over old roots and trampling upon moles. He saw that when he came out of the rank weeds he would have to cross a field, and that beyond it lay a dark thicket of blackthorn, in which he thought he would be safe. He expected after making his way through it to find the road leading straight to Kiev. He ran across the field at once and found himself in the thicket.

He crawled through the prickly bushes, paying a toll of rags from his coat on every thorn, and came out into a little hollow. A willow with spreading branches bent down almost to the earth. A little brook sparkled pure as silver. The first thing the philosopher did was to lie down and drink, for he was insufferably thirsty. "Good water!" he said, wiping his lips; "I might rest here!"

"No, we had better go straight ahead; they'll be coming to look for you!"

These words rang out above his ears. He looked round—before him was standing Yavtuh. "Curse Yavtuh!" the philosopher thought in his wrath; "I could take you and fling you . . . And I could batter in your ugly face and all of you with an oak post."

"You needn't have gone such a long way round," Yavtuh went on, "you'd have done better to keep to the road I have come by, straight by the stable. And it's a pity about your coat. It's good cloth. What did you pay a yard for it? But we've walked far enough; it's time to go home."

The philosopher trudged after Yavtuh, scratching himself. "Now the cursed witch will give it to me!" he thought. "Though, after all, what am I thinking about? What am I afraid of? Am I not a Cossack? Why, I've been through two nights, God will succour me the third also. The cursed witch committed a fine lot of sins, it seems, since the Evil One makes such a fight for her."

Such were the reflections that absorbed him as he walked into the courtyard. Keeping up his spirits with these thoughts, he asked Dorosh, who through the patronage of the butler sometimes had access to the cellars, to pull out a keg of vodka; and the two friends, sitting in the barn, put away not much less than half a pailful, so that the philosopher, getting on his feet, shouted: "Musicians! I must have musicians!" and without waiting for the latter fell to dancing a jig in a clear space in the middle of the yard. He danced till it was time for the afternoon snack, and the servants who stood round him in a circle, as is the custom on such occasions, at last spat on the ground and walked away, saying: "Good gracious, what a time the fellow keeps it up!" At last the philosopher lay down to sleep on the spot, and a good sousing of cold water was needed to wake him up for supper. At supper he talked of what it meant to be a Cossack, and how he should not be afraid of anything in the world.

"Time is up," said Yavtuh, "let us go."

"A splinter through your tongue, you damned hog!" thought the philosopher, and getting to his feet he said: "Come along."

On the way the philosopher kept glancing from side to side and made faint attempts. at conversation with his companions. But Yavtuh said nothing; and even Dorosh was disinclined to talk. It was a hellish night. A whole pack of wolves was howling in the distance, and even the barking of the dogs had a dreadful sound.

"I fancy something else is howling; that's not a wolf," said Dorosh. Yavtuh was silent. The philosopher could find nothing to say.

They drew near the church and stepped under the decaying wooden domes that showed how little the owner of the place thought about God and his own soul. Yavtuh and Dorosh withdrew as before, and the philosopher was left alone.

Everything was the same, everything wore the same sinister familiar aspect. He stood still for a minute. The horrible witch's coffin was still standing motionless in the middle of the church.

"I won't be afraid; by God, I will not!" he said, and, drawing a circle around himself as before, he began recalling all his spells and exorcisms. There was an awful stillness; the candles spluttered and flooded the whole church with light. The philosopher turned one page, then turned another and noticed that he was not reading what was written in the book. With horror he crossed himself and began chanting. This gave him a little more courage; the reading made progress, and the pages turned rapidly one after the other.

All of a sudden . . . in the midst of the stillness . . . the iron lid of the coffin burst with a crash and the corpse rose up. It was more terrible than the first time. Its teeth clacked horribly against each other, its lips twitched convulsively, and incantations came from them in wild shrieks. A whirl-wind swept through the church, the ikons fell to the ground, broken glass came flying down from the windows. The doors were burst from their hinges and a countless multitude of monstrous beings trooped into the church of God. A terrible noise of wings and scratching claws filled the church. All flew and raced about looking for the philosopher.

All trace of drink had disappeared, and Homa's head was quite clear now. He kept crossing himself and repeating prayers at random. And all the while he heard the unclean horde whirring round him, almost touching him with their loathsome tails and the tips of their wings. He had not the courage to look at them; he only saw a huge monster, the whole width of the wall, standing in the shade of its matted locks as of a forest; through the tangle of hair two eyes glared horribly with eyebrows slightly lifted. Above it something was hanging in the air like an immense bubble with a thousand claws and scorpion-stings stretching from the centre; black earth hung in clods on them. They were all looking at him, seeking him, but could not see him, surrounded by his mysterious circle. "Bring Viy! Fetch Viy!" he heard the corpse cry.

And suddenly a stillness fell upon the church; the wolves' howling was heard in the distance, and soon there was the thud of heavy footsteps re-sounding through the church. With a sidelong glance he saw they were bringing a squat, thick-set, bandy-legged figure. He was covered all over with black earth. His arms and legs grew out like strong sinewy roots.. He trod heavily, stumbling at every step. His long eyelids hung down to the very ground. Homa saw with horror that his face was of iron. He was supported under the arms and led straight to the spot where Homa was standing.

"Lift up my eyelids. I do not see!" said Viy in a voice that seemed to come from underground—and all the company flew to raise his eyelids. "Do not look!" an inner voice whispered to the philosopher. He could not restrain himself, and he looked.

"There he is!" shouted Viy, and thrust an iron finger at him. And all pounced upon the philosopher together. He fell expiring to the ground, and his soul fled from his body in terror

There was the sound of a cock crowing. It was the second cock-crow; the first had been missed by the gnomes. In panic they rushed pell-mell to the doors and windows to fly out in utmost haste; but they could not; and so they remained there, stuck in the doors and windows.

When the priest went in, he stopped short at the sight of this defamation of God's holy place, and dared not serve the requiem on such a spot. And so the church was left for ever, with monsters stuck in the doors and windows, was overgrown with forest trees, roots, rough grass and wild thorns, and no one can now find the way to it.

When the rumours of this reached Kiev, and the theologian, Halyava, heard at last of the fate of the philosopher Homa, he spent a whole hour plunged in thought. Great changes had befallen him during that time. Fortune had smiled on him; on the conclusion of his course of study, he was made bell-ringer of the very highest belfry, and he was almost always to be seen with a damaged nose, as the wooden staircase to the belfry had been extremely carelessly made.

"Have you heard what has happened to Homa?" Tibery Gorobets, who by now was a philosopher and had a newly-grown moustache, asked, coming up to him.

"Such was the lot God sent him," said Halyava the bell-ringer. "Let us go to the pot-house and drink to his memory!"

The young philosopher, who was beginning to enjoy his privileges with the ardour of an enthusiast, so that his full trousers and his coat and even his cap reeked of spirits and coarse tobacco, instantly signified his readiness.

"He was a fine fellow, Homa!" said the bell-ringer, as the lame inn-keeper set the third mug before him. "He was a fine man! And he came to grief for nothing."

"I know why he came to grief: it was because he was afraid; if he had not been afraid, the witch could not have done anything to him. You have only to cross yourself and spit just on her tail, and nothing will happen. I know all about it. Why, all the old women who sit in our market in Kiev are all witches."

To this the bell-ringer bowed his head in token of agreement. But, observing that his tongue was incapable of uttering a single word, he cautiously got up from the table, and, lurching to right and to left, went to hide in a remote spot in the rough grass; from the force of habit, how-ever, did not forget to carry off the sole of an old boot that was lying about on the bench.

How Much Land Does A Man Need?

Leo Tolstoy

I

An elder sister came to visit her younger sister in the country. The elder was married to a shopkeeper in town, the younger to a peasant in the village. As the sisters sat over their tea talking, the elder began to boast of the advantages of town life, saying how comfortably they lived there, how well they dressed, what fine clothes her children wore, what good things they ate and drank, and how she went to the theater, promenades, and entertainments.

The younger sister was piqued, and in turn disparaged the life of a shopkeeper, and stood up for that of a peasant.

"I wouldn't change my way of life for yours," said she. "We may live roughly, but at least we're free from worry. You live in better style than we do, but though you often earn more than you need, you're very likely to lose all you have. You know the proverb, `Loss and gain are brothers twain.' It often happens that people who're wealthy one day are begging their bread the next. Our way is safer. Though a peasant's life is not a rich one, it's long. We'll never grow rich, but we'll always have enough to eat."

The elder sister said sneeringly:

"Enough? Yes, if you like to share with the pigs and the calves! What do you know of elegance or manners! However much your good man may slave, you'll die as you live—on a dung heap—and your children the same."

"Well, what of that?" replied the younger sister. "Of course our work is rough and hard. But on the other hand, it's sure, and we need not bow to anyone. But you, in your towns, are surrounded by temptations; today all may be right, but tomorrow the Evil One may tempt your husband with cards, wine, or women, and all will go to ruin. Don't such things happen often enough?"

Pahom, the master of the house, was lying on the top of the stove and he listened to the women's chatter.

"It is perfectly true," thought he. "Busy as we are from childhood tilling mother earth, we peasants have no time to let any nonsense settle in our heads. Our only trouble is that we haven't land enough. If I had plenty of land, I shouldn't fear the Devil himself!"

The women finished their tea, chatted a while about dress, and then cleared away the tea things and lay down to sleep.

But the Devil had been sitting behind the stove, and had heard all that had been said. He was pleased that the peasant's wife had led her husband into boasting, and that he had said that if he had plenty of land he would not fear the Devil himself.

"All right," thought the Devil. "We'll have a tussle. I'll give you land enough; and by means of that land I'll get you into my power."

II

Close to the village there lived a lady, a small landowner who had an estate of about three hundred acres. She had always lived on good terms with the peasants until she engaged as her manager an old soldier, who took to burdening the people with fines. However careful Pahom tried to be, it happened again and again that now a horse of his got among the lady's oats, now a cow strayed into her garden, now his calves found their way into her meadows—and he always had to pay a fine.

Pahom paid up, but grumbled, and, going home in a temper, was rough with his family. All through that summer Pahom had much trouble because of this manager, and he was actually glad when winter came and the cattle had to be stabled. Though he grudged the fodder hen they could no longer graze on the pasture land, at least he was free from anxiety about them.

In the winter the news got about that the lady was going to sell her land and that the keeper of the inn on the high road was bargaining for it. When the peasants heard this they were very much alarmed.

"Well," thought they, "if the innkeeper gets the land, he'll worry with fines worse than the lady's manager. We all depend on that rate."

So the peasants went on behalf of their village Council and asked the lady not to sell the land to the innkeeper, offering her a better price for it themselves. The lady agreed to let them have it. Then the peasants tried to arrange for the village Council to buy the whole estate, so that it might be held by them all in common. They met twice to discuss it, but could not settle the matter; the Evil One sowed discord among them and they could not agree. So they decided to buy the land individually, each according to his means; and the lady agreed to this plan as she had to the other.

Presently Pahom heard that a neighbor of his was buying fifty acres, and that the lady had consented to accept one-half in cash and to wait year for the other half. Pahom felt envious.

"Look at that," thought he, "the land is all being sold, and I'll get none of it." So he spoke to his wife.

"Other people are buying," said he, "and we must also buy twenty acres or so. Life is becoming impossible. That manager is simply crushing us with his fines."

So they put their heads together and considered how they could manage to buy it. They had one hundred rubles laid by. They sold a colt and one half of their bees, hired out one of their sons as a farm hand, and took his wages in advance; borrowed the rest from a brother-in-law, and so scraped together half the purchase money.

Having done this, Pahom chose a farm of forty acres, some of it wooded, and went to the lady to bargain for it. They came to an agreement, and he shook hands with her upon it and paid her a deposit in advance. Then they went to town and signed the deeds, he paying half the price down, and undertaking to pay the remainder within two years.

So now Pahom had land of his own. He borrowed seed, and sowed it on the land he had bought. The harvest was a good one, and within a year he had managed to pay off his debts both to the lady and to his brother-in-law. So he became a landowner, plowing and sowing his own land, making hay on his own land, cutting his own trees, and feeding his cattle on his own pasture. When he went out to plow his fields, or to look at his growing corn, or at his grass meadows, his heart would fill with joy. The grass that grew and the flowers that bloomed there seemed to him unlike any that grew elsewhere. Formerly, when he had passed by that land, it had appeared the same as any other land, but now it seemed quite different.

III

So Pahom was well contented, and everything would have been right if the neighboring peasants would only not have trespassed on his wheatfields and meadows. He appealed to them most civilly, but they still went on: now the herdsmen would let the village cows stray into his meadows, then horses from the night pasture would get among his corn. Pahom turned them out again and again, and forgave their owners, and for a long time he forbore to prosecute anyone. But at last he lost patience and complained to the District Court. He knew it was the peasants' want of land, and no evil intent on their part, that caused trouble, but he thought:

"I can't go on overlooking it, or they'll destroy all I have. They must be taught a lesson."

So he had them up, gave them one lesson, and then another, and or three of the peasants were fined. After a time Pahom's neighbors began to bear him a grudge for this, and would now and then let their cattle on to his land on purpose. One peasant even got into Pahom's wood at night and cut down five young lime trees for their bark. Pahom, passing through the wood one day, noticed something white. He came nearer and saw the stripped trunks lying on the ground, and close by stood the stumps where the trees had been. Pahom was furious.

"If he'd only cut one here and there it would have been bad enough," thought Pahom, "but the rascal has actually cut down a whole clump. If I could only find out who did this, I'd get even with him."

He racked his brains as to who it could be. Finally he decided: "It must be Simon—no one else could have done it." So he went to Simon's homestead to have a look around, but he found nothing, and only had an angry scene. However, he now felt more certain than ever that Simon had done it, and he lodged a complaint. Simon was summoned. The case was tried, and retried, and at

Leo Tolstoy   How Much Land Does A Man Need?

the end of it all Simon was acquitted, there being no evidence against him. Pahom felt still more aggrieved, and let his anger loose upon the Elder and the Judges.

"You let thieves grease your palms," said he. "If you were honest folk yourselves you wouldn't let a thief go free."

So Pahom quarreled with the judges and with his neighbors. Threats to burn his hut began to be uttered. So though Pahom had more land, his place in the community was much worse than before.

About this time a rumor got about that many people were moving to new parts.

"There's no need for me to leave my land," thought Pahom. "But some of the others may leave our village and then there'd be more room for us. I'd take over their land myself and make my estate somewhat bigger. I could then live more at ease. As it is, I'm still too cramped to be comfortable."

One day Pahom was sitting at home, when a peasant, passing through the village, happened to drop in. He was allowed to stay the night, and supper was given him. Pahom had a talk with this peasant and asked him where he came from. The stranger answered that he came from beyond the Volga, where he had been working. One word led to another, and the man went on to say that many people were settling in those parts. He told how some people from his village had settled there. They had joined the community there and had had twenty-five acres per man granted them. The land was so good, he said, that the rye sown on it grew as high as a horse, and so thick that five cuts of a sickle made a sheaf. One peasant, he said, had brought nothing with him but his bare hands, and now he had six horses and two cows of his own. Pahom's heart kindled with desire.

"Why should I suffer in this narrow hole, if one can live so well elsewhere?" he thought. "I'll sell my land and my homestead here, and with the money I'll start afresh over there and get everything new. In this crowded place one is always having trouble. But I must first go and find out all about it myself."

Toward summer he got ready and started out. He went down the Volga on a steamer to Samara, then walked another three hundred miles on foot, and at last reached the place. It was just as the stranger had said. The peasants had plenty of land: every man had twenty-five acres of communal land given him for his use, and anyone who had money could buy, besides, at a ruble-and-a-half an acre, as much good freehold land as he wanted.

Having found out all he wished to know, Pahom returned home as autumn came on, and began selling off his belongings. He sold his land at a profit, sold his homestead and all his cattle, and withdrew from membership in the village. He only waited till the spring, and then started with his family for the new settlement.

IV

As soon as Pahom and his family reached their new abode, he applied tor admission into the Council of a large village. He stood treat to the Elders and obtained the necessary documents. Five shares of communal land were given him for his own and his sons' use: that is to say—125 acres (not all together, but in different fields) besides the use of the communal pasture. Pahom put up the buildings he needed and bought cattle. Of the communal land alone he had three times as much as at his former home, and the land was good wheat land. He was ten times better off than he had been. He had plenty of arable land and pasturage, and could keep as many head of cattle as he liked.

At first, in the bustle of building and settling down, Pahom was pleased with it all, but when he got used to it he began to think that even here he hadn't enough land. The first year he sowed wheat on his share of the communal land and had a good crop. He wanted to go on sowing wheat, but had not enough communal land for the purpose, and what he had already used was not available, for in those parts wheat is sown only on virgin soil or on fallow land. It is sown for one or two years, and then the land lies fallow till it is again overgrown with steppe grass. There were many who wanted such land, and there was not enough for all, so that people quarreled about it. Those who were better off wanted it for growing wheat, and those who were poor wanted it to let to dealers, so that they might raise money to pay their taxes. Pahom wanted to sow more wheat, so he rented land from a dealer for a year. He sowed much wheat and had a fine crop, but the land was too far from the village—the wheat had to be carted more than ten miles. After a time Pahom noticed that some peasant-dealers were living on separate farms and were growing wealthy, and he thought:

"If I were to buy some freehold land and have a homestead on it, it would be a different thing altogether. Then it would all be fine and close together."

The question of buying freehold land recurred to him again and again.

He went on in the same way for three years, renting land and sowing wheat. The seasons turned out well and the crops were good, so that he began to lay by money. He might have gone on living contentedly, but he grew tired of having to rent other people's land every year, and having to scramble for it. Wherever there was good land to be had, the peasants would rush for it and it was taken up at once, so that unless you were sharp about it you got none. It happened in the third year that he and a dealer together rented a piece of pasture land from some peasants, and they had already plowed it up, when there was some dispute and the peasants went to law about it, and things fell out so that the labor was all lost.

"If it were my own land," thought Pahom, "I should be independent, and there wouldn't be all this unpleasantness."

So Pahom began looking out for land which he could buy, and he came across a peasant who had bought thirteen hundred acres, but having got into difficulties was willing to sell again cheap. Pahom bargained and haggled with him, and at last they settled the price at fifteen hundred rubles, part in cash and part to be paid later. They had all but clinched the matter when a passing dealer happened to stop at Pahom's one day to get feed for his horses. He drank tea with Pahom, and they had a talk. The dealer said that he was just returning from the land of the Bashkirs, far away, where he had bought thirteen thousand acres of land, all for a thousand rubles. Pahom questioned him further, and the dealer said:

"All one has to do is to make friends with the chiefs. I gave away about one hundred rubles' worth of silk robes and carpets, besides a case of tea, and I gave wine to those who would drink it; and I got the land for less than three kopecks an acre." And he showed Pahom the title deed, saying:

"The land lies near a river, and the whole steppe is virgin soil."

Pahom plied him with questions, and the dealer said:

"There's more land there than you could cover if you walked a year, and it all belongs to the Bashkirs. They're as simple as sheep, and land can be got almost for nothing."

"There, now," thought Pahom, "with my one thousand rubles, why should I get only thirteen hundred acres, and saddle myself with a debt besides? If I take it out there, I can get more than ten times as much for my money."

V

Pahom inquired how to get to the place, and as soon as the grain dealer had left him, he prepared to go there himself. He left his wife to look after the homestead, and started on his journey, taking his hired man with him. They stopped at a town on their way and bought a case of tea, some wine, and other presents, as the grain dealer had advised.

On and on they went until they had gone more than three hundred miles, and on the seventh day they came to a place where the Bashkirs had pitched their round tents. It was all just as the dealer had said. The people lived on the steppe, by a river, in felt-covered tents. They neither tilled the ground nor ate bread. Their cattle and horses grazed in herds on the steppe. The colts were tethered behind the tents, and the mares were driven to them twice a day. The mares were milked, and from the milk kumiss was made. It was the women who prepared the kumiss, and they also made cheese. As far as the men were concerned, drinking kumiss and tea, eating mutton, and playing on their pipes was all they cared about. They were all stout and merry, and all the summer long they never thought of doing any work. They were quite ignorant, and knew no Russian, but were good-natured enough.

As soon as they saw Pahom, they came out of their tents and gathered around their visitor. An interpreter was found, and Pahom told them he had come about some land. The Bashkirs seemed very glad; they took Pahom and led him into one of the best tents, where they made him sit on some down cushions placed on a carpet, while they sat around him. They gave him some tea and kumiss, and had a sheep killed, and gave him mutton to eat. Pahom took presents out of his cart and distributed them among the Bashkirs, and divided the tea amongst them. The Bashkirs were delighted. They talked a great deal among themselves, and then told the interpreter what to say.

"They wish to tell you," said the interpreter, "that they like you, and that it's our custom to do all we can to please a guest and to repay him for his gifts. You have given us presents, now tell us which of the things we possess please you best, that we may present them to you."

"What pleases me best here," answered Pahom, "is your land. Our land is crowded and the soil is worn out, but you have plenty of land, and it is good land. I never saw the likes of it."

The interpreter told the Bashkirs what Pahom had said. They talked among themselves for a while. Pahom could not understand what they were saying, but saw that they were much amused and heard them shout and laugh. Then they were silent and looked at Pahom while the interpreter said:

"They wish me to tell you that in return for your presents they will gladly give you as much land as you want. You have only to point it out with your hand and it is yours."

The Bashkirs talked again for a while and began to dispute. Pahom asked what they were disputing about, and the interpreter told him that some of them thought they ought to ask their Chief about the land and not act in his absence, while others thought there was no need to wait for his return.

VI

While the Bashkirs were disputing, a man in a large fox-fur cap appeared on the scene. They all became silent and rose to their feet. The interpreter said: "This is our Chief himself."

Pahom immediately fetched the best dressing gown and five pounds tea, and offered these to the Chief. The Chief accepted them, and seated himself in the place of honor. The Bashkirs at once began telling him something. The Chief listened for a while, then made a sign with his head for them to be silent, and addressing himself to Pahom, said in Russian:

"Well, so be it. Choose whatever piece of land you like; we have plenty of it."

"How can I take as much as I like?" thought Pahom. "I must get a deed to make it secure, or else they may say: 'It is yours,' and afterward may take it away again."

"Thank you for your kind words," he said aloud. "You have much land, and I only want a little. But I should like to be sure which portion is mine. Could it not be measured and made over to me? Life and death are in God's hands. You good people give it to me, but your children might wish to take it back again."

"You are quite right," said the Chief. "We will make it over to you."

"I heard that a dealer had been here," continued Pahom, "and that you gave him a little land, too, and signed title deeds to that effect. I should like to have it done in the same way."

The Chief understood.

"Yes," replied he, "that can be done quite easily. We have a scribe, and we will go to town with you and have the deed properly sealed."

"And what will be the price?" asked Pahom.

"Our price is always the same: one thousand rubles a day." Pahom did not understand.

"A day? What measure is that? How many acres would that be?"

"We do not know how to reckon it out," said the Chief. "We sell it by the day. As much as you can go around on your feet in a day is yours, and the price is one thousand rubles a day."

Pahom was surprised.

"But in a day you can get around a large tract of land," he said.

The Chief laughed.

"It will all be yours!" said he. "But there is one condition: If you don't return on the same day to the spot whence you started, your money is lost."

"But how am I to mark the way that I have gone?"

"Why, we shall go to any spot you like, and stay there. You must start from that spot and make your round, taking a spade with you. Wherever you think necessary, make a mark. At every turning, dig a hole and pile up the turf; then afterward we will go around with a plow from hole to hole. You may make as large a circuit as you please, but before the sun sets you must return to the place you started from. All the land you cover will be yours."

Pahom was delighted. It was decided to start early next morning. They talked a while, and after drinking some more kumiss and eating some more mutton, they had tea again, and then the night came on. They gave Pahom a feather bed to sleep on, and the Bashkirs dispersed for the night, promising to assemble the next morning at daybreak and de out before sunrise to the appointed spot.

VII

Pahom lay on the feather bed, but could not sleep. He kept thinking about the land.

"What a large tract I'll mark off!" thought he. "I can easily do thirty-five miles in a day. The days are long now, and within a circuit of thirty-five miles what a lot of land there will be! I'll sell the poorer land, or let it to peasants, but I'll pick out the best and farm it myself. I'll buy two ox teams and hire two more laborers. About a hundred and fifty acres shall be plowland, and I'll pasture cattle on the rest."

Pahom lay awake all night, and dozed off only just before dawn. Hardly were his eyes dosed when he had a dream. He thought he was lying in that same tent and heard somebody chuckling outside. He wondered who it could be, and rose and went out, and he saw the Bashkir Chief sitting in front of the tent holding his sides and rolling about with laughter. Going nearer to the Chief, Pahom asked: "What are you laughing at?" But he saw that it was no longer the Chief, but the grain dealer who had recently stopped at his house and had told him about the land. Just as Pahom was going to ask: "Have you been here long?" he saw that it was not the dealer, but the peasant who had come up from the Volga, long ago, to Pahom's old home. Then he saw that it was not the peasant either, but the Devil himself with hoofs and horns, Sitting there and chuckling, and before him lay a man, prostrate on the ground, barefooted, with only trousers and a shirt on. And Pahom dreamed that he looked more attentively to see what sort of man it was lying there, and he saw that the man was dead, and that it was himself. Horror-struck, he awoke.

"What things one dreams about!" thought he.

Looking around he saw through the open door that the dawn was breaking.

"It's time to wake them up," thought he. "We ought to be starting." He got up, roused his man (who was sleeping in his cart), bade him harness, and went to call the Bashkirs.

"It's time to go to the steppe to measure the land," he said.

The Bashkirs rose and assembled, and the Chief came, too. Then they began drinking kumiss again, and offered Pahom some tea, but he would not wait.

"If we are to go, let's go. It's high time," said he.

VIII

The Bashkirs got ready and they all started: some mounted on horses and some in carts. Pahom drove in his own small cart with his servant and took a spade with him. When they reached the steppe, the red dawn was beginning to They ascended a hillock (called by the Bashkirs a *shikhan*) and, dismounting from their carts and their horses, gathered in one spot. The Chief came up to Pahom and, stretching out his arm toward the plain:

"See," said he, "all this, as far as your eye can reach, is ours. You may have any part of it you like."

Pahom's eyes glistened: it was all virgin soil, as flat as the palm of your hand, as black as the seed of a poppy, and in the hollows different kinds of grasses grew breast-high.

The Chief took off his fox-fur cap, placed it on the ground, and said: "'this will be the mark. Start from here, and return here again. All the land you go around shall be yours."

Pahom took out his money and put it on the cap. Then he took off his outer coat, remaining in his sleeveless undercoat. He unfastened his girdle and tied it tight below his stomach, put a little bag of bread into the breast of his coat, and, tying a flask of water to his girdle, he drew up the tops of his boots, took the spade from his man, and stood ready to start. He considered for some moments which way he had better go—it was tempting everywhere.

"No matter," he concluded, "I'll go toward the rising sun."

He turned his face to the east, stretched himself, and waited for the sun to appear above the rim.

"I must lose no time," he thought, "and it's easier walking while it's still cool."

Leo Tolstoy   How Much Land Does A Man Need?

The sun's rays had hardly flashed above the horizon when Pahom, carrying the spade over his shoulder, went down into the steppe.

Pahom started walking neither slowly nor quickly. After having gone a thousand yards he stopped, dug a hole, and placed pieces of turf one on another to make it more visible. Then he went on; and now that he had walked off his stiffness he quickened his pace. After a while he dug another hole.

Pahom looked back. The hillock could be distinctly seen in the sun-light, with the people on it, and the glittering iron rims of the cart-wheels. At a rough guess Pahom concluded that he had walked three miles. It was growing warmer; he took off his undercoat, slung it across his shoulder, and went on again. It had grown quite warm now; he looked at the sun—it was time to think of breakfast.

"The first shift is done, but there are four in a day, and it's too soon yet to turn. But I'll just take off my boots," said he to himself.

He sat down, took off his boots, stuck them into his girdle, and went on. It was easy walking now.

"I'll go on for another three miles," thought he, "and then turn to the left. This spot is so fine that it would be a pity to lose it. The further one goes, the better the land seems."

He went straight on for a while, and when he looked around, the hillock was scarcely visible and the people on it looked like black ants, and he could just see something glistening there in the sun.

"Ah," thought Pahom, "I have gone far enough in this direction; it's time to turn. Besides, I'm in a regular sweat, and very thirsty."

He stopped, dug a large hole, and heaped up pieces of turf. Next he untied his flask, had a drink, and then turned sharply to the left. He went on and on; the grass was high, and it was very hot.

Pahom began to grow tired: he looked at the sun and saw that it was noon.

"Well," he thought, "I must have a rest."

He sat down, and ate some bread and drank some water; but he did not lie down, thinking that if he did he might fall asleep. After sitting a little while, he went on again. At first he walked easily; the food had strengthened him; but it had become terribly hot and he felt sleepy. Still he went on, thinking: "An hour to suffer, a lifetime to live."

He went a long way in this direction also, and was about to turn to the left again, when he perceived a damp hollow: "It would be a pity to leave that out," he thought. "Flax would do well there." So he went on past the hollow and dug a hole on the other side of it before he made a sharp turn. Pahom looked toward the hillock. The heat made the air hazy: it seemed to be quivering, and through the haze the people on the hillock could scarcely be seen.

"Ah," thought Pahom, "I have made the sides too long; I must make this one shorter." And he went along the third side, stepping faster. He looked at the sun: it was nearly halfway to the horizon, and he had not yet done two miles of the third side of the square. He was still ten miles from the goal.

"No," he thought, "though it will make my land lopsided, I must hurry back in a straight line now. I might go too far, and as it is I have a great deal of land."

So Pahom hurriedly dug a hole and turned straight toward the hillock.

IX

Pahom went straight toward the hillock, but he now walked with difficulty. He was exhausted from the heat, his bare feet were cut and bruised, and his legs began to fail. He longed to rest, but it was impossible if he meant to get back before sunset. The sun waits for no man, and it was sinking lower and lower.

"Oh, Lord," he thought, "if only I have not blundered trying for too much! What if I am too late?"

He looked toward the hillock and at the sun. He was still far from his goal, and the sun was already near the rim of the sky.

Pahom walked on and on; it was very hard walking, but he went quicker and quicker. He pressed on, but was still far from the place. He began running, threw away his coat, his boots, his flask, and his cap, and kept only the spade which he used as a support.

"What am I to do?" he thought again. "I've grasped too much and ruined the whole affair. I can't get there before the sun sets."

Leo Tolstoy   How Much Land Does A Man Need?

And this fear made him still more breathless. Pahom kept on running; his soaking shirt and trousers stuck to him, and his mouth was parched. His breast was working like a blacksmith's bellows, his bean was beating like a hammer, and his legs were giving way as if they did not belong to him. Pahom was seized with terror lest he should die of the strain.

Though afraid of death, he could not stop.

"After having run all that way they will call me a fool if I stop now," thought he.

And he ran on and on, and drew near and heard the Bashkirs yelling and shouting to him, and their cries inflamed his heart still more. He gathered his last strength and ran on.

The sun was close to the rim of the sky and, cloaked in mist, looked large, and red as blood. Now, yes, now, it was about to set! The sun was quite low, but he was also quite near his goal. Pahom could already see the people on the hillock waving their arms to make him hurry. He could see the fox-fur cap on the ground and the money in it, and the Chief sitting on the ground holding his sides. And Pahom remembered his dream.

"There's plenty of land," thought he, "but will God let me live on it? I have lost my life, I have lost my life! Never will I reach that spot!"

Pahom looked at the sun, which had reached the earth: one side of it had already disappeared. With all his remaining strength he rushed on, bending his body forward so that his legs could hardly follow fast enough to keep him from falling. Just as he reached the hillock it suddenly grew dark. He looked up—the sun had already set!

He gave a cry: "All my labor has been in vain," thought he, and was about to stop, but he heard the Bashkirs still shouting, and remembered that though to him, from below, the sun seemed to have set, they on the hillock could still see it. He took a long breath and ran up the hillock. It was still light there. He reached the top and saw the cap. Before it sat the Chief, laughing and holding his sides. Again Pahom remembered his dream, and he uttered a cry: his legs gave way beneath him, he fell forward and reached the cap with his hands.

"Ah, that's a fine fellow!" exclaimed the Chief. "He has gained much land!"

Pahom's servant came running up and tried to raise him, but he saw that blood was flowing from his mouth. Pahom was dead.

Stories That Scared Even Stalin

The Bashkirs clicked their tongues to show their pity.

His servant picked up the spade and dug a grave long enough for Pahom to lie in, and buried him in it.

Six feet from his head to his heels was all he needed.

The Queen of Spades
Alexander Pushkin

I

There was a card party at the rooms of Naroumoff, of the Horse Guards. The long winter night passed away imperceptibly, and it was five o'clock in the morning before the company sat down to supper. Those who had won ate with a good appetite; the others sat staring absently at their empty plates. When the champagne appeared, however, the conversation became more animated, and all took a part in it.

"And how did you fare, Souirin?" asked the host.

"Oh, I lost, as usual. I must confess that I am unlucky. I play mirandole, I always keep cool, I never allow anything to put me out, and yet I always lose!"

"And you did not once allow yourself to be tempted to back the red? Your firmness astonishes me."

"But what do you think of Hermann?" said one of the guests, pointing to a young engineer. "He has never had a card in his hand in his life, he has never in his life laid a wager; and yet he sits here till five o'clock in the morning watching our play."

"Play interests me very much," said Hermann, "but I am not in the position to sacrifice the necessary in the hope of winning the superfluous."

"Hermann is a German; he is economical--that is all!" observed Tomsky. "But if there is one person that I cannot understand, it is my grandmother, the Countess Anna Fedorovna!"

"How so?" inquired the guests.

"I cannot understand," continued Tomsky, "how it is that my grandmother does not punt."

"Then you do not know the reason why?"

"No, really; I haven't the faintest idea. But let me tell you the story. You must know that about sixty years ago my grandmother went to Paris, where she created quite a sensation. People used to run after her to catch a glimpse of the 'Muscovite Venus.' Richelieu made love to her, and my grandmother maintains that he almost blew out his brains in consequence of her cruelty. At that time ladies used to play at faro. On one occasion at the Court, she lost a very considerable sum to the Duke of Orleans. On returning home, my grandmother removed the patches from her face, took off her hoops, informed my grandfather of her loss at the gaming-table, and ordered him to pay the money. My deceased grandfather, as far as I remember, was a sort of house-steward to my grandmother. He dreaded her like fire; but, on hearing of such a heavy loss, he almost went out of his mind. He calculated the various sums she had lost, and pointed out to her that in six months she had spent half a million of francs; that neither their Moscow nor Saratoff estates were in Paris; and, finally, refused point-blank to pay the debt. My grandmother gave him a box on the ear and slept by herself as a sign of her displeasure. The next day she sent for her husband, hoping that this domestic punishment had produced an effect upon him, but she found him inflexible. For the first time in her life she entered into reasonings and explanations with him, thinking to be able to convince him by pointing out to him that there are debts and debts, and that there is a great difference between a prince and a coachmaker.

"But it was all in vain, my grandfather still remained obdurate. But the matter did not rest there. My grandmother did not know what to do. She had shortly before become acquainted with a very remarkable man. You have heard of Count St. Germain, about whom so many marvelous stories are told. You know that he represented himself as the Wandering Jew, as the discoverer of the elixir of life, of the philosopher's stone, and so forth. Some laughed at him as a charlatan; but Casnova, in his memoirs, says that he was a spy. But be that as it may, St.

Germain, in spite of the mystery surrounding him, was a very fascinating person, and was much sought after in the best circles of society. Even to this day my grandmother retains an affectionate recollection of him, and becomes quite angry if anyone speaks disrespectfully of him. My grandmother knew that St. Germain had large sums of money at his disposal. She resolved to have recourse to him, and she wrote a letter to him asking him to come to her without delay. The queer old man immediately waited upon her, and found her overwhelmed with grief. She described to him in the blackest colors the barbarity of her husband, and ended by declaring that her whole hope depended upon his friendship and amiability.

"St. Germain reflected.

"'I could advance you the sum you want,' said he, 'but I know that you would not rest easy until you had paid me back, and I should not like to bring fresh troubles upon you. But there is another way of getting out of your difficulty: you can win back your money.'

"'But, my dear Count,' replied my grandmother, 'I tell you that I haven't any money left!'

"'Money is not necessary,' replied St. Germain, 'be pleased to listen to me.'

"Then he revealed to her a secret, for which each of us would give a good deal."

The young officers listened with increased attention. Tomsky lit his pipe, puffed away for a moment, and then continued:

"That same evening my grandmother went to Versailles to the jeu de la reine. The Duke of Orleans kept the bank; my grandmother excused herself in an offhanded manner for not having yet paid her debt by inventing some little story, and then began to play against him. She chose three cards and played them one after the other; all three won sonika,* and my grandmother recovered every farthing that she lost."

"Mere chance!" said one of the guests.

"A tale!" observed Hermann.

"Perhaps they were marked cards!" said a third.

---

* Said of a card when it wins or loses in the quickest possible time.

"I do not think so," replied Tomsky, gravely.

"What!" said Naroumoff, "you have a grandmother who knows how to hit upon three lucky cards in succession, and you have never yet succeeded in getting the secret of it out of her?"

"That's the deuce of it!" replied Tomsky, "she had four sons, one of whom was my father; all four were determined gamblers, and yet not to one of them did she ever reveal her secret, although it would not have been a bad thing either for them or for me. But this is what I heard from my uncle, Count Ivan Ilitch, and he assured me, on his honor, that it was true. The late Chaplitsky-- the same who died in poverty after having squandered millions—once lost, in his youth, about three hundred thousand roubles—to Zoritch, if I remember rightly. He was in despair. My grandmother, who was always very severe upon the extravagance of young men, took pity, however, upon Chaplitsky. She gave him three cards telling him to play them one after the other, at the same time exacting from him a solemn promise that he would never play at cards again as long as he lived. Chaplitsky then went to his victorious opponent, and they began a fresh game. On the first card he staked fifty thousand roubles, and won sonika; he doubled the stake, and won again; till at last, by pursuing the same tactics, he won back more than he had lost."

"But it is time to go to bed, it is a quarter to six already."

And, indeed, it was already beginning to dawn; the young men emptied their glasses and then took leave of each other.

II

The old Countess A---- was seated in her dressing-room in front of her looking-glass. Three waiting maids stood around her. One held a small pot of rouge, another a box of hairpins, and the third a tall cap with bright red ribbons. The Countess had no longer the slightest pretensions to beauty, but she still preserved the habits of her youth, dressed in strict accordance with the fashion of seventy years before, and made as long and as careful a toilette as she would have done sixty years previously. Near the window, at an embroidery frame, sat a young lady, her ward.

"Good-morning, grandmamma," said a young officer, entering the room. "Bonjour, Mademoiselle Lise. Grandmamma, I want to ask you something."

Alexander Pushkin   The Queen of Spades

"What is it, Paul?"

"I want you to let me introduce one of my friends to you, and to allow me to bring him to the ball on Friday."

"Bring him direct to the ball and introduce him to me there. Were you at B----'s yesterday?"

"Yes; everything went off very pleasantly, and dancing was kept up until five o'clock. How charming Eletskaia was!"

"But, my dear, what is there charming about her? Isn't she like her grandmother, the Princess Daria Petrovna? By the way, she must be very old, the Princess Daria Petrovna?"

"How do you mean, old?" cried Tomsky, thoughtlessly, "she died seven years ago."

The young lady raised her head, and made a sign to the young officer. He then remembered that the old Countess was never to be informed of the death of her contemporaries, and he bit his lips. But the old Countess heard the news with the greatest indifference.

"Dead!" said she, "and I did not know it. We were appointed maids of honor at the same time, and when we were presented to the Empress--"

And the Countess for the hundredth time related to her grandson one of her anecdotes.

"Come, Paul," said she, when she had finished her story, "help me to get up. Lizanka,* where is my snuffbox?"

And the Countess with her three maids went behind a screen to finish her toilette. Tomsky was left alone with the young lady.

"Who is the gentleman you wish to introduce to the Countess?" asked Lizaveta Ivanovna in a whisper.

"Naroumoff. Do you know him?"

"No. Is he a soldier or a civilian?"

"A soldier."

"Is he in the Engineers?"

"No, in the Cavalry. What made you think that he was in the Engineers?"

- Diminutive of Lizaveta (Elizabeth).

57

The young lady smiled, but made no reply.

"Paul," cried the Countess from behind the screen, "send me some new novel, only pray don't let it be one of the present day style."

"What do you mean, grandmother?"

"That is, a novel, in which the hero strangles neither his father nor his mother, and in which there are no drowned bodies. I have a great horror of drowned persons."

"There are no such novels nowadays. Would you like a Russian one?"

"Are there any Russian novels? Send me one, my dear, pray send me one!"

"Good-bye, grandmother. I am in a hurry. . . . Goodby Lizavetta Ivanovna. What made you think that Naroumoff was in the Engineers?"

And Tomsky left the boudoir.

Lizaveta Ivanovna was left alone. She laid aside her work, and began to look out of the window. A few moments afterwards, at a corner house on the other side of the street, a young officer appeared. A deep flush covered her cheeks; she took up her work again, and bent her head down over the frame. At the same moment the Countess returned, completely dressed.

"Order the carriage, Lizaveta," said she, "we will go out for a drive."

Lizaveta rose from the frame, and began to arrange her work.

"What is the matter with you, my child, are you deaf?" cried the Countess. "Order the carriage to be got ready at once."

"I will do so this moment," replied the young lady, hastening into the anteroom.

A servant entered and gave the Countess some books from Prince Paul Alexandrovitch.

"Tell him that I am much obliged to him," said the Countess.

"Lizaveta! Lizaveta! where are you running to?"

"I am going to dress."

"There is plenty of time, my dear. Sit down here. Open the first volume and read to me aloud."

Her companion took the book and read a few lines.

"Louder," said the Countess. "What is the matter with you, my child? Have you lost your voice? Wait--Give me that footstool--a little nearer--that will do!"

Lizaveta read two more pages. The Countess yawned.

"Put the book down," said she, "what a lot of nonsense! Send it back to Prince Paul with my thanks. . . . But where is the carriage?"

"The carriage is ready," said Lizaveta, looking out into the street.

"How is it that you are not dressed?" said the Countess. "I must always wait for you. It is intolerable, my dear!"

Liza hastened to her room. She had not been there two minutes before the Countess began to ring with all her might. The three waiting-maids came running in at one door, and the valet at another.

"How is it that you cannot hear me when I ring for you?" said the Countess. "Tell Lizaveta Ivanovna that I am waiting for her."

Lizaveta returned with her hat and cloak on.

"At last you are here!" said the Countess. "But why such an elaborate toilette? Whom do you intend to captivate? What sort of weather is it? It seems rather windy."

"No, your Ladyship, it is very calm," replied the valet.

"You never think of what you are talking about. Open the window. So it is; windy and bitterly cold. Unharness the horses, Lizaveta, we won't go out--there was no need to deck yourself like that."

"What a life is mine!" thought Lizaveta Ivanovna.

And, in truth, Lizaveta Ivanovna was a very unfortunate creature.

"The bread of the stranger is bitter," says Dante, "and his staircase hard to climb." But who can know what the bitterness of dependence is so well as the poor companion of an old lady of quality? The Countess A---- had by no means a bad heart, but she was capricious, like a woman who had been spoiled by the world, as well as being avaricious and egotistical, like all old people, who have seen their best days, and whose thoughts are with the past, and not the present. She participated in all the vanities of the great world, went to balls, where she sat in a corner, painted and dressed in old-fashioned style, like a deformed but indispensable ornament of the ballroom; all the guests on entering approached her and made a profound bow, as if in accordance with a set ceremony, but after that nobody took any further notice of her. She received the whole town at her house, and observed the strictest etiquette, although she could no longer recognize the faces of people. Her numerous domestics, growing fat and old in her antechamber and servants' hall, did just as they liked, and vied with each other in robbing the aged Countess in the most bare-faced manner. Lizaveta Ivanovna was the martyr of the household. She made tea, and was reproached with using too much sugar; she read novels aloud to the Countess, and the faults of the author were visited upon her head; she accompanied the Countess in her walks, and was held answerable for the weather or the state of the pavement. A salary was attached to the post, but she very rarely received it, although she was expected to dress like everybody else, that is to say, like very few indeed. In society she played the most pitiable role. Everybody knew her, and nobody paid her any attention. At balls she danced only when a partner was wanted, and ladies would only take hold of her arm when it was necessary to lead her out of the room to attend to their dresses. She was very self-conscious, and felt her position keenly, and she looked about her with impatience for a deliverer to come to her rescue; but the young men, calculating in their giddiness, honored her with but very little attention, although Lizaveta Ivanovna was a hundred times prettier than the bare-faced, cold-hearted marriageable girls around whom they hovered. Many a time did she quietly slink away from the glittering, but wearisome, drawing-room, to go and cry in her own poor little room, in which stood a screen, a chest of drawers, a looking-glass, and a painted bedstead, and where a tallow candle burnt feebly in a copper candlestick.

One morning--this was about two days after the evening party described at the beginning of this story, and a week previous to the scene at which we have just assisted--Lizaveta Ivanovna was seated near the window at her embroidery frame, when, happening to look out into the street, she caught sight of a young Engineer officer, standing motionless with his eyes fixed upon her window. She lowered her head, and went on again with her work. About five minutes afterwards she looked out again--the young officer was still standing in the same place. Not being in the habit of coquetting with passing officers, she did not continue to gaze out into the street, but went on sewing for a couple of hours, without raising her head. Dinner was announced. She rose up and began to put her embroidery away, but glancing casually out of the window, she perceived the officer again. This seemed to her very strange. After dinner she went to the window with a certain feeling of uneasiness, but the officer was no longer there--and she thought no more about him.

A couple of days afterwards, just as she was stepping into the carriage with the Countess, she saw him again. He was standing close behind the door, with his face half-concealed by his fur collar, but his dark eyes sparkled beneath his cap. Lizaveta felt alarmed, though she knew not why, and she trembled as she seated herself in the carriage.

On returning home, she hastened to the window--the officer was standing in his accustomed place, with his eyes fixed upon her. She drew back, a prey to curiosity, and agitated by a feeling which was quite new to her.

From that time forward not a day passed without the young officer making his appearance under the window at the customary hour, and between him and her there was established a sort of mute acquaintance. Sitting in her place at work, she used to feel his approach, and, raising her head, she would look at him longer and longer each day. The young man seemed to be very grateful to her; she saw with the sharp eye of youth, how a sudden flush covered his pale cheeks each time that their glances met. After about a week she commenced to smile at him. . . .

When Tomsky asked permission of his grandmother, the Countess, to present one of his friends to her, the young girl's heart beat violently. But hearing that Naroumoff was not an Engineer, she regretted that by her thoughtless question, she had betrayed her secret to the volatile Tomsky.

Hermann was the son of a German who had become a naturalized Russian, and from whom he had inherited a small capital. Being firmly convinced of the necessity of preserving his independence, Hermann did not touch his private income, but lived on his pay, without allowing himself the slightest luxury. Moreover, he was reserved and ambitious, and his companions rarely had an opportunity of making merry at the expense of his extreme parsimony. He had strong passions and an ardent imagination, but his firmness of disposition preserved him from the ordinary errors of young men. Thus, though a gamester at heart, he never touched a card, for he considered his position did not allow him--as he said--

"To risk the necessary in the hope of winning the superfluous," yet he would sit for nights together at the card table and follow with feverish anxiety the different turns of the game.

The story of the three cards had produced a powerful impression upon his imagination, and all night long he could think of nothing else. "If," he thought to himself the following evening, as he walked along the streets of St. Petersburg, "if the old Countess would not reveal her secret to me! If she would only tell me the names of the three winning cards. Why should I not try my fortune?

I must get introduced to her and win her favor--become her lover. . . . But all that will take time, and she is eighty-seven years old. She might be dead in a week, in a couple of days even.

But the story itself? Can it really be true? No! Economy, temperance, and industry; those are my three winning cards; by means of them I shall be able to double my capital--increase it sevenfold, and procure for myself ease and independence."

Musing in this manner, he walked on until he found himself in one of the principal streets of St. Petersburg, in front of a house of antiquated architecture. The street was blocked with equipages; carriages one after the other drew up in front of the brilliantly illuminated doorway. At one moment there stepped out onto the pavement the well-shaped little foot of some young beauty, at another the heavy boot of a cavalry officer, and then the silk stockings and shoes of a member of the diplomatic world. Fur and cloaks passed in rapid succession before the gigantic porter at the entrance. Hermann stopped. "Whose house is this?" he asked of the watchman at the corner.

"The Countess A----'s," replied the watchman.

Hermann started. The strange story of the three cards again presented itself to his imagination. He began walking up and down before the house, thinking of its owner and her strange secret.

Returning late to his modest lodging, he could not go to sleep for a long time, and when at last he did doze off, he could dream of nothing but cards, green tables, piles of banknotes, and heaps of ducats. He played one card after the other, winning uninterruptedly, and then he gathered up the gold and filled his pockets with the notes. When he woke up late the next morning, he sighed over the loss of his imaginary wealth, and then sallying out into the town, he found himself once more in front of the Countess's residence. Some unknown power seemed to have attracted him thither. He stopped and looked up at the windows. At one of these he saw a head with luxuriant black hair, which was bent down, probably over some book or an embroidery frame. The head was raised. Hermann saw a fresh complexion, and a pair of dark eyes. That moment decided his fate.

III

Lizaveta Ivanovna had scarcely taken off her hat and cloak, when the Countess sent for her, and again ordered her to get the carriage ready. The vehicle drew up before the door, and they prepared to take their seats. Just at the moment when two footmen were assisting the old lady to enter the carriage, Lizaveta saw her Engineer standing close beside the wheel; he grasped her hand; alarm caused her to lose her presence of mind, and the young man disappeared--but not before he had left a letter between her fingers. She concealed it in her glove, and during the whole of the drive she neither saw nor heard anything. It was the custom of the Countess, when out for an airing in her carriage, to be constantly asking such questions as "Who was that person that met us just now? What is the name of this bridge? What is written on that sign-board?" On this occasion, however, Lizaveta returned such vague and absurd answers, that the Countess became angry with her.

"What is the matter with you, my dear?" she exclaimed. "Have you taken leave of your senses, or what is it? Do you not hear me or understand what I say? Heaven be thanked, I am still in my right mind and speak plainly enough!"

Lizaveta Ivanovna did not hear her. On returning home she ran to her room, and drew the letter out of her glove: it was not sealed. Lizaveta read it. The letter contained a declaration of love; it was tender, respectful, and copied word for word from a German novel. But Lizaveta did not know anything of the German language, and she was quite delighted.

For all that, the letter caused her to feel exceedingly uneasy. For the first time in her life she was entering into secret and confidential relations with a young man. His boldness alarmed her. She reproached herself for her imprudent behavior, and knew not what to do. Should she cease to sit at the window, and, by assuming an appearance of indifference towards him, put a check upon the young officer's desire for further acquaintance with her? Should she send his letter back to him, or should she answer him in a cold and decided manner? There was nobody to whom she could turn in her perplexity, for she had neither female friend nor adviser. At length she resolved to reply to him.

She sat down at her little writing table, took pen and paper, and began to think. Several times she began her letter and then tore it up; the way she had expressed herself seemed to her either too inviting or too cold and decisive. At last she succeeded in writing a few lines with which she felt satisfied.

"I am convinced," she wrote, "that your intentions are honorable, and that you do not wish to offend me by any imprudent behavior, but our acquaintance must not begin in such a manner. I return you your letter, and I hope that I shall never have any cause to complain of this undeserved slight."

The next day, as soon as Hermann made his appearance, Lizaveta rose from her embroidery, went into the drawing-room, opened the ventilator, and threw the letter into the street, trusting that the young officer would have the perception to pick it up.

Hermann hastened forward, picked it up, and then repaired to a confectioner's shop. Breaking the seal of the envelope, he found inside it his own letter and Lizaveta's reply. He had expected this, and he returned home, his mind deeply occupied with his intrigue.

Three days afterwards a bright-eyed young girl from a milliner's establishment brought Lizaveta a letter. Lizaveta opened it with great uneasiness, fearing that it was a demand for money, when, suddenly, she recognized Hermann's handwriting.

"You have made a mistake, my dear," said she. "This letter is not for me."

"Oh, yes, it is for you," replied the girl, smiling very knowingly. "Have the goodness to read it."

Lizaveta glanced at the letter. Hermann requested an interview.

"It cannot be," she cried, alarmed at the audacious request and the manner in which it was made. "This letter is certainly not for me," and she tore it into fragments.

"If the letter was not for you, why have you torn it up?" said the girl. "I should have given it back to the person who sent it."

"Be good enough, my dear," said Lizaveta, disconcerted by this remark, "not to bring me any more letters for the future, and tell the person who sent you that he ought to be ashamed."

But Hermann was not the man to be thus put off. Every day Lizaveta received from him a letter, sent now in this way, now in that. They were no longer translated from the German. Hermann wrote them under the inspiration of passion, and spoke in his own language, and they bore full testimony to the inflexibility of his desire, and the disordered condition of his uncontrollable imagination. Lizaveta no longer thought of sending them back to him; she became intoxicated with them, and began to reply to them, and little by little her answers became longer and more affectionate. At last she threw out of the window to him the following letter:

"This evening there is going to be a ball at the Embassy. The Countess will be there. We shall remain until two o'clock. You have now an opportunity of seeing me alone. As soon as the Countess is gone, the servants will very probably go out, and there will be nobody left but the Swiss, but he usually goes to sleep in his lodge. Come about half-past eleven. Walk straight upstairs. If you meet anybody in the anteroom, ask if the Countess is at home. You will be told 'No,' in which case there will be nothing left for you to do but to go away again. But it is most probable that you will meet nobody. The maidservants will all be together in one room. On leaving the anteroom, turn to the left, and walk straight on until you reach the Countess's bedroom. In the bedroom, behind a screen, you will find two doors: the one on the right leads to a cabinet, which the Countess never enters; the one on the left leads to a corridor, at the end of which is a little winding staircase; this leads to my room."

Hermann trembled like a tiger as he waited for the appointed time to arrive. At ten o'clock in the evening he was already in front of the Countess's house. The weather was terrible; the wind blew with great violence, the sleety snow fell in large flakes, the lamps emitted a feeble light, the streets were deserted; from time to time a sledge drawn by a sorry-looking hack, passed by on the lookout for a belated passenger. Hermann was enveloped in a thick overcoat, and felt neither wind nor snow.

At last the Countess's carriage drew up. Hermann saw two footmen carry out in their arms the bent form of the old lady, wrapped in sable fur, and immediately behind her, clad in a warm mantle, and with her head ornamented with a wreath of fresh flowers, followed Lizaveta. The door was closed. The carriage rolled heavily away through the yielding snow. The porter shut the street door, the windows became dark.

Hermann began walking up and down near the deserted house; at length he stopped under a lamp, and glanced at his watch: it was twenty minutes past eleven. He remained standing under the lamp, his eyes fixed upon the watch impatiently waiting for the remaining minutes to pass. At half-past eleven precisely Hermann ascended the steps of the house and made his way into the brightly-illuminated vestibule. The porter was not there. Hermann hastily ascended the staircase, opened the door of the anteroom, and saw a footman sitting asleep in an antique chair by the side of a lamp. With a light, firm step Hermann passed by him. The drawing-room and dining-room were in darkness, but a feeble reflection penetrated thither from the lamp in the anteroom.

Hermann reached the Countess's bedroom. Before a shrine, which was full of old images, a golden lamp was burning. Faded stuffed chairs and divans with soft cushions stood in melancholy symmetry around the room, the walls of which were hung with china silk. On one side of the room hung two portraits painted in Paris by Madame Lebrun. One of these represented a stout, red-faced man of about forty years of age, in a bright green uniform, and with a star upon his breast; the other--a beautiful young woman, with an aquiline nose, forehead curls, and a rose in her powdered hair. In the corner stood porcelain shepherds and shepherdesses, dining-room clocks from the workshop of the celebrated Lefroy, bandboxes, roulettes, fans, and the various playthings for the amusement of ladies that were in vogue at the end of the last century, when Montgolfier's balloons and Niesber's magnetism were the rage. Hermann stepped behind the screen. At the back of it stood a little iron bedstead; on the right was the door which led to the cabinet; on the left, the other which led to the corridor. He opened the latter, and saw the little winding staircase which led to the room of the poor companion. But he retraced his steps and entered the dark cabinet.

The time passed slowly. All was still. The clock in the drawing-room struck twelve, the strokes echoed through the room one after the other, and everything was quiet again. Hermann stood leaning against the cold stove. He was calm, his heart beat regularly, like that of a man resolved upon a dangerous but inevitable undertaking. One o'clock in the morning struck; then two, and he heard the distant noise of carriage-wheels. An involuntary agitation took possession of him. The carriage drew near and stopped. He heard the sound of the carriage steps being let down. All was bustle within the house. The servants were running hither and thither, there was a confusion of voices, and the rooms were lit up. Three antiquated chambermaids entered the bedroom, and they were shortly afterwards followed by the Countess, who, more dead than alive, sank into a Voltaire armchair. Hermann peeped through a chink. Lizaveta Ivanovna passed close by him, and he heard her hurried steps as she hastened up the little spiral staircase. For a moment his heart was assailed by something like a pricking of conscience, but the emotion was only transitory, and his heart became petrified as before.

The Countess began to undress before her looking-glass. Her rose-bedecked cap was taken off, and then her powdered wig was removed from off her white and closely cut hair. Hairpins fell in showers around her. Her yellow satin dress, brocaded with silver, fell down at her swollen feet.

Hermann was a witness of the repugnant mysteries of her toilette; at last the Countess was in her night-cap and dressing-gown, and in this costume, more suitable to her age, she appeared less hideous and deformed.

Like all old people, in general, the Countess suffered from sleeplessness. Having undressed, she seated herself at the window in a Voltaire armchair, and dismissed her maids. The candles were taken away, and once more the room was left with only one lamp burning in it. The Countess sat there looking quite yellow, mumbling with her flaccid lips and swaying to and fro. Her dull eyes expressed complete vacancy of mind, and, looking at her, one would have thought that the rocking of her body was not a voluntary action of her own, but was produced by the action of some concealed galvanic mechanism.

Suddenly the death-like face assumed an inexplicable expression. The lips ceased to tremble, the eyes became animated: before the Countess stood an unknown man.

"Do not be alarmed, for Heaven's sake, do not be alarmed!" said he in a low but distinct voice. "I have no intention of doing you any harm; I have only come to ask a favor of you."

The old woman looked at him in silence, as if she had not heard what he had said. Hermann thought that she was deaf, and, bending down towards her ear, he repeated what he had said. The aged Countess remained silent as before.

"You can insure the happiness of my life," continued Hermann, "and it will cost you nothing. I know that you can name three cards in order--"

Hermann stopped. The Countess appeared now to understand what he wanted; she seemed as if seeking for words to reply.

"It was a joke," she replied at last. "I assure you it was only a joke."

"There is no joking about the matter," replied Hermann, angrily. "Remember Chaplitsky, whom you helped to win."

The Countess became visibly uneasy. Her features expressed strong emotion, but they quickly resumed their former immobility.

"Can you not name me these three winning cards?" continued Hermann.

The Countess remained silent; Hermann continued:

"For whom are you preserving your secret? For your grandsons? They are rich enough without it, they do not know the worth of money. Your cards would be of no use to a spendthrift. He who cannot preserve his paternal inheritance will die in want, even though he had a demon at his service. I am not a man of that sort. I know the value of money. Your three cards will not be thrown away upon me. Come!"

He paused and tremblingly awaited her reply. The Countess remained silent. Hermann fell upon his knees.

"If your heart has ever known the feeling of love," said be, "if you remember its rapture, if you have ever smiled at the cry of your new-born child, if any human feeling has ever entered into your breast, I entreat you by the feelings of a wife, a lover, a mother, by all that is most sacred in life, not to reject my prayer. Reveal to me your secret. Of what use is it to you? May be it is connected with some terrible sin, with the loss of eternal salvation, with some bargain with the devil. Reflect, you are old, you have not long to live--I am ready to take your sins upon my soul. Only reveal to me your secret. Remember that the happiness of a man is in your hands, that not only I, but my children and my grandchildren, will bless your memory and reverence you as a saint."

The old Countess answered not a word.

Hermann rose to his feet.

"You old hag!" he exclaimed, grinding his teeth, "then I will make you answer!" With these words he drew a pistol from his pocket. At the sight of the pistol, the Countess for the second time exhibited strong emotions. She shook her head, and raised her hands as if to protect herself from the shot. Then she fell backwards, and remained motionless.

"Come, an end to this childish nonsense!" said Hermann, taking hold of her hand. "I ask you for the last time: will you tell me the names of your three cards, or will you not?"

The Countess made no reply. Hermann perceived that she was dead!

IV

Lizaveta Ivanovna was sitting in her room, still in her ball dress, lost in deep thought. On returning home, she had hastily dismissed the chambermaid, who very reluctantly came forward to assist her, saying that she would undress herself, and with a trembling heart had gone up to her own room, expecting to find Hermann there, but yet hoping not to find him. At the first glance he was not there, and she thanked her fate for having prevented him keeping the appointment. She sat down without undressing, and began to call to mind all the circumstances which in a short time had carried her so far. It was not three weeks since the time when she had first seen the young officer from the window--and yet she was already in correspondence with him, and he had succeeded in inducing her to grant him a nocturnal interview. She knew his name only through his having written it at the bottom of some of his letters; she had never spoken to him, had never heard his voice, and had never heard him spoken of until that evening. But, strange to say, that very evening at the ball, Tomsky, being piqued with the young Princess Pauline N----, who, contrary to her usual custom, did not flirt with him, wished to revenge himself by assuming an air of indifference: he therefore engaged Lizaveta Ivanovna, and danced an endless mazurka with her. During the whole of the time he kept teasing her about her partiality for Engineer officers, he assured her that he knew far more than she imagined, and some of his jests were so happily aimed, that Lizaveta thought several times that her secret was known to him.

"From whom have you learned all this?" she asked, smiling.

"From a friend of a person very well known to you," replied Tomsky, "from a very distinguished man."

"And whom is this distinguished man?"

"His name is Hermann." Lizaveta made no reply, but her hands and feet lost all sense of feeling.

"This Hermann," continued Tomsky, "is a man of romantic personality. He has the profile of a Napoleon, and the soul of a Mephistopheles. I believe that he has at least three crimes upon his conscience. How pale you have become!"

"I have a headache. But what did this Hermann, or whatever his name is, tell you?"

"Hermann is very dissatisfied with his friend. He says that in his place he would act very differently. I even think that Hermann himself has designs upon you; at least, he listens very attentively to all that his friend has to say about you."

"And where has he seen me?"

"In church, perhaps; or on the parade. God alone knows where. It may have been in your room, while you were asleep, for there is nothing that he--"

Three ladies approaching him with the question: "oubli ou regret?" interrupted the conversation, which had become so tantalizingly interesting to Lizaveta.

The lady chosen by Tomsky was the Princess Pauline herself. She succeeded in effecting a reconciliation with him during the numerous turns of the dance, after which he conducted her to her chair. On returning to his place, Tomsky thought no more either of Hermann or Lizaveta. She longed to renew the interrupted conversation, but the mazurka came to an end, and shortly afterwards the old Countess took her departure.

Tomsky's words were nothing more than the customary small talk of the dance, but they sank deep into the soul of the young dreamer. The portrait, sketched by Tomsky, coincided with the picture she had formed within her own mind, and, thanks to the latest romances, the ordinary countenance of her admirer became invested with attributes capable of alarming her and fascinating her imagination at the same time. She was now sitting with her bare arms crossed, and with her head, still adorned with flowers, sunk upon her uncovered bosom. Suddenly the door opened and Hermann entered. She shuddered.

"Where were you?" she asked in a terrified whisper.

"In the old Countess's bedroom," replied Hermann. "I have just left her. The Countess is dead."

"My God! What do you say?"

"And I am afraid," added Hermann, "that I am the cause of her death."

Lizaveta looked at him, and Tomsky's words found an echo in her soul: "This man has at least three crimes upon his conscience!" Hermann sat down by the window near her, and related all that had happened.

Lizaveta listened to him in terror. So all those passionate letters, those ardent desires, this bold, obstinate pursuit—all this was not love! Money--that was what his soul yearned for! She could not satisfy his desire and make him happy. The poor girl had been nothing but the blind tool of a robber, of the murderer of her aged benefactress! She wept bitter tears of agonized repentance. Hermann gazed at her in silence; his heart, too, was a prey to violent emotion, but neither the tears of the poor girl, nor the wonderful charm of her beauty, enhanced by her grief, could produce any impression upon his hardened soul. He felt no pricking of conscience at the thought of the dead old woman. One thing only grieved him: the irreparable loss of the secret from which he had expected to obtain great wealth.

"You are a monster!" said Lizaveta at last.

"I did not wish for her death," replied Hermann, "my pistol was not loaded." Both remained silent. The day began to dawn. Lizaveta extinguished her candle, a pale light illumined her room. She wiped her tear-stained eyes, and raised them towards Hermann. He was sitting near the window, with his arms crossed, and with a fierce frown upon his forehead. In this attitude he bore a striking resemblance to the portrait of Napoleon. This resemblance struck Lizaveta even.

"How shall I get you out of the house?" said she at last. "I thought of conducting you down the secret staircase."

"I will go alone," he answered.

Lizaveta arose, took from her drawer a key, handed it to Hermann, and gave him the necessary instructions. Hermann pressed her cold, inert hand, kissed her bowed head, and left the room.

He descended the winding staircase, and once more entered the Countess's bedroom. The dead old lady sat as if petrified, her face expressed profound tranquillity. Hermann stopped before her, and gazed long and earnestly at her, as if he wished to convince himself of the terrible reality. At last he entered the cabinet, felt behind the tapestry for the door, and then began to descend the dark staircase, filled with strange emotions. "Down this very staircase," thought he, "perhaps coming from the very same room, and at this very same hour sixty years ago, there may have glided, in an embroidered coat, with his hair dressed a l'oiseau royal, and pressing to his heart his three-cornered hat, some youn gallant who has long been mouldering in the grave, but the heart of his aged mistress has only today ceased to beat."

At the bottom of the staircase Hermann found a door, which he opened with a key, and then traversed a corridor which conducted him into the street.

V

Three days after the fatal night, at nine o'clock in the morning, Hermann repaired to the Convent of -----, where the last honors were to be paid to the mortal remains of the old Countess. Although feeling no remorse, he could not altogether stifle the voice of conscience, which said to him: "You are the murderer of the old woman!" In spite of his entertaining very little religious belief, he was exceedingly superstitious; and believing that the dead Countess might exercise an evil influence on his life, he resolved to be present at her obsequies in order to implore her pardon.

The church was full. It was with difficulty that Herman made his way through the crowd of people. The coffin was placed upon a rich catafalque beneath a velvet baldachin. The deceased Countess lay within it, with her hands crossed upon her breast, with a lace cap upon her head, and dressed in a white satin robe. Around the catafalque stood the members of her household; the servants in black caftans, with armorial ribbons upon their shoulders and candles in their hands; the relatives--children, grandchildren, and great-grandchildren--in deep mourning.

Nobody wept, tears would have been an affectation. The Countess was so old that her death could have surprised nobody, and her relatives had long looked upon her as being out of the world. A famous preacher delivered the funeral sermon. In simple and touching words he described the peaceful passing away of the righteous, who had passed long years in calm preparation for a Christian end. "The angel of death found her," said the orator, "engaged in pious meditation and waiting for the midnight bridegroom."

The service concluded amidst profound silence. The relatives went forward first to take a farewell of the corpse. Then followed the numerous guests, who had come to render the last homage to her who for so many years had been a participator in their frivolous amusements. After these followed the members of the

Countess's household. The last of these an old woman of the same age as the deceased. Two young women led her forward by the hand. She had not strength enough to bow down to the ground--she merely shed a few tears, and kissed the cold hand of the mistress.

Herman now resolved to approach the coffin. He knelt down upon the cold stones, and remained in that position for some minutes; at last he arose as pale as the deceased Countess herself; he ascended the steps of the catafalque and bent over the corpse. . . . At that moment it seemed to him that the dead woman darted a mocking look at him and winked with one eye. Hermann started back, took a false step, and fell to the ground. Several persons hurried forward and raised him up. At the same moment Lizaveta Ivanovna was borne fainting into the porch of the church. This episode disturbed for some minutes the solemnity of the gloomy ceremony. Among the congregation arose a deep murmur, and a tall, thin chamberlain, a near relative of the deceased, whispered in the ear of an Englishman, who was standing near him, that the young officer was a natural son of the Countess, to which the Englishman coldly replied "Oh!"

During the whole of that day Hermann was strangely excited. Repairing to an out of the way restaurant to dine, be drank a great deal of wine, contrary to his usual custom, in the hope of deadening his inward agitation. But the wine only served to excite his imagination still more. On returning home he threw himself upon his bed without undressing, and fell into a deep sleep.

When he woke up it was already night, and the moon was shining into the room. He looked at his watch: it was a quarter to three. Sleep had left him; he sat down upon his bed, and thought of the funeral of the old Countess.

At that moment somebody in the street looked in at his window and immediately passed on again. Hermann paid no attention to this incident. A few moments afterwards he heard the door of his anteroom open. Hermann thought that it was his orderly, drunk as usual, returning from some nocturnal expedition, but presently he heard footsteps that were unknown to him: somebody was walking softly over the floor in slippers. The door opened, and a woman dressed in white entered the room. Hermann mistook her for his old nurse, and wondered what could bring her there at that hour of the night. But the white woman glided rapidly across the room and stood before him--and Hermann thought he recognized the Countess.

"I have come to you against my wish," she said in a firm voice, "but I have been ordered to grant your request. Three, seven, ace, will win for you if played in succession, but only on these conditions: that you do not play more than one card in twenty-four- hours, and that you never play again during the rest of your life. I forgive you my death, on condition that you marry my companion, Lizaveta Ivanovna."

With these words she turned round very quietly, walked with a shuffling gait towards the door, and disappeared. Hermann heard the street door open and shut, and again he saw someone look in at him through the window.

For a long time Hermann could not recover himself. He then rose up and entered the next room. His orderly was lying asleep upon the floor, and he had much difficulty in waking him. The orderly was drunk as usual, and no information could be obtained from him. The street door was locked. Hermann returned to his room, lit his candle, and wrote down all the details of his vision.

VI

Two fixed ideas can no more exist together in the moral world than two bodies can occupy one and the same physical world. "Three, seven, ace" soon drove out of Hermann's mind the thought of the dead Countess. "Three, seven, ace" were perpetually running through his head, and continually being repeated by his lips. If he saw a young girl, he would say: "How slender she is; quite like the three of hearts." If anybody asked "What is the time?" he would reply: "Five minutes to seven." Every stout man that he saw reminded him of the ace. "Three, seven, ace" haunted him in his sleep, and assumed all possible shapes. The threes bloomed before him in the forms of magnificent flowers, the sevens were represented by Gothic portals, and the aces became transformed into gigantic spiders. One thought alone occupied his whole mind—to make a profitable use of the secret which he had purchased so dearly. He thought of applying for a furlough so as to travel abroad. He wanted to go to Paris and tempt fortune in some gambling houses that abounded there. Chance spared him all this trouble.

There was in Moscow a society of rich gamesters, presided over by the celebrated Chekalinsky, who had passed all his life at the card table, and had amassed millions, accepting bills of exchange for his winnings, and paying his losses in ready money.

His long experience secured for him the confidence of his companions, and his open house, his famous cook, and his agreeable and fascinating manners, gained for him the respect of the public. He came to St. Petersburg. The young men of the capital flocked to his rooms, forgetting balls for cards, and preferring the emotions of faro to the seductions of flirting. Naroumoff conducted Hermann to Chekalinsky's residence.

They passed through a suite of rooms, filled with attentive domestics. The place was crowded. Generals and Privy Counsellors were playing at whist, young men were lolling carelessly upon the velvet-covered sofas, eating ices and smoking pipes. In the drawing-room, at the head of a long table, around which were assembled about a score of players, sat the master of the house keeping the bank. He was a man of about sixty years of age, of a very dignified appearance; his head was covered with silvery white hair; his full, florid countenance expressed good-nature, and his eyes twinkled with a perpetual smile. Naroumoff introduced Hermann to him. Chekalinsky shook him by the hand in a friendly manner, requested him not to stand on ceremony, and then went on dealing.

The game occupied some time. On the table lay more than thirty cards. Chekalinsky paused after each throw, in order to give the players time to arrange their cards and note down their losses, listened politely to their requests, and more politely still, straightened the corners of cards that some player's hand had chanced to bend. At last the game was finished. Chekalinsky shuffled the cards, and prepared to deal again.

"Will you allow me to take a card?" said Hermann, stretching out his hand from behind a stout gentleman who was punting.

Chekalinsky smiled and bowed silently, as a sign of acquiescence. Naroumoff laughingly congratulated Hermann on his abjuration of that abstention from cards which he had practised for so long a period, and wished him a lucky beginning.

"Stake!" said Hermann, writing some figures with chalk on the back of his card.

"How much?" asked the banker, contracting the muscles of his eyes, "excuse me, I cannot see quite clearly."

"Forty-seven thousand roubles," replied Hermann. At these words every head in the room turned suddenly round, and all eyes were fixed upon Hermann.

"He has taken leave of his senses!" thought Naroumoff.

"Allow me to inform you," said Chekalinsky, with his eternal smile, "that you are playing very high; nobody here has ever staked more than two hundred and seventy-five roubles at once."

"Very well," replied Hermann, "but do you accept my card or not?"

Chekalinsky bowed in token of consent.

"I only wish to observe," said he, "that although I have the greatest confidence in my friends, I can only play against ready money. For my own part I am quite convinced that your word is sufficient, but for the sake of the order of the game, and to facilitate the reckoning up, I must ask you to put the money on your card."

Hermann drew from his pocket a bank-note, and handed it to Chekalinsky, who, after examining it in a cursory manner, placed it on Hermann's card. He began to deal. On the right a nine turned up, and on the left a three.

"I have won!" said Hermann, showing his card.

A murmur of astonishment arose among the players. Chekalinsky frowned, but the smile quickly returned to his face. "Do you wish me to settle with you?" he said to Hermann.

"If you please," replied the latter.

Chekalinsky drew from his pocket a number of banknotes and paid at once. Hermann took up his money and left the table. Naroumoff could not recover from his astonishment. Hermann drank a glass of lemonade and returned home.

The next evening he again repaired to Chekalinsky's. The host was dealing. Hermann walked up to the table; the punters immediately made room for him. Chekalinsky greeted him with a gracious bow.

Hermann waited for the next deal, took a card and placed upon it his forty-seven thousand roubles, together with his winnings of the previous evening. Chekalinsky began to deal. A knave turned up on the right, a seven on the left.

Hermann showed his seven. There was a general exclamation. Chekalinsky was evidently ill at ease, but he counted out the ninety-four thousand roubles and handed them over to Hermann, who pocketed them in the coolest manner possible, and immediately left the house.

The next evening Hermann appeared again at the table. Everyone was expecting him. The generals and privy counsellors left their whist in order to watch such extraordinary play. The young officers quitted their sofas, and even the servants crowded into the room. All pressed round Hermann. The other players left off punting, impatient to see how it would end. Hermann stood at the table, and prepared to play alone against the pale, but still smiling Chekalinsky. Each opened a pack of cards. Chekalinsky shuffled. Hermann took a card and covered it with a pile of banknotes. It was like a duel. Deep silence reigned around.

Chekalinsky began to deal, his hands trembled. On the right a queen turned up, and on the left an ace.

"Ace has won!" cried Hermann, showing his card.

"Your queen has lost," said Chekalinsky, politely.

Hermann started; instead of an ace, there lay before him the queen of spades! He could not believe his eyes, nor could he understand how he had made such a mistake.

At that moment it seemed to him that the queen of spades smiled ironically, and winked her eye at him. He was struck by her remarkable resemblance. . . .

"The old Countess!" he exclaimed, seized with terror. Chekalinsky gathered up his winnings. For some time Hermann remained perfectly motionless. When at last he left the table, there was a general commotion in the room.

"Splendidly punted!" said the players. Chekalinsky shuffled the cards afresh, and the game went on as usual.

. . . . .

Hermann went out of his mind, and is now confined in room number seventeen of the Oboukhoff Hospital. He never answers any questions, but he constantly mutters with unusual rapidity: "Three, seven, ace! Three, seven, queen!"

Lizaveta Ivanovna has married a very amiable young man, a son of the former steward of the old Countess. He is in the service of the State somewhere, and is in receipt of a good income. Lizaveta is also supporting a poor relative.

Tomsky has been promoted to the rank of captain, and has become the husband of the Princess Pauline.

The Crooked Mirror
(A Christmas Story)
Anton Chekhov

We went into the reception hall, my wife and I. It smelled of moss and damp. Hordes of rats and mice leaped aside as we brought light to walls that had not seen it for a century. As we shut the door behind us, a puff of wind rustled papers piled in corners; light fell on them and we noticed ancient lettering and medieval pictures. On walls green with age hung portraits of my ancestors. They stared down, stern and disdainful, as if about to say:

"A whipping for you, my man!"

Our steps resounded through the building. I coughed and there came an echo, the very one that replied once to my ancestors . . .

And the wind moaned and howled. There was a sobbing in the chimney stack like someone in despair and big drops of rain beat a melancholy patter on the glimmering windows.

"Oh, ancestors of mine," I murmured with a sigh, "if I were a writer, looking at your portraits, I could write a long novel. For each of these old people was young once and each man or woman of them was a fitting subject. And what a story it would be! Look, say, at that old lady, my great-grandmother That ugly misshapen woman had a remarkable history."

"Do you see the mirror," I asked my wife, "do you see it, hanging there in the corner?"

And I pointed out to her a large mirror in a frame of blackened bronze that hung in a corner near the portrait of my great-grandmother.

"That mirror has magic powers: it was the ruin of my great-grandmother. For it she paid an enormous sum and she did not part with it until the moment of her death. Day and night, incessantly, she looked into it, looked even when she ate and drank. As she went to sleep, she laid the mirror by her in the bed and, dying, begged that it be laid beside her in the coffin. It was only because it would not fit into the coffin that her wish was unfulfilled."

"She was a vain coquette, wasn't she?" said my wife.

"I admit it. But hadn't she other mirrors, then? Why was it just that mirror that she loved and not another? Hadn't she better mirrors even? No, my dear, some terrible secret is hidden there. How else do you explain it? Legend has it there's a devil in the mirror and that my great-grandmother was fascinated by devils."

I brushed dust from the mirror, looked into it and began to laugh. A dull echo replied. It was a crooked mirror that twisted my features in all directions: my nose appeared on my left cheek and my chin was cleft and turned askew.

"What strange tastes my great grandmother had!" I said.

My wife went hesitantly to the mirror and she too glanced there—and at once a terrible thing happened. She went pale, trembled all over and cried out. The candlestick dropped from her hand and rolled on the floor and the candle went out. Darkness closed over us.

And at that very moment I heard something heavy falling: my wife had lost consciousness.

The wind moaned on as sadly as ever, rats scampered, mice rustled among the papers. The hairs bristled and stirred on my head as a shutter broke from a window and clattered down, and the moon came into view ... .

I lifted my wife in my arms and carried her from the house of my ancestors. And it was not till the evening of the next day that she came to herself.

"The mirror! Give me the mirror!" she said. "Where is the mirror?"

For a full week afterwards she neither ate nor drank nor slept and all the time kept asking for the mirror to be brought to her. She sobbed, tore her hair and tossed to and fro till at last, when the doctor said she might die of exhaustion, her condition being extremely grave, I mastered my fear and went down there again and brought back for her the mirror of my great-grandmother. As she saw it, she laughed with joy, then clutched at it and kissed it, and devoured it with her eyes.

More than ten years have passed by since then and still she stares incessantly into the mirror, not turning away an instant.

"Is it really me?" she whispers and her face, as she blushes, shines with serene delight. "Yes, it is! All things tell lies to me except this mirror. People lie, my husband lies. Oh, if only I had seen myself earlier, I would have known what I truly am and would never have married that man! He is quite unworthy of me. The most handsome and noble of knights should be at my feet."

Once, as I stood behind my wife, I glanced inadvertantly into the mirror—and learned a terrible secret. I saw there a woman of such dazzling beauty as I have never seen in all my life, a wonder of nature, a figure of comeliness, grace and love.

How can I explain it? What had happened? Why did my ugly lumbering wife look so lovely in the mirror? Why?

Because, indeed, the distorting mirror distorted every line of my wife's ugly face and by this changing of the features chanced to make it beautiful. A minus times a minus is a plus.

And now both of us, my wife and I, sit at the mirror, not turning away an instant, looking: my nose twists up my left cheek, my chin is cleft and turned askew but my wife's face is fascinating—and an insane passion overcomes me.

"Ha, ha, ha!"

I laugh savagely. And my wife whispers, scarcely heard. "How lovely I am!

The Death of Ivan Ilyich
Leo Tolstoy

Chapter I

During an interval in the Melvinski trial in the large building of the Law Courts the members and public prosecutor met in Ivan Egorovich Shebek's private room, where the conversation turned on the celebrated Krasovski case. Fedor Vasilievich warmly maintained that it was not subject to their jurisdiction, Ivan Egorovich maintained the contrary, while Peter Ivanovich, not having entered into the discussion at the start, took no part in it but looked through the *Gazette* which had just been handed in.

"Gentlemen," he said, "Ivan Ilych has died!"

"You don't say so!"

"Here, read it yourself," replied Peter Ivanovich, handing Fedor Vasilievich the paper still damp from the press. Surrounded by a black border were the words: "Praskovya Fedorovna Golovina, with profound sorrow, informs relatives and friends of the demise of her beloved husband Ivan Ilych Golovin, Member of the Court of Justice, which occurred on February the 4th of this year 1882. The funeral will take place on Friday at one o'clock in the afternoon."

Ivan Ilych had been a colleague of the gentlemen present and was liked by them all. He had been ill for some weeks with an illness said to be incurable. His post had been kept open for him, but there had been conjectures that in case of his death Alexeev might receive his appointment, and that either Vinnikov or Shtabel would succeed Alexeev. So on receiving the news of Ivan

Ilych's death the first thought of each of the gentlemen in that private room was of the changes and promotions it might occasion among themselves or their acquaintances.

"I shall be sure to get Shtabel's place or Vinnikov's," thought Fedor Vasilievich. "I was promised that long ago, and the promotion means an extra eight hundred rubles a year for me besides the allowance."

"Now I must apply for my brother-in-law's transfer from Kaluga," thought Peter Ivanovich. "My wife will be very glad, and then she won't be able to say that I never do anything for her relations."

"I thought he would never leave his bed again," said Peter Ivanovich aloud. "It's very sad."

"But what really was the matter with him?"

"The doctors couldn't say — at least they could, but each of them said something different. When last I saw him I though he was getting better."

"And I haven't been to see him since the holidays. I always meant to go."

"Had he any property?"

"I think his wife had a little — but something quiet trifling."

"We shall have to go to see her, but they live so terribly far away."

"Far away from you, you mean. Everything's far away from your place."

"You see, he never can forgive my living on the other side of the river," said Peter Ivanovich, smiling at Shebek. Then, still talking of the distances between different parts of the city, they returned to the Court.

Besides considerations as to the possible transfers and promotions likely to result from Ivan Ilych's death, the mere fact of the death of a near acquaintance aroused, as usual, in all who heard of it the complacent feeling that, "it is he who is dead and not I."

Each one thought or felt, "Well, he's dead but I'm alive!" But the more intimate of Ivan Ilych's acquaintances, his so-called friends, could not help thinking also that they would now have to fulfill the very tiresome demands of propriety by attending the funeral service and paying a visit of condolence to the widow.

Leo Tolstoy   The Death of Ivan Ilyich

Fedor Vasilievich and Peter Ivanovich had been his nearest acquaintances. Peter Ivanovich had studied law with Ivan Ilych and had considered himself to be under obligations to him.

Having told his wife at dinner-time of Ivan Ilych's death, and of his conjecture that it might be possible to get her brother transferred to their circuit, Peter Ivanovich sacrificed his usual nap, put on his evening clothes and drove to Ivan Ilych's house.

At the entrance stood a carriage and two cabs. Leaning against the wall in the hall downstairs near the cloakstand was a coffin-lid covered with cloth of gold, ornamented with gold cord and tassels, that had been polished up with metal powder. Two ladies in black were taking off their fur cloaks. Peter Ivanovich recognized one of them as Ivan Ilych's sister, but the other was a stranger to him. His colleague Schwartz was just coming downstairs, but on seeing Peter Ivanovich enter he stopped and winked at him, as if to say: "Ivan Ilych has made a mess of things — not like you and me."

Schwartz's face with his Piccadilly whiskers, and his slim figure in evening dress, had as usual an air of elegant solemnity which contrasted with the playfulness of his character and had a special piquancy here, or so it seemed to Peter Ivanovich.

Peter Ivanovich allowed the ladies to precede him and slowly followed them upstairs. Schwartz did not come down but remained where he was, and Peter Ivanovich understood that he wanted to arrange where they should play bridge that evening. The ladies went upstairs to the widow's room, and Schwartz with seriously compressed lips but a playful looking his eyes, indicated by a twist of his eyebrows the room to the right where the body lay.

Peter Ivanovich, like everyone else on such occasions, entered feeling uncertain what he would have to do. All he knew was that at such times it is always safe to cross oneself. But he was not quite sure whether one should make obseisances while doing so. He therefore adopted a middle course. On entering the room he began crossing himself and made a slight movement resembling a bow. At the same time, as far as the motion of his head and arm allowed, he surveyed the room. Two young men — apparently nephews, one of whom was a high-school pupil — were leaving the room, crossing themselves as they did so. An old woman was standing motionless, and a lady with strangely arched eyebrows was saying something to her in a whisper. A vigorous, resolute Church Reader, in a frock-coat, was reading something in a loud voice with an expression that precluded any contradiction. The butler's assistant, Gerasim, stepping lightly in front of Peter Ivanovich, was strewing something on the floor. Noticing this, Peter Ivanovich was immediately aware of a faint odour of a decomposing body.

The last time he had called on Ivan Ilych, Peter Ivanovich had seen Gerasim in the study. Ivan Ilych had been particularly fond of him and he was performing the duty of a sick nurse.

Peter Ivanovich continued to make the sign of the cross slightly inclining his head in an intermediate direction between the coffin, the Reader, and the icons on the table in a corner of the room. Afterwards, when it seemed to him that this movement of his arm in crossing himself had gone on too long, he stopped and began to look at the corpse.

The dead man lay, as dead men always lie, in a specially heavy way, his rigid limbs sunk in the soft cushions of the coffin, with the head forever bowed on the pillow. His yellow waxen brow with bald patches over his sunken temples was thrust up in the way peculiar to the dead, the protruding nose seeming to press on the upper lip. He was much changed and grown even thinner since Peter Ivanovich had last seen him, but, as is always the case with the dead, his face was handsomer and above all more dignified than when he was alive. the expression on the face said that what was necessary had been accomplished, and accomplished rightly. Besides this there was in that expression a reproach and a warning to the living. This warning seemed to Peter Ivanovich out of place, or at least not applicable to him. He felt a certain discomfort and so he hurriedly crossed himself once more and turned and went out of the door — too hurriedly and too regardless of propriety, as he himself was aware.

Schwartz was waiting for him in the adjoining room with legs spread wide apart and both hands toying with his top-hat behind his back. The mere sight of that playful, well-groomed, and elegant figure refreshed Peter Ivanovich. He felt that Schwartz was above all these happenings and would not surrender to any depressing influences. His very look said that this incident of a church service for Ivan Ilych could not be a sufficient reason for infringing the order of the session — in other words, that it would certainly not prevent his unwrapping a new pack of cards and shuffling them that evening while a footman placed fresh candles on the table: in fact, that there was no reason for supposing that this incident would hinder their spending the evening agreeably.

Indeed he said this in a whisper as Peter Ivanovich passed him, proposing that they should meet for a game at Fedor

Vasilievich's. But apparently Peter Ivanovich was not destined to play bridge that evening. Praskovya Fedorovna (a short, fat woman who despite all efforts to the contrary had continued to broaden steadily from her shoulders downwards and who had the same extraordinarily arched eyebrows as the lady who had been standing by the coffin), dressed all in black, her head covered with lace, came out of her own room with some other ladies, conducted them to the room where the dead body lay, and said: "The service will begin immediately. Please go in."

Schwartz, making an indefinite bow, stood still, evidently neither accepting nor declining this invitation. Praskovya Fedorovna recognizing Peter Ivanovich, sighed, went close up to him, took his hand, and said: "I know you were a true friend to Ivan Ilych..." and looked at him awaiting some suitable response. And Peter Ivanovich knew that, just as it had been the right thing to cross himself in that room, so what he had to do here was to press her hand, sigh, and say, "Believe me..." So he did all this and as he did it felt that the desired result had been achieved: that both he and she were touched.

"Come with me. I want to speak to you before it begins," said the widow. "Give me your arm."

Peter Ivanovich gave her his arm and they went to the inner rooms, passing Schwartz who winked at Peter Ivanovich compassionately.

"That does for our bridge! Don's object if we find another player. Perhaps you can cut in when you do escape," said his playful look.

Peter Ivanovich sighed still more deeply and despondently, and Praskovya Fedorovna pressed his arm gratefully. When they reached the drawing-room, upholstered in pink cretonne and lighted by a dim lamp, they sat down at the table — she on a sofa and Peter Ivanovich on a low pouffe, the springs of which yielded spasmodically under his weight. Praskovya Fedorovna had been on the point of warning him to take another seat, but felt that such a warning was out of keeping with her present condition and so changed her mind. As he sat down on the pouffe Peter Ivanovich recalled how Ivan Ilych had arranged this room and had consulted him regarding this pink cretonne with green leaves. The whole room was full of furniture and knick-knacks, and on her way to the sofa the lace of the widow's black shawl caught on the edge of the table. Peter Ivanovich rose to detach it, and the springs of the pouffe, relieved of his weight, rose also and gave him a push. The widow began detaching her shawl herself, and Peter Ivanovich again sat down, suppressing the rebellious springs of the pouffe under him. But the widow had not quite freed herself and Peter Ivanovich got up again, and again the pouffe rebelled and even creaked. When this was all over she took out a clean cambric handkerchief and began to weep. The episode with the shawl and the struggle with the pouffe had cooled Peter Ivanovich's emotions and he sat there with a sullen look on his face. This awkward situation was interrupted by Sokolov, Ivan Ilych's butler, who came to report that the plot in the cemetery that Praskovya Fedorovna had chosen would cost tow hundred rubles. She stopped weeping and, looking at Peter Ivanovich with the air of a victim, remarked in French that it was very hard for her. Peter Ivanovich made a silent gesture signifying his full conviction that it must indeed be so.

"Please smoke," she said in a magnanimous yet crushed voice, and turned to discuss with Sokolov the price of the plot for the grave.

Peter Ivanovich while lighting his cigarette heard her inquiring very circumstantially into the prices of different plots in the cemetery and finally decide which she would take. when that was done she gave instructions about engaging the choir. Sokolov then left the room.

"I look after everything myself," she told Peter Ivanovich, shifting the albums that lay on the table; and noticing that the table was endangered by his cigarette-ash, she immediately passed him an ash-tray, saying as she did so: "I consider it an affectation to say that my grief prevents my attending to practical affairs. On the contrary, if anything can — I won't say console me, but — distract me, it is seeing to everything concerning him." She again took out her handkerchief as if preparing to cry, but suddenly, as if mastering her feeling, she shook herself and began to speak calmly. "But there is something I want to talk to you about."

Peter Ivanovich bowed, keeping control of the springs of the pouffe, which immediately began quivering under him.

"He suffered terribly the last few days."

"Did he?" said Peter Ivanovich.

"Oh, terribly! He screamed unceasingly, not for minutes but for hours. for the last three days he screamed incessantly. It was unendurable. I cannot understand how I bore it; you could hear him three rooms off. Oh, what I have suffered!"

"Is it possible that he was conscious all that time?" asked Peter Ivanovich.

"Yes," she whispered. "To the last moment. He took leave of us a quarter of an hour before he died, and asked us to take Volodya away."

The thought of the suffering of this man he had known so intimately, first as a merry little boy, then as a schoolmate, and later as a grown-up colleague, suddenly struck Peter Ivanovich with horror, despite an unpleasant consciousness of his own and this woman's dissimulation. He again saw that brow, and that nose pressing down on the lip, and felt afraid for himself.

"Three days of frightful suffering and the death! Why, that might suddenly, at any time, happen to me," he thought, and for a moment felt terrified. But — he did not himself know how — the customary reflection at once occurred to him that this had happened to Ivan Ilych and not to him, and that it should not and could not happen to him, and that to think that it could would be yielding to depressing which he ought not to do, as Schwartz's expression plainly showed. After which reflection Peter Ivanovich felt reassured, and began to ask with interest about the details of Ivan Ilych's death, as though death was an accident natural to Ivan Ilych but certainly not to himself.

After many details of the really dreadful physical sufferings Ivan Ilych had endured (which details he learnt only from the effect those sufferings had produced on Praskovya Fedorovna's nerves) the widow apparently found it necessary to get to business.

"Oh, Peter Ivanovich, how hard it is! How terribly, terribly hard!" and she again began to weep.

Peter Ivanovich sighed and waited for her to finish blowing her nose. When she had don so he said, "Believe me..." and she again began talking and brought out what was evidently her chief concern with him — namely, to question him as to how she could obtain a grant of money from the government on the occasion of her husband's death. She made it appear that she was asking Peter Ivanovich's advice about her pension, but he soon saw that she already knew about that to the minutest detail, more even than he did himself. She knew how much could be got out of the government in consequence of her husband's death, but wanted to find out whether she could not possibly extract something more. Peter Ivanovich tried to think of some means of doing so, but after reflecting for a while and, out of propriety, condemning the government for its niggardliness, he said he thought that nothing more could be got. Then she sighed and evidently began to devise means of getting rid of her visitor. Noticing this, he put out his cigarette, rose, pressed her hand, and went out into the anteroom.

In the dining-room where the clock stood that Ivan Ilych had liked so much and had bought at an antique shop, Peter Ivanovich met a priest and a few acquaintances who had come to attend the service, and he recognized Ivan Ilych's daughter, a handsome young woman. She was in black and her slim figure appeared slimmer than ever. She had a gloomy, determined, almost angry expression, and bowed to Peter Ivanovich as though he were in some way to blame.

Behind her, with the same offended look, stood a wealthy young man, and examining magistrate, whom Peter Ivanovich also knew and who was her fiance, as he had heard. He bowed mournfully to them and was about to pass into the death-chamber, when from under the stairs appeared the figure of Ivan Ilych's schoolboy son, who was extremely like his father. He seemed a little Ivan Ilych, such as Peter Ivanovich remembered when they studied law together. His tear-stained eyes had in them the look that is seen in the eyes of boys of thirteen or fourteen who are not pure-minded. When he saw Peter Ivanovich he scowled morosely and shamefacedly. Peter Ivanovich nodded to him and entered the death-chamber. The service began: candles, groans, incense, tears, and sobs. Peter Ivanovich stood looking gloomily down at his feet. He did not look once at the dead man, did not yield to any depressing influence, and was one of the first to leave the room. There was no one in the anteroom, but Gerasim darted out of the dead man's room, rummaged with his strong hands among the fur coats to find Peter Ivanovich's and helped him on with it.

"Well, friend Gerasim," said Peter Ivanovich, so as to say something. "It's a sad affair, isn't it?"

"It's God will. We shall all come to it some day," said Gerasim, displaying his teeth — the even white teeth of a healthy peasant — and, like a man in the thick of urgent work, he briskly opened the front door, called the coachman, helped Peter Ivanovich into the sledge, and sprang back to the porch as if in readiness for what he had to do next.

Peter Ivanovich found the fresh air particularly pleasant after the smell of incense, the dead body, and carbolic acid.

"Where to sir?" asked the coachman.

"It's not too late even now....I'll call round on Fedor Vasilievich."

He accordingly drove there and found them just finishing the first rubber, so that it was quite convenient for him to cut in.

Chapter II

Ivan Ilych's life had been most simple and most ordinary and therefore most terrible.

He had been a member of the Court of Justice, and died at the age of forty-five. His father had been an official who after serving in various ministries and departments in Petersburg had made the sort of career which brings men to positions from which by reason of their long service they cannot be dismissed, though they are obviously unfit to hold any responsible position, and for whom therefore posts are specially created, which though fictitious carry salaries of from six to ten thousand rubles that are not fictitious, and in receipt of which they live on to a great age.

Such was the Privy Councillor and superfluous member of various superfluous institutions, Ilya Epimovich Golovin.

He had three sons, of whom Ivan Ilych was the second. The eldest son was following in his father's footsteps only in another department, and was already approaching that stage in the service at which a similar sinecure would be reached. the third son was a failure. He had ruined his prospects in a number of positions and was not serving in the railway department. His father and brothers, and still more their wives, not merely disliked meeting him, but avoided remembering his existence unless compelled to do so. His sister had married Baron Greff, a Petersburg official of her father's type. Ivan Ilych was *le phenix de la famille* as people said. He was neither as cold and formal as his elder brother nor as wild as the younger, but was a happy mean between them — an intelligent polished, lively and agreeable man. He had studied with his younger brother at the School of Law, but the latter had failed to complete the course and was expelled when he was in the fifth class. Ivan Ilych finished the course well. Even when he was at the School of Law he was just what he remained for the rest of his life: a capable, cheerful, good-natured, and sociable man, though strict in the fulfillment of what he considered to be his duty: and he considered his duty to be what was so considered by those in authority. Neither as a boy nor as a man was he a toady, but from early youth was by nature attracted to people of high station as a fly is drawn to the light, assimilating their ways and views of life and establishing friendly relations with them. All the enthusiasms of childhood and youth passed without leaving much trace on him; he succumbed to sensuality, to vanity, and latterly among the highest classes to liberalism, but always within limits which his instinct unfailingly indicated to him as correct.

At school he had done things which had formerly seemed to him very horrid and made him feel disgusted with himself when he did them; but when later on he saw that such actions were done by people of good position and that they did not regard them as wrong, he was able not exactly to regard them as right, but to forget about them entirely or not be at all troubled at remembering them.

Having graduated from the School of Law and qualified for the tenth rank of the civil service, and having received money from his father for his equipment, Ivan Ilych ordered himself clothes at Scharmer's, the fashionable tailor, hung a medallion inscribed *respice finem* on his watch-chain, took leave of his professor and the prince who was patron of the school, had a farewell dinner with his comrades at Donon's first-class restaurant, and with his new and fashionable portmanteau, linen, clothes, shaving and other toilet appliances, and a travelling rug, all purchased at the best shops, he set off for one of the provinces where through his father's influence, he had been attached to the governor as an official for special service.

In the province Ivan Ilych soon arranged as easy and agreeable a position for himself as he had had at the School of Law. He performed his official task, made his career, and at the same time amused himself pleasantly and decorously. Occasionally he paid official visits to country districts where he behaved with dignity both to his superiors and inferiors, and performed the duties entrusted to him, which related chiefly to the sectarians, with an exactness and incorruptible honesty of which he could not but feel proud.

In official matters, despite his youth and taste for frivolous gaiety, he was exceedingly reserved, punctilious, and even severe; but in society he was often amusing and witty, and always good-natured, correct in his manner, and *bon enfant*, as the governor and his wife — with whom he was like one of the family — used to say of him.

In the province he had an affair with a lady who made advances to the elegant young lawyer, and there was also a milliner; and there were carousals with aides-de-camp who visited the district, and after-supper visits to a certain outlying street of doubtful reputation; and there was too some obsequiousness to his chief and even to his chief's wife, but all this was done with such a tone of good breeding that no hard names could be applied to it. It all came under the heading of the French saying: *"Il faut que jeunesse se passe."* It was all done with clean hands, in clean linen, with French phrases, and above all among people of the best society and consequently with the approval of people of rank.

So Ivan Ilych served for five years and then came a change in his official life. The new and reformed judicial institutions were introduced, and new men were needed. Ivan Ilych became such a new man. He was offered the post of examining magistrate, and he accepted it though the post was in another province and obliged him to give up the connexions he had formed and to make new ones. His friends met to give him a send-off; they had a group photograph taken and presented him with a silver cigarette-case, and he set off to his new post.

As examining magistrate Ivan Ilych was just as *comme il faut* and decorous a man, inspiring general respect and capable of separating his official duties from his private life, as he had been when acting as an official on special service. His duties now as examining magistrate were fare more interesting and attractive than before. In his former position it had been pleasant to wear an undress uniform made by Scharmer, and to pass through the crowd of petitioners and officials who were timorously awaiting an audience with the governor, and who envied him as with free and easy gait he went straight into his chief's private room to have a cup of tea and a cigarette with him. But not many people had then been directly dependent on him — only police officials and the sectarians when he went on special missions — and he liked to treat them politely, almost as comrades, as if he were letting them feel that he who had the power to crush them was treating them in this simple, friendly way. There were then but few such people.

But now, as an examining magistrate, Ivan Ilych felt that everyone without exception, even the most important and self-satisfied, was in his power, and that he need only write a few words on a sheet of paper with a certain heading, and this or that important, self- satisfied person would be brought before him in the role of an accused person or a witness, and if he did not choose to allow him to sit down, would have to stand before him and answer his questions. Ivan Ilych never abused his power; he tried on the contrary to soften its expression, but the consciousness of it and the possibility of softening its effect, supplied the chief interest and attraction of his office. In his work itself, especially in his examinations, he very soon acquired a method of eliminating all considerations irrelevant to the legal aspect of the case, and reducing even the most complicated case to a form in which it would be presented on paper only in its externals, completely excluding his personal opinion of the matter, while above all observing every prescribed formality. The work was new and Ivan Ilych was one of the first men to apply the new Code of 1864.

On taking up the post of examining magistrate in a new town, he made new acquaintances and connections, placed himself on a new footing and assumed a somewhat different tone. He took up an attitude of rather dignified aloofness towards the provincial authorities, but picked out the best circle of legal gentlemen and wealthy gentry living in the town and assumed a tone of slight dissatisfaction with the government, of moderate liberalism, and of enlightened citizenship. At the same time, without at all altering the elegance of his toilet, he ceased shaving his chin and allowed his beard to grow as it pleased.

Ivan Ilych settled down very pleasantly in this new town. The society there, which inclined towards opposition to the governor was friendly, his salary was larger, and he began to play *vint* [a form of bridge], which he found added not a little to the pleasure of life, for he had a capacity for cards, played good-humouredly, and calculated rapidly and astutely, so that he usually won.

After living there for two years he met his future wife, Praskovya Fedorovna Mikhel, who was the most attractive, clever, and brilliant girl of the set in which he moved, and among other amusements and relaxations from his labours as examining magistrate, Ivan Ilych established light and playful relations with her.

While he had been an official on special service he had been accustomed to dance, but now as an examining magistrate it was exceptional for him to do so. If he danced now, he did it as if to show that though he served under the reformed order of things, and had reached the fifth official rank, yet when it came to dancing he could do it better than most people. So at the end of an evening he sometimes danced with Praskovya Fedorovna, and it was chiefly during these dances that he captivated her. She fell in love with him. Ivan Ilych had at first no definite intention of marrying, but when the girl fell in love with him he said to himself: "Really, why shouldn't I marry?"

Praskovya Fedorovna came of a good family, was not bad looking, and had some little property. Ivan Ilych might have aspired to a more brilliant match, but even this was good. He had his salary, and she, he hoped, would have an equal income. She was well connected, and was a sweet, pretty, and thoroughly correct young woman. to say that Ivan Ilych married because he fell in love with Praskovya Fedorovna and found that she sympathized with his views of life would be as incorrect as to say that he married because his social circle approved of the match. He was swayed by both these considerations: the marriage gave him personal satisfaction, and at the same time it was considered the right thing by the most highly placed of his associates.

So Ivan Ilych got married.

The preparations for marriage and the beginning of married life, with its conjugal caresses, the new furniture, new crockery, and new linen, were very pleasant until his wife became pregnant — so that Ivan Ilych had begun to think that marriage would not impair the easy, agreeable, gay and always decorous character of his life, approved of by society and regarded by himself as natural, but would even improve it. But from the first months of his wife's pregnancy, something new, unpleasant, depressing, and unseemly, and from which there was no way of escape, unexpectedly showed itself.

His wife, without any reason — *de gaiete de coeur* as Ivan Ilych expressed it to himself — began to disturb the pleasure and propriety of their life. She began to be jealous without any cause, expected him to devote his whole attention to her, found fault with everything, and made coarse and ill-mannered scenes.

At first Ivan Ilych hoped to escape from the unpleasantness of this state of affairs by the same easy and decorous relation to life that had served him heretofore: he tried to ignore his wife's disagreeable moods, continued to live in his usual easy and pleasant way, invited friends to his house for a game of cards, and also tried going out to his club or spending his evenings with friends. But one day his wife began upbraiding him so vigorously, using such coarse words, and continued to abuse him every time he did not fulfill her demands, so resolutely and with such evident determination not to give way till he submitted — that is, till he stayed at home and was bored just as she was — that he became alarmed. He now realized that matrimony — at any rate with Praskovya Fedorovna — was not always conducive to the pleasures and amenities of life, but on the contrary often infringed both comfort and propriety, and that he must therefore entrench himself against such infringement. And Ivan Ilych began to seek for means of doing so. His official duties were the one thing that imposed upon Praskovya Fedorovna, and by means of his official work and the duties attached to it he began struggling with his wife to secure his own independence.

With the birth of their child, the attempts to feed it and the various failures in doing so, and with the real and imaginary illnesses of mother and child, in which Ivan Ilych's sympathy was demanded but about which he understood nothing, the need of securing for himself an existence outside his family life became still more imperative.

As his wife grew more irritable and exacting and Ivan Ilych transferred the center of gravity of his life more and more to his official work, so did he grow to like his work better and became more ambitious than before.

Very soon, within a year of his wedding, Ivan Ilych had realized that marriage, though it may add some comforts to life, is in fact a very intricate and difficult affair towards which in order to perform one's duty, that is, to lead a decorous life approved of by society, one must adopt a definite attitude just as towards one's official duties.

And Ivan Ilych evolved such an attitude towards married life. He only required of it those conveniences — dinner at home, housewife, and bed — which it could give him, and above all that propriety of external forms required by public opinion. For the rest he looked for lighthearted pleasure and propriety, and was very thankful when he found them, but if he met with antagonism and querulousness he at once retired into his separate fenced-off world of official duties, where he found satisfaction.

Ivan Ilych was esteemed a good official, and after three years was made Assistant Public Prosecutor. His new duties, their importance, the possibility of indicting and imprisoning anyone he chose, the publicity his speeches received, and the success he had in all these things, made his work still more attractive.

More children came. His wife became more and more querulous and ill-tempered, but the attitude Ivan Ilych had adopted towards his home life rendered him almost impervious to her grumbling.

After seven years' service in that town he was transferred to another province as Public Prosecutor. They moved, but were short of money and his wife did not like the place they moved to. Though the salary was higher the cost of living was greater, besides which two of their children died and family life became still more unpleasant for him.

Praskovya Fedorovna blamed her husband for every inconvenience they encountered in their new home. Most of the conversations between husband and wife, especially as to the children's education, led to topics which recalled former disputes, and these disputes were apt to flare up again at any moment. There remained only those rare periods of amorousness which still came to them at times but did not last long. These were islets at which they anchored for a while and then again set out upon that ocean of veiled hostility which showed itself in their aloofness from one another. This aloofness might have grieved Ivan Ilych had he considered that it ought not to exist, but he now regarded the position as normal, and even made it the goal at which he aimed in family life. His aim was to free himself more and more from those unpleasantness and to give them a semblance of harmlessness and propriety. He attained this by spending less and less time with his family, and when obliged to be at home he tried to safeguard his position by the presence of outsiders. The chief thing however was that he had his official duties. The whole interest of his life now centered in the official world and that interest absorbed him. The consciousness of his power, being able to ruin anybody he wished to ruin, the importance, even the external dignity of his entry into court, or meetings with his subordinates, his success with superiors and inferiors, and above all his masterly handling of cases, of which he was conscious — all this gave him pleasure and filled his life, together with chats with his colleagues, dinners, and bridge. So that on the whole Ivan Ilych's life continued to flow as he considered it should do — pleasantly and properly.

So things continued for another seven years. His eldest daughter was already sixteen, another child had died, and only one son was left, a schoolboy and a subject of dissension. Ivan Ilych wanted to put him in the School of Law, but to spite him Praskovya Fedorovna entered him at the High School. The daughter had been educated at home and had turned out well: the boy did not learn badly either.

Chapter III

So Ivan Ilych lived for seventeen years after his marriage. He was already a Public Prosecutor of long standing, and had declined several proposed transfers while awaiting a more desirable post, when an unanticipated and unpleasant occurrence quite upset the peaceful course of his life. He was expecting to be offered the post of presiding judge in a University town, but Happe somehow came to the front and obtained the appointment instead. Ivan Ilych became irritable, reproached Happe, and quarreled both him and with his immediate superiors — who became colder to him and again passed him over when other appointments were made.

This was in 1880, the hardest year of Ivan Ilych's life. It was then that it became evident on the one hand that his salary was insufficient for them to live on, and on the other that he had been forgotten, and not only this, but that what was for him the greatest and most cruel injustice appeared to others a quite ordinary occurrence. Even his father did not consider it his duty to help him. Ivan Ilych felt himself abandoned by everyone, and that they regarded his position with a salary of 3,500 rubles as quite normal and even fortunate. He alone knew that with the consciousness of the injustices done him, with his wife's incessant nagging, and with the debts he had contracted by living beyond his means, his position was far from normal.

In order to save money that summer he obtained leave of absence and went with his wife to live in the country at her brother's place.

In the country, without his work, he experienced *ennui* for the first time in his life, and not only *ennui* but intolerable depression, and he decided that it was impossible to go on living like that, and that it was necessary to take energetic measures.

Having passed a sleepless night pacing up and down the veranda, he decided to go to Petersburg and bestir himself, in order to punish those who had failed to appreciate him and to get transferred to another ministry.

Next day, despite many protests from his wife and her brother, he started for Petersburg with the sole object of obtaining a post with a salary of five thousand rubles a year. He was no longer bent on any particular department, or tendency, or kind of activity. All he now wanted was an appointment to another post with a salary of five thousand rubles, either in the administration, in the banks, with the railways in one of the Empress Marya's

Institutions, or even in the customs — but it had to carry with it a salary of five thousand rubles and be in a ministry other than that in which they had failed to appreciate him.

And this quest of Ivan Ilych's was crowned with remarkable and unexpected success. At Kursk an acquaintance of his, F. I. Ilyin, got into the first-class carriage, sat down beside Ivan Ilych, and told him of a telegram just received by the governor of Kursk announcing that a change was about to take place in the ministry: Peter Ivanovich was to be superseded by Ivan Semonovich.

The proposed change, apart from its significance for Russia, had a special significance for Ivan Ilych, because by bringing forward a new man, Peter Petrovich, and consequently his friend Zachar Ivanovich, it was highly favourable for Ivan Ilych, since Sachar Ivanovich was a friend and colleague of his.

In Moscow this news was confirmed, and on reaching Petersburg Ivan Ilych found Zachar Ivanovich and received a definite promise of an appointment in his former Department of Justice.

A week later he telegraphed to his wife: "Zachar in Miller's place. I shall receive appointment on presentation of report."

Thanks to this change of personnel, Ivan Ilych had unexpectedly obtained an appointment in his former ministry which placed him two states above his former colleagues besides giving him five thousand rubles salary and three thousand five hundred rubles for expenses connected with his removal. All his ill humour towards his former enemies and the whole department vanished, and Ivan Ilych was completely happy.

He returned to the country more cheerful and contented than he had been for a long time. Praskovya Fedorovna also cheered up and a truce was arranged between them. Ivan Ilych told of how he had been feted by everybody in Petersburg, how all those who had been his enemies were put to shame and now fawned on him, how envious they were of his appointment, and how much everybody in Petersburg had liked him.

Praskovya Fedorovna listened to all this and appeared to believe it. She did not contradict anything, but only made plans for their life in the town to which they were going. Ivan Ilych saw with delight that these plans were his plans, that he and his wife agreed, and that, after a stumble, his life was regaining its due and natural character of pleasant lightheartedness and decorum.

Ivan Ilych had come back for a short time only, for he had to take up his new duties on the 10th of September. Moreover, he needed time to settle into the new place, to move all his belongings from the province, and to buy and order many additional things: in a word, to make such arrangements as he had resolved on, which were almost exactly what Praskovya Fedorovna too had decided on.

Now that everything had happened so fortunately, and that he and his wife were at one in their aims and moreover saw so little of one another, they got on together better than they had done since the first years of marriage. Ivan Ilych had thought of taking his family away with him at once, but the insistence of his wife's brother and her sister-in-law, who had suddenly become particularly amiable and friendly to him and his family, induced him to depart alone.

So he departed, and the cheerful state of mind induced by his success and by the harmony between his wife and himself, the one intensifying the other, did not leave him. He found a delightful house, just the thing both he and his wife had dreamt of. Spacious, lofty reception rooms in the old style, a convenient and dignified study, rooms for his wife and daughter, a study for his son — it might have been specially built for them. Ivan Ilych himself superintended the arrangements, chose the wallpapers, supplemented the furniture (preferably with antiques which he considered particularly 'comme il faut'), and supervised the upholstering. Everything progressed and progressed and approached the ideal he had set himself: even when things were only half completed they exceeded his expectations. He saw what a refined and elegant character, free from vulgarity, it would all have when it was ready. On falling asleep he pictured to himself how the reception room would look. Looking at the yet unfinished drawing room he could see the fireplace, the screen, the what-not, the little chairs dotted here and there, the dishes and plates on the walls, and the bronzes, as they would be when everything was in place. He was pleased by the thought of how his wife and daughter, who shared his taste n this matter, would be impressed by it. They were certainly not expecting as much. He had been particularly successful in finding, and buying cheaply, antiques which gave a particularly aristocratic character to the whole place. But in his letters he intentionally understated everything in order to be able to surprise them. All this so absorbed him that his new duties — though he liked his official work — interested him less than he had expected. Sometimes he even had moments of absent-mindedness during the court sessions and would consider whether he should have straight or curved cornices for his curtains. He was so interested in it all that he often did things himself, rearranging the furniture, or re-hanging the curtains. Once when mounting a step-ladder to show the upholsterer, who did not understand, how he wanted the hangings draped, he mad a false step and slipped, but being a strong and agile man he clung on and only knocked his side against the knob of the window frame. The bruised place was painful but the pain soon passed, and he felt particularly bright and well just then. He wrote: "I feel fifteen years younger." He thought he would have everything ready by September, but it dragged on till mid-October. But the result was charming not only in his eyes but to everyone who saw it.

In reality it was just what is usually seen in the houses of people of moderate means who want to appear rich, and therefore succeed only in resembling others like themselves: there are damasks, dark wood, plants, rugs, and dull and polished bronzes — all the things people of a certain class have in order to resemble other people of that class. His house was so like the others that it would never have been noticed, but to him it all seemed to be quite exceptional. He was very happy when he met his family at the station and brought them to the newly furnished house all lit up, where a footman in a white tie opened the door into the hall decorated with plants, and when they went on into the drawing-room and the study uttering exclamations of delight. He conducted them everywhere, drank in their praises eagerly, and beamed with pleasure. At tea that evening, when Praskovya Fedorovna among others things asked him about his fall, he laughed, and showed them how he had gone flying and had frightened the upholsterer.

"It's a good thing I'm a bit of an athlete. Another man might have been killed, but I merely knocked myself, just here; it hurts when it's touched, but it's passing off already — it's only a bruise."

So they began living in their new home — in which, as always happens, when they got thoroughly settled in they found they were just one room short — and with the increased income, which as always was just a little (some five hundred rubles) too little, but it was all very nice.

Things went particularly well at first, before everything was finally arranged and while something had still to be done: this thing bought, that thing ordered, another thing moved, and something else adjusted. Though there were some disputes between husband and wife, they were both so well satisfied and had so much to do that it all passed off without any serious quarrels. When nothing was left to arrange it became rather dull and something seemed to be lacking, but they were then making acquaintances, forming habits, and life was growing fuller.

Ivan Ilych spent his mornings at the law court and came home to diner, and at first he was generally in a good humour, though he occasionally became irritable just on account of his house. (Every spot on the tablecloth or the upholstery, and every broken window- blind string, irritated him. He had devoted so much trouble to arranging it all that every disturbance of it distressed him.) But on the whole his life ran its course as he believed life should do: easily, pleasantly, and decorously.

He got up at nine, drank his coffee, read the paper, and then put on his undress uniform and went to the law courts. there the harness in which he worked had already been stretched to fit him and he donned it without a hitch: petitioners, inquiries at the chancery, the chancery itself, and the sittings public and administrative. In all this the thing was to exclude everything fresh and vital, which always disturbs the regular course of official business, and to admit only official relations with people, and then only on official grounds. A man would come, for instance, wanting some information. Ivan Ilych, as one in whose sphere the matter did not lie, would have nothing to do with him: but if the man had some business with him in his official capacity, something that could be expressed on officially stamped paper, he would do everything, positively everything he could within the limits of such relations, and in doing so would maintain the semblance of friendly human relations, that is, would observe the courtesies of life. As soon as the official relations ended, so did everything else. Ivan Ilych possessed this capacity to separate his real life from the official side of affairs and not mix the two, in the highest degree, and by long practice and natural aptitude had brought it to such a pitch that sometimes, in the manner of a virtuoso, he would even allow himself to let the human and official relations mingle. He let himself do this just because he felt that he could at any time he chose resume the strictly official attitude again and drop the human relation. and he did it all easily, pleasantly, correctly, and even artistically. In the intervals between the sessions he smoked, drank tea, chatted a little about politics, a little about general topics, a little about cards, but most of all about official appointments. Tired, but with the feelings of a virtuoso — one of the first violins who has played his part in an orchestra with precision — he would return home to find that his wife and daughter had been out paying calls, or had a visitor, and that his son had been to school, had done his homework with his tutor, and was surely learning what is taught at High Schools. Everything was as it should be. After dinner, if they had no visitors, Ivan Ilych sometimes read a book that was being much discussed at the time, and in the evening settled down to work, that is, read official papers, compared the depositions of witnesses, and noted paragraphs of the Code applying to them. This was neither dull nor amusing. It was dull when he might have been playing bridge, but if no bridge was available it was at any rate better than doing nothing or sitting with his wife. Ivan Ilych's chief pleasure was giving little dinners to which he invited men and women of good social position, and just as his drawing-room resembled all other drawing-rooms so did his enjoyable little parties resemble all other such parties.

Once they even gave a dance. Ivan Ilych enjoyed it and everything went off well, except that it led to a violent quarrel with his wife about the cakes and sweets. Praskovya Fedorovna had made her own plans, but Ivan Ilych insisted on getting everything from an expensive confectioner and ordered too many cakes, and the quarrel occurred because some of those cakes were left over and the confectioner's bill came to forty-five rubles. It was a great and disagreeable quarrel. Praskovya Fedorovna called him "a fool and an imbecile," and he clutched at his head and made angry allusions to divorce.

But the dance itself had been enjoyable. The best people were there, and Ivan Ilych had danced with Princess Trufonova, a sister of the distinguished founder of the Society "Bear My Burden".

The pleasures connected with his work were pleasures of ambition; his social pleasures were those of vanity; but Ivan Ilych's greatest pleasure was playing bridge. He acknowledged that whatever disagreeable incident happened in his life, the pleasure that beamed like a ray of light above everything else was to sit down to bridge with good players, not noisy partners, and of course to four-handed bridge (with five players it was annoying to have to stand out, though one pretended not to mind), to play a clever and serious game (when the cards allowed it) and then to have supper and drink a glass of wine. After a game of bridge, especially if he had won a little (to win a large sum was unpleasant), Ivan Ilych went to bed in a specially good humour.

So they lived. They formed a circle of acquaintances among the best people and were visited by people of importance and by young folk. In their views as to their acquaintances, husband, wife and daughter were entirely agreed, and tacitly and unanimously kept at arm's length and shook off the various shabby friends and relations who, with much show of affection, gushed into the drawing-room with its Japanese plates on the walls. Soon these shabby friends ceased to obtrude themselves and only the best people remained in the Golovins' set.

Young men made up to Lisa, and Petrishchev, an examining magistrate and Dmitri Ivanovich Petrishchev's son and sole heir, began to be so attentive to her that Ivan Ilych had already spoken to Praskovya Fedorovna about it, and considered whether they should not arrange a party for them, or get up some private theatricals.

So they lived, and all went well, without change, and life flowed pleasantly.

Chapter IV

They were all in good health. It could not be called ill health if Ivan Ilych sometimes said that he had a queer taste in his mouth and felt some discomfort in his left side.

But this discomfort increased and, though not exactly painful, grew into a sense of pressure in his side accompanied by ill humour. And his irritability became worse and worse and began to mar the agreeable, easy, and correct life that had established itself in the Golovin family. Quarrels between husband and wife became more and more frequent, and soon the ease and amenity disappeared and even the decorum was barely maintained. Scenes again became frequent, and very few of those islets remained on which husband and wife could meet without an explosion. Praskovya Fedorovna now had good reason to say that her husband's temper was trying. With characteristic exaggeration she said he had always had a dreadful temper, and that it had needed all her good nature to put up with it for twenty years. It was true that now the quarrels were started by him. His bursts of temper always came just before dinner, often just as he began to eat his soup. Sometimes he noticed that a plate or dish was chipped, or the food was not right, or his son put his elbow on the table, or his daughter's hair was not done as he liked it, and for all this he blamed Praskovya Fedorovna. At first she retorted and said disagreeable things to him, but once or twice he fell into such a rage at the beginning of dinner that she realized it was due to some physical derangement brought on by taking food, and so she restrained herself and did not answer, but only hurried to get the dinner over. She regarded this self-restraint as highly praiseworthy. Having come to the conclusion that her husband had a dreadful temper and made her life miserable, she began to feel sorry for herself, and the more she pitied herself the more she hated her husband. She began to wish he would die; yet she did not want him to die because then his salary would cease. And this irritated her against him still more. She considered herself dreadfully unhappy just because not even his death could save her, and though she concealed her exasperation, that hidden exasperation of hers increased his irritation also.

After one scene in which Ivan Ilych had been particularly unfair and after which he had said in explanation that he certainly was irritable but that it was due to his not being well, she said that he was ill it should be attended to, and insisted on his going to see a celebrated doctor.

He went. Everything took place as he had expected and as it always does. There was the usual waiting and the important air assumed by the doctor, with which he was so familiar (resembling that which he himself assumed in court), and the sounding and listening, and the questions which called for answers that were foregone conclusions and were evidently unnecessary, and the look of importance which implied that "if only you put yourself in our hands we will arrange everything — we know indubitably how it has to be done, always in the same way for everybody alike." It was all just as it was in the law courts. The doctor put on just the same air towards him as he himself put on towards an accused person.

The doctor said that so-and-so indicated that there was so-and-so inside the patient, but if the investigation of so-and-so did not confirm this, then he must assume that and that. If he assumed that and that, then. . .and so on. To Ivan Ilych only one question was important: was his case serious or not? But the doctor ignored that inappropriate question. From his point of view it was not the one under consideration, the real question was to decide between a floating kidney, chronic catarrh, or appendicitis. It was not a question the doctor solved brilliantly, as it seemed to Ivan Ilych, in favour of the appendix, with the reservation that should an examination of the urine give fresh indications the matter would be reconsidered. All this was just what Ivan Ilych had himself brilliantly accomplished a thousand times in dealing with men on trial. The doctor summed up just as brilliantly, looking over his spectacles triumphantly and even gaily at the accused. From the doctor's summing up Ivan Ilych concluded that things were bad, but that for the doctor, and perhaps for everybody else, it was a matter of indifference, though for him it was bad. And this conclusion struck him painfully, arousing in him a great feeling of pity for himself and of bitterness towards the doctor's indifference to a matter of such importance.

He said nothing of this, but rose, placed the doctor's fee on the table, and remarked with a sigh: "We sick people probably often put inappropriate questions. But tell me, in general, is this complaint dangerous, or not?..."

The doctor looked at him sternly over his spectacles with one eye, as if to say: "Prisoner, if you will not keep to the questions put to you, I shall be obliged to have you removed from the court."

"I have already told you what I consider necessary and proper. The analysis may show something more." And the doctor bowed.

Ivan Ilych went out slowly, seated himself disconsolately in his sledge, and drove home. All the way home he was going over what the doctor had said, trying to translate those complicated, obscure, scientific phrases into plain language and find in them an answer to the question: "Is my condition bad? Is it very bad? Or is there as yet nothing much wrong?" And it seemed to him that the meaning of what the doctor had said was that it was very bad. Everything in the streets seemed depressing. The cabmen, the houses, the passers-by, and the shops, were dismal. His ache, this dull gnawing ache that never ceased for a moment, seemed to have acquired a new and more serious significance from the doctor's dubious remarks. Ivan Ilych now watched it with a new and oppressive feeling.

He reached home and began to tell his wife about it. She listened, but in the middle of his account his daughter came in with her hat on, ready to go out with her mother. She sat down reluctantly to listen to this tedious story, but could not stand it long, and her mother too did not hear him to the end.

"Well, I am very glad," she said. "Mind now to take your medicine regularly. Give me the prescription and I'll send Gerasim to the chemist's." And she went to get ready to go out.

While she was in the room Ivan Ilych had hardly taken time to breathe, but he sighed deeply when she left it.

"Well," he thought, "perhaps it isn't so bad after all."

He began taking his medicine and following the doctor's directions, which had been altered after the examination of the urine. but then it happened that there was a contradiction between the indications drawn from the examination of the urine and the symptoms that showed themselves. It turned out that what was happening differed from what the doctor had told him, and that he had either forgotten or blundered, or hidden something from him. He could not, however, be blamed for that, and Ivan Ilych still obeyed his orders implicitly and at first derived some comfort from doing so.

From the time of his visit to the doctor, Ivan Ilych's chief occupation was the exact fulfillment of the doctor's instructions regarding hygiene and the taking of medicine, and the observation of his pain and his excretions. His chief interest came to be people's ailments and people's health. When sickness, deaths, or recoveries were mentioned in his presence, especially when the illness resembled his own, he listened with agitation which he tried to hide, asked questions, and applied what he heard to his own case.

The pain did not grow less, but Ivan Ilych made efforts to force himself to think that he was better. And he could do this so long as nothing agitated him. But as soon as he had any unpleasantness with his wife, any lack of success in his official work, or held bad cards at bridge, he was at once acutely sensible of his disease. He had formerly borne such mischances, hoping soon to adjust what was wrong, to master it and attain success, or make a grand slam. But now every mischance upset him and plunged him into despair. He would say to himself: "there now, just as I was beginning to get better and the medicine had begun to take effect, comes this accursed misfortune, or unpleasantness. . ." And he was furious with the mishap, or with the people who were causing the unpleasantness and killing him, for he felt that this fury was killing him but he could not restrain it. One would have thought that it should have been clear to him that this exasperation with circumstances and people aggravated his illness, and that he ought therefore to ignore unpleasant occurrences. But he drew the very opposite conclusion: he said that he needed peace, and he watched for everything that might disturb it and became irritable at the slightest infringement of it. His condition was rendered worse by the fact that he read medical books and consulted doctors. The progress of his disease was so gradual that he could deceive himself when comparing one day with another — the difference was so slight. But when he consulted the doctors it seemed to him that he was getting worse, and even very rapidly. Yet despite this he was continually consulting them.

That month he went to see another celebrity, who told him almost the same as the first had done but put his questions rather differently, and the interview with this celebrity only increased Ivan Ilych's doubts and fears. A friend of a friend of his, a very good doctor, diagnosed his illness again quite differently from the others, and though he predicted recovery, his questions and suppositions bewildered Ivan Ilych still more and increased his doubts. A homeopathist diagnosed the disease in yet another way, and prescribed medicine which Ivan Ilych took secretly for a week. But after a week, not feeling any improvement and having lost confidence both in the former doctor's treatment and in this one's, he became still more despondent. One day a lady acquaintance mentioned a cure effected by a wonder-working icon. Ivan Ilych caught himself listening attentively and beginning to believe that it had occurred. This incident alarmed him. "Has my mind really weakened to such an extent?" he asked himself. "Nonsense! It's all rubbish. I mustn't give way to nervous fears but having chosen a doctor must keep strictly to his treatment. That is what I will do. Now it's all settled. I won't think about it, but will follow the treatment seriously till summer, and then we shall see. From now there must be no more of this wavering!" this was easy to say but impossible to carry out. The pain in his side oppressed him and seemed to grow worse and more incessant, while the taste in his mouth grew stranger and stranger. It seemed to him that his breath had a disgusting smell, and he was conscious of a loss of appetite and strength. There was no deceiving himself: something terrible, new, and more important than anything before in his life, was taking place within him of which he alone was aware. Those about him did not understand or would not understand it, but thought everything in the world was going on as usual. That tormented Ivan Ilych more than anything. He saw that his household, especially his wife and daughter who were in a perfect whirl of visiting, did not understand anything of it and were annoyed that he was so depressed and so exacting, as if he were to blame for it. Though they tried to disguise it he saw that he was an obstacle in their path, and that his wife had adopted a definite line in regard to his illness and kept to it regardless of anything he said or did. Her attitude was this: "You know," she would say to her friends, "Ivan Ilych can't do as other people do, and keep to the treatment prescribed for him. One day he'll take his drops and keep strictly to his diet and go to bed in good time, but the next day unless I watch him he'll suddenly forget his medicine, eat sturgeon —

Leo Tolstoy   The Death of Ivan Ilyich

which is forbidden — and sit up playing cards till one o'clock in the morning."

"Oh, come, when was that?" Ivan Ilych would ask in vexation. "Only once at Peter Ivanovich's."

"And yesterday with shebek."

"Well, even if I hadn't stayed up, this pain would have kept me awake."

"Be that as it may you'll never get well like that, but will always make us wretched."

Praskovya Fedorovna's attitude to Ivan Ilych's illness, as she expressed it both to others and to him, was that it was his own fault and was another of the annoyances he caused her. Ivan ilych felt that this opinion escaped her involuntarily — but that did not make it easier for him.

At the law courts too, Ivan Ilych noticed, or thought he noticed, a strange attitude towards himself. It sometimes seemed to him that people were watching him inquisitively as a man whose place might soon be vacant. Then again, his friends would suddenly begin to chaff him in a friendly way about his low spirits, as if the awful, horrible, and unheard-of thing that was going on within him, incessantly gnawing at him and irresistibly drawing him away, was a very agreeable subject for jests. Schwartz in particular irritated him by his jocularity, vivacity, and *savoir-faire*, which reminded him of what he himself had been ten years ago.

Friends came to make up a set and they sat down to cards. They dealt, bending the new cards to soften them, and he sorted the diamonds in his hand and found he had seven. His partner said "No trumps" and supported him with two diamonds. What more could be wished for? It ought to be jolly and lively. They would make a grand slam. But suddenly Ivan Ilych was conscious of that gnawing pain, that taste in his mouth, and it seemed ridiculous that in such circumstances he should be pleased to make a grand slam.

He looked at his partner Mikhail Mikhaylovich, who rapped the table with his strong hand and instead of snatching up the tricks pushed the cards courteously and indulgently towards Ivan Ilych that he might have the pleasure of gathering them up without the trouble of stretching out his hand for them. "Does he think I am too weak to stretch out my arm?" thought Ivan Ilych, and forgetting what he was doing he over-trumped his partner, missing the grand slam by three tricks. And what was most awful of all was that he saw how upset Mikhail Mikhaylovich was about it but did not himself care. And it was dreadful to realize why he did not care.

They all saw that he was suffering, and said: "We can stop if you are tired. Take a rest." Lie down? No, he was not at all tired, and he finished the rubber. All were gloomy and silent. Ivan Ilych felt that he had diffused this gloom over them and could not dispel it. They had supper and went away, and Ivan Ilych was left alone with the consciousness that his life was poisoned and was poisoning the lives of others, and that this poison did not weaken but penetrated more and more deeply into his whole being.

With this consciousness, and with physical pain besides the terror, he must go to bed, often to lie awake the greater part of the night. Next morning he had to get up again, dress, go to the law courts, speak, and write; or if he did not go out, spend at home those twenty-four hours a day each of which was a torture. And he had to live thus all alone on the brink of an abyss, with no one who understood or pitied him.

Chapter V

So one month passed and then another. Just before the New Year his brother-in-law came to town and stayed at their house. Ivan Ilych was at the law courts and Praskovya Fedorovna had gone shopping. When Ivan Ilych came home and entered his study he found his brother-in-law there — a healthy, florid man — unpacking his portmanteau himself. He raised his head on hearing Ivan Ilych's footsteps and looked up at him for a moment without a word. That stare told Ivan Ilych everything. His brother-in-law opened his mouth to utter an exclamation of surprise but checked himself, and that action confirmed it all. "I have changed, eh?" "Yes, there is a change." And after that, try as he would to get his brother-in-law to return to the subject of his looks, the latter would say nothing about it. Praskovya Fedorovna came home and her brother went out to her. Ivan Ilych locked to door and began to examine himself in the glass, first full face, then in profile. He took up a portrait of himself taken with his wife, and compared it with what he saw in the glass. The change in him was immense. Then he bared his arms to the elbow, looked at them, drew the sleeves down again, sat down on an ottoman, and grew blacker than night.

"No, no, this won't do!" he said to himself, and jumped up, went to the table, took up some law papers and began to read them, but could not continue. He unlocked the door and went into the reception-room. The door leading to the drawing-room was shut. He approached it on tiptoe and listened.

"No, you are exaggerating!" Praskovya Fedorovna was saying.

"Exaggerating! Don't you see it? Why, he's a dead man! Look at his eyes — there's no life in them. But what is it that is wrong with him?"

"No one knows. Nikolaevich [that was another doctor] said something, but I don't know what. And Seshchetitsky [this was the celebrated specialist] said quite the contrary. . ."

Ivan Ilych walked away, went to his own room, lay down, and began musing; "The kidney, a floating kidney." He recalled all the doctors had told him of how it detached itself and swayed about. And by an effort of imagination he tried to catch that kidney and arrest it and support it. So little was needed for this, it seemed to him. "No, I'll go to see Peter Ivanovich again." [That was the friend whose friend was a doctor.] He rang, ordered the carriage, and got ready to go.

"Where are you going, Jean?" asked his wife with an especially sad and exceptionally kind look.

This exceptionally kind look irritated him. He looked morosely at her.

"I must go to see Peter Ivanovich."

He went to see Peter Ivanovich, and together they went to see his friend, the doctor. He was in, and Ivan Ilych had a long talk with him.

Reviewing the anatomical and physiological details of what in the doctor's opinion was going on inside him, he understood it all.

There was something, a small thing, in the vermiform appendix. It might all come right. Only stimulate the energy of one organ and check the activity of another, then absorption would take place and everything would come right. He got home rather late for dinner, ate his dinner, and conversed cheerfully, but could not for a long time bring himself to go back to work in his room. At last, however, he went to his study and did what was necessary, but the consciousness that he had put something aside — an important, intimate matter which he would revert to when his work was done — never left him. When he had finished his work he remembered that this intimate matter was the thought of his vermiform appendix. But he did not give himself up to it, and went to the drawing-room for tea. There were callers there, including the examining magistrate who was a desirable match for his daughter, and they were conversing, playing the piano, and singing. Ivan Ilych, as Praskovya Fedorovna remarked, spent that evening more cheerfully than usual, but he never for a moment forgot that he had postponed the important matter of the appendix. At eleven o'clock he said goodnight and went to his bedroom. Since his illness he had slept alone in a small room next to his study. He undressed and took up a novel by Zola, but instead of reading it he fell into thought, and in his imagination that desired improvement in the vermiform appendix occurred. There was the absorption and evacuation and the re-establishment of normal activity. "Yes, that's it!" he said to himself. "One need only assist nature, that's all." He remembered his medicine, rose, took it, and lay down on his back watching for the beneficent action of the medicine and for it to lessen the pain. "I need only take it regularly and avoid all injurious influences. I am already feeling better, much better." He began touching his side: it was not painful to the touch. "There, I really don't feel it. It's much better already." He put out the light and turned on his side . . . "The appendix is getting better, absorption is occurring." Suddenly he felt the old, familiar, dull, gnawing pain, stubborn and serious. There was the same familiar loathsome taste in his mouth. His heart sand and he felt dazed. "My God! My God!" he muttered. "Again, again! And it will never cease." And suddenly the matter presented itself in a quite different aspect. "Vermiform appendix! Kidney!" he said to himself. "It's not a question of appendix or kidney, but of life and...death. Yes, life was there and now it is going, going and I cannot stop it. Yes. Why deceive myself? Isn't it obvious to everyone but me that I'm dying, and that it's only a question of weeks, days...it may happen this moment. There was light and now there is darkness. I was here and now I'm going there! Where?" A chill came over him, his breathing ceased, and he felt only the throbbing of his heart.

"When I am not, what will there be? There will be nothing. Then where shall I be when I am no more? Can this be dying? No, I don't want to!" He jumped up and tried to light the candle, felt for it with trembling hands, dropped candle and candlestick on the floor, and fell back on his pillow.

"What's the use? It makes no difference," he said to himself, staring with wide-open eyes into the darkness. "Death. Yes, death. And none of them knows or wishes to know it, and they have no pity for me. Now they are playing." (He heard through the door the distant sound of a song and its accompaniment.) "It's all the same to them, but they will die too! Fools! I first, and they later, but it will be the same for them. And now they are merry...the beasts!"

Anger choked him and he was agonizingly, unbearably miserable. "It is impossible that all men have been doomed to suffer this awful horror!" He raised himself.

"Something must be wrong. I must calm myself — must think it all over from the beginning." And he again began thinking. "Yes, the beginning of my illness: I knocked my side, but I was still quite well that day and the next. It hurt a little, then rather more. I saw the doctors, then followed despondency and anguish, more doctors, and I drew nearer to the abyss. My strength grew less and I kept coming nearer and nearer, and now I have wasted away and there is no light in my eyes. I think of the appendix — but this is death! I think of mending the appendix, and all the while here is death! Can it really be death?" Again terror seized him and he gasped for breath. He leant down and began feeling for the matches, pressing with his elbow on the stand beside the bed. It was in his way and hurt him, he grew furious with it, pressed on it still harder, and upset it. Breathless and in despair he fell on his back, expecting death to come immediately.

Meanwhile the visitors were leaving. Praskovya Fedorovna was seeing them off. She heard something fall and came in.

"What has happened?"

"Nothing. I knocked it over accidentally."

She went out and returned with a candle. He lay there panting heavily, like a man who has run a thousand yards, and stared upwards at her with a fixed look.

"What is it, Jean?"

"No...o...thing. I upset it." ("Why speak of it? She won't understand," he thought.)

And in truth she did not understand. She picked up the stand, lit his candle, and hurried away to see another visitor off. When she came back he still lay on his back, looking upwards.

"What is it? Do you feel worse?"

"Yes."

She shook her head and sat down.

"Do you know, Jean, I think we must ask Leshchetitsky to come and see you here."

This meant calling in the famous specialist, regardless of expense. He smiled malignantly and said "No." She remained a little longer and then went up to him and kissed his forehead.

While she was kissing him he hated her from the bottom of his soul and with difficulty refrained from pushing her away.

"Good night. Please God you'll sleep."

"Yes."

Chapter VI

Ivan Ilych saw that he was dying, and he was in continual despair.

In the depth of his heart he knew he was dying, but not only was he not accustomed to the thought, he simply did not and could not grasp it.

The syllogism he had learnt from Kiesewetter's Logic: "Caius is a man, men are mortal, therefore Caius is mortal," had always seemed to him correct as applied to Caius, but certainly not as applied to himself. That Caius — man in the abstract — was mortal, was perfectly correct, but he was not Caius, not an abstract man, but a creature quite, quite separate from all others. He had been little Vanya, with a mamma and a papa, with Mitya and Volodya, with the toys, a coachman and a nurse, afterwards with Katenka and will all the joys, griefs, and delights of childhood, boyhood, and youth. What did Caius know of the smell of that striped leather ball Vanya had been so fond of? Had Caius kissed his mother's hand like that, and did the silk of her dress rustle so for Caius? Had he rioted like that at school when the pastry was bad? Had Caius been in love like that? Could Caius preside at a session as he did? "Caius really was mortal, and it was right for him to die; but for me, little Vanya, Ivan Ilych, with all my thoughts and emotions, it's altogether a different matter. It cannot be that I ought to die. That would be too terrible."

Such was his feeling.

"If I had to die like Caius I would have known it was so. An inner voice would have told me so, but there was nothing of the sort in me and I and all my friends felt that our case was quite different from that of Caius. and now here it is!" he said to himself. "It can't be. It's impossible! But here it is. How is this? How is one to understand it?"

He could not understand it, and tried to drive this false, incorrect, morbid thought away and to replace it by other proper and healthy thoughts. But that thought, and not the thought only but the reality itself, seemed to come and confront him.

And to replace that thought he called up a succession of others, hoping to find in them some support. He tried to get back into the former current of thoughts that had once screened the thought of death from him. But strange to say, all that had formerly shut off, hidden, and destroyed his consciousness of death, no longer had that effect. Ivan Ilych now spent most of his time in attempting to re-establish that old current. He would say to himself: "I will take up my duties again — after all I used to live by them." And banishing all doubts he would go to the law courts, enter into conversation with his colleagues, and sit carelessly as was his wont, scanning the crowd with a thoughtful look and leaning both his emaciated arms on the arms of his oak chair; bending over as usual to a colleague and drawing his papers nearer he would interchange whispers with him, and then suddenly raising his eyes and sitting erect would pronounce certain words and open the proceedings. But suddenly in the midst of those proceedings the pain in his side, regardless of the stage the proceedings had reached, would begin its own gnawing work. Ivan Ilych would turn his attention to it and try to drive the thought of it away, but without success. *It* would come and stand before him and look at him, and he would be petrified and the light would die out of his eyes, and he would again begin asking himself whether *It* alone was true. And his colleagues and subordinates would see with surprise and distress that he, the brilliant and subtle judge, was becoming confused and making mistakes. He would shake himself, try to pull himself together, manage somehow to bring the sitting to a close, and return home with the sorrowful consciousness that his judicial labours could not as formerly hide from him what he wanted them to hide, and could not deliver him from *It*. And what was worst of all was that *It* drew his attention to itself not in order to make him take some action but only that he should look at *It*, look it straight in the face: look at it and without doing anything, suffer inexpressibly.

And to save himself from this condition Ivan Ilych looked for consolations — new screens — and new screens were found and for a while seemed to save him, but then they immediately fell to pieces or rather became transparent, as if *It* penetrated them and nothing could veil *It*.

In these latter days he would go into the drawing-room he had arranged — that drawing-room where he had fallen and for the sake of which (how bitterly ridiculous it seemed) he had sacrificed his life — for he knew that his illness originated with that knock. He would enter and see that something had scratched the polished table. He would look for the cause of this and find that it was the bronze ornamentation of an album, that had got bent. He would take up the expensive album which he had lovingly arranged, and feel vexed with his daughter and her friends for their untidiness - - for the album was torn here and there and some of the photographs turned upside down. He would put it carefully in order and bend the ornamentation back into position. Then it would occur to him to place all those things in another corner of the room, near the plants. He would call the footman, but his daughter or wife would come to help him. They would not agree, and his wife would contradict him, and he would dispute and grow angry. But that was all right, for then he did not think about 'It'. 'It' was invisible.

But then, when he was moving something himself, his wife would say: "Let the servants do it. You will hurt yourself again." And suddenly *It* would flash through the screen and he would see it. It was just a flash, and he hoped it would disappear, but he would involuntarily pay attention to his side. "It sits there as before, gnawing just the same!" And he could no longer forget 'It', but could distinctly see it looking at him from behind the flowers. "What is it all for?"

"It really is so! I lost my life over that curtain as I might have done when storming a fort. Is that possible? How terrible and how stupid. It can't be true! It can't, but it is."

He would go to his study, lie down, and again be alone with 'It': face to face with 'It'. And nothing could be done with 'It' except to look at it and shudder.

Chapter VII

How it happened it is impossible to say because it came about step by step, unnoticed, but in the third month of Ivan Ilych's illness, his wife, his daughter, his son, his acquaintances, the doctors, the servants, and above all he himself, were aware that the whole interest he had for other people was whether he would soon vacate his place, and at last release the living from the discomfort caused by his presence and be himself released from his sufferings.

He slept less and less. He was given opium and hypodermic injections of morphine, but this did not relieve him. The dull depression he experienced in a somnolent condition at first gave him a little relief, but only as something new, afterwards it became as distressing as the pain itself or even more so.

Special foods were prepared for him by the doctors' orders, but all those foods became increasingly distasteful and disgusting to him.

For his excretions also special arrangements had to be made, and this was a torment to him every time — a torment from the uncleanliness, the unseemliness, and the smell, and from knowing that another person had to take part in it.

But just through his most unpleasant matter, Ivan Ilych obtained comfort. Gerasim, the butler's young assistant, always came in to carry the things out. Gerasim was a clean, fresh peasant lad, grown stout on town food and always cheerful and bright. At first the sight of him, in his clean Russian peasant costume, engaged on that disgusting task embarrassed Ivan Ilych.

Once when he got up from the commode to weak to draw up his trousers, he dropped into a soft armchair and looked with horror at his bare, enfeebled thighs with the muscles so sharply marked on them.

Gerasim with a firm light tread, his heavy boots emitting a pleasant smell of tar and fresh winter air, came in wearing a clean Hessian apron, the sleeves of his print shirt tucked up over his strong bare young arms; and refraining from looking at his sick master out of consideration for his feelings, and restraining the joy of life that beamed from his face, he went up to the commode.

"Gerasim!" said Ivan Ilych in a weak voice.

"Gerasim started, evidently afraid he might have committed some blunder, and with a rapid movement turned his fresh, kind, simple young face which just showed the first downy signs of a beard.

"Yes, sir?"

"That must be very unpleasant for you. You must forgive me. I am helpless."

"Oh, why, sir," and Gerasim's eyes beamed and he showed his glistening white teeth, "what's a little trouble? It's a case of illness with you, sir."

And his deft strong hands did their accustomed task, and he went out of the room stepping lightly. five minutes later he as lightly returned.

Ivan Ilych was still sitting in the same position in the armchair.

"Gerasim," he said when the latter had replaced the freshly-washed utensil. "Please come here and help me." Gerasim went up to him. "Lift me up. It is hard for me to get up, and I have sent Dmitri away."

Gerasim went up to him, grasped his master with his strong arms deftly but gently, in the same way that he stepped — lifted him, supported him with one hand, and with the other drew up his trousers and would have set him down again, but Ivan Ilych asked to be led to the sofa. Gerasim, without an effort and without apparent pressure, led him, almost lifting him, to the sofa and placed him on it.

"That you. How easily and well you do it all!"

Gerasim smiled again and turned to leave the room. But Ivan Ilych felt his presence such a comfort that he did not want to let him go.

"One thing more, please move up that chair. No, the other one — under my feet. It is easier for me when my feet are raised."

Gerasim brought the chair, set it down gently in place, and raised Ivan Ilych's legs on it. It seemed to Ivan Ilych that he felt better while Gerasim was holding up his legs.

"It's better when my legs are higher," he said. "Place that cushion under them."

Gerasim did so. He again lifted the legs and placed them, and again Ivan Ilych felt better while Gerasim held his legs. When he set them down Ivan Ilych fancied he felt worse.

"Gerasim," he said. "Are you busy now?"

"Not at all, sir," said Gerasim, who had learnt from the townsfolk how to speak to gentlefolk.

"What have you still to do?"

"What have I to do? I've done everything except chopping the logs for tomorrow."

"Then hold my legs up a bit higher, can you?"

"Of course I can. Why not?" and Gerasim raised his master's legs higher and Ivan Ilych thought that in that position he did not feel any pain at all.

"And how about the logs?"

"Don't trouble about that, sir. There's plenty of time."

Ivan Ilych told Gerasim to sit down and hold his legs, and began to talk to him. And strange to say it seemed to him that he felt better while Gerasim held his legs up.

After that Ivan Ilych would sometimes call Gerasim and get him to hold his legs on his shoulders, and he liked talking to him. Gerasim did it all easily, willingly, simply, and with a good nature that touched Ivan Ilych. Health, strength, and vitality in other people were offensive to him, but Gerasim's strength and vitality did not mortify but soothed him.

What tormented Ivan Ilych most was the deception, the lie, which for some reason they all accepted, that he was not dying but was simply ill, and the only need keep quiet and undergo a treatment and then something very good would result. He however knew that do what they would nothing would come of it, only still more agonizing suffering and death. This deception tortured him — their not wishing to admit what they all knew and what he knew, but wanting to lie to him concerning his terrible condition, and wishing and forcing him to participate in that lie. Those lies — lies enacted over him on the eve of his death and destined to degrade this awful, solemn act to the level of their visitings, their curtains, their sturgeon for dinner — were a terrible agony for Ivan Ilych. And strangely enough, many times when they were going through their antics over him he had been within a hairbreadth of calling out to them: "Stop lying! You know and I know that I am dying. Then at least stop lying about it!" But he had never had the spirit to do it. The awful, terrible act of his dying was, he could see, reduced by those about him to the level of a casual, unpleasant, and almost indecorous incident (as if someone entered a drawing room defusing an unpleasant odour) and this was done by that very decorum which he had served all his life long. He saw that no one felt for him, because no one even wished to grasp his position. Only Gerasim recognized it and pitied him. And so Ivan Ilych felt at ease only with him. He felt comforted when Gerasim supported his legs (sometimes all night long) and refused to go to bed, saying: "Don't you worry, Ivan Ilych. I'll get sleep enough later on," or when he suddenly became familiar and exclaimed: "If you weren't sick it would be another matter, but as it is, why should I grudge a little trouble?" Gerasim alone did not lie; everything showed that he alone understood the facts of the case and did not consider it necessary to disguise them, but simply felt sorry for his emaciated and enfeebled master. Once when Ivan Ilych was sending him away he even said straight out: "We shall all of us die, so why should I grudge a little trouble?" — expressing the fact that he did not think his work burdensome, because he was doing it for a dying man and hoped someone would do the same for him when his time came.

Apart from this lying, or because of it, what most tormented Ivan Ilych was that no one pitied him as he wished to be pitied. At certain moments after prolonged suffering he wished most of all (though he would have been ashamed to confess it) for someone to pity him as a sick child is pitied. He longed to be petted and comforted. he knew he was an important functionary, that he had a beard turning grey, and that therefore what he long for was impossible, but still he longed for it. and in Gerasim's attitude towards him there was something akin to what he wished for, and so that attitude comforted him. Ivan Ilych wanted to weep, wanted to be petted and cried over, and then his colleague Shebek would come, and instead of weeping and being petted, Ivan Ilych would assume a serious, severe, and profound air, and by force of habit would express his opinion on a decision of the Court of Cassation and would stubbornly insist on that view. This falsity around him and within him did more than anything else to poison his last days.

Chapter VIII

It was morning. He knew it was morning because Gerasim had gone, and Peter the footman had come and put out the candles, drawn back one of the curtains, and begun quietly to tidy up. Whether it was morning or evening, Friday or Sunday, made no difference, it was all just the same: the gnawing, unmitigated, agonizing pain, never ceasing for an instant, the consciousness of life inexorably waning but not yet extinguished, the approach of that ever dreaded and hateful Death which was the only reality, and always the same falsity. What were days, weeks, hours, in such a case?

"Will you have some tea, sir?"

"He wants things to be regular, and wishes the gentlefolk to drink tea in the morning," thought ivan Ilych, and only said "No."

"Wouldn't you like to move onto the sofa, sir?"

"He wants to tidy up the room, and I'm in the way. I am uncleanliness and disorder," he thought, and said only:

"No, leave me alone."

The man went on bustling about. Ivan Ilych stretched out his hand. Peter came up, ready to help.

"What is it, sir?"

"My watch."

Peter took the watch which was close at hand and gave it to his master.

"Half-past eight. Are they up?"

"No sir, except Vladimir Ivanovich" (the son) "who has gone to school. Praskovya Fedorovna ordered me to wake her if you asked for her. Shall I do so?"

"No, there's no need to." "Perhaps I'd better have some tea," he thought, and added aloud: "Yes, bring me some tea."

Peter went to the door, but Ivan Ilych dreaded being left alone. "How can I keep him here? Oh yes, my medicine." "Peter, give me my medicine." "Why not? Perhaps it may still do some good." He took a spoonful and swallowed it. "No, it won't help. It's all tomfoolery, all deception," he decided as soon as he became aware of the familiar, sickly, hopeless taste. "No, I can't believe in it any longer. But the pain, why this pain? If it would only cease just for a moment!" And he moaned. Peter turned towards him. "It's all right. Go and fetch me some tea."

Peter went out. Left alone Ivan Ilych groaned not so much with pain, terrible thought that was, as from mental anguish. Always and for ever the same, always these endless days and nights. If only it would come quicker! If only *what* would come quicker? Death, darkness?...No, no! anything rather than death!

when Peter returned with the tea on a tray, Ivan Ilych stared at him for a time in perplexity, not realizing who and what he was. Peter was disconcerted by that look and his embarrassment brought Ivan Ilych to himself.

"Oh, tea! All right, put it down. Only help me to wash and put on a clean shirt."

And Ivan Ilych began to wash. With pauses for rest, he washed his hands and then his face, cleaned his teeth, brushed his hair, looked in the glass. He was terrified by what he saw, especially by the limp way in which his hair clung to his pallid forehead.

While his shirt was being changed he knew that he would be still more frightened at the sight of his body, so he avoided looking at it. Finally he was ready. He drew on a dressing-gown, wrapped himself in a plaid, and sat down in the armchair to take his tea. For a moment he felt refreshed, but as soon as he began to drink the tea he was again aware of the same taste, and the pain also returned. He finished it with an effort, and then lay down stretching out his legs, and dismissed Peter.

Always the same. Now a spark of hope flashes up, then a sea of despair rages, and always pain; always pain, always despair, and always the same. When alone he had a dreadful and distressing desire to call someone, but he knew beforehand that with others present it would be still worse. "Another dose of morphine—to lose consciousness. I will tell him, the doctor, that he must think of something else. It's impossible, impossible, to go on like this."

An hour and another pass like that. But now there is a ring at the door bell. Perhaps it's the doctor? It is. He comes in fresh, hearty, plump, and cheerful, with that look on his face that seems to say: "There now, you're in a panic about something, but we'll arrange it all for you directly!" The doctor knows this expression is out of place here, but he has put it on once for all and can't take it off — like a man who has put on a frock-coat in the morning to pay a round of calls.

The doctor rubs his hands vigorously and reassuringly.

"Brr! How cold it is! There's such a sharp frost; just let me warm myself!" he says, as if it were only a matter of waiting till he was warm, and then he would put everything right.

"Well now, how are you?"

Ivan Ilych feels that the doctor would like to say: "Well, how are our affairs?" but that even he feels that this would not do, and says instead: "What sort of a night have you had?"

Ivan Ilych looks at him as much as to say: "Are you really never ashamed of lying?" But the doctor does not wish to understand this question, and Ivan Ilych says: "Just as terrible as ever. The pain never leaves me and never subsides. If only something . . ."

"Yes, you sick people are always like that.... There, now I think I am warm enough. Even Praskovya Fedorovna, who is so particular, could find no fault with my temperature. Well, now I can say good-morning," and the doctor presses his patient's hand.

Then dropping his former playfulness, he begins with a most serious face to examine the patient, feeling his pulse and taking his temperature, and then begins the sounding and auscultation.

Ivan Ilych knows quite well and definitely that all this is nonsense and pure deception, but when the doctor, getting down on his knee, leans over him, putting his ear first higher then lower, and performs various gymnastic movements over him with a significant expression on his face, Ivan Ilych submits to it all as he used to submit to the speeches of the lawyers, though he knew very well that they were all lying and why they were lying.

The doctor, kneeling on the sofa, is still sounding him when Praskovya Fedorovna's silk dress rustles at the door and she is heard scolding Peter for not having let her know of the doctor's arrival.

She comes in, kisses her husband, and at once proceeds to prove that she has been up a long time already, and only owing to a misunderstanding failed to be there when the doctor arrived.

Ivan Ilych looks at her, scans her all over, sets against her the whiteness and plumpness and cleanness of her hands and neck, the gloss of her hair, and the sparkle of her vivacious eyes. He hates her with his whole soul. And the thrill of hatred he feels for her makes him suffer from her touch.

Her attitude towards him and his diseases is still the same. Just as the doctor had adopted a certain relation to his patient which he could not abandon, so had she formed one towards him — that he was not doing something he ought to do and was himself to blame, and that she reproached him lovingly for this — and she could not now change that attitude.

"You see he doesn't listen to me and doesn't take his medicine at the proper time. And above all he lies in a position that is no doubt bad for him — with his legs up."

She described how he made Gerasim hold his legs up.

The doctor smiled with a contemptuous affability that said: "What's to be done? These sick people do have foolish fancies of that kind, but we must forgive them."

When the examination was over the doctor looked at his watch, and then Praskovya Fedorovna announced to Ivan Ilych that it was of course as he pleased, but she had sent today for a celebrated specialist who would examine him and have a consultation with Michael Danilovich (their regular doctor).

"Please don't raise any objections. I am doing this for my own sake," she said ironically, letting it be felt that she was doing it all for his sake and only said this to leave him no right to refuse. He remained silent, knitting his brows. He felt that he was surrounded and involved in a mesh of falsity that it was hard to unravel anything.

Everything she did for him was entirely for her own sake, and she told him she was doing for herself what she actually was doing for herself, as if that was so incredible that he must understand the opposite.

At half-past eleven the celebrated specialist arrived. Again the sounding began and the significant conversations in his presence and in another room, about the kidneys and the appendix, and the questions and answers, with such an air of importance that again, instead of the real question of life and death which now alone confronted him, the question arose of the kidney and appendix which were not behaving as they ought to and would now be attached by Michael Danilovich and the specialist and forced to amend their ways.

The celebrated specialist took leave of him with a serious though not hopeless look, and in reply to the timid question Ivan Ilych, with eyes glistening with fear and hope, put to him as to whether there was a chance of recovery, said that he could not vouch for it but there was a possibility. The look of hope with which Ivan Ilych watched the doctor out was so pathetic that Praskovya Fedorovna, seeing it, even wept as she left the room to hand the doctor his fee.

The gleam of hope kindled by the doctor's encouragement did not last long. The same room, the same pictures, curtains, wallpaper, medicine bottles, were all there, and the same aching suffering body, and Ivan Ilych began to moan. They gave him a subcutaneous injection and he sank into oblivion.

Leo Tolstoy   The Death of Ivan Ilyich

It was twilight when he came to. They brought him his dinner and he swallowed some beef tea with difficulty, and then everything was the same again and night was coming on.

After dinner, at seven o'clock, Praskovya Fedorovna came into the room in evening dress, her full bosom pushed up by her corset, and with traces of powder on her face. She had reminded him in the morning that they were going to the theatre. Sarah Bernhardt was visiting the town and they had a box, which he had insisted on their taking. Now he had forgotten about it and her toilet offended him, but he concealed his vexation when he remembered that he had himself insisted on their securing a box and going because it would be an instructive and aesthetic pleasure for the children.

Praskovya Fedorovna came in, self-satisfied but yet with a rather guilty air. She sat down and asked how he was, but, as he saw, only for the sake of asking and not in order to learn about it, knowing that there was nothing to learn — and then went on to what she really wanted to say: that she would not on any account have gone but that the box had been taken and Helen and their daughter were going, as well as Petrishchev (the examining magistrate, their daughter's fiancé) and that it was out of the question to let them go alone; but that she would have much preferred to sit with him for a while; and he must be sure to follow the doctor's orders while she was away.

"Oh, and Fedor Petrovich" (the fiancé) "would like to come in. May he? And Lisa?"

"All right."

Their daughter came in in full evening dress, her fresh young flesh exposed (making a show of that very flesh which in his own case caused so much suffering), strong, healthy, evidently in love, and impatient with illness, suffering, and death, because they interfered with her happiness.

Fedor petrovich came in too, in evening dress, his hair curled 'a la Capoul', a tight stiff collar round his long sinewy neck, an enormous white shirt-front and narrow black trousers tightly stretched over his strong thighs. He had one white glove tightly drawn on, and was holding his opera hat in his hand.

Following him the schoolboy crept in unnoticed, in a new uniform, poor little fellow, and wearing gloves. Terribly dark shadows showed under his eyes, the meaning of which Ivan Ilych knew well.

His son had always seemed pathetic to him, and now it was dreadful to see the boy's frightened look of pity. It seemed to Ivan Ilych that Vasya was the only one besides Gerasim who understood and pitied him.

They all sat down and again asked how he was. A silence followed. Lisa asked her mother about the opera glasses, and there was an altercation between mother and daughter as to who had taken them and where they had been put. This occasioned some unpleasantness.

Fedor Petrovich inquired of Ivan Ilych whether he had ever seen Sarah Bernhardt. Ivan Ilych did not at first catch the question, but then replied: "No, have you seen her before?"

"Yes, in 'Adrienne Lecouvreur'."

Praskovya Fedorovna mentioned some roles in which Sarah Bernhardt was particularly good. Her daughter disagreed. Conversation sprang up as to the elegance and realism of her acting — the sort of conversation that is always repeated and is always the same.

In the midst of the conversation Fedor Petrovich glanced at Ivan Ilych and became silent. The others also looked at him and grew silent. Ivan Ilych was staring with glittering eyes straight before him, evidently indignant with them. This had to be rectified, but it was impossible to do so. The silence had to be broken, but for a time no one dared to break it and they all became afraid that the conventional deception would suddenly become obvious and the truth become plain to all. Lisa was the first to pluck up courage and break that silence, but by trying to hide what everybody was feeling, she betrayed it.

"Well, if we are going it's time to start," she said, looking at her watch, a present from her father, and with a faint and significant smile at Fedor Petrovich relating to something known only to them. She got up with a rustle of her dress.

They all rose, said good-night, and went away.

When they had gone it seemed to Ivan Ilych that he felt better; the falsity had gone with them. But the pain remained — that same pain and that same fear that made everything monotonously alike, nothing harder and nothing easier. Everything was worse.

Again minute followed minute and hour followed hour. Everything remained the same and there was no cessation. And the inevitable end of it all became more and more terrible.

"Yes, send Gerasim here," he replied to a question Peter asked.

Chapter IX

His wife returned late at night. She came in on tiptoe, but he heard her, opened his eyes, and made haste to close them again. She wished to send Gerasim away and to sit with him herself, but he opened his eyes and said: "No, go away."

"Are you in great pain?"

"Always the same."

"Take some opium."

He agreed and took some. She went away.

Till about three in the morning he was in a state of stupefied misery. It seemed to him that he and his pain were being thrust into a narrow, deep black sack, but though they were pushed further and further in they could not be pushed to the bottom. And this, terrible enough in itself, was accompanied by suffering. He was frightened yet wanted to fall through the sack, he struggled but yet co-operated. And suddenly he broke through, fell, and regained consciousness. Gerasim was sitting at the foot of the bed dozing quietly and patiently, while he himself lay with his emaciated stockinged legs resting on Gerasim's shoulders; the same shaded candle was there and the same unceasing pain.

"Go away, Gerasim," he whispered.

"It's all right, sir. I'll stay a while."

"No. Go away."

He removed his legs from Gerasim's shoulders, turned sideways onto his arm, and felt sorry for himself. He only waited till Gerasim had gone into the next room and then restrained himself no longer but wept like a child. He wept on account of his helplessness, his terrible loneliness, the cruelty of man, the cruelty of God, and the absence of God.

"Why hast Thou done all this? Why hast Thou brought me here? Why, why dost Thou torment me so terribly?"

He did not expect an answer and yet wept because there was no answer and could be none. The pain again grew more acute, but he did not stir and did not call. He said to himself: "Go on!

Strike me! But what is it for? What have I done to Thee? What is it for?"

Then he grew quiet and not only ceased weeping but even held his breath and became all attention. It was as though he were listening not to an audible voice but to the voice of his soul, to the current of thoughts arising within him.

"What is it you want?" was the first clear conception capable of expression in words, that he heard.

"What do you want? What do you want?" he repeated to himself.

"What do I want? To live and not to suffer," he answered.

And again he listened with such concentrated attention that even his pain did not distract him.

"To live? How?" asked his inner voice.

"Why, to live as I used to — well and pleasantly."

"As you lived before, well and pleasantly?" the voice repeated.

And in imagination he began to recall the best moments of his pleasant life. But strange to say none of those best moments of his pleasant life now seemed at all what they had then seemed — none of them except the first recollections of childhood. There, in childhood, there had been something really pleasant with which it would be possible to live if it could return. But the child who had experienced that happiness existed no longer, it was like a reminiscence of somebody else.

As soon as the period began which had produced the present Ivan Ilych, all that had then seemed joys now melted before his sight and turned into something trivial and often nasty.

And the further he departed from childhood and the nearer he came to the present the more worthless and doubtful were the joys. This began with the School of Law. A little that was really good was still found there — there was light-heartedness, friendship, and hope. But in the upper classes there had already been fewer of such good moments. Then during the first years of his official career, when he was in the service of the governor, some pleasant moments again occurred: they were the memories of love for a woman. Then all became confused and there was still less of what was good; later on again there was still less that was good, and the further he went the less there was. His marriage, a mere accident, then the disenchantment that followed it, his wife's bad breath and the sensuality and hypocrisy: then that deadly official life and those preoccupations about money, a year of it, and two, and ten, and twenty, and always the same thing. And the longer it lasted the more deadly it became. "It is as if I had been going downhill while I imagined I was going up. And that is really what it was. I was going up in public opinion, but to the same extent life was ebbing away from me. And now it is all done and there is only death.

"Then what does it mean? Why? It can't be that life is so senseless and horrible. But if it really has been so horrible and senseless, why must I die and die in agony? There is something wrong!

"Maybe I did not live as I ought to have done," it suddenly occurred to him. "But how could that be, when I did everything properly?" he replied, and immediately dismissed from his mind this, the sole solution of all the riddles of life and death, as something quite impossible.

"Then what do you want now? To live? Live how? Live as you lived in the law courts when the usher proclaimed 'The judge is coming!' The judge is coming, the judge!" he repeated to himself. "Here he is, the judge. But I am not guilty!" he exclaimed angrily. "What is it for?" And he ceased crying, but turning his face to the wall continued to ponder on the same question: Why, and for what purpose, is there all this horror? But however much he pondered he found no answer. And whenever the thought occurred to him, as it often did, that it all resulted from his not having lived as he ought to have done, he at once recalled the correctness of his whole life and dismissed so strange an idea.

Chapter X

Another fortnight passed. Ivan Ilych now no longer left his sofa. He would not lie in bed but lay on the sofa, facing the wall nearly all the time. He suffered ever the same unceasing agonies and in his loneliness pondered always on the same insoluble question: "What is this? Can it be that it is Death?" And the inner voice answered: "Yes, it is Death."

"Why these sufferings?" And the voice answered, "For no reason — they just are so." Beyond and besides this there was nothing.

From the very beginning of his illness, ever since he had first been to see the doctor, Ivan Ilych's life had been divided between two contrary and alternating moods: now it was despair and the expectation of this uncomprehended and terrible death, and now hope and an intently interested observation of the functioning of his organs. Now before his eyes there was only a kidney or an intestine that temporarily evaded its duty, and now only that incomprehensible and dreadful death from which it was impossible to escape.

These two states of mind had alternated from the very beginning of his illness, but the further it progressed the more doubtful and fantastic became the conception of the kidney, and the more real the sense of impending death.

He had but to call to mind what he had been three months before and what he was now, to call to mind with what regularity he had been going downhill, for every possibility of hope to be shattered.

Latterly during the loneliness in which he found himself as he lay facing the back of the sofa, a loneliness in the midst of a populous town and surrounded by numerous acquaintances and relations but that yet could not have been more complete anywhere - - either at the bottom of the sea or under the earth — during that terrible loneliness Ivan ilych had lived only in memories of the past. Pictures of his past rose before him one after another. they always began with what was nearest in time and then went back to what was most remote — to his childhood — and rested there. If he thought of the stewed prunes that had been offered him that day, his mind went back to the raw shriveled French plums of his childhood, their peculiar flavour and the flow of saliva when he sucked their stones, and along with the memory of that taste came a whole series of memories of those days: his nurse, his brother, and their toys. "No, I mustn't thing of that....It is too painful," Ivan Ilych said to himself, and brought himself back to the present — to the button on the back of the sofa and the creases in its morocco. "Morocco is expensive, but it does not wear well: there had been a quarrel about it. It was a different kind of quarrel and a different kind of morocco that time when we tore father's portfolio and were punished, and mamma brought us some tarts...." And again his thoughts dwelt on his childhood, and again it was painful and he tried to banish them and fix his mind on something else.

Then again together with that chain of memories another series passed through his mind — of how his illness had progressed and grown worse. There also the further back he looked the more life there had been. There had been more of what was good in life and more of life itself. The two merged together.

"Just as the pain went on getting worse and worse, so my life grew worse and worse," he thought. "There is one bright spot there at the back, at the beginning of life, and afterwards all becomes blacker and blacker and proceeds more and more rapidly — in inverse ration to the square of the distance from death," thought Ivan Ilych. And the example of a stone falling downwards with increasing velocity entered his mind. Life, a series of increasing sufferings, flies further and further towards its end — the most terrible suffering. "I am flying...." He shuddered, shifted himself, and tried to resist, but was already aware that resistance was impossible, and again with eyes weary of gazing but unable to cease seeing what was before them, he stared at the back of the sofa and waited — awaiting that dreadful fall and shock and destruction.

"Resistance is impossible!" he said to himself. "If I could only understand what it is all for! But that too is impossible. An explanation would be possible if it could be said that I have not lived as I ought to. But it is impossible to say that," and he remembered all the legality, correctitude, and propriety of his life. "That at any rate can certainly not be admitted," he thought, and his lips smiled ironically as if someone could see that smile and be taken in by it. "There is no explanation! Agony, death....What for?"

Chapter XI

Another two weeks went by in this way and during that fortnight an even occurred that Ivan Ilych and his wife had desired. Petrishchev formally proposed. It happened in the evening. The next day Praskovya Fedorovna came into her husband's room considering how best to inform him of it, but that very night there had been a fresh change for the worse in his condition. She found him still lying on the sofa but in a different position. He lay on his back, groaning and staring fixedly straight in front of him.

She began to remind him of his medicines, but he turned his eyes towards her with such a look that she did not finish what she was saying; so great an animosity, to her in particular, did that look express.

"For Christ's sake let me die in peace!" he said.

She would have gone away, but just then their daughter came in and went up to say good morning. He looked at her as he had done at his wife, and in reply to her inquiry about his health said dryly that he would soon free them all of himself. They were both silent and after sitting with him for a while went away.

"Is it our fault?" Lisa said to her mother. "It's as if we were to blame! I am sorry for papa, but why should we be tortured?"

The doctor came at his usual time. Ivan Ilych answered "Yes" and "No," never taking his angry eyes from him, and at last said: "You know you can do nothing for me, so leave me alone."

"We can ease your sufferings."

"You can't even do that. Let me be."

The doctor went into the drawing room and told Praskovya Fedorovna that the case was very serious and that the only resource left was opium to allay her husband's sufferings, which must be terrible.

It was true, as the doctor said, that Ivan Ilych's physical sufferings were terrible, but worse than the physical sufferings were his mental sufferings which were his chief torture.

His mental sufferings were due to the fact that that night, as he looked at Gerasim's sleepy, good-natured face with it prominent cheek-bones, the question suddenly occurred to him: "What if my whole life has been wrong?"

It occurred to him that what had appeared perfectly impossible before, namely that he had not spent his life as he should have done, might after all be true. It occurred to him that his scarcely perceptible attempts to struggle against what was considered good by the most highly placed people, those scarcely noticeable impulses which he had immediately suppressed, might have been the real thing, and all the rest false. And his professional duties and the whole arrangement of his life and of his family, and all his social and official interests, might all have been false. He tried to defend all those things to himself and suddenly felt the weakness of what he was defending. There was nothing to defend.

"But if that is so," he said to himself, "and i am leaving this life with the consciousness that I have lost all that was given me and it is impossible to rectify it — what then?"

He lay on his back and began to pass his life in review in quite a new way. In the morning when he saw first his footman, then his wife, then his daughter, and then the doctor, their every word and movement confirmed to him the awful truth that had been revealed to him during the night. In them he saw himself — all that for which he had lived — and saw clearly that it was not real at all, but a terrible and huge deception which had hidden both life and death. This consciousness intensified his physical suffering tenfold. He groaned and tossed about, and pulled at his clothing which choked and stifled him. And he hated them on that account.

He was given a large dose of opium and became unconscious, but at noon his sufferings began again. He drove everybody away and tossed from side to side.

His wife came to him and said:

"Jean, my dear, do this for me. It can't do any harm and often helps. Healthy people often do it."

He opened his eyes wide.

"What? Take communion? Why? It's unnecessary! However..."

She began to cry.

"Yes, do, my dear. I'll send for our priest. He is such a nice man."

"All right. Very well," he muttered.

When the priest came and heard his confession, Ivan Ilych was softened and seemed to feel a relief from his doubts and consequently from his sufferings, and for a moment there came a ray of hope. He again began to think of the vermiform appendix and the possibility of correcting it. He received the sacrament with tears in his eyes.

When they laid him down again afterwards he felt a moment's ease, and the hope that he might live awoke in him again. He began to think of the operation that had been suggested to him. "To live! I want to live!" he said to himself.

His wife came in to congratulate him after his communion, and when uttering the usual conventional words she added:

"You feel better, don't you?"

Without looking at her he said "Yes."

Her dress, her figure, the expression of her face, the tone of her voice, all revealed the same thing. "This is wrong, it is not as it should be. All you have lived for and still live for is falsehood and deception, hiding life and death from you." And as soon as he admitted that thought, his hatred and his agonizing physical suffering again sprang up, and with that suffering a consciousness of the unavoidable, approaching end. And to this was added a new sensation of grinding shooting pain and a feeling of suffocation.

The expression of his face when he uttered that "Yes" was dreadful. Having uttered it, he looked her straight in the eyes, turned on his face with a rapidity extraordinary in his weak state and shouted:

"Go away! Go away and leave me alone!"

Chapter XII

From that moment the screaming began that continued for three days, and was so terrible that one could not hear it through two closed doors without horror. At the moment he answered his wife realized that he was lost, that there was no return, that the end had come, the very end, and his doubts were still unsolved and remained doubts.

"Oh! Oh! Oh!" he cried in various intonations. He had begun by screaming "I won't!" and continued screaming on the letter "O".

For three whole days, during which time did not exist for him, he struggled in that black sack into which he was being thrust by an invisible, resistless force. He struggled as a man condemned to death struggles in the hands of the executioner, knowing that he cannot save himself. And every moment he felt that despite all his efforts he was drawing nearer and nearer to what terrified him. he felt that his agony was due to his being thrust into that black hole and still more to his not being able to get right into it. He was hindered from getting into it by his conviction that his life had been a good one. That very justification of his life held him fast and prevented his moving forward, and it caused him most torment of all.

Suddenly some force struck him in the chest and side, making it still harder to breathe, and he fell through the hole and there at the bottom was a light. What had happened to him was like the sensation one sometimes experiences in a railway carriage when one thinks one is going backwards while one is really going forwards and suddenly becomes aware of the real direction.

"Yes, it was not the right thing," he said to himself, "but that's no matter. It can be done. But what *is* the right thing? he asked himself, and suddenly grew quiet.

This occurred at the end of the third day, two hours before his death. Just then his schoolboy son had crept softly in and gone up to the bedside. The dying man was still screaming desperately and waving his arms. His hand fell on the boy's head, and the boy caught it, pressed it to his lips, and began to cry.

At that very moment Ivan Ilych fell through and caught sight of the light, and it was revealed to him that though his life had not been what it should have been, this could still be rectified. He asked himself, "What *is* the right thing?" and grew still, listening. Then he felt that someone was kissing his hand. He opened his eyes, looked at his son, and felt sorry for him. His wife camp up to him and he glanced at her. She was gazing at him open-mouthed, with undried tears on her nose and cheek and a despairing look on her face. He felt sorry for her too.

"Yes, I am making them wretched," he thought. "They are sorry, but it will be better for them when I die." He wished to say this but had not the strength to utter it. "Besides, why speak? I must act," he thought. with a look at his wife he indicated his son and said: "Take him away. . .sorry for him...sorry for you too. . . ." He tried to add, "Forgive me," but said "Forego" and waved his hand, knowing that He whose understanding mattered would understand.

And suddenly it grew clear to him that what had been oppressing him and would not leave his was all dropping away at once from two sides, from ten sides, and from all sides. He was sorry for them, he must act so as not to hurt them: release them and free himself from these sufferings. "How good and how simple!" he thought. "And the pain?" he asked himself. "What has become of it? Where are you, pain?"

He turned his attention to it.

"Yes, here it is. Well, what of it? Let the pain be."

"And death...where is it?"

He sought his former accustomed fear of death and did not find it. "Where is it? What death?" There was no fear because there was no death.

In place of death there was light.

"So that's what it is!" he suddenly exclaimed aloud. "What joy!"

To him all this happened in a single instant, and the meaning of that instant did not change. For those present his agony continued for another two hours. Something rattled in his throat, his emaciated body twitched, then the gasping and rattle became less and less frequent.

"It is finished!" said someone near him.

He heard these words and repeated them in his soul.

"Death is finished," he said to himself. "It is no more!"

He drew in a breath, stopped in the midst of a sigh, stretched out, and died.

The Adventure of
Second Lieutenant Bubnov
Ivan Turgenev

Second Lieutenant Bubnov was promenading along one of the streets of a country town. Along the whole length of this street, which was over half a mile, stood only three houses, of which two were on the right and one on the left.

Since no more than two hours remained till dusk, the elderly townsfolk, women owners of the said three houses, had closed the shutters, driven the hens into the roosts and gone to bed. Second Lieutenant Bubnov walked along, his hands buried in his pockets, abandoning himself, as his custom was, to his favorite reflection as to how he would act if he were Napoleon.

Suddenly a man of short stature, attired in very unusual garments, approached him. Bubnov took him at first to be the landowner Telushkin, who had just returned from abroad, not because personally he had the honour of knowing Mr. Telushkin, but he had heard tales of the queer and strangely outlandish garments this gentleman wore. On the stranger's very first words he was undeceived.

Approaching the Second Lieutenant Bubnov, the man declared in off-hand tones, as if repeating a formula: "I am the Devil."

"Either he is drunk, or I am," thought the Lieutenant. "In either case it's unwise to remain here."

But the stranger smilingly made it impossible for him to budge an inch.

"You are not drunk, dear Ivan Andreevich Bubnov, for I really am the Devil."

Ivan thought again: "Either he is mad, or I am mad, so why should I stay with him?"

The stranger caught the lapel of his coat and spoke again loudly and decisively. "Bubnov! What would you do if you were Napoleon?"

Thought Bubnov, reassured: "Surely he must be the Devil . . ." and then aloud: "What do you want?"

"First, I want to convince you that I really am the Devil. Look over there. You see those nettles, now look carefully at what they shall do. What about a Cossack dance? A proper one?"

The nettles which were growing in profusion along the fences immediately broke into a Cossack dance in first-rate style.

"Good!" said the Devil, "and there will be no hitch as far as I am personally concerned either."

Then he began to play some astonishing personal tricks. He placed both his feet into his mouth and pulled them through the back of his neck. He took out his own eyes, and using both hands, merrily threw them about in the air; finally he presented his nose to Ivan Andreevich as a souvenir. The lieutenant unbuttoned his coat and put the nose into his side pocket.

"Now do you believe that I am the Devil?"

"Yes! Yes, I do. What do you want from me, my good friend?"

"Nothing, nothing at all! The fact is, I've been suffering from boredom, so I just dropped in to have a chat with you. Would you care to take a little stroll?"

"Delighted, I am sure." They started off together side by side like two old friends.

"What an extraordinary experience!" thought Ivan Andreevich, "I must be having the D.T.'s." He caught at his moustache and tugged it as bard as he could. . . . His head creaked like wood.

No need for you to worry, friend Ivan Andreevich, and besides, you may accidentally pull your head right off if you keep tugging like that . . . and without a head, as you know very well yourself, a man is not so handy as with one. But there! We'll try it."

Ivan Turgenev   The Adventure of Second Lieutenant Bubnov

The Devil caught Second Lieutenant Bubnov by his fore-lock and pulled off his head completely. Bubnov had every intention of wondering at this action, but without a head a man cannot even wonder. The Devil played about with Ivan's head; raised it to his nose and sniffed at it. Then he replaced it on the Second Lieutenant's body. Immediately the Lieutenant opened his mouth and made a jovial remark. Thus conversing, the two wandered out of the town and at last found themselves in a large wood.

"Look here, now," said Ivan Andreevich, "you aren't going to lead me into some gully to the vultures, are you? I cannot stand vultures." "Oh, dear me, no! Of course not!" retorted the Devil.

They came to a great withered oak. On a branch of the tree an old raven was perched, croaking in a dreary drawl. In reality this raven was a crow, but in deeper reality it was the Devil's grandmother. The Devil never had a mother, only a grandmother. How this came about, even the Devil himself never knew.

"I am going to present you to my granny," he said to Ivan Andreevich. "But I am wearing only my morning clothes," replied Bubnov. "That will be all right," said the Devil, "but I must politely request you not on any account whatsoever to make the sign of the Cross, for this would deprive us of your pleasant company. And now will you do me the favour of biting off the tip of my tail?"

With these remarkable words the Devil raised his tail, which was fluffy and soft as a cat's paw, right up to Ivan Andreevich's very lips.

"No! I shall not bite your tail!" cried Ivan Andreevich.

"Why not?"

"It would give you pain."

"Me? Goodness! Please be so kind as to bite it. Do not stand on ceremony. Please. . . ."

While he was speaking the accursed tail kept on thrusting itself into Ivan Andreevich's mouth. . . .

"But is this absolutely necessary?"

"Absolutely."

Second Lieutenant Bubnov was about to catch the Devil's tail with his right hand, but suddenly stopped, glanced at the Devil over his shoulder, and said: "I suppose your tail tastes rotten?"

"Not at all! Just wish for whichever dish you happen to like, and my tail will taste like that dish."

"I would like cucumber with honey!" said Ivan, after reflection. And then he bit. . . . !

Indeed the Devil was right. The tail smacked of cucumber and honey, with just a shade of sulphur. But who would notice such a trifle?

Second Lieutenant Bubnov had hardly swallowed the fragment of tail when he suddenly found himself in a moderately tidy room. In a large old-fashioned arm-chair was seated an old hag with a largish nose, cracking nuts. The Devil led Ivan Andreevich to her.

"Granny," he said, "this is Second Lieutenant Ivan Andreevich Bubnov. Ivan Andreevich—my granny."

Having thus introduced them to each other, he pushed a chair towards the Second Lieutenant and left them in order to don his horns.

The Lieutenant did not know how to begin; not because he was unable, as the saying is, "to make conversation," but he did not know the name and patronymic of the Devil's grandmother, and could not think of how to address her: just "Madam" seemed somewhat awkward. . . . At last he made up his mind and began: "Dear Mistress . . ."

But the old woman opened her mouth in a strange manner and in a very hoarse voice uttered: "No needless words! No needless words, Second Lieutenant Ivan Bubnov!".

It seemed to Ivan that the old woman's words took shape and were flying towards him in a kind of spiral screw. His embarrassment left him and he only nodded his head. The old woman went on cracking her nuts but kept staring at him, as if she expected him to speak. Ivan Andreevich was at his wit's end and sat in silence like a stone idol. Evidently this wearied the old woman, for suddenly she jumped up, caught Ivan Andreevich by his hands and started dancing all over the room with him,. displaying incredible agility.

"Second Lieutenant, my little Cupid. Dance with me, darling!" she crooned as they danced.

Bubnov felt dizzy and cried out at last in despair: "Devil! Devil! Your granny has gone crazy!"

The Devil hurried in, now wearing his horns. He caught his grand-mother by the armpits and deferentially sat her down in her place. Then in humble expressions he begged Ivan Andreevich to pardon his grand-mother.

"But," he added, "I want to give you a good time. So now I will introduce you to my little grandchild. She is still very young, she has only a tiny tail as yet; but you are an honourable gentleman. You will not take advantage of her inexperience. . . . Babebibobu, come here!"

From the next room came the Devil's grandchild. She dropped a polite curtsy to Ivan Andreevich, and bashfully fell on her great-great-grandmother's neck.

Ivan Andreevich bowed to her, clicking his heels together. "What's her name?" he asked the Devil.

"Babebibobu," replied the Devil.

"Babeb . . . and so on isn't a Russian name," remarked the Second Lieutenant.

"We are foreigners," explained Babebibobu's grandfather.

Ivan Andreevich pulled himself together and went over to kiss Babebibobu's hand, which she extended to him. He had time to notice that the little nails of her dainty little fingers were slightly bent down in the form of claws; besides, at the very instant of the kiss he felt a stinging sensation on his lips.

"Will you take a stroll with me in the garden?" Babebibobu asked in a whisper.

"I shall be delighted," replied Ivan Bubnov. The old woman whispered to the Devil. Evidently she was not in favour of the suggested walk. But the Devil shrugged his shoulders and turned away. . . . Bubnov left the room with the Devil's grandchild.

The Devil's garden was like many other gardens, nothing exceptional. But Ivan Andreevich noticed one peculiarity; all the plants were emitting groans as if growing were painful. Such was the arrangement of the Devil.

Babebibobu walked on in silence for a long time, but at last she lifted her little head, looked at Ivan Andreevich, sighed and said: "I love you, Bubnov."

The Second Lieutenant remembered her grandfather's admonition and replied good-naturedly: "Please compose yourself."

"I love you, Bubnov, and you must return my love," she repeated more endearingly. "I shall crown you with poppy, red as my cheeks; I shall feed you with the freshest of acorns; I shall make you drunk with the juice of bracken and we shall be happy and virtuous! Bubnov, I love you."

Bubnov looked at her. He was about to say: "And I love you, too, Babebi . . ." but suddenly it seemed to him that Babebibobu's eyes began contracting and expanding like those of a feline, while her nostrils distended and her teeth sharpened. . . . It suddenly seemed to him as if he were a mouse and she had become a cat. . . .

"No!" he said suddenly, "I cannot return your love. Let us return home."

"But where is home?" she asked in a strange voice.

Ivan looked around. He was standing on the very top of a very high pillar and even so only on one leg; his other leg was fluttering in the breeze like a flag. Up the pillar which was lathered and smeared with oil, many kinds of little imps were climbing with great difficulty. They were endeavouring to reach the top . . . and no doubt, Ivan Andreevich must have been appointed the reward for the winner of the race. Babebibobu was floating around him in the air, laughing malignantly. . . .

"Devil, you prove yourself a traitor," the Second Lieutenant said with difficulty.

"Children! Children! Have you got lost, or what?" the Devil's voice resounded around them.

Both Ivan Andreevich and Babebibobu again found themselves in the garden. Not far away from them stood the Devil smiling pleasantly. . . .

"You do not know how to entertain a dear guest, little Babebi!" (so he always addressed her when displeased). "Please, come right over here with me, Ivan Andreevich, and leave this silly chit of a girl."

"Oh, indeed! Silly chit of a girl, am I," retorted Babebibobu. "Why, already my horns are shooting. . . ." And bending her head down, she pulled her hair asunder and showed Ivan Andreevich two tiny, dainty little horns.

Ivan Andreevich, who never in his life had learned any dancing, suddenly jumped, turned three times on one leg, made a *glissade, jetee assemblee, pas de zephire*, stooped down and kissed the tip of Babebibobu's right horn; but as if jubilant at such a recognition the horn itself suddenly grew up and painfully struck the Second Lieutenant.

Half an hour later they were all seated round the table.

"Let's see," thought Ivan Andreevich, "what do these people have for dinner?"

They were seated in the following order: at the top of the table the old woman, the Devil's grandmother; on her right the Lieutenant; on the left of the old woman, her grandson, the Devil; to the left of the Devil and opposite the old lady, Babebibobu.

An enormously big covered tureen entered the room, pushed up close, curtsied and jumped on to the table.

"What do they eat?" wondered Bubnov. "But we'll soon see."

The old woman addressed her grandson: "Dear grandchild, we'd better marry Second Lieutenant Bubnov and Babebibobu, don't you think?" "Of course," answered the grandchild.

Marry the Devil's granddaughter, what a strange idea! How curious the results to Second Lieutenant Bubnov! Suppose there were children, what then? What would be their social rank? Would they be nobles, or not? Or what condition of people? They would scarcely be able to enter a military college! "A most difficult situation this," he mused. "Why on earth did I eat the Devil's tail?"

"However," observed the Devil, "there can be no marriage without mutual consent. I am a good-hearted old grandfather, and love my Babebibobu; equally, for many years I have the greatest esteem for my friend Iran Andreevich. . . . Babebibobu! Tell me, do you love Second Lieutenant Bubnov?"

"Just doesn't she love him," exclaimed the old demon. "Only look at her. She is already licking her lips.... "

In very truth, the Devil's granddaughter, cocking her eyes and smiling grimly, was passing her red, red little tongue over her sharp little white teeth. . . .

"She will devour me," shouted Bubnov.

"May good digestion wait on appetite," remarked the Devil.

"How, appetite? What does it mean—appetite? I am an officer! I am a guest! Does one ever eat an officer? Does one ever eat a guest?"

"You ask for information and evidence," retorted the Devil, "that's easy at once! I have staying with me a German doctor who will prove to you as plain as twice two are four, that to devour you is possible, essential, becoming and pleasant."

"Were he even a thousand doctors he can prove nothing to me! Absolutely nothing! Decidedly nothing." The Second Lieutenant got furious, and began waving his arms about like a windmill. "I shall depart, confound you! I am going! What an idiot I was to eat part of your tail! I am going!"

Ivan Andreevich tried to rise, but in vain. The arm-chair in which he sat turned into some kind of ugly spider and seized him with demoniacal force.

The Devil and his family almost split their sides with laughter watching the Lieutenant's frenzied and fruitless efforts. . . . The old woman's laughter extraordinarily resembled the old goat's bleating; Babebibobu screamed with enjoyment.

"Let me go!" groaned Ivan Andreevich. "Away with you, you devilish tribe in the name of . . ."

"Stop! Stop him!" shouted the Devil. "Do not let him make the sign of the Cross. . . ."

Babebibobu sprang, with a bloodthirsty smile, at the Second Lieutenant, and in one snap bit his right arm off. . . . At the same instant the lid came off the tureen, the poor Second Lieutenant was caught and thrown into the tureen. . . . When he had been seasoned with vinegar, oil, pep-per, grated powder, sulphur, cranberry juice, they devoured him, devoured him to the last little bone. All through the dinner singers and musicians were performing various overtures. . . . Babebibobu with especial relish ate the Second Lieutenant's heart, and the Devil nearly choked himself with an epaulette.

Next morning Second Lieutenant Bubnov was found in the same street of the town. He lay with his face to the fence and was as red as a poppy. They brought him back to consciousness. With terror he looked around, talking all sorts of nonsense; assuring them that he was feeling himself not there, but far away in three entirely alien stomachs. Only towards evening did he finally come to himself. After that he could never forget his meeting with the Devil, and often would say: "Were I Napoleon, I should exterminate all devils!"

He lived, however, to a great old age, did not resign his commission, and died a junior lieutenant.

A Terrible Night

Anton Chekhov

Ivan Petrovitch Panikhidin went pale, turned down the lamp and spoke with deep feeling:

"A dark shadow lay over the land that Christmas Eve in 1883 as I made my way home from the house of a friend, now dead, where we had taken part in a séance. The lane I had to go along was unlit and I made my way almost by touch. My room in Moscow was in a large boarding house owned by Troopov, a civil servant, in a very dreary district. My thoughts, as I moved forward, were gloomy and oppressive ...

" 'Your life is ebbing to its close ... Go to confession.' "

"Those were the words spoken to me by Spinoza, the spirit we had dared to conjure up. I asked him to repeat them and the saucer not only did so but added: 'Tonight.' I don't believe in spiritualism but the thought of death, even in casual reference, depresses me. Death, gentlemen, is unavoidable, common to all, but nevertheless repugnant to the nature of man

... And now, as cold darkness gathered about me, raindrops whirling furiously in moaning wind, with not a living soul to see, no human sound to hear, a vague and inexplicable terror came upon me. I, a man quite free from superstition, hurried forward, afraid to look back or glance to the side. I felt that, if I did, I would surely see death in ghostly form."

Panikhidin breathed deeply, drank some water and went on:

Stories That Scared Even Stalin

"This vague but very natural terror didn't leave me even as I climbed to the fourth floor of Troopov's boarding house, opened my door and went into the room. It was dark in my modest dwelling and a soft wind moaned above the stove and, as if seeking warmth, rattled the air-vent.

" 'If we're to believe Spinoza . . .' "—I smiled ironically—'. . . then, there, beneath that stove, my death will come to-night . . . A rather horrible thought, though!'

"I lit a match . . . Frantic gusts of wind scurried over the roof of the building. The quiet moaning became a low spiteful howl and somewhere down below a loose shutter clattered . .

" 'How grim it must be for homeless people on a night like this . . .' I thought.

"But there was no time to ponder in this way. As the sulphur of my match flared in little blue flame, I glanced round the room and an astonishing and terrible sight confronted me . . . If only a gust of wind had blown out the match! Then perhaps I'd have seen nothing and the hairs would not have reared up on my head. I gave a cry, stepped back towards the door and, full of horror, shut my eyes . . .

"In the middle of the room was a coffin.

"In the brief blue flame I had made out its shape . . . had seen silk brocade, pink and shimmering with glints . . . and a cross of fretted gold on top. Some things, gentlemen, impress themselves on the memory, even if we see them only for a moment. So it was with that coffin. I saw it only for a second or two but I remember its slightest features . . . It was for someone of medium height and, to judge by the pink colour, a young girl. The expensive brocade, the supports, the bronze handles—all suggested that she was rich.

"I ran headlong from my room and without reflection, with-out thought, knowing only fear, rushed down the stairs. In the dark my legs got tangled in the skirts of my overcoat: it's a wonder I didn't fall and break my neck. I came out into the street, leaned against a wet lamppost and tried to compose myself. My heart was beating fearfully and I couldn't get my breath . . ."

One of the listeners turned up the lamp and moved closer to the storyteller who continued:

"To find my room on fire, or a thief there, or a mad dog . . that wouldn't have astounded me. Nor would it if the ceiling had come down, the floor caved in or the walls given way. Those are natural phenomena and can be understood. But how could a coffin have come in my room? Where could it have come from? . . . Expensive, for a young woman of high rank apparently—how could it have come to the dingy room of a petty clerk? Was it empty, or was there . . . a dead body in it? Who was she, then, taken prematurely from a life of riches to pay me this strange and terrible visit? It was an agonizing mystery!

" 'If this is not a supernatural thing , . .'—the thought flashed into my mind—'then it must be a crime. . .

"I was lost in wonder and conjecture. My door had been locked when I was out and only my closest friends knew where the key was. Friends wouldn't bring me a coffin. Perhaps undertaker's men brought it there by mistake, chose the wrong floor or wrong door and put the coffin where it wasn't intended.

But it's well known that undertaker's men don't leave a room before they're paid or at least given a tip.

"'The spirits foretold my death.' I remembered. 'Did they provide a coffin too?'

"Gentlemen, I do not believe in spirits, nor did I then, but a coincidence of that sort would put even a philosopher into a sombre mood.

"'But this is all nonsense!' I decided. 'I'm as frightened as a schoolboy. It was an optical illusion—nothing more! I was feeling so gloomy when I came in, no wonder my strained nerves made me imagine a coffin . . . Of course, an optical illusion. What else could it have been?'

"The rain lashed my face and battered my cap and the skirts of my overcoat . . . I was cold and fearfully wet . . . I had to go somewhere . . . But where? To go back to my room might mean seeing the coffin again and that sight would be more than I could stand. To be alone with a coffin, perhaps with a dead body inside it, when there wasn't a living soul to see, no human sound to hear . . . : it could cost me my reason . . . But to stay in the street in the cold and pouring rain was out of the question.

"I decided to go and spend the night with my friend Upokoev, who later shot himself, you'll remember. He lived in furnished rooms in the house of Cherepov, the merchant, on Dead Street."

Panikhidin wiped perspiration from his pale face and, with a sigh, continued:

"I didn't find my friend at home. When I had knocked till I was sure he wasn't there, I groped for the key over the door, opened it and went in. I flung my wet overcoat to the floor and, stumbling against a dim sofa, sat down on it to rest . . . It was very dark . . . The wind droned mournfully in the ventilator shaft and in the stove a cricket chirped a monotonous song. From the Kremlin came the peal of Christmas bells . . . I hurriedly lit a match. But its light did not lighten my gloom—quite the reverse. A fearful horror once again overwhelmed me. I cried out, reeled and, not knowing what I did, ran from the room . . .

"For in my friend's flat, as in my own, there was—a coffin!

"It was almost twice as big as mine and its brown upholstery gave it a particularly sombre hue. How had it come there? My eyes were deceiving me—impossible to doubt that any longer. There couldn't be a coffin in both rooms. It must be a sickness of the nerves, an hallucination. Wherever I went now, I would see before my death's terrible dwelling place. Perhaps I'd gone out of my mind, was suffering from a kind of 'coffin-mania,' and the cause of that madness wasn't hard to find: I had only to remember the spiritualist séance and Spinoza's words . . .

"'I'm going mad!' I thought in horror, clutching my brow. 'My God! What will become of me?'

"I'd a splitting headache and my legs were giving way . . .

"The rain was pouring down in bucketfuls, there was a piercing wind and now I had neither fur coat nor cap. To go back to the flat for them was out of the question, quite beyond my powers ... Terror clutched me fiercely in an icy grip. Even though I knew I had suffered an hallucination, the hairs rose up on my head and sweat poured from my brow.

"What was I to do?" went on Panikhidin. "I was out of my wits and likely to catch my death of cold. Luckily I remembered that a good friend lived not far from Dead Street: Pogostov, a doctor recently qualified, who had been with me that evening at the séance. I hurried to his dwelling . . . At that time he wasn't yet married to his rich wife and lived on the fifth floor of the big boarding house owned by Kladbishenski, the counselor of state.

"There my overwrought nerves were to suffer further torment. As I climbed to the fifth floor, I heard a terrible noise. Someone was running overhead, thudding heavily and slamming doors.

" 'Help me!' I heard a heart-rending cry. 'Help me! Caretaker!'

"And a moment later there came down the stairs towards me a dark figure in fur coat and flabby top hat.

"'Pogostov!' I shouted, as I recognized my friend. 'It's you. What's the matter?'

"As he reached me, Pogostov stopped and clutched my arm convulsively. He was pale, breathing heavily and trembling. His eyes were distracted and his chest heaved . . .

"'Is it you, Panikhidin?' he asked in hollow voice. 'But is it really you? You're as pale as if you'd come from the grave . . . But enough of that ... You're not an hallucination, are you? . . . My God! You look terrible!'

" 'And what about you? You look pretty awful.'

" 'Oh, my dear chap, give me time to pull myself together ... I'm glad to see you, if it's really you and not an optical illusion. That damned séance! ... It shook up my nerves so much that, imagine, as soon as I got home, I saw . . . there in my room . . . a coffin!'

"I couldn't believe my ears and asked him to repeat what he'd said.

" 'A coffin, a real coffin!' said the doctor, sitting down, quite worn out, on a step. 'I'm not a coward but the devil himself would be scared if, after a séance, he stumbled on a coffin in the dark.'

"Confused and trying to console him a little, I told the doctor about the coffins that I had seen . . .

"For a minute we stared at one another, wide-eyed and open-mouthed. Then, to convince ourselves we weren't hallucinations, we started to punch each other.

" 'It's hurting both of us,' said the doctor. 'That means we're not asleep and seeing one another in dreams. So the coffins, mine and both of yours, can't be illusions but really do exist. Well, what do we do now, old chap?'

"We stayed a full hour on the cold staircase, then decided, lost in wonder and conjecture and terribly cold, to cast off our mean fears, wake up the caretaker and go with him to the doctor's room. We did so. As we went in, we lit a candle and at once saw a coffin upholstered in white silk brocade with gold fringes and tassels. The caretaker piously crossed himself.

" 'Now we can find out . . .' said the pallid doctor, his body trembling, '. . . whether this coffin is empty . . . or occupied . . .'

"After long hesitation, very natural in the circumstances, the doctor stooped and, gritting his teeth in fearful expectation, pulled off the coffin lid. We looked in and . . .

"It was empty . . .

"Instead of a dead body we found a letter which read as follows:

" 'Dear Pogostov,

" 'You know that my father-in-law has got his business into a fearful mess. He's up to the ears in debt. Tomorrow or the day after there will be distraint on his goods, and that will ruin his family and mine, and stain our honour too, which I hold more dear. At a family conference last night we decided to put away all things of value. Since my father-in-law's property consists of coffins—as you know, he's a master coffin-maker, the best in town—we decided to conceal all the best coffins. I implore you as a friend to help us save our property and honour. In the hope that you can store our property I am bringing you, my dear fellow, one coffin which I beg you to conceal in your room till I can take it back. I hope you will not refuse me, especially as the coffin will not be with you for more than a week. To all whom I count our sincere friends I am sending a coffin and putting my trust in their generosity and kindness.

" 'Your dear friend,

" 'Ivan Cheloustin.'

"For three months after this terrible experience I was treated for nervous exhaustion; and our friend, the coffin-maker's son-in-law, saved both his property and honour. He has a monumental mason's business now and trades in tombstones and memorial tablets. He is not doing very well and every night, when I come home, I fear that I'll see beside my bed a statue in white marble or a catafalque."

The Dog
Ivan Turgenev

But if you once admit the existence of the supernatural, and that it can enter into the ordinary affairs of everyday life, allow me to ask what scope is left for the exercise of reason?"

And so saying, Anthony Stephanich crossed his arms.

Anthony Stephanich was a Councilor to the Minister in some department or other, and this circumstance, joined with those of his possessing a grave bass voice, and of his speaking with great precision, rendered him an object of universal consideration. He had just been compelled, as his detractors phrased it, to accept the Cross of St Stanislaus.

"There can be no doubt of that," said Skorevich.

"It is impossible to dispute it," said Cinarevich.

"I assent entirely," said the master of the house, Phinoplentoff, in his thin little voice.

Now there was a short, plump, bald, middle-aged little man who was sitting silent close to the stove, and he suddenly said

"I confess that I don't agree with you, for something which was certainly supernatural once happened to me myself."

Everybody looked at him, and there was a pause. The little man in question was a small landed proprietor in Kalouga who had only come to live at St Petersburg a short time before. He had once been in the hussars and lost his money at play, resigned his commission, and returned to cultivate cabbages at his native village. Recent events had greatly reduced his income, and he had come to town in order to try and obtain some small employment. For this object he had none of the ordinary means of success, nor influential acquaintances, but he placed great confidence in the friendship of an old comrade in his regiment, who had certainly become a great personage, how or why nobody knew, and whom he had once helped to thrash a card-sharper. Besides this, he was a great believer in his own luck, and, as a matter of fact, his confidence turned out not to have been misplaced. After some days he was appointed inspector of certain government factories. The place was a good one, it stood rather high, and did not call for the exercise of any striking talents even if the factories in question had existed anywhere except upon paper, or if it had been settled what was to be manufactured in them when they did exist. But then they formed part of a new scheme of administrative economy.

Anthony Stephanich was the first to speak.

"Surely, my dear sir, you cannot mean seriously to tell us that you ever met with anything supernatural; I mean, any departure from the laws of nature."

"Yes, I did," said the "dear sir", whose name was Porphyry Capitonovich.

"A departure from the laws of nature," sharply repeated Anthony Stephanich, who had evidently got hold of a favourite phrase.

"Quite so; just as you are kind enough to express it," said the little man.

"This is very extraordinary. What do you think, gentlemen?"

Anthony Stephanich had tried to put on a sarcastic expression, but had failed; or, to be more exact, had given his features an expression such as would have been produced by perceiving a bad smell. He turned to the gentlemen from Kalouga and continued -

"Could you be so kind as to give us some details of such a strange occurrence?"

"Do you want to hear about it?" said the gentleman. "All right."

He got up, went to the middle of the room, and began.

Ivan Turgenev The Dog

"You may possibly know, gentlemen, or more probably you don't, that I possess a small property in the district of Kozelsk. I used to get something from it once upon a time, but, as you may well conceive, it brings me in nothing now, except business and quarrels. However, I don't want to talk politics. Well, on this property I had a small farm with a kitchen-garden to match, a pond with tenth in it, divers buildings, and among others a little house for myself. I am not married. One fine day, six years ago, I came home rather late. I had been dining with one of the neighbours, but I assure you I was all right so far as that went. I took off my clothes, got into bed, and blew out the candle. I had hardly blown it out when I heard something move underneath the bed. I wondered what it could be. At first I thought it was mice. But it wasn't mice. I could hear it scratching and walking about and shaking itself. It was obvious that it was a dog, but I couldn't think what dog it could be. I hadn't got one. So I thought that it must be a stray one. I called the servant and scolded him for being careless, and letting a dog get hidden under the bed. He asked, "What dog?" I answered him, "How should I know?" It was his business to prevent that sort of thing happening. He stooped down with the candle and looked under the bed. He said there was not any dog there. I looked underneath myself, and sure enough there was no dog there. I stared at him, and he began to grin. I called him a fool, and said the dog must have slipped out and got away when he opened the door, that he had been half asleep and hadn't noticed it. I asked if he thought that I had been drinking? However, I did not await the reply which he was about to make, but told him to clear out. When he was gone, I curled myself up, and I heard nothing more that night.

"However, the night afterwards the whole thing began again. I had hardly put the candle out when I heard the beast shake itself. I called the servant again. He looked under the bed. There wasn't anything there. So I sent him away again, and put out the candle the second time. Then I heard the dog again. There couldn't be any doubt about it. I could hear it breathe. I could hear it biting at its own coat and hunting for fleas, so I called the man to come again, without bringing a candle. He came, and I told him to listen. He said he heard. I couldn't see him, but I knew by the sound of his voice that he was frightened. I asked him how he could explain it. He said it was the Evil One. I told him to hold his stupid tongue, but we were both pretty frightened. I lighted the candle, and then there was no more dog and no more noise. I left the candle burning all night, and whether you like to believe it or not, I assure you that the same thing went on every night for six weeks. I got quite used to it, and I used to put out

153

the candle, because light prevents my sleeping, and I did not mind the thing, as it didn't do me any harm."

"You are certainly brave," said Anthony Stephanich, with a smile of mingled pity and contempt. "One can see that you have been a trooper."

"I certainly shouldn't be afraid of you, at any rate," answered Porphyry Capitonovich, with a decided ring of the soldier in his tone. "Anyhow, I'll tell you what happened. The same neighbour with whom I had dined before came to dine with me in turn. He took pot-luck with me, and I won fifteen roubles from him afterwards. He looked out into the night, and said he would have to be going. However, I had a plan, and I asked him to stay and sleep, and try and win his money back the next day. He considered, and then he agreed to stay. I had a bed made up for him in my own room. We went to bed and smoked and talked and discussed women, as men do. At last I saw that Basil Basilich put out his light and turned his back towards me, as much as to say Schlafen Sie wohl. I waited a little, and then I put out my own candle, and before I had time to think the game began. The beast did more than move; he came out from under the bed, and walked across the room. I could hear his feet on the wooden floor. He shook himself, and then there was a thump. He knocked against a chair, which was standing beside Basil Basilich's bed. Basil called out to me quite naturally, in his ordinary voice, to ask me if the dog that I had got was a pointer. I told him that I hadn't got any dog, and never had had. He asked me what the noise was then? I told him to light his candle and see. He asked me again if it wasn't a dog. Then I heard him turn round. He told me I was joking; and I told him I was not.

"After this I heard him scraping away with a match while the dog was scratching itself. Suddenly the match struck, and there was nothing to be seen or heard. Basil Basilich stared at me, and I stared at him. He asked me what all the nonsense was. I told him that if you made Socrates and Frederick the Great put their heads together over it, they couldn't explain it; and I told him all about it. He jumped out of bed like a scalded cat, and wanted to have his carriage called, to go away at once. I wanted to argue with him, but he only made more noise. He told me there must be some curse upon me, and that nothing would make him stay. I got him more or less quiet at last, but he insisted on having a bed in another room, and a light all night.

"When he was having his tea in the morning, he was calmer, and he gave me his advice to go away from home for some days, and then, perhaps, the thing would come to an end.

"He was a decidedly clever man, and I had great respect for his acumen. He got round his mother-in-law quite amazingly. He got her to accept letters of exchange, and she was as tame as a sheep. She made him commissioner for the administration of all her property. Fools don't do that sort of thing with their mothers-in-law. However, he was in a bad temper when he went away for I won a hundred more roubles from him, and he was cross. He told me I was behaving unthankfully towards him. How on earth could the luck be my fault? But I did as he advised, and I started for the town the same day. I knew an old man there who kept an inn, and who was a Dissenter, and it was to his house that I went. He was a little old creature, and a bit snappish, because he had lost his wife and all his children, and he was alone. He couldn't bear the smell of tobacco, and dogs were his particular horror. Rather than see a dog in his rooms he would have left the house. 'Behold,' he would say, 'the all-holy Virgin, who is graciously pleased to hang inside my room, and then how could I allow the unclean brutes to come sniffing in there.' Of course it is want of education. As far as I am concerned, I am content that everybody should use the common sense that God gives him. That's my Gospel."

"You seem to be a philosopher," said Anthony Stephanich, with the same smile as before.

Porphyry Capitonovich made a slight movement of the eyebrows, and also moved his moustache a little. He said:

"As to my being a philosopher, no proof has yet been adduced, but I teach philosophy to other people."

This made everybody look at Anthony Stephanich. We expected some startling reply, or at least a glance of scathing indignation. We were mistaken. The smile of the Ministerial Councillor changed from one of contempt to one of indifference. He yawned; he changed the position of his feet. There was nothing more.

"Well," said Capitonovich, "I took up my quarters in this old man's house; for the sake of his acquaintance with me, he put me in his own room, and made himself up a bed behind a screen. It wasn't a good room, at its best, and it was hot and stuffy beyond all belief. Everything was sticky, and the flies were all over the place. In one corner there was a cupboard full of old holy pictures covered with tarnished plates all bulging out. There was a smell of oil and drugs like a chemist's shop. There were two pillows on the bed, and black beetles ran out if you touched them. For want of something to do I drank more tea than I wanted, and then, beastly as the place was I got into bed. I could hear the old Dissenter on the other side of the screen sighing and groaning and mumbling his prayers. Then he went to sleep. It wasn't long before he began snoring. I listened to him. He began gently, and then it got worse and worse. I became irritated. It was a long time since I put out my own light, but it was not dark, because there was a lamp burning in front of the holy pictures. It was this that put me out. I got out of bed as quietly as I could, walked barefoot to the lamp, and blew it out. Nothing happened. So I thought it was all right, and got back into bed again. But I was hardly in before I heard the old story again. The dog was scratching and shaking himself the whole thing as before. I lay still in bed, listening to see what would happen next. My landlord woke up. I heard him call out, `Sir, what's the matter; have you put out the lamp, sir?' I made no answer, and I heard him get out of bed and say, `What's the matter? What's the matter?—dog—dog—the d—d Niconian.' I called to him not to put himself out, but to come to me, as something very odd was happening. He emerged from behind his screen with the end of an unbleached wax taper in his hand. Such a figure I had never seen—his fierce eyes and hairy figure, with the hair growing even in his ears, were just like a badger. On his head he had a white felt hat; his white beard went down to his girdle, and over his chest he had a waistcoat with brass buttons. His feet were thrust into a pair of old furred slippers, and he diffused around him a pervading odour of gin. In this guise he proceeded to the holy pictures, before which he crossed himself three times with his two forefingers. Then he relighted the lamp, crossed himself again, and having done so, turned round to me, and said in a thick voice

" `Well, what's the matter?'

"I told him the whole story. He did not utter a syllable; he scratched his head. When I had done, he sat down, still silent, on the foot of my bed. Here he proceeded to scratch his stomach and the nape of his neck, and to rub himself. But still he never uttered a word. At last I said to him

" `Well, Theodoulos Ivanovich, I want to know what you think about it. Don't you think it's a temptation of the Evil One?'

"The old man looked at me.

" 'Temptation of the Evil One!' said he. 'You think that, do you? It would be all very well in your own tobacco reek, but how about this house? This house is an holy place. A temptation of the Evil One? If it is not a temptation of the Evil One, what is it?'

"Then he sat silent, thinking and scratching himself. At last he said to me, though not very distinctly, because the hair got into his mouth

" 'Go to Belev. There's only one man that I know of that can help you. He lives at Belev. He is one of our people. If he likes to help you, so much the better for you. If he does not like, you've got nothing more to do.'

"I asked him how I could find the man.

" 'I'll tell you,' said the Nonconformist, 'but, after all, why should it be a temptation of the Evil One? It's a vision; it may become even a revelation, but you're not up to all that. That's beyond you. Well, now, try to get to sleep, with God the Father and His Christ watching over you. I am going to bum some incense. We will think about it tomorrow. You know that second thoughts are almost always best.'

"In the morning, accordingly, we took counsel together, although he had nearly choked me in the night with his incense. The address which he gave me was this. When I got to Belev I was to go into the square and to ask at the second shop on the right hand for a certain Prochorovich, and give him a letter. The letter was a scrap of paper on which was written, 'In the Name of the Father, and of the Son, and of the Holy Ghost. Amen. To Sergius Prochorovich Pervoushine. Trust this man. Theodoulus Ivanovich. Send some cabbages, and praised be God's Holy Name.' I thanked my old Dissenter, and forthwith ordered a carriage, and went to Belev. My argument was, 'This thing in the night has not done me any harm yet, but it's very tiresome, and it's not the thing for a man like me or an officer.' What do you think?"

"And you went to Belev?" said Phinoplentoff.

"Yes, I went there straight. When I got to the square, I asked at the second shop on the right for Prochorovich. They told me he was not there. I asked where he lived, and they told me, in his own house in the suburb on the Oka. I accordingly crossed the Oka, and found the house in question, which might more fitly have been described as a shanty. I found a man in a darned blue shirt, with a torn cap, working among cabbages, with his back to me. I came up to him and said, 'Are you so and so?' He turned round, and I give you my word of honour, I never saw such a pair of eyes. He was old, he had no teeth, his face was as small as one's hand, and he had a beard like a he-goat.

" 'Yes,' he said, 'I am he. What can I do to serve you?'

" 'There,' said I, and gave him the letter.

"He stared hard at me, and then said

" 'Be pleased to come into my room, I am not able to read without glasses.'

"We went into his room. It was a perfect kennel, bare and wretched, and with hardly space enough in which to turn round. On the wall there was a sacred picture, as black as coal, with black heads of Saints with gleaming whites to their eyes. He pulled out the drawer in an old table, took out a pair of spectacles mounted in iron, fixed them upon his nose and read the letter, after which he fixed his eyes on me through the spectacles.

" 'Have you need of me?'

" 'Yes.'

" 'Well, tell me what it is. I am listening.'

"He sat down, took out of his pocket an old checked pocket-handkerchief, full of holes, and spread it upon his knees. Me he never invited to sit down. He fixed upon me a look of power and dignity which might have become a Senator or a Minister of the Government. To my amazement I suddenly found myself seized with an emotion of terror. My heart seemed to sink within my shoes. Then he averted his gaze. This seemed to be enough, and when I had recovered myself a little, I told him my story. He said nothing, but frowned and bit his lips. Then, with an air of majesty and dignity, he slowly asked me my name, my age, who had been my parents, and whether I was married or single. After I told him this, he bit his lips and frowned again; then he held up one finger, and said, 'Cast yourself down before the holy images of the pure and helpful Saints, Sabbatius and Zosimus of the Solovetsky.'

"I threw myself down flat upon my face, and I might almost as well have remained lying there, such was the awe and fear with which this man inspired me. I would have done anything that he told me. Gentlemen, I see that you are laughing at me, but I assure you that I didn't feel anything like laughing. At last he said -

" 'Get up, sir, it is possible to help you. What has been sent to you is not a punishment, but a warning, that means to say that you are in danger, but, fortunately for you, there is some one praying for you. Go to the market-place and buy a young dog, keep it always with you both day and night; your visions will stop, and, moreover, you will find the dog useful.'

"Heaven seemed to open before me. His words filled me with gladness. I bowed profoundly to him, and was turning to go away when it struck me that I ought to give him something. I took out a three-rouble note, but he pushed it away with his hand and said :

" 'Give it to a chapel or to the poor; things like this are not paid for.'

"I bowed before him again, down to his very girdle, and walked off straight to the market-place. As I reached the shops, the first thing I saw was a man in a long grey gabardine, carrying a liver-coloured dog about two months old. I asked the man to stop and tell me the price of his dog. He said, 'Two roubles', and I proposed to give him three. He thought I was mad, but I gave him the bank-note to hold in his teeth while he carried the dog for me to my carriage. The coachman was soon ready, and I was at home the same evening. I kept the dog on my knees the whole time, and when he whined I called him my treasure. I gave him food and water, and had straw brought up to my room and made him a bed there. When I had blown the candle out and found myself in the dark, I wondered what was going to happen, but nothing happened. I began to feel quite bold, and called on the unseen power to begin its usual performance, but there was no response. Then I called in my servant and asked him if he could hear anything, but he could hear nothing either."

"Was that the end of it?" said Anthony Stephanich, but without sneering.

"It was the end of the noises," said Porphyry Capitonovich, "but it was not the end of the whole story. The dog grew, and became a large, strong setter. He showed an extraordinarily strong attachment to me. There is very little sport down in our part of the world, but whenever I took him out with me I always found it good. I used to take him all about with me. Sometimes he started a hare, or a partridge, or a wild duck, but he never went far from me. Wherever I went, he came too. I took him with me even when I went to bathe. A lady of my acquaintance wanted to turn him out of the drawing-room one day. We had a downright battle. I ended by breaking the affected creature's windows for her. Well, one fine day in summer there was the worst drought that I have ever known. There was a sort of haze in the air. Everything was burnt up. It was dark. The sun was like a red ball, and the dust was enough to make one sneeze. The earth gaped with cracks. I got tired of staying in the house, half-undressed, with shutters shut, and as it got a little cooler I made up my mind to go and call on a lady who lived about a verst off. She was a kind-hearted woman, still pretty young, and always smart. She was a little original, but that is rather an advantage in women than otherwise. I got to the steps of her door most frightfully thirsty, but I knew that Nymphodora Semenovna would pick me up with whortleberry-water and other refreshments. I had my hand on the door-handle, when I suddenly heard a tremendous row, and children shrieking, on the other side of a cottage, and in an instant a great red brute, that at first I did not see was a dog, made straight for me with his mouth open, his eyes red, and his hair all up. I had hardly gasped when it flew full at my chest. I almost had a fit. I shall never forget the white teeth and the foaming tongue close to my face. In an instant my own dog flew to my rescue like a flash of lightning, and hung on to the other's neck like a leech. The other one choked, snapped, and fell back. I opened the door, and jumped into the hall. I did not know where I was. I threw myself against a door with all my strength and yelled for help—while the two dogs fought upon the steps. The whole house was roused. Nymphodora ran out with her hair down. There was a lull in the noise, and I heard somebody call out to shut the gate. I peeped through the door. There was nothing on the steps, but men were running about the court seizing logs of wood as if they were mad themselves. I saw an old woman poke her cap out of a dormer window, and heard her call out that the dog had run down through the village, and I went out to look for mine. Presently he came into the court, limping, and hurt, and bloody. I asked what on earth was the matter, for there was a crowd gathered as if there had been a fire. They told me it was one of the Count's dogs that had gone mad, and that it had been about since the day before. This was a Count who was a neighbour of mine, and who had all sorts of strange dogs.

"I was in an awful fright, and I went to a looking-glass to see if I had got hurt. There was nothing, thank God, but I looked as green as grass, and Nymphodora Semenovna was lying on the sofa sobbing like a hen clucking. No wonder, too. It was her nerves, and her kind-heartedness. When she came to a little she said to me in a hollow voice

" `Are you still alive?'

" `Yes,' I said, `I am still alive. My dog saved me.' She said

"`What a noble thing! Did the mad dog kill him?'

Ivan Turgenev   The Dog

" 'No,' said I, 'he is not killed, but he is very much hurt.' "She answered, 'Then he ought to be shot at once.' "I told her I would not. I was going to try to cure him. "Then the dog himself came and scratched at the door, and I at once let him in.

" 'Oh, what are you doing?' she said, 'he will bite us all.'

"I said, 'Forgive me; it does not come out all at once like that.'

"She said, 'How can you? You have gone off your head.'

"I said, 'Nymphodora, do be quiet and talk sense,' but she called out to me to go away with my horrid dog.

"I said I was going to go.

"She said, 'Go away at once, don't stay a moment. Go away; you're a brute. Never you dare to see me again. I daresay you have got hydrophobia, too.'

"I said, 'All right, but just be good enough to let me have the carriage; there might be danger if I walked all the way back.'

"She stared at me. 'You can have the carriage or anything that you want, if only you will go away at once. Just look at its eyes.'

"She bolted out of the room, and hit one of the maids whom she met, and then I heard her taken ill next door. You can take it as what you like, but Nymphodora Semenovna and I were never friends again from that day onwards, and the more I think about it the more I feel that if it was for nothing else, I ought to be thankful for that to my dog to my dying day. I ordered the carriage and took the dog home with me in it. When I got home I examined him and washed his wounds. I thought the best thing I could do would be to take him next day to the wise man of the country. He was an astonishing old man. He mumbles something or other over water. Some people say he puts snakes' slime into it. He gives it you to drink, and it makes you all right at once. I thought that I would get myself bled at the same time. Bleeding is a good thing for fits. Of course you ought not to be bled in the arm, but in the dimple."

"Where is the dimple?" asked Phinoplentoff, timidly.

"Do you not know? It is the place under the hand, at the end of the thumb, where you put the snuff when you want to take a good lot of it. See. That is the right place to be bled, you can see that for yourself. The blood that comes out of the hand is the vein blood. In the other place it is the silly blood. Doctors don't know about those sort of things. The Germans know nothing about it.

Farriers do it a great deal. They are very good at it. They just put their scissors there and give them a tap with the hammer, and the whole thing is done. The night came on while I was thinking about it, and it was time to go to bed. So I went, and of course, I kept the dog with me; but I don't know whether it was the heat or the shock that I had had, or the fleas, or what I was thinking about, but I could not get to sleep. I got restless. I drank water, I opened the window. I got the guitar and played the Moujik of Koumarino with Italian variations. But it would not do. I thought it was the room that I could not stand, so I took a pillow and two sheets and a coverlet and went across the garden, and made myself a bed in the hay under the shed. I was more comfortable there. It was a calm night. Every now and then there was a little breath of air that touched you on the face, like a woman's hand. The fresh hay smelt good, like tea. The crickets sang in the apple trees. Every now and then you'd hear a hen quail clucking, and you felt that she was happy in the dew beside her mate. The sky was quite still. The stars were shining, and there were little light clouds, like flakes of cotton wool, that hardly changed.

"Well," continued Porphyry Capitonovich, "I lay down, but I didn't get to sleep. I kept thinking, and especially about presentiments, and what that man Prochorovich had said to me, when he told me to look out for squalls, and now how such an extraordinary thing had happened. I could not understand it. It was impossible to understand it. All of a sudden the dog jumped up and whined. I thought his wounds were hurting him. Then the moon kept me awake. Do you not believe me? I assure you it did. The moon was straight in front of me, round, and flat, and big, and yellow, and I thought that she was there to tease me. I put out my tongue at her. Did she want to know what I was thinking about? I turned over, but I felt her upon my ear, and upon the back of my neck. It was like rain all over me. I opened my eyes again. The moon showed every little point of grass, every little twig in the hay, every little spider's web, as if it was cut out sharp, and she said, 'There you are, look at it.' There was nothing more to be done. I rested my head upon my hand and looked. I have strong eyes and I could not sleep. The gate of the shed was wide open and I looked through. One could see the country for five versts. It was patchy, clear in some places and dark in others, as is the case in moonlight. I was looking out over it when I thought I saw something moving a long distance off. Then I saw some-thing pass quickly much nearer. Then I saw a dark figure leap. It had come much nearer then. I wondered if it was a hare. I supposed so, and it was coming nearer. Then I saw it was bigger than a hare. It came out of the shadow on to the meadow, which lay quite white in the moonlight, and the thing moved upon it like a great black spot. Evidently it was some kind of wild beast—a fox, perhaps, or a wolf. My heart began to beat. But what was there to be afraid of? There are plenty of beasts that run about at night. My curiosity overcame my fear. I got up and rubbed my eyes, when all of a sudden I turned cold as if ice had been put down my back. The shadowy creature grew larger and darted in at the gate of the yard. I then saw that it was an enormous brute with a great head. It shot past like a bullet, then stopped and began to snuff. It was the mad dog. I could neither move nor cry. It bounded in at the door of the shed with sparkling eyes, howled, and leaped upon me as I lay upon the hay. At that moment my own dog sprang forward wide-awake. The two beasts fought and fell. I don't remember what followed. I only remember that I fell over them somehow in a heap, escaped through the garden, and got to my own bedroom. When I recovered myself a little, I woke up the whole house, and we all armed ourselves and sallied out. I got a sword and a revolver. I had bought the revolver just after the emancipation of the serfs, for reasons which I need not mention, and a bad one it was. I missed two shots out of every three. We went to the shed with burning sticks; we went forward and shouted, but we could not hear anything. At last we went in, and there we found my dog lying dead and the other disappeared.

'I am not ashamed to tell you that I cried like a child.

"I knelt down and kissed the body of the poor beast who had saved my life twice, and I was there still when my old housekeeper Prascovia came and said to me, `What's the matter with you? To get into such a state about a dog. God forgive you. You ought to be ashamed of yourself, and you'll catch cold.' It is true I had hardly anything on. `If the dog has got killed to save your life, it is an honour for him.' I did not agree with Prascovia, but I went back to the house. As to the mad dog, it was shot by a soldier the next day, which must have been providential, as the soldier had never fired off a gun before, although he possessed a medal for having been one of the saviours of the country in 1812. Now, gentlemen, that is why I told you that something supernatural had once happened to me."

With these words, Porphyry Capitonovich was silent and filled his pipe. We all looked at one another without speaking. At last Phinoplentoff said, "No doubt you lead an holy life, and this is a reward"—but here he stopped short, for he saw that Porphyry got red in the face.

"But if you once admit the existence of the supernatural," said Anthony Stephanich, "and that it can enter into the ordinary affairs of every-day life, allow me to ask what scope is left for the exercise of reason?"

Nobody had anything to answer.

A Dead Body

Anton Chekhov

A still August night. A mist is rising slowly from the fields and casting an opaque veil over everything within eyesight. Lighted up by the moon, the mist gives the impression at one moment of a calm, boundless sea, at the next of an immense white wall. The air is damp and chilly. Morning is still far off. A step from the bye-road which runs along the edge of the forest a little fire is gleaming. A dead body, covered from head to foot with new white linen, is lying under a young oak tree. A wooden ikon is lying on its breast. Beside the corpse almost on the road sits the "watch"—two peasants performing one of the most disagreeable and uninviting of peasants' duties. One, a tall young fellow with a scarcely perceptible moustache and thick black eyebrows, in a tattered sheepskin and bark shoes, is sitting on the wet grass, his feet stuck out straight in front of him, and is trying to while away the time with work. He bends his long neck, and breathing loudly through his nose, makes a spoon out of a big crooked bit of wood; the other--a little scraggy, pock-marked peasant with an aged face, a scanty moustache, and a little goat's beard--sits with his hands dangling loose on his knees, and without moving gazes listlessly at the light. A small camp-fire is lazily burning down between them, throwing a red glow on their faces. There is perfect stillness. The only sounds are the scrape of the knife on the wood and the crackling of damp sticks in the fire.

"Don't you go to sleep, Syoma . . ." says the young man.

"I . . . I am not asleep . . ." stammers the goat-beard.

"That's all right. . . . It would be dreadful to sit here alone, one would be frightened. You might tell me something, Syoma."

"You are a queer fellow, Syomushka! Other people will laugh and tell a story and sing a song, but you--there is no making you out. You sit like a scarecrow in the garden and roll your eyes at the fire. You can't say anything properly . . . when you speak you seem frightened. I dare say you are fifty, but you have less sense than a child. Aren't you sorry that you are a simpleton?"

"I am sorry," the goat-beard answers gloomily.

"And we are sorry to see your foolishness, you may be sure. You are a good-natured, sober peasant, and the only trouble is that you have no sense in your head. You should have picked up some sense for yourself if the Lord has afflicted you and given you no understanding. You must make an effort, Syoma. . . . You should listen hard when anything good's being said, note it well, and keep thinking and thinking. . . . If there is any word you don't understand, you should make an effort and think over in your head in what meaning the word is used. Do you see? Make an effort! If you don't gain some sense for yourself you'll be a simpleton and of no account at all to your dying day."

All at once a long drawn-out, moaning sound is heard in the forest.

Something rustles in the leaves as though torn from the very top of the tree and falls to the ground. All this is faintly repeated by the echo. The young man shudders and looks enquiringly at his companion.

"It's an owl at the little birds," says Syoma, gloomily.

"Why, Syoma, it's time for the birds to fly to the warm countries!"

"To be sure, it is time."

"It is chilly at dawn now. It is co-old. The crane is a chilly creature, it is tender. Such cold is death to it. I am not a crane, but I am frozen. . . . Put some more wood on!"

Syoma gets up and disappears in the dark undergrowth. While he is busy among the bushes, breaking dry twigs, his companion puts his hand over his eyes and starts at every sound. Syoma brings an armful of wood and lays it on the fire. The flame irresolutely licks the black twigs with its little tongues, then suddenly, as though at the word of command, catches them and throws a crimson light on the faces, the road, the white linen with its prominences where the hands and feet of the corpse raise it, the ikon. The "watch" is silent. The young man bends his neck still lower and sets to work with still more nervous haste. The goat-beard sits motionless as before and keeps his eyes fixed on the fire. . . .

"Ye that love not Zion . . . shall be put to shame by the Lord." A falsetto voice is suddenly heard singing in the stillness of the night, then slow footsteps are audible, and the dark figure of a man in a short monkish cassock and a broad-brimmed hat, with a wallet on his shoulders, comes into sight on the road in the crimson firelight.

"Thy will be done, O Lord! Holy Mother!" the figure says in a husky falsetto. "I saw the fire in the outer darkness and my soul leapt for joy. . . . At first I thought it was men grazing a drove of horses, then I thought it can't be that, since no horses were to be seen. 'Aren't they thieves,' I wondered, 'aren't they robbers lying in wait for a rich Lazarus? Aren't they the gypsy people offering sacrifices to idols?' And my soul leapt for joy. 'Go, Feodosy, servant of God,' I said to myself, 'and win a martyr's crown!' And I flew to the fire like a light-winged moth. Now I stand before you, and from your outer aspect I judge of your souls: you are not thieves and you are not heathens. Peace be to you!"

"Good-evening."

"Good orthodox people, do you know how to reach the Makuhinsky Brickyards from here?"

"It's close here. You go straight along the road; when you have gone a mile and a half there will be Ananova, our village. From the village, father, you turn to the right by the river-bank, and so you will get to the brickyards. It's two miles from Ananova."

"God give you health. And why are you sitting here?

"We are sitting here watching. You see, there is a dead body. . . ."

"What? what body? Holy Mother!"

The pilgrim sees the white linen with the ikon on it, and starts so violently that his legs give a little skip. This unexpected sight has an overpowering effect upon him. He huddles together and stands as though rooted to the spot, with wide-open mouth and staring eyes. For three minutes he is silent as though he could not believe his eyes, then begins muttering:

"O Lord! Holy Mother! I was going along not meddling with anyone, and all at once such an affliction."

"What may you be?" enquires the young man. "Of the clergy?"

"No . . . no. . . . I go from one monastery to another. . . . Do you know Mi . . . Mihail Polikarpitch, the foreman of the brickyard? Well, I am his nephew. . . . Thy will be done, O Lord! Why are you here?"

"We are watching . . . we are told to."

"Yes, yes . . ." mutters the man in the cassock, passing his hand over his eyes. "And where did the deceased come from?"

"He was a stranger."

"Such is life! But I'll . . . er . . . be getting on, brothers. . . . I feel flustered. I am more afraid of the dead than of anything, my dear souls! And only fancy! while this man was alive he wasn't noticed, while now when he is dead and given over to corruption we tremble before him as before some famous general or a bishop. . . . Such is life; was he murdered, or what?"

"The Lord knows! Maybe he was murdered, or maybe he died of himself."

"Yes, yes. . . . Who knows, brothers? Maybe his soul I now tasting the joys of Paradise."

"His soul is still hovering here, near his body," says the young man. "It does not depart from the body for three days."

"H'm, yes! . . . How chilly the nights are now! It sets one's teeth chattering. . . . So then I am to go straight on and on? . . ."

"Till you get to the village, and then you turn to the right by the river-bank."

"By the river-bank. . . . To be sure. . . . Why am I standing still? I must go on. Farewell, brothers."

The man in the cassock takes five steps along the road and stops.

"I've forgotten to put a kopeck for the burying," he says. "Good orthodox friends, can I give the money?"

"You ought to know best, you go the round of the monasteries. If he died a natural death it would go for the good of his soul; if it's a suicide it's a sin."

"That's true. . . . And maybe it really was a suicide! So I had better keep my money. Oh, sins, sins! Give me a thousand roubles and I would not consent to sit here. . . . Farewell, brothers."

The cassock slowly moves away and stops again.

"I can't make up my mind what I am to do," he mutters. "To stay here by the fire and wait till daybreak. . . . I am frightened; to go on is dreadful, too. The dead man will haunt me all the way in the darkness. . . . The Lord has chastised me indeed! Over three hundred miles I have come on foot and nothing happened, and now I am near home and there's trouble. I can't go on. . . ."

"It is dreadful, that is true."

"I am not afraid of wolves, of thieves, or of darkness, but I am afraid of the dead. I am afraid of them, and that is all about it. Good orthodox brothers, I entreat you on my knees, see me to the village."

"We've been told not to go away from the body."

"No one will see, brothers. Upon my soul, no one will see! The Lord will reward you a hundredfold! Old man, come with me, I beg! Old man! Why are you silent?"

"He is a bit simple," says the young man.

"You come with me, friend; I will give you five kopecks."

"For five kopecks I might," says the young man, scratching his head, "but I was told not to. If Syoma here, our simpleton, will stay alone, I will take you. Syoma, will you stay here alone?"

"I'll stay," the simpleton consents.

"Well, that's all right, then. Come along!" The young man gets up, and goes with the cassock. A minute later the sound of their steps and their talk dies away. Syoma shuts his eyes and gently dozes. The fire begins to grow dim, and a big black shadow falls on the dead body.

The Overcoat
Nikolai Gogol

In the department of -- but it is better not to mention the department. There is nothing more irritable than departments, regiments, courts of justice, and, in a word, every branch of public service. Each individual attached to them nowadays thinks all society insulted in his person. Quite recently a complaint was received from a justice of the peace, in which he plainly demonstrated that all the imperial institutions were going to the dogs, and that the Czar's sacred name was being taken in vain; and in proof he appended to the complaint a romance in which the justice of the peace is made to appear about once every ten lines, and sometimes in a drunken condition. Therefore, in order to avoid all unpleasantness, it will be better to describe the department in question only as a certain department.

So, in a certain department there was a certain official -- not a very high one, it must be allowed -- short of stature, somewhat pock-marked, red-haired, and short-sighted, with a bald forehead, wrinkled cheeks, and a complexion of the kind known as sanguine. The St. Petersburg climate was responsible for this. As for his official status, he was what is called a perpetual titular councillor, over which, as is well known, some writers make merry, and crack their jokes, obeying the praiseworthy custom of attacking those who cannot bite back.

His family name was Bashmatchkin. This name is evidently derived from "bashmak" (shoe); but when, at what time, and in what manner, is not known. His father and grandfather, and all the Bashmatchkins, always wore boots, which only had new heels two or three times a year. His name was Akakiy Akakievitch. It may strike the reader as rather singular and far-fetched, but he may rest assured that it was by no means far-fetched, and that the circumstances were such that it would have been impossible to give him any other.

This is how it came about.

Akakiy Akakievitch was born, if my memory fails me not, in the evening of the 23rd of March. His mother, the wife of a Government official and a very fine woman, made all due arrangements for having the child baptised. She was lying on the bed opposite the door; on her right stood the godfather, Ivan Ivanovitch Eroshkin, a most estimable man, who served as presiding officer of the senate, while the godmother, Anna Semenovna Byelobrushkova, the wife of an officer of the quarter, and a woman of rare virtues. They offered the mother her choice of three names, Mokiya, Sossiya, or that the child should be called after the martyr Khozdazat. "No," said the good woman, "all those names are poor." In order to please her they opened the calendar to another place; three more names appeared, Triphiliy, Dula, and Varakhasiy. "This is a judgment," said the old woman. "What names! I truly never heard the like. Varada or Varukh might have been borne, but not Triphiliy and Varakhasiy!" They turned to another page and found Pavsikakhiy and Vakhtisiy. "Now I see," said the old woman, "that it is plainly fate. And since such is the case, it will be better to name him after his father. His father's name was Akakiy, so let his son's be Akakiy too." In this manner he became Akakiy Akakievitch. They christened the child, whereat he wept and made a grimace, as though he foresaw that he was to be a titular councillor.

In this manner did it all come about. We have mentioned it in order that the reader might see for himself that it was a case of necessity, and that it was utterly impossible to give him any other name. When and how he entered the department, and who appointed him, no one could remember. However much the directors and chiefs of all kinds were changed, he was always to be seen in the same place, the same attitude, the same occupation; so that it was afterwards affirmed that he had been born in undress uniform with a bald head. No respect was shown him in the department. The porter not only did not rise from his seat when he passed, but never even glanced at him, any more than if a fly had flown through the reception-room. His superiors treated him in coolly despotic fashion. Some sub-chief would thrust a paper under his nose without so much as saying, "Copy," or "Here's a nice interesting affair," or anything else agreeable, as is customary amongst well-bred officials. And he took it, looking only at the paper and not observing who handed it to him, or whether he had the right to do so; simply took it, and set about copying it.

The young officials laughed at and made fun of him, so far as their official wit permitted; told in his presence various stories concocted about him, and about his landlady, an old woman of seventy; declared that she beat him; asked when the wedding was to be; and strewed bits of paper over his head, calling them snow. But Akakiy Akakievitch answered not a word, any more than if there had been no one there besides himself. It even had no effect upon his work: amid all these annoyances he never made a single mistake in a letter. But if the joking became wholly unbearable, as when they jogged his hand and prevented his attending to his work, he would exclaim, "Leave me alone! Why do you insult me?" And there was something strange in the words and the voice in which they were uttered. There was in it something which moved to pity; so much that one young man, a new-comer, who, taking pattern by the others, had permitted himself to make sport of Akakiy, suddenly stopped short, as though all about him had undergone a transformation, and presented itself in a different aspect. Some unseen force repelled him from the comrades whose acquaintance he had made, on the supposition that they were well-bred and polite men. Long afterwards, in his gayest moments, there recurred to his mind the little official with the bald forehead, with his heart-rending words, "Leave me alone! Why do you insult me?" In these moving words, other words resounded --"I am thy brother." And the young man covered his face with his hand; and many a time afterwards, in the course of his life, shuddered at seeing how much inhumanity there is in man, how much savage coarseness is concealed beneath delicate, refined worldliness, and even, O God! in that man whom the world acknowledges as honourable and noble.

It would be difficult to find another man who lived so entirely for his duties. It is not enough to say that Akakiy laboured with zeal: no, he laboured with love. In his copying, he found a varied and agreeable employment. Enjoyment was written on his face: some letters were even favourites with him; and when he encountered these, he smiled, winked, and worked with his lips, till it seemed as though each letter might be read in his face, as his pen traced it. If his pay had been in proportion to his zeal, he would, perhaps, to his great surprise, have been made even a councillor of state. But he worked, as his companions, the wits, put it, like a horse in a mill.

Moreover, it is impossible to say that no attention was paid to him. One director being a kindly man, and desirous of rewarding him for his long service, ordered him to be given something more important than mere copying. So he was ordered to make a report of an already concluded affair to another department: the duty consisting simply in changing the heading and altering a few words from the first to the third person. This caused him so much toil that he broke into a perspiration, rubbed his forehead, and finally said, "No, give me rather something to copy." After that they let him copy on forever.

Outside this copying, it appeared that nothing existed for him. He gave no thought to his clothes: his undress uniform was not green, but a sort of rusty- meal colour. The collar was low, so that his neck, in spite of the fact that it was not long, seemed inordinately so as it emerged from it, like the necks of those plaster cats which wag their heads, and are carried about upon the heads of scores of image sellers. And something was always sticking to his uniform, either a bit of hay or some trifle. Moreover, he had a peculiar knack, as he walked along the street, of arriving beneath a window just as all sorts of rubbish were being flung out of it: hence he always bore about on his hat scraps of melon rinds and other such articles. Never once in his life did he give heed to what was going on every day in the street; while it is well known that his young brother officials train the range of their glances till they can see when any one's trouser straps come undone upon the opposite sidewalk, which always brings a malicious smile to their faces. But Akakiy Akakievitch saw in all things the clean, even strokes of his written lines; and only when a horse thrust his nose, from some unknown quarter, over his shoulder, and sent a whole gust of wind down his neck from his nostrils, did he observe that he was not in the middle of a page, but in the middle of the street.

On reaching home, he sat down at once at the table, supped his cabbage soup up quickly, and swallowed a bit of beef with onions, never noticing their taste, and gulping down everything with flies and anything else which the Lord happened to send at the moment. His stomach filled, he rose from the table, and copied papers which he had brought home. If there happened to be none, he took copies for himself, for his own gratification, especially if the document was noteworthy, not on account of its style, but of its being addressed to some distinguished person.

Nikolai Gogol   The Overcoat

Even at the hour when the grey St. Petersburg sky had quite dispersed, and all the official world had eaten or dined, each as he could, in accordance with the salary he received and his own fancy; when all were resting from the departmental jar of pens, running to and fro from their own and other people's indispensable occupations, and from all the work that an uneasy man makes willingly for himself, rather than what is necessary; when officials hasten to dedicate to pleasure the time which is left to them, one bolder than the rest going to the theatre; another, into the street looking under all the bonnets; another wasting his evening in compliments to some pretty girl, the star of a small official circle; another -- and this is the common case of all -- visiting his comrades on the fourth or third floor, in two small rooms with an ante-room or kitchen, and some pretensions to fashion, such as a lamp or some other trifle which has cost many a sacrifice of dinner or pleasure trip; in a word, at the hour when all officials disperse among the contracted quarters of their friends, to play whist, as they sip their tea from glasses with a kopek's worth of sugar, smoke long pipes, relate at times some bits of gossip which a Russian man can never, under any circumstances, refrain from, and, when there is nothing else to talk of, repeat eternal anecdotes about the commandant to whom they had sent word that the tails of the horses on the Falconet Monument had been cut off, when all strive to divert themselves, Akakiy Akakievitch indulged in no kind of diversion. No one could ever say that he had seen him at any kind of evening party. Having written to his heart's content, he lay down to sleep, smiling at the thought of the coming day -- of what God might send him to copy on the morrow.

Thus flowed on the peaceful life of the man, who, with a salary of four hundred rubles, understood how to be content with his lot; and thus it would have continued to flow on, perhaps, to extreme old age, were it not that there are various ills strewn along the path of life for titular councillors as well as for private, actual, court, and every other species of councillor, even for those who never give any advice or take any themselves.

There exists in St. Petersburg a powerful foe of all who receive a salary of four hundred rubles a year, or thereabouts. This foe is no other than the Northern cold, although it is said to be very healthy. At nine o'clock in the morning, at the very hour when the streets are filled with men bound for the various official departments, it begins to bestow such powerful and piercing nips on all noses impartially that the poor officials really do not know what to do with them. At an hour when the foreheads of even those who occupy exalted positions ache with the cold, and tears start to their eyes, the poor titular councillors are sometimes quite unprotected. Their only salvation lies in traversing as quickly as possible, in their thin little cloaks, five or six streets, and then warming their feet in the porter's room, and so thawing all their talents and qualifications for official service, which had become frozen on the way.

Akakiy Akakievitch had felt for some time that his back and shoulders suffered with peculiar poignancy, in spite of the fact that he tried to traverse the distance with all possible speed. He began finally to wonder whether the fault did not lie in his cloak. He examined it thoroughly at home, and discovered that in two places, namely, on the back and shoulders, it had become thin as gauze: the cloth was worn to such a degree that he could see through it, and the lining had fallen into pieces. You must know that Akakiy Akakievitch's cloak served as an object of ridicule to the officials: they even refused it the noble name of cloak, and called it a cape. In fact, it was of singular make: its collar diminishing year by year, but serving to patch its other parts. The patching did not exhibit great skill on the part of the tailor, and was, in fact, baggy and ugly. Seeing how the matter stood, Akakiy Akakievitch decided that it would be necessary to take the cloak to Petrovitch, the tailor, who lived somewhere on the fourth floor up a dark stair-case, and who, in spite of his having but one eye, and pock-marks all over his face, busied himself with considerable success in repairing the trousers and coats of officials and others; that is to say, when he was sober and not nursing some other scheme in his head.

It is not necessary to say much about this tailor; but, as it is the custom to have the character of each personage in a novel clearly defined, there is no help for it, so here is Petrovitch the tailor. At first he was called only Grigoriy, and was some gentleman's serf; he commenced calling himself Petrovitch from the time when he received his free papers, and further began to drink heavily on all holidays, at first on the great ones, and then on all church festivities without discrimination, wherever a cross stood in the calendar. On this point he was faithful to ancestral custom; and when quarrelling with his wife, he called her a low female and a German. As we have mentioned his wife, it will be necessary to say a word or two about her. Unfortunately, little is known of her beyond the fact that Petrovitch has a wife, who wears a cap and a dress; but cannot lay claim to beauty, at least, no one but the soldiers of the guard even looked under her cap when they met her.

Ascending the staircase which led to Petrovitch's room -- which staircase was all soaked with dish-water, and reeked with the smell of spirits which affects the eyes, and is an inevitable adjunct to all dark stairways in St. Petersburg houses -- ascending the stairs, Akakiy Akakievitch pondered how much Petrovitch would ask, and mentally resolved not to give more than two rubles. The door was open; for the mistress, in cooking some fish, had raised such a smoke in the kitchen that not even the beetles were visible. Akakiy Akakievitch passed through the kitchen unperceived, even by the housewife, and at length reached a room where he beheld Petrovitch seated on a large unpainted table, with his legs tucked under him like a Turkish pasha. His feet were bare, after the fashion of tailors who sit at work; and the first thing which caught the eye was his thumb, with a deformed nail thick and strong as a turtle's shell. About Petrovitch's neck hung a skein of silk and thread, and upon his knees lay some old garment. He had been trying unsuccessfully for three minutes to thread his needle, and was enraged at the darkness and even at the thread, growling in a low voice, "It won't go through, the barbarian! you pricked me, you rascal!"

Akakiy Akakievitch was vexed at arriving at the precise moment when Petrovitch was angry; he liked to order something of Petrovitch when the latter was a little downhearted, or, as his wife expressed it, "when he had settled himself with brandy, the one-eyed devil!" Under such circumstances, Petrovitch generally came down in his price very readily, and even bowed and returned thanks. Afterwards, to be sure, his wife would come, complaining that her husband was drunk, and so had fixed the price too low; but, if only a ten-kopek piece were added, then the matter was settled. But now it appeared that Petrovitch was in a sober condition, and therefore rough, taciturn, and inclined to demand, Satan only knows what price. Akakiy Akakievitch felt this, and would gladly have beat a retreat; but he was in for it. Petrovitch screwed up his one eye very intently at him, and Akakiy Akakievitch involuntarily said: "How do you do, Petrovitch?"

"I wish you a good morning, sir," said Petrovitch, squinting at Akakiy Akakievitch's hands, to see what sort of booty he had brought.

"Ah! I -- to you, Petrovitch, this --" It must be known that Akakiy Akakievitch expressed himself chiefly by prepositions, adverbs, and scraps of phrases which had no meaning whatever. If the matter was a very difficult one, he had a habit of never completing his sentences; so that frequently, having begun a phrase with the words, "This, in fact, is quite --" he forgot to go on, thinking that he had already finished it.

"What is it?" asked Petrovitch, and with his one eye scanned Akakievitch's whole uniform from the collar down to the cuffs, the back, the tails and the button- holes, all of which were well known to him, since they were his own handiwork. Such is the habit of tailors; it is the first thing they do on meeting one.

"But I, here, this -- Petrovitch -- a cloak, cloth -- here you see, everywhere, in different places, it is quite strong -- it is a little dusty, and looks old, but it is new, only here in one place it is a little -- on the back, and here on one of the shoulders, it is a little worn, yes, here on this shoulder it is a little -- do you see? that is all. And a little work --"

Petrovitch took the cloak, spread it out, to begin with, on the table, looked hard at it, shook his head, reached out his hand to the window-sill for his snuff-box, adorned with the portrait of some general, though what general is unknown, for the place where the face should have been had been rubbed through by the finger, and a square bit of paper had been pasted over it. Having taken a pinch of snuff, Petrovitch held up the cloak, and inspected it against the light, and again shook his head once more. After which he again lifted the general-adorned lid with its bit of pasted paper, and having stuffed his nose with snuff, closed and put away the snuff-box, and said finally, "No, it is impossible to mend it; it's a wretched garment!"

Akakiy Akakievitch's heart sank at these words.

"Why is it impossible, Petrovitch?" he said, almost in the pleading voice of a child; "all that ails it is, that it is worn on the shoulders. You must have some pieces --"

"Yes, patches could be found, patches are easily found," said Petrovitch, "but there's nothing to sew them to. The thing is completely rotten; if you put a needle to it -- see, it will give way."

"Let it give way, and you can put on another patch at once."

"But there is nothing to put the patches on to; there's no use in strengthening it; it is too far gone. It's lucky that it's cloth; for, if the wind were to blow, it would fly away."

"Well, strengthen it again. How will this, in fact --"

"No," said Petrovitch decisively, "there is nothing to be done with it. It's a thoroughly bad job. You'd better, when the cold winter weather comes on, make yourself some gaiters out of it, because stockings are not warm. The Germans invented them in order to make more money." Petrovitch loved, on all occasions, to have a fling at the Germans. "But it is plain you must have a new cloak."

At the word "new," all grew dark before Akakiy Akakievitch's eyes, and everything in the room began to whirl round. The only thing he saw clearly was the general with the paper face on the lid of Petrovitch's snuff-box. "A new one?" said he, as if still in a dream: "why, I have no money for that."

"Yes, a new one," said Petrovitch, with barbarous composure.

"Well, if it came to a new one, how would it -- ?"

"You mean how much would it cost?"

"Yes."

"Well, you would have to lay out a hundred and fifty or more," said Petrovitch, and pursed up his lips significantly. He liked to produce powerful effects, liked to stun utterly and suddenly, and then to glance sideways to see what face the stunned person would put on the matter.

"A hundred and fifty rubles for a cloak!" shrieked poor Akakiy Akakievitch, perhaps for the first time in his life, for his voice had always been distinguished for softness.

"Yes, sir," said Petrovitch, "for any kind of cloak. If you have a marten fur on the collar, or a silk-lined hood, it will mount up to two hundred."

"Petrovitch, please," said Akakiy Akakievitch in a beseeching tone, not hearing, and not trying to hear, Petrovitch's words, and disregarding all his "effects," "some repairs, in order that it may wear yet a little longer."

"No, it would only be a waste of time and money," said Petrovitch; and Akakiy Akakievitch went away after these words, utterly discouraged. But Petrovitch stood for some time after his departure, with significantly compressed lips, and without betaking himself to his work, satisfied that he would not be dropped, and an artistic tailor employed.

Akakiy Akakievitch went out into the street as if in a dream. "Such an affair!" he said to himself: "I did not think it had come to --" and then after a pause, he added, "Well, so it is! See what it has come to at last! and I never imagined that it was so!" Then followed a long silence, after which he exclaimed, "Well, so it is! See what already -- nothing unexpected that -- it would be nothing -- what a strange circumstance!" So saying, instead of going home, he went in exactly the opposite direction without himself suspecting it. On the way, a chimney-sweep bumped up against him, and blackened his shoulder, and a whole hatful of rubbish landed on him from the top of a house which was building. He did not notice it; and only when he ran against a watchman, who, having planted his halberd beside him, was shaking some snuff from his box into his horny hand, did he recover himself a little, and that because the watchman said, "Why are you poking yourself into a man's very face? Haven't you the pavement?" This caused him to look about him, and turn towards home.

There only, he finally began to collect his thoughts, and to survey his position in its clear and actual light, and to argue with himself, sensibly and frankly, as with a reasonable friend with whom one can discuss private and personal matters. "No," said Akakiy Akakievitch, "it is impossible to reason with Petrovitch now; he is that -- evidently his wife has been beating him. I'd better go to him on Sunday morning; after Saturday night he will be a little cross-eyed and sleepy, for he will want to get drunk, and his wife won't give him any money; and at such a time, a ten-kopek piece in his hand will -- he will become more fit to reason with, and then the cloak, and that --" Thus argued Akakiy Akakievitch with himself, regained his courage, and waited until the first Sunday, when, seeing from afar that Petrovitch's wife had left the house, he went straight to him.

Petrovitch's eye was, indeed, very much askew after Saturday: his head drooped, and he was very sleepy; but for all that, as soon as he knew what it was a question of, it seemed as though Satan jogged his memory. "Impossible," said he: "please to order a new one." Thereupon Akakiy Akakievitch handed over the ten-kopek piece. "Thank you, sir; I will drink your good health," said Petrovitch: "but as for the cloak, don't trouble yourself about it; it is good for nothing. I will make you a capital new one, so let us settle about it now."

Akakiy Akakievitch was still for mending it; but Petrovitch would not hear of it, and said, "I shall certainly have to make you a new one, and you may depend upon it that I shall do my best. It may even be, as the fashion goes, that the collar can be fastened by silver hooks under a flap."

Then Akakiy Akakievitch saw that it was impossible to get along without a new cloak, and his spirit sank utterly. How, in fact, was it to be done? Where was the money to come from? He might, to be sure, depend, in part, upon his present at Christmas; but that money had long been allotted beforehand. He must have some new trousers, and pay a debt of long standing to the shoemaker for putting new tops to his old boots, and he must order three shirts from the seamstress, and a couple of pieces of linen. In short, all his money must be spent; and even if the director should be so kind as to order him to receive forty-five rubles instead of forty, or even fifty, it would be a mere nothing, a mere drop in the ocean towards the funds necessary for a cloak: although he knew that Petrovitch was often wrong-headed enough to blurt out some outrageous price, so that even his own wife could not refrain from exclaiming, "Have you lost your senses, you fool?" At one time he would not work at any price, and now it was quite likely that he had named a higher sum than the cloak would cost.

But although he knew that Petrovitch would undertake to make a cloak for eighty rubles, still, where was he to get the eighty rubles from? He might possibly manage half, yes, half might be procured, but where was the other half to come from? But the reader must first be told where the first half came from. Akakiy Akakievitch had a habit of putting, for every ruble he spent, a groschen into a small box, fastened with a lock and key, and with a slit in the top for the reception of money. At the end of every half-year he counted over the heap of coppers, and changed it for silver. This he had done for a long time, and in the course of years, the sum had mounted up to over forty rubles. Thus he had one half on hand; but where was he to find the other half? Where was he to get another forty rubles from? Akakiy Akakievitch thought and thought, and decided that it would be necessary to curtail his ordinary expenses, for the space of one year at least, to dispense with tea in the evening; to burn no candles, and, if there was anything which he must do, to go into his landlady's room, and work by her light. When he went into the street, he must walk as lightly as he could, and as cautiously, upon the stones, almost upon tiptoe, in order not to wear his heels down in too short a time; he must give the laundress as little to wash as possible; and, in order not to wear out his clothes, he must take them off, as soon as he got home, and wear only his cotton dressing-gown, which had been long and carefully saved.

To tell the truth, it was a little hard for him at first to accustom himself to these deprivations; but he got used to them at length, after a fashion, and all went smoothly. He even got used to being hungry in the evening, but he made up for it by treating himself, so to say, in spirit, by bearing ever in mind the idea of his future cloak. From that time forth his existence seemed to become, in some way, fuller, as if he were married, or as if some other man lived in him, as if, in fact, he were not alone, and some pleasant friend had consented to travel along life's path with him, the friend being no other than the cloak, with thick wadding and a strong lining incapable of wearing out. He became more lively, and even his character grew firmer, like that of a man who has made up his mind, and set himself a goal. From his face and gait, doubt and indecision, all hesitating and wavering traits disappeared of themselves. Fire gleamed in his eyes, and occasionally the boldest and most daring ideas flitted through his mind; why not, for instance, have marten fur on the collar? The thought of this almost made him absent-minded. Once, in copying a letter, he nearly made a mistake, so that he exclaimed almost aloud, "Ugh!" and crossed himself. Once, in the course of every month, he had a conference with Petrovitch on the subject of the cloak, where it would be better to buy the cloth, and the colour, and the price. He always returned home satisfied, though troubled, reflecting that the time would come at last when it could all be bought, and then the cloak made.

The affair progressed more briskly than he had expected. Far beyond all his hopes, the director awarded neither forty nor forty-five rubles for Akakiy Akakievitch's share, but sixty. Whether he suspected that Akakiy Akakievitch needed a cloak, or whether it was merely chance, at all events, twenty extra rubles were by this means provided. This circumstance hastened matters. Two or three months more of hunger and Akakiy Akakievitch had accumulated about eighty rubles. His heart, generally so quiet, began to throb. On the first possible day, he went shopping in company with Petrovitch. They bought some very good cloth, and at a reasonable rate too, for they had been considering the matter for six months, and rarely let a month pass without their visiting the shops to inquire prices. Petrovitch himself said that no better cloth could be had. For lining, they selected a cotton stuff, but so firm and thick that Petrovitch declared it to be better than silk, and even prettier and more glossy. They did not buy the marten fur, because it was, in fact, dear, but in its stead, they picked out the very best of cat-skin which could be found in the shop, and which might, indeed, be taken for marten at a distance.

Petrovitch worked at the cloak two whole weeks, for there was a great deal of quilting: otherwise it would have been finished sooner. He charged twelve rubles for the job, it could not possibly have been done for less. It was all sewed with silk, in small, double seams; and Petrovitch went over each seam afterwards with his own teeth, stamping in various patterns.

It was -- it is difficult to say precisely on what day, but probably the most glorious one in Akakiy Akakievitch's life, when Petrovitch at length brought home the cloak. He brought it in the morning, before the hour when it was necessary to start for the department. Never did a cloak arrive so exactly in the nick of time; for the severe cold had set in, and it seemed to threaten to increase. Petrovitch brought the cloak himself as befits a good tailor. On his countenance was a significant expression, such as Akakiy Akakievitch had never beheld there. He seemed fully sensible that he had done no small deed, and crossed a gulf separating tailors who only put in linings, and execute repairs, from those who make new things. He took the cloak out of the pocket handkerchief in which he had brought it. The handkerchief was fresh from the laundress, and he put it in his pocket for use. Taking out the cloak, he gazed proudly at it, held it up with both hands, and flung it skilfully over the shoulders of Akakiy Akakievitch. Then he pulled it and fitted it down behind with his hand, and he draped it around Akakiy Akakievitch without buttoning it. Akakiy Akakievitch, like an experienced man, wished to try the sleeves. Petrovitch helped him on with them, and it turned out that the sleeves were satisfactory also. In short, the cloak appeared to be perfect, and most seasonable. Petrovitch did not neglect to observe that it was only because he lived in a narrow street, and had no signboard, and had known Akakiy Akakievitch so long, that he had made it so cheaply; but that if he had been in business on the Nevsky Prospect, he would have charged seventy-five rubles for the making alone. Akakiy Akakievitch did not care to argue this point with Petrovitch. He paid him, thanked him, and set out at once in his new cloak for the department. Petrovitch followed him, and, pausing in the street, gazed long at the cloak in the distance, after which he went to one side expressly to run through a crooked alley, and emerge again into the street beyond to gaze once more upon the cloak from another point, namely, directly in front.

Meantime Akakiy Akakievitch went on in holiday mood. He was conscious every second of the time that he had a new cloak on his shoulders; and several times he laughed with internal satisfaction. In fact, there were two advantages, one was its warmth, the other its beauty. He saw nothing of the road, but suddenly found himself at the department. He took off his cloak in the ante-room, looked it over carefully, and confided it to the especial care of the attendant. It is impossible to say precisely how it was that every one in the department knew at once that Akakiy Akakievitch had a new cloak, and that the "cape" no longer existed. All rushed at the same moment into the ante-room to inspect it. They congratulated him and said pleasant things to him, so that he began at first to smile and then to grow ashamed. When all surrounded him, and said that the new cloak must be "christened," and that he must give a whole evening at least to this, Akakiy Akakievitch lost his head completely, and did not know where he stood, what to answer, or how to get out of it. He stood blushing all over for several minutes, and was on the point of assuring them with great simplicity that it was not a new cloak, that it was so and so, that it was in fact the old "cape."

At length one of the officials, a sub-chief probably, in order to show that he was not at all proud, and on good terms with his inferiors, said, "So be it, only I will give the party instead of Akakiy Akakievitch; I invite you all to tea with me to-night; it happens quite a propos, as it is my name-day." The officials naturally at once offered the sub-chief their congratulations and accepted the invitations with pleasure. Akakiy Akakievitch would have declined, but all declared that it was discourteous, that it was simply a sin and a shame, and that he could not possibly refuse. Besides, the notion became pleasant to him when he recollected that he should thereby have a chance of wearing his new cloak in the evening also.

That whole day was truly a most triumphant festival day for Akakiy Akakievitch. He returned home in the most happy frame of mind, took off his cloak, and hung it carefully on the wall, admiring afresh the cloth and the lining. Then he brought out his old, worn-out cloak, for comparison. He looked at it and laughed, so vast was the difference. And long after dinner he laughed again when the condition of the "cape" recurred to his mind. He dined cheerfully, and after dinner wrote nothing, but took his ease for a while on the bed, until it got dark. Then he dressed himself leisurely, put on his cloak, and stepped out into the street. Where the host lived, unfortunately we cannot say: our memory begins to fail us badly; and the houses and streets in St. Petersburg have become so mixed up in our head that it is very difficult to get anything out of it again in proper form. This much is certain, that the official lived in the best part of the city; and therefore it must have been anything but near to Akakiy Akakievitch's residence. Akakiy Akakievitch was first obliged to traverse a kind of wilderness of deserted, dimly-lighted streets; but in proportion as he approached the official's quarter of the city, the streets became more lively, more populous, and more brilliantly illuminated.

Pedestrians began to appear; handsomely dressed ladies were more frequently encountered; the men had otter skin collars to their coats; peasant waggoners, with their grate-like sledges stuck over with brass-headed nails, became rarer; whilst on the other hand, more and more drivers in red velvet caps, lacquered sledges and bear-skin coats began to appear, and carriages with rich hammer-cloths flew swiftly through the streets, their wheels scrunching the snow. Akakiy Akakievitch gazed upon all this as upon a novel sight. He had not been in the streets during the evening for years. He halted out of curiosity before a shop-window to look at a picture representing a handsome woman, who had thrown off her shoe, thereby baring her whole foot in a very pretty way; whilst behind her the head of a man with whiskers and a handsome moustache peeped through the doorway of another room. Akakiy Akakievitch shook his head and laughed, and then went on his way. Why did he laugh? Either because he had met with a thing utterly unknown, but for which every one cherishes, nevertheless, some sort of feeling; or else he thought, like many officials, as follows: "Well, those French! What is to be said? If they do go in anything of that sort, why --" But possibly he did not think at all.

Akakiy Akakievitch at length reached the house in which the sub-chief lodged. The sub-chief lived in fine style: the staircase was lit by a lamp; his apartment being on the second floor. On entering the vestibule, Akakiy Akakievitch beheld a whole row of goloshes on the floor. Among them, in the centre of the room, stood a samovar or tea-urn, humming and emitting clouds of steam. On the walls hung all sorts of coats and cloaks, among which there were even some with beaver collars or velvet facings. Beyond, the buzz of conversation was audible, and became clear and loud when the servant came out with a trayful of empty glasses, cream-jugs, and sugar-bowls. It was evident that the officials had arrived long before, and had already finished their first glass of tea.

Akakiy Akakievitch, having hung up his own cloak, entered the inner room. Before him all at once appeared lights, officials, pipes, and card-tables; and he was bewildered by the sound of rapid conversation rising from all the tables, and the noise of moving chairs. He halted very awkwardly in the middle of the room, wondering what he ought to do. But they had seen him. They received him with a shout, and all thronged at once into the ante-room, and there took another look at his cloak. Akakiy Akakievitch, although somewhat confused, was frank-hearted, and could not refrain from rejoicing when he saw how they praised his cloak. Then, of course, they all dropped him and his cloak, and returned, as was proper, to the tables set out for whist.

All this, the noise, the talk, and the throng of people was rather overwhelming to Akakiy Akakievitch. He simply did not know where he stood, or where to put his hands, his feet, and his whole body. Finally he sat down by the players, looked at the cards, gazed at the face of one and another, and after a while began to gape, and to feel that it was wearisome, the more so as the hour was already long past when he usually went to bed. He wanted to take leave of the host; but they would not let him go, saying that he must not fail to drink a glass of champagne in honour of his new garment. In the course of an hour, supper, consisting of vegetable salad, cold veal, pastry, confectioner's pies, and champagne, was served. They made Akakiy Akakievitch drink two glasses of champagne, after which he felt things grow livelier.

Still, he could not forget that it was twelve o'clock, and that he should have been at home long ago. In order that the host might not think of some excuse for detaining him, he stole out of the room quickly, sought out, in the ante-room, his cloak, which, to his sorrow, he found lying on the floor, brushed it, picked off every speck upon it, put it on his shoulders, and descended the stairs to the street.

In the street all was still bright. Some petty shops, those permanent clubs of servants and all sorts of folk, were open. Others were shut, but, nevertheless, showed a streak of light the whole length of the door-crack, indicating that they were not yet free of company, and that probably some domestics, male and female, were finishing their stories and conversations whilst leaving their masters in complete ignorance as to their whereabouts. Akakiy Akakievitch went on in a happy frame of mind: he even started to run, without knowing why, after some lady, who flew past like a flash of lightning. But he stopped short, and went on very quietly as before, wondering why he had quickened his pace. Soon there spread before him those deserted streets, which are not cheerful in the daytime, to say nothing of the evening. Now they were even more dim and lonely: the lanterns began to grow rarer, oil, evidently, had been less liberally supplied. Then came wooden houses and fences: not a soul anywhere; only the snow sparkled in the streets, and mournfully veiled the low-roofed cabins with their closed shutters. He approached the spot where the street crossed a vast square with houses barely visible on its farther side, a square which seemed a fearful desert.

Afar, a tiny spark glimmered from some watchman's box, which seemed to stand on the edge of the world. Akakiy Akakievitch's cheerfulness diminished at this point in a marked degree. He entered the square, not without an involuntary sensation of fear, as though his heart warned him of some evil. He glanced back and on both sides, it was like a sea about him. "No, it is better not to look," he thought, and went on, closing his eyes. When he opened them, to see whether he was near the end of the square, he suddenly beheld, standing just before his very nose, some bearded individuals of precisely what sort he could not make out. All grew dark before his eyes, and his heart throbbed.

"But, of course, the cloak is mine!" said one of them in a loud voice, seizing hold of his collar. Akakiy Akakievitch was about to shout "watch," when the second man thrust a fist, about the size of a man's head, into his mouth, muttering, "Now scream!"

Akakiy Akakievitch felt them strip off his cloak and give him a push with a knee: he fell headlong upon the snow, and felt no more. In a few minutes he recovered consciousness and rose to his feet; but no one was there. He felt that it was cold in the square, and that his cloak was gone; he began to shout, but his voice did not appear to reach to the outskirts of the square. In despair, but without ceasing to shout, he started at a run across the square, straight towards the watchbox, beside which stood the watchman, leaning on his halberd, and apparently curious to know what kind of a customer was running towards him and shouting. Akakiy Akakievitch ran up to him, and began in a sobbing voice to shout that he was asleep, and attended to nothing, and did not see when a man was robbed. The watchman replied that he had seen two men stop him in the middle of the square, but supposed that they were friends of his; and that, instead of scolding vainly, he had better go to the police on the morrow, so that they might make a search for whoever had stolen the cloak.

Akakiy Akakievitch ran home in complete disorder; his hair, which grew very thinly upon his temples and the back of his head, wholly disordered; his body, arms, and legs covered with snow. The old woman, who was mistress of his lodgings, on hearing a terrible knocking, sprang hastily from her bed, and, with only one shoe on, ran to open the door, pressing the sleeve of her chemise to her bosom out of modesty; but when she had opened it, she fell back on beholding Akakiy Akakievitch in such a state. When he told her about the affair, she clasped her hands, and said that he must go straight to the district chief of police, for his subordinate would turn up his nose, promise well, and drop the matter there. The very best thing to do, therefore, would be to go to the district chief, whom she knew, because Finnish Anna, her former cook, was now nurse at his house. She often saw him passing the house; and he was at church every Sunday, praying, but at the same time gazing cheerfully at everybody; so that he must be a good man, judging from all appearances. Having listened to this opinion, Akakiy Akakievitch betook himself sadly to his room; and how he spent the night there any one who can put himself in another's place may readily imagine.

Early in the morning, he presented himself at the district chief's; but was told that this official was asleep. He went again at ten and was again informed that he was asleep; at eleven, and they said: "The superintendent is not at home;" at dinner time, and the clerks in the ante-room would not admit him on any terms, and insisted upon knowing his business. So that at last, for once in his life, Akakiy Akakievitch felt an inclination to show some spirit, and said curtly that he must see the chief in person; that they ought not to presume to refuse him entrance; that he came from the department of justice, and that when he complained of them, they would see.

The clerks dared make no reply to this, and one of them went to call the chief, who listened to the strange story of the theft of the coat. Instead of directing his attention to the principal points of the matter, he began to question Akakiy Akakievitch: Why was he going home so late? Was he in the habit of doing so, or had he been to some disorderly house? So that Akakiy Akakievitch got thoroughly confused, and left him without knowing whether the affair of his cloak was in proper train or not.

All that day, for the first time in his life, he never went near the department. The next day he made his appearance, very pale, and in his old cape, which had become even more shabby. The news of the robbery of the cloak touched many; although there were some officials present who never lost an opportunity, even such a one as the present, of ridiculing Akakiy Akakievitch. They decided to make a collection for him on the spot, but the officials had already spent a great deal in subscribing for the director's portrait, and for some book, at the suggestion of the head of that division, who was a friend of the author; and so the sum was trifling.

One of them, moved by pity, resolved to help Akakiy Akakievitch with some good advice at least, and told him that he ought not to go to the police, for although it might happen that a police-officer, wishing to win the approval of his superiors, might hunt up the cloak by some means, still his cloak would remain in the possession of the police if he did not offer legal proof that it belonged to him. The best thing for him, therefore, would be to apply to a certain prominent personage; since this prominent personage, by entering into relations with the proper persons, could greatly expedite the matter.

As there was nothing else to be done, Akakiy Akakievitch decided to go to the prominent personage. What was the exact official position of the prominent personage remains unknown to this day. The reader must know that the prominent personage had but recently become a prominent personage, having up to that time been only an insignificant person. Moreover, his present position was not considered prominent in comparison with others still more so. But there is always a circle of people to whom what is insignificant in the eyes of others, is important enough. Moreover, he strove to increase his importance by sundry devices; for instance, he managed to have the inferior officials meet him on the staircase when he entered upon his service; no one was to presume to come directly to him, but the strictest etiquette must be observed; the collegiate recorder must make a report to the government secretary, the government secretary to the titular councillor, or whatever other man was proper, and all business must come before him in this manner. In Holy Russia all is thus contaminated with the love of imitation; every man imitates and copies his superior. They even say that a certain titular councillor, when promoted to the head of some small separate room, immediately partitioned off a private room for himself, called it the audience chamber, and posted at the door a lackey with red collar and braid, who grasped the handle of the door and opened to all comers; though the audience chamber could hardly hold an ordinary writing-table.

The manners and customs of the prominent personage were grand and imposing, but rather exaggerated. The main foundation of his system was strictness. "Strictness, strictness, and always strictness!" he generally said; and at the last word he looked significantly into the face of the person to whom he spoke. But there was no necessity for this, for the half-score of subordinates who formed the entire force of the office were properly afraid; on catching sight of him afar off they left their work and waited, drawn up in line, until he had passed through the room. His ordinary converse with his inferiors smacked of sternness, and consisted chiefly of three phrases: "How dare you?" "Do you know whom you are speaking to?" "Do you realize who stands before you?"

Otherwise he was a very kind-hearted man, good to his comrades, and ready to oblige; but the rank of general threw him completely off his balance. On receiving any one of that rank, he became confused, lost his way, as it were, and never knew what to do. If he chanced to be amongst his equals he was still a very nice kind of man, a very good fellow in many respects, and not stupid; but the very moment that he found himself in the society of people but one rank lower than himself he became silent; and his situation aroused sympathy, the more so as he felt himself that he might have been making an incomparably better use of his time. In his eyes there was sometimes visible a desire to join some interesting conversation or group; but he was kept back by the thought, "Would it not be a very great condescension on his part? Would it not be familiar? and would he not thereby lose his importance?" And in consequence of such reflections he always remained in the same dumb state, uttering from time to time a few monosyllabic sounds, and thereby earning the name of the most wearisome of men.

To this prominent personage Akakiy Akakievitch presented himself, and this at the most unfavourable time for himself though opportune for the prominent personage. The prominent personage was in his cabinet conversing gaily with an old acquaintance and companion of his childhood whom he had not seen for several years and who had just arrived when it was announced to him that a person named Bashmatchkin had come. He asked abruptly, "Who is he?" --"Some official," he was informed. "Ah, he can wait! this is no time for him to call," said the important man.

It must be remarked here that the important man lied outrageously: he had said all he had to say to his friend long before; and the conversation had been interspersed for some time with very long pauses, during which they merely slapped each other on the leg, and said, "You think so, Ivan Abramovitch!" "Just so, Stepan Varlamitch!" Nevertheless, he ordered that the official should be kept waiting, in order to show his friend, a man who had not been in the service for a long time, but had lived at home in the country, how long officials had to wait in his anteroom.

At length, having talked himself completely out, and more than that, having had his fill of pauses, and smoked a cigar in a very comfortable arm-chair with reclining back, he suddenly seemed to recollect, and said to the secretary, who stood by the door with papers of reports, "So it seems that there is a tchinovnik waiting to see me. Tell him that he may come in." On perceiving Akakiy Akakievitch's modest mien and his worn undress uniform, he turned abruptly to him and said, "What do you want?" in a curt hard voice, which he had practised in his room in private, and before the looking-glass, for a whole week before being raised to his present rank.

Akakiy Akakievitch, who was already imbued with a due amount of fear, became somewhat confused: and as well as his tongue would permit, explained, with a rather more frequent addition than usual of the word "that," that his cloak was quite new, and had been stolen in the most inhuman manner; that he had applied to him in order that he might, in some way, by his intermediation -- that he might enter into correspondence with the chief of police, and find the cloak.

For some inexplicable reason this conduct seemed familiar to the prominent personage. "What, my dear sir!" he said abruptly, "are you not acquainted with etiquette? Where have you come from? Don't you know how such matters are managed? You should first have entered a complaint about this at the court below: it would have gone to the head of the department, then to the chief of the division, then it would have been handed over to the secretary, and the secretary would have given it to me."

"But, your excellency," said Akakiy Akakievitch, trying to collect his small handful of wits, and conscious at the same time that he was perspiring terribly, "I, your excellency, presumed to trouble you because secretaries -- are an untrustworthy race."

"What, what, what!" said the important personage. "Where did you get such courage? Where did you get such ideas? What impudence towards their chiefs and superiors has spread among the young generation!" The prominent personage apparently had not observed that Akakiy Akakievitch was already in the neighbourhood of fifty. If he could be called a young man, it must have been in comparison with some one who was twenty. "Do you know to whom you speak? Do you realise who stands before you? Do you realise it? do you realise it? I ask you!" Then he stamped his foot and raised his voice to such a pitch that it would have frightened even a different man from Akakiy Akakievitch.

Akakiy Akakievitch's senses failed him; he staggered, trembled in every limb, and, if the porters had not run to support him, would have fallen to the floor. They carried him out insensible. But the prominent personage, gratified that the effect should have surpassed his expectations, and quite intoxicated with the thought that his word could even deprive a man of his senses, glanced sideways at his friend in order to see how he looked upon this, and perceived, not without satisfaction, that his friend was in a most uneasy frame of mind, and even beginning, on his part, to feel a trifle frightened.

Akakiy Akakievitch could not remember how he descended the stairs and got into the street. He felt neither his hands nor feet. Never in his life had he been so rated by any high official, let alone a strange one. He went staggering on through the snow-storm, which was blowing in the streets, with his mouth wide open; the wind, in St. Petersburg fashion, darted upon him from all quarters, and down every cross-street. In a twinkling it had blown a quinsy into his throat, and he reached home unable to utter a word. His throat was swollen, and he lay down on his bed. So powerful is sometimes a good scolding!

The next day a violent fever showed itself. Thanks to the generous assistance of the St. Petersburg climate, the malady progressed more rapidly than could have been expected: and when the doctor arrived, he found, on feeling the sick man's pulse, that there was nothing to be done, except to prescribe a fomentation, so that the patient might not be left entirely without the beneficent aid of medicine; but at the same time, he predicted his end in thirty-six hours. After this he turned to the landlady, and said, "And as for you, don't waste your time on him: order his pine coffin now, for an oak one will be too expensive for him." Did Akakiy Akakievitch hear these fatal words? and if he heard them, did they produce any overwhelming effect upon him? Did he lament the bitterness of his life? -- We know not, for he continued in a delirious condition. Visions incessantly appeared to him, each stranger than the other. Now he saw Petrovitch, and ordered him to make a cloak, with some traps for robbers, who seemed to him to be always under the bed; and cried every moment to the landlady to pull one of them from under his coverlet. Then he inquired why his old mantle hung before him when he had a new cloak. Next he fancied that he was standing before the prominent person, listening to a thorough setting-down, and saying, "Forgive me, your excellency!" but at last he began to curse, uttering the most horrible words, so that his aged landlady crossed herself, never in her life having heard anything of the kind from him, the more so as those words followed directly after the words "your excellency." Later on he talked utter nonsense, of which nothing could be made: all that was evident being, that his incoherent words and thoughts hovered ever about one thing, his cloak.

At length poor Akakiy Akakievitch breathed his last. They sealed up neither his room nor his effects, because, in the first place, there were no heirs, and, in the second, there was very little to inherit beyond a bundle of goose-quills, a quire of white official paper, three pairs of socks, two or three buttons which had burst off his trousers, and the mantle already known to the reader. To whom all this fell, God knows. I confess that the person who told me this tale took no interest in the matter. They carried Akakiy Akakievitch out and buried him.

And St. Petersburg was left without Akakiy Akakievitch, as though he had never lived there. A being disappeared who was protected by none, dear to none, interesting to none, and who never even attracted to himself the attention of those students of human nature who omit no opportunity of thrusting a pin through a common fly, and examining it under the microscope. A being who bore meekly the jibes of the department, and went to his grave without having done one unusual deed, but to whom, nevertheless, at the close of his life appeared a bright visitant in the form of a cloak, which momentarily cheered his poor life, and upon whom, thereafter, an intolerable misfortune descended, just as it descends upon the mighty of this world!

Several days after his death, the porter was sent from the department to his lodgings, with an order for him to present himself there immediately; the chief commanding it. But the porter had to return unsuccessful, with the answer that he could not come; and to the question, "Why?" replied, "Well, because he is dead! he was buried four days ago." In this manner did they hear of Akakiy Akakievitch's death at the department, and the next day a new official sat in his place, with a handwriting by no means so upright, but more inclined and slanting.

But who could have imagined that this was not really the end of Akakiy Akakievitch, that he was destined to raise a commotion after death, as if in compensation for his utterly insignificant life? But so it happened, and our poor story unexpectedly gains a fantastic ending.

A rumour suddenly spread through St. Petersburg that a dead man had taken to appearing on the Kalinkin Bridge and its vicinity at night in the form of a tchinovnik seeking a stolen cloak, and that, under the pretext of its being the stolen cloak, he dragged, without regard to rank or calling, every one's cloak from his shoulders, be it cat-skin, beaver, fox, bear, sable; in a word, every sort of fur and skin which men adopted for their covering. One of the department officials saw the dead man with his own eyes and immediately recognised in him Akakiy Akakievitch. This, however, inspired him with such terror that he ran off with all his might, and therefore did not scan the dead man closely, but only saw how the latter threatened him from afar with his finger. Constant complaints poured in from all quarters that the backs and shoulders, not only of titular but even of court councillors, were exposed to the danger of a cold on account of the frequent dragging off of their cloaks.

Arrangements were made by the police to catch the corpse, alive or dead, at any cost, and punish him as an example to others in the most severe manner. In this they nearly succeeded; for a watchman, on guard in Kirushkin Alley, caught the corpse by the collar on the very scene of his evil deeds, when attempting to pull off the frieze coat of a retired musician. Having seized him by the collar, he summoned, with a shout, two of his comrades, whom he enjoined to hold him fast while he himself felt for a moment in his boot, in order to draw out his snuff-box and refresh his frozen nose. But the snuff was of a sort which even a corpse could not endure. The watchman having closed his right nostril with his finger, had no sooner succeeded in holding half a handful up to the left than the corpse sneezed so violently that he completely filled the eyes of all three. While they raised their hands to wipe them, the dead man vanished completely, so that they positively did not know whether they had actually had him in their grip at all. Thereafter the watchmen conceived such a terror of dead men that they were afraid even to seize the living, and only screamed from a distance, "Hey, there! Go your way!" So the dead tchinovnik began to appear even beyond the Kalinkin Bridge, causing no little terror to all timid people.

But we have totally neglected that certain prominent personage who may really be considered as the cause of the fantastic turn taken by this true history. First of all, justice compels us to say that after the departure of poor, annihilated Akakiy Akakievitch he felt something like remorse. Suffering was unpleasant to him, for his heart was accessible to many good impulses, in spite of the fact that his rank often prevented his showing his true self. As soon as his friend had left his cabinet, he began to think about poor Akakiy Akakievitch. And from that day forth, poor Akakiy Akakievitch, who could not bear up under an official reprimand, recurred to his mind almost every day. The thought troubled him to such an extent that a week later he even resolved to send an official to him, to learn whether he really could assist him; and when it was reported to him that Akakiy Akakievitch had died suddenly of fever, he was startled, hearkened to the reproaches of his conscience, and was out of sorts for the whole day.

Wishing to divert his mind in some way, and drive away the disagreeable impression, he set out that evening for one of his friends' houses, where he found quite a large party assembled. What was better, nearly every one was of the same rank as himself, so that he need not feel in the least constrained. This had a marvellous effect upon his mental state. He grew expansive, made himself agreeable in conversation, in short, he passed a delightful evening. After supper he drank a couple of glasses of champagne -- not a bad recipe for cheerfulness, as every one knows. The champagne inclined him to various adventures; and he determined not to return home, but to go and see a certain well-known lady of German extraction, Karolina Ivanovna, a lady, it appears, with whom he was on a very friendly footing.

It must be mentioned that the prominent personage was no longer a young man, but a good husband and respected father of a family. Two sons, one of whom was already in the service, and a good-looking, sixteen-year-old daughter, with a rather retrousse but pretty little nose, came every morning to kiss his hand and say, "Bonjour, papa." His wife, a still fresh and good-looking woman, first gave him her hand to kiss, and then, reversing the procedure, kissed his. But the prominent personage, though perfectly satisfied in his domestic relations, considered it stylish to have a friend in another quarter of the city. This friend was scarcely prettier or younger than his wife; but there are such puzzles in the world, and it is not our place to judge them. So the important personage descended the stairs, stepped into his sledge, said to the coachman, "To Karolina Ivanovna's," and, wrapping himself luxuriously in his warm cloak, found himself in that delightful frame of mind than which a Russian can conceive no better, namely, when you think of nothing yourself, yet when the thoughts creep into your mind of their own accord, each more agreeable than the other, giving you no trouble either to drive them away or seek them. Fully satisfied, he recalled all the gay features of the evening just passed, and all the mots which had made the little circle laugh. Many of them he repeated in a low voice, and found them quite as funny as before; so it is not surprising that he should laugh heartily at them. Occasionally, however, he was interrupted by gusts of wind, which, coming suddenly, God knows whence or why, cut his face, drove masses of snow into it, filled out his cloak-collar like a sail, or suddenly blew it over his head with supernatural force, and thus caused him constant trouble to disentangle himself.

Suddenly the important personage felt some one clutch him firmly by the collar. Turning round, he perceived a man of short stature, in an old, worn uniform, and recognised, not without terror, Akakiy Akakievitch. The official's face was white as snow, and looked just like a corpse's. But the horror of the important personage transcended all bounds when he saw the dead man's mouth open, and, with a terrible odour of the grave, gave vent to the following remarks: "Ah, here you are at last! I have you, that -- by the collar! I need your cloak; you took no trouble about mine, but reprimanded me; so now give up your own."

The pallid prominent personage almost died of fright. Brave as he was in the office and in the presence of inferiors generally, and although, at the sight of his manly form and appearance, every one said, "Ugh! how much character he had!" at this crisis, he, like many possessed of an heroic exterior, experienced such terror, that, not without cause, he began to fear an attack of illness. He flung his cloak hastily from his shoulders and shouted to his coachman in an unnatural voice, "Home at full speed!" The coachman, hearing the tone which is generally employed at critical moments and even accompanied by something much more tangible, drew his head down between his shoulders in case of an emergency, flourished his whip, and flew on like an arrow. In a little more than six minutes the prominent personage was at the entrance of his own house. Pale, thoroughly scared, and cloakless, he went home instead of to Karolina Ivanovna's, reached his room somehow or other, and passed the night in the direst distress; so that the next morning over their tea his daughter said, "You are very pale to-day, papa." But papa remained silent, and said not a word to any one of what had happened to him, where he had been, or where he had intended to go.

This occurrence made a deep impression upon him. He even began to say: "How dare you? Do you realize who stands before you?" less frequently to the under-officials, and if he did utter the words, it was only after having first learned the bearings of the matter. But the most noteworthy point was, that from that day forward the apparition of the dead tchinovnik ceased to be seen. Evidently the prominent personage's cloak just fitted his shoulders; at all events, no more instances of his dragging cloaks from people's shoulders were heard of. But many active and apprehensive persons could by no means reassure themselves, and asserted that the dead tchinovnik still showed himself in distant parts of the city.

In fact, one watchman in Kolomna saw with his own eyes the apparition come from behind a house. But being rather weak of body, he dared not arrest him, but followed him in the dark, until, at length, the apparition looked round, paused, and inquired, "What do you want?" at the same time showing a fist such as is never seen on living men. The watchman said, "It's of no consequence," and turned back instantly. But the apparition was much too tall, wore huge moustaches, and, directing its steps apparently towards the Obukhoff bridge, disappeared in the darkness of the night.

Christmas Eve
Nikolai Gogol

The last day before Christmas had passed. A clear winter night had come; the stars peeped out; the moon rose majestically in the sky to light good people and all the world so that all might enjoy singing kolyadkil and praising the Lord. It was freezing harder than in the morning; but it was so still that the crunch of the snow under the boot could be heard half a mile away. Not one group of boys had appeared under the hut windows yet; only the moon peeped in at them stealthily as though calling to the girls who were dressing in their best to make haste and run out on the crunching snow. that moment the smoke rose in puffs from a hut chimney . passed like a cloud over the sky, and a witch on a broomstick rose up in the air with the smoke.

If the assessor of Sorochintsy, in his cap edged with lambs and cut like a Turk's, in his dark blue overcoat lined with black astrakhan, had driven by at that moment with his three hired horses and the fiendishly braided whip with which it is his habit to urge on his coachman, he would certainly have noticed her, for there is not a witch in the world who could elude the eyes of the Sorochintsy assessor. He can count on his fingers how many suckling Digs every peasant woman's sow has farrowed and how much linen is lying in her chest and just which of her clothes and house-hold belongings her good man pawns on Sunday at the tavern. But the Sorochintsy assessor did not drive by, and, indeed, what business is it of his? He has his own district. Meanwhile, the witch rose so high in the air that she was only a little black patch gleaming aloft. But wherever that little patch appeared, there the stars one after another vanished. Soon the witch had gathered a whole sleeveful of them. Three or four were still shining. All at once from the opposite side another little patch appeared, grew larger, began to lengthen out, and was no longer a little patch. A shortsighted man would never have made out what it was, even if he had put the wheels of the commissar's chaise on his nose as spectacles. At first It looked like a regular German:2 the narrow little face, continually twisting and turning and sniffing at everything, ended in a little round heel, like our pigs' snouts; the legs were so thin that if the mayor of Yareski had had legs like that, he would certainly have broken them in the first Cossack dance. But from behind he was for all the world a district attorney in uniform, for he had a tail as long and pointed as the uniform coattails are nowadays. It was only from the goat-beard under his chin, from the little horns sticking from his forehead, and from his being no whiter than a chimney sweep, that one could tell that he was not a German or a district attorney, but simply the devil, who had one last night left him to wander about the wide world and teach good folk to sin. On the morrow when the first bells rang for prayer, he would run with his tail between his legs straight off to his lair.

Meanwhile the devil stole silently up to the moon and stretched his hand out to seize it, but drew it back quickly as though he were scorched, sucked his fingers and danced about, then ran up from the other side and again skipped away and drew back his hand. But in spite of all his failures the sly devil did not give up his tricks. Running up, he suddenly seized the moon with both hands; grim-acing and blowing, he kept flinging it from one hand to the other, like a peasant who has picked up an ember for his pipe with bare fingers; at last, he hurriedly put it in his pocket and ran on as though nothing had happened.

No one in Dikanka noticed that the devil had stolen the moon. It is true the district clerk, crawling out of the tavern on all fours, saw the moon for no reason whatever dancing in the sky, and he swore that he had to the whole village; but people shook their heads and even made fun of him. But what motive led the devil to this illegal act? Why, this was how it was: he knew that the rich Cossack, Chub, had been invited by the sexton to a supper of rice soup at which a kinsman of the sexton's, who had come from the bishop's choir, wore a dark blue coat and could take the very lowest bass note, the mayor, the Cossack Sverbiguz, and some others were to be present, and at which besides the Christmas soup there were to be spiced vodka, saffron vodka, and good things of all sorts. And meanwhile his daughter, the greatest beauty in the village, was left at home, and there was no doubt that the blacksmith, a very strong and fine young fellow, would pay her a visit, and him the devil hated more than Father Kondrat's sermons. In his spare time the blacksmith had taken up painting and was reckoned the finest artist in the whole countryside. Even the Cossack officer L-----ko, who was still strong and hearty in those days, sent for him to Poltava expressly to paint a picket fence around his house. All the bowls from which the Cossacks of Dikanka gulped their borsht had been painted by the blacksmith. He was a God-fearing man and often painted icons of the saints: even now you may find his Luke the Evangelist in the church of T----- But the triumph of his art was a picture painted on the church wall in the chapel on the right. In it he depicted St. Peter on the Day of Judgment with the keys in his hand driving the Evil Spirit out of hell; the frightened devil was running in all directions, foreseeing his doom, while the sinners, who had been imprisoned before, were chasing him and striking him with whips, blocks of wood, and anything they could get hold of. While the artist was working at this picture and painting it on a big wooden board, the devil did all he could to hinder him; he gave him a nudge on the arm, unseen, blew some ashes from the forge in the smithy, and scattered them on the picture; but, in spite of it all, the work was finished, the picture was brought into the church and put on the wall of the side chapel, and from that day the devil had sworn to revenge himself on the blacksmith.

    He had only one night left to wander upon earth; but he was looking for some means of venting his anger on the blacksmith that night. And that was why he made up his mind to steal the moon, reckoning that old Chub was lazy and slow to move, and the sex-ton's hut a good distance away: the road passed by cross paths be-side the mills and the graveyard and went around a ravine. On a moonlight night spiced vodka and saffron vodka might have tempted Chub; but in such darkness it was doubtful whether anyone could drag him from the stove and bring him out of the cottage. And the blacksmith, who had for a long time been on bad terms with him, would on no account have ventured, strong as he was, to visit the daughter when the father was at home.

And so, as soon as the devil had hidden the moon in his pocket, it became so dark all over the world that not everyone could have found the way to the tavern, let alone to the sexton's. The witch shrieked when she suddenly found herself in darkness. Then the devil running up, all bows and smiles, put his arm around her, and began whispering in her ear the sort of thing that is usually whispered to all females. Things are oddly arranged in our world! All who live in it are always trying to outdo and imitate one another. In the old days the judge and the police captain were the only ones in Mirgorod who used to wear cloth overcoats lined with sheepskin in the winter, while all the minor officials wore plain sheepskin; but nowadays the assessor and the chamberlain have managed to get themselves new cloth overcoats lined with astrakhan. The year before last the treasury clerk and the district clerk bought dark blue duck at sixty kopeks a yard. The sexton has got himself cotton trousers for the summer and a striped vest of camel's hair. In fact everyone tries to be somebody! When will folks give up being vain! I am ready to bet that many would be surprised to see the devil carrying on in that way. What is most annoying is that, no doubt, he fancies himself a handsome fellow, though his figure is a shameful sight. With a face, as Foma Grigorievich used to say, the abomination of abominations, yet even he plays the dashing hero! But in the sky and under the sky it was growing so dark that there was no seeing what followed between them.

"So you have not been to see the sexton in his new hut, friend?" said the Cossack Chub, coming out at his door, to a tall lean peasant in a short sheepskin, whose stubby beard showed that for at least two weeks it had not been touched by the broken piece of scythe with which, for lack of a razor, peasants usually shave their beards. "There will be a fine drinking party there tonight!" Chub went on, grinning as he spoke. "If only we are not late!"

Hereupon Chub set straight the belt that closely girt his sheep-skin, pulled his cap more firmly on his head, and gripped his whip, the terror and the enemy of tiresome dogs; but glancing upward, he stopped. "What the hell! Look! look, Panas . . . !"

"What?" articulated his friend, and he too turned his face upward.

"What, indeed! There is no moon!"

"What a nuisance! There really is no moon."

"That's just it, there isn't!" Chub said, with some annoyance at his friend's imperturbable indifference. "You don't care, I'll bet."

"Well, what can I do about it?"

"Some devil," Chub went on, wiping his mustaches with his sleeve, "has to go and meddle—may he never have a glass of vodka to drink in the mornings, the dog! I swear it's as though to mock us. ... As I sat indoors I looked out of the window and the night was lovely! It was light, the snow was sparkling in the moonlight; you could see everything as though it were day. And here, before I'm out of the door, you can't see your hand before your face! May he break his teeth on a crust of buckwheat bread!"

Chub went on grumbling and swearing for a long while, and at the same time he was hesitant about what to decide. He had a desperate longing to gossip about all sorts of nonsense at the sexton's where no doubt the mayor was already sitting, as well as the bass choir singer, and Mikita, the tar dealer, who used to come once every two weeks on his way to Poltava, and who cracked such jokes that all the village worthies held their sides from laughing. Already in his mind's eye Chub saw the spiced vodka on the table. All this was enticing, it is true, but the darkness of the night recalled the charms of laziness so dear to every Cossack. How nice it would be now to lie on the stove with his legs tucked under him, quietly smoking his pipe and listening through a delicious drowsiness to the songs and carols of the lighthearted boys and girls who gathered in groups under the windows! He would undoubtedly have decided on the latter course had he been alone; but for the two together, it was not so dreary and terrible to go through the dark night; besides he did not care to seem sluggish and cowardly to others. When he had finished swearing he turned again to his friend.

"So there is no moon, friend?"

"No!"

"It's strange, really! Let me have a pinch of snuff! You have splendid snuff, friend! Where do you get it?"

"Splendid! What the hell do you mean by splendid?" answered the friend, shutting the birchbark snuffbox with patterns pricked out upon it. "It wouldn't make an old hen sneeze!"

"I remember," Chub still went on, "the innkeeper, Zuzulya, once brought me some snuff from Nyezhin. Ah, that was snuff! it was good snuff! So what is it to be? It's dark, you know!"

"So maybe we'll stay at home," his friend said, taking hold of the door handle.

If his friend had not said that, Chub would certainly have made up his mind to stay at home; but now something seemed egging him on to oppose it. "No, friend, let us go! It won't do; we must go!"

Even as he was saying it, he was angry with himself for having said it. He very much disliked going out on such a night, but it was a comfort to him that he was acting on his own decision and not following advice.

His friend looked around and scratched his shoulders with the handle of his whip, without the slightest sign of anger on his face, like a man to whom it is a matter of complete indifference whether he sits at home or goes out—and the two friends set off on their road.

Now let us see what Chub's daughter, the beauty, was doing all by herself. Before Oksana was seventeen, people were talking about nothing but her in almost the whole world, both on this side of Dikanka and on the other side of Dikanka. The young men were unanimous in declaring that there never had been and never would be a finer girl in the village. Oksana heard and knew all that was said about her and, like a beauty, was full of caprices. If, instead of a checked skirt and an apron, she had been dressed as a lady, she could never have kept a servant. The young men ran after her in crowds, but, losing patience, by degrees gave up on the obstinate beauty, and turned to others who were not so spoiled. Only the blacksmith was persistent and would not abandon his courtship, although he was treated not a bit better than the rest. When her father went out, Oksana spent a long while dressing herself in her best and preening before a little mirror in a pewter frame; she could not tear herself away from admiring herself.

"What put it into folks' heads to spread it abroad that I am pretty?" she said, as it were without thinking, simply to talk to her-self about something. "Folks lie, I am not pretty at all!"

But the fresh animated face reflected in the mirror, its youthfulness, its sparkling black eyes and inexpressibly charming smile that stirred the soul, at once proved the contrary.

"Can my black eyebrows and my eyes," the beauty went on, still holding the mirror, "be so beautiful that there are none like them in the world? What is there pretty in that turned-up nose, and in those cheeks and those lips? Is my black hair pretty?

Ough, my curls might frighten one in the evening, they twist and twine around my head like long snakes! I see now that I am not pretty at all!" And, moving the mirror a little further away, she cried out: "No, I am pretty! Ah, how pretty! Wonderful! What a joy I shall be to the man whose wife I become! How my husband will admire me! He'll be wild with joy. He will kiss me to death!"

"Wonderful girl!" whispered the blacksmith, coming in softly. "And hasn't she a little conceit! She's been standing looking in the mirror for an hour and can't tear herself away, and praising herself aloud, too!"

"Yes, boys, I am a match for you! Just look at me!" the pretty coquette went on: "how gracefully I step; my chemise is embroidered with red silk. And the ribbons on my head! You will never see_ richer braid! My father bought me all this so that the finest young man in the world may marry me." And, laughing, she turned around and saw the blacksmith. .

She uttered a shriek and stood still, coldly facing him.

The blacksmith's hands dropped helplessly to his sides.

It is hard to describe what the dark face of the lovely girl expressed. There was sternness in it, and through the sternness a sort of defiance of the embarrassed blacksmith, and at the same time a hardly perceptible flush of anger delicately suffused her face; and all this was so mingled and so indescribably pretty that to give her a million kisses was the best thing that could have been done at the moment.

"Why have you come here?" was how Oksana began. "Do you want me to shove you out of the door with a spade? You are all very clever at coming to see us. You sniff out in a minute when there are no fathers in the house. Oh, I know you! Well, is my chest ready?"

"It will be ready, my little heart, it will be ready after Christmas. If only you knew how I have worked at it; for two nights I didn't leave the smithy. But then, no priest's wife will have a chest like it. The iron I bound it with is better than what I put on the officer's chariot, when I worked at Poltava. And how it will be painted! You won't find one like it if you wander over the whole neighborhood with your little white feet! Red and blue flowers will be scattered over the whole ground. It will glow like fire. Don't be angry with me! Allow me at least to speak to you, to look at you!"

"Who's forbidding you? Speak and look!"

Then she sat down on the bench, glanced again in the mirror, and began arranging her hair. She looked at her neck, at her chemise embroidered in red silk, and a subtle feeling of complacency could be read on her lips and fresh cheeks, and was reflected in her eyes.

"Allow me to sit beside you," said the blacksmith.

"Sit down," said Oksana, with the same emotion still perceptible on her lips and in her gratified eyes.

"Wonderful, lovely Oksana, allow me to kiss you!" ventured the blacksmith, growing bolder, and he drew her toward him with the intention of snatching a kiss. But Oksana turned away her cheek, which had been very close to the blacksmith's lips, and pushed him away.

"What more do you want? When there's honey he must have a spoonful! Go away, your hands are harder than iron. And you smell of smoke. I believe you have smeared me all over with your soot."

Then she picked up the mirror and began preening again.

"She does not love me!" the blacksmith thought to himself, hanging his head. "It's all a game to her while I stand before her like a fool and cannot take my eyes off her. And I should like to stand before her always and never to take my eyes off her! Wonderful girl! What would I not give to know what is in her heart, and whom she loves. But no, she cares for nobody. She is admiring herself; she is tormenting poor me, while I am so sad that everything is darkness to me. I love her as no man in the world ever has loved or ever will."

"Is it true that your mother's a witch?" Oksana said, and she laughed. And the blacksmith felt that everything within him was laughing. That laugh echoed as if it were at once in his heart and in his softly tingling veins, and for all that, his soul was angry that he had not the right to kiss that sweetly laughing face.

"What care I for Mother? You are father and mother to me and all that is precious in the world. If the Czar summoned me and said: `Smith Vakula, ask me for all that is best in my kingdom; I will give you anything. I will bid them make you a golden forge and you shall work with silver hammers."I don't care,' I should say to the Czar, `for precious stones or a golden forge nor for all your kingdom: give me rather my Oksana.' "

"You see, what a fellow you are! Only my father's no fool either. You'll see that, when he doesn't marry your mother!"

Oksana said, smiling slyly. "But the girls are not here. . . . What's the meaning of it? We ought to have been singing long ago. I am getting tired of waiting."

"Let them stay away, my beauty!"

"I should hope not! I expect the boys will come with them. And then there will be dances. I can imagine what funny stories they will tell!"

"So you'll be merry with them?"

"Yes, merrier than with you. Ah! someone knocked; I expect it is the girls and the boys."

"What's the use of my staying longer?" the blacksmith said to himself. "She is jeering at me. I am no more to her than an old rusty horseshoe. But if that's so, anyway I won't let another man laugh at me. If only I see for certain that she likes someone better than me, I'll teach him to keep away . ."

A knock at the door and a cry of "Open!" ringing out sharply in the frost interrupted his reflections.

"Stop, I'll open the door," said the blacksmith, and he went out, intending in his anger to break the ribs of anyone who might be there.

The frost grew sharper, and up above it turned so cold that the devil kept hopping from one hoof to the other and blowing into his fists, trying to warm his frozen hands. And indeed it is small wonder that he should be cold, being used day after day to knocking about in hell, where, as we all know, it is not so cold as it is with us in winter, and where, putting on his cap and standing before the hearth, like a real cook, he fries sinners with as much satisfaction as a peasant woman fries a sausage at Christmas.

The witch herself felt that it was cold, although she was warmly clad; and so, throwing her arms upward, she stood with one foot out, and putting herself into the attitude of a man flying along on skates, without moving a single muscle, she dropped through the air, as though on an icy slope, and straight into her chimney.

The devil started after her in the same way. But as the creature is nimbler than any dandy in stockings, there is no wonder that he reached the top of the chimney almost on the neck of his mistress, and both found themselves in a roomy oven among the pots.

The witch stealthily moved back the oven door to see whether her son, Vakula, had invited visitors to the hut; but seeing that there was no one, except the sacks that lay in the middle of the floor, she crept out of the oven, flung off her warm pelisse, rearranged her clothing, and no one could have told that she had been riding on a broom the minute before.

Vakula's mother was not more than forty years old. She was neither pretty nor ugly. Indeed, it is hard to be pretty at such an age. However, she was so clever at attracting even the resolute Cossacks (who, it may not be amiss to observe, do not care much about beauty) that the mayor and the sexton, Osip Nikiforovich (if his wife were not at home, of course), and the Cossack Korny Chub, and the Cossack Kasian Sverbiguz, were all lavishing attentions on her. And it must be said to her credit that she was very skillful in managing them: not one of them dreamed that he had a rival. If a God-fearing peasant or a gentleman (as the Cossacks call them-selves) wearing a cape with a hood went to church on Sunday or, if the weather was bad, to the tavern, how could he fail to look in on Solokha, eat curd dumplings with sour cream, and gossip in the warm hut with its chatty and agreeable mistress? And the Cossack would purposely go a long way around before reaching the tavern, and would call that "looking in on his way." And when Solokha went to church on a holiday, dressed in a bright-checked plakhta with a cotton zapaska, and above it a dark blue overskirt on the back of which gold flourishes were embroidered, and took up her stand close to the right side of the choir, the sexton would be sure to begin coughing and unconsciously screw up his eyes in her direction; the mayor would smooth his mustaches, begin twisting the curl behind his ear, and say to the man standing next to him: "Ah, a nice woman, a hell of a woman!" Solokha would bow to each one of them, and each one would think that she was bowing to him alone.

But anyone fond of meddling in other people's business would notice at once that Solokha was most gracious to the Cossack Chub. Chub was a widower. Eight stacks of wheat always stood before his hut. Two pairs of stalwart oxen poked their heads out of the barn with the thatched roof by the roadside and mooed every time they saw their crony, the cow, or their uncle, the fat bull, pass. A bearded billygoat used to clamber onto the roof, from which he would bleat in a harsh voice like the police captain's, taunting the turkeys when they came out into the yard, and turning his back when he saw his enemies, the boys, who used to jeer at his beard. In Chub's trunks there was plenty of linen and many caftans and old-fashioned overcoats with gold braid on them; his wife had been fond of fine clothes. In his vegetable patch, besides poppies, cabbages, and sunflowers, two beds were sown every year with tobacco. All this Solokha thought would not be improper to join to her own farm, and, already reckoning in what good condition it would be when it passed into her hands, she felt doubly well-disposed to old Chub. And to prevent her son Vakula from courting Chub's daughter and succeeding in getting possession of it all himself (then he would very likely not let her interfere in anything), she had recourse to the common maneuver of all women of forty—that is, setting Chub against the blacksmith as often as she could. Possibly these sly tricks and subtleties were the reason that the old women were beginning here and there, particularly when they had drunk a drop too much at some merry gathering, to say that Solokha was certainly a witch, that the boy Kizyakolupenko had seen a tail on her back no bigger than a peasant woman's spindle; that, no longer ago than the Thursday before last, she had run across the road in the form of a black cat; that on one occasion a sow had run up to the priest's wife, had crowed like a cock, put Father Kondrat's cap on her head, and run away again. .

It happened that just when the old women were talking about this, a cowherd, Tymish Korostyavy, came up. He did not fail to tell them how in the summer, just before St. Peter's Fast, when he had lain down to sleep in the stable, putting some straw under his head, he saw with his own eyes a witch, with her hair down, in nothing but her chemise, begin milking the cows, and he could not stir he was so spellbound, and she had smeared his lips with something so nasty that he was spitting the whole day afterwards. But all that was somewhat doubtful, for the only one who can see a witch is the assessor of Sorochintsy. And so all the notable Cossacks waved their hands impatiently when they heard such tales. "They are lying, the bitches!" was their usual answer.

After she had crept out of the stove and rearranged herself, Solokha, like a good housewife, began tidying up and putting everything in its place; but she did not touch the sacks. "Vakula brought those in, let him take them out himself!" she thought. Meanwhile the devil, who had chanced to turn around just as he was flying into the chimney, had caught sight of Chub arm-in-arm with his neighbor already a long way from home. Instantly he flew out of the chimney, cut across their road, and began flinging up heaps of frozen snow in all directions. A blizzard sprang up. All was whiteness in the air. The snow zigzagged behind and in front and threatened to plaster up the eyes, the mouth, and the ears of the friends. And the devil flew back to the chimney again, certain that Chub would go back home with his neighbor, would find the black-smith there and probably give him such a scolding that it would be a long time before he would be able to handle a brush and paint offensive caricatures.

As a matter of fact, as soon as the blizzard began and the wind blew straight in their faces, Chub expressed his regret, and pulling his hood further down on his head showered abuse on himself, the devil, and his friend. His annoyance was feigned, however. Chub was really glad of the snowstorm. They had still eight times as far to go as they had gone already before they would reach the sexton's. They turned around. The wind blew on the back of their heads, but they could see nothing through the whirling snow.

"Stop, friend! I think we are going wrong," said Chub, after walking on a little. "I do not see a single hut. Oh, what a snowstorm! You go a little that way and see whether you find the road, and meanwhile I'll look this way. It was the foul fiend put it into my head to go trudging out in such a storm! Don't forget to shout when you find the road. Oh, what a heap of snow Satan has driven into my eyes!"

The road was not to be seen, however. Chub's friend, turning off, wandered up and down in his high boots, and at last came straight upon the tavern. This lucky find so cheered him that he forgot everything and, shaking the snow off, walked straight in, not worrying himself in the least about the friend he had left on the road. Meanwhile Chub thought that he had found the road. Standing still, he started shouting at the top of his voice, but, seeing that his friend did not appear, he made up his mind to go on alone. After walking on a little he saw his own hut. Snowdrifts lay all about it and on the roof. Clapping his frozen hands together, he began knocking on the door and shouting peremptorily to his daughter to open it.

"What do you want here?" the blacksmith called grimly, as he came out.

Chub, recognizing the blacksmith's voice, stepped back a little. "Ah, no, it's not my hut," he said to himself. "The blacksmith doesn't come into my hut. Though, as I look it over, it is not the blacksmith's either. Whose place can it be? I know! I didn't recognize it! It's where lame Levchenko lives, who has lately married a young wife. His is the only hut that is like mine. I did think it was a little strange that I had reached home so soon. But

Levchenko is at the sexton's now, I know that. Why is the blacksmith here . . . ? Ah, a-ha! he comes to see his young wife. So that's it! Good . . . ! Now I understand it all."

"Who are you and what are you hanging about at people's doors for?" said the blacksmith more grimly than before, coming closer to him.

"No, I am not going to tell him who I am," thought Chub. "I wouldn't be surprised if he gave me a good beating, the damned brute." And, disguising his voice, he answered: "It's me, good man! I have come for your pleasure, to sing carols under your windows."

"Go to hell with your carols!" Vakula shouted angrily. "Why are you standing there? Do you hear! Get out of here!"

Chub already had that prudent intention; but it annoyed him to be forced to obey the blacksmith's orders. It seemed as though some evil spirit nudged his arm and compelled him to say something contradictory. "Why are you screaming like that?" he said in the same voice. "I want to sing carols and that's all there is to it!"

"Aha! I see words aren't enough for you!" And with that Chub felt a very painful blow on his shoulder.

"So I see you are beginning to fight now!" he said, stepping back a little.

"Get away, get away!" shouted the blacksmith, giving Chub an-other shove.

"Well, you are the limit!" said Chub in a voice that betrayed pain, annoyance, and timidity. "You are fighting in earnest, I see, and hitting pretty hard, too."

"Get away, get away!" shouted the blacksmith, and slammed the door.

"Look, how he swaggered!" said Chub when he was left alone in the road. "Just try going near him! What a fellow! He's a somebody! Do you suppose I won't have the law on you? No, my dear boy, I am going straight to the commissar. I'll teach you! I don't care if you are a blacksmith and a painter. But I must look at my back and shoulders; I believe they are black and blue. The bastard must have hit hard. It's a pity that it is cold, and I don't want to take off my pelisse. You wait, you fiend of a blacksmith; may the devil give you a beating and your smithy, too; I'll make you dance! Ah, the damned rascal! But he is not at home, now. I expect Solokha is all alone. H'm . . . it's not far off, I might go! It's such weather now that no one will interrupt us. There's no saying what may happen. . . . Aie, how hard that damned blacksmith did hit!"

Here Chub, rubbing his back, started off in a different direction. The agreeable possibilities awaiting him in a tryst with Solokha eased the pain a little and made him insensible even to the frost, the crackling of which could be heard on all the roads in spite of the howling of the storm. At moments a look of mawkish sweetness came into his face, though the blizzard soaped his beard and mustaches with snow more briskly than any barber who tyrannically holds his victim by the nose. But if everything had not been hidden by the flying snow, Chub might have been seen long afterward stopping and rubbing his back as he said: "The damned blacksmith did hit hard!" and then going on his way again.

While the nimble dandy with the tail and goat-beard was flying out of the chimney and back again into the chimney, the pouch which hung on a shoulder-belt at his side, and in which he had put the stolen moon, chanced to catch in something in the stove and came open—and the moon took advantage of this accident to fly up through the chimney of Solokha's hut and to float smoothly through the sky. Everything was flooded with light. It was as though there had been no snowstorm. The snow sparkled, a broad silvery plain, studded with crystal stars. The frost seemed less cold. Groups of boys and girls appeared with sacks. Songs rang out, and under almost every hut window were crowds of carol singers.

How wonderful is the light of the moon! It is hard to put into words how pleasant it is on such a night to mingle in a group of singing, laughing girls and among boys ready for every jest and sport which the gaily smiling night can suggest. It is warm under the thick pelisse; the cheeks glow brighter than ever from the frost, and the devil himself prompts to mischief.

Groups of girls with sacks burst into Chub's hut and gathered around Oksana. The blacksmith was deafened by the shouts, the laughter, the stories. They fought with one another in telling the beauty some bit of news, in emptying their sacks and boasting of the little loaves, sausages, and curd dumplings of which they had already gathered a fair harvest from their singing. Oksana seemed to be highly pleased and delighted; she chatted first with one and then with another and laughed without ceasing.

With what envy and anger the blacksmith looked at this gaiety, and this time he cursed the carol singing, though he was passionately fond of it himself.

"Ah, Odarka!" said the lighthearted beauty, turning to one of the girls, "you have some new slippers. Ah, how pretty! And with gold on them! It's nice for you, Odarka, you have a man who will buy you anything, but I have no one to get me such splendid slippers."

"Don't grieve, my precious Oksana!" said the blacksmith. "I will get you slippers such as not many a lady wears."

"You!" said Oksana, with a quick and proud glance at him. "I should like to know where you'll get hold of slippers such as I could put on my feet. Perhaps you will bring me the very ones the Czarina wears?"

"You see the sort she wants!" cried the crowd of girls, laughing.

"Yes!" the beauty went on proudly, "all of you be my witnesses: if the blacksmith Vakula brings me the very slippers the Czarina wears, here's my word on it: I'll marry him that very day."

The girls carried off the capricious beauty with them.

"Laugh away! Laugh away!" thought the blacksmith as he followed them out. "I laugh at myself! I wonder and can't think what I have done with my senses! She does not love me—well, let her go! As though there were no one in the world but Oksana. Thank God, there are lots of fine girls besides her in the village. And what is Oksana? She'll never make a good housewife; the only thing she is good at is dressing up. No, it's enough! It's time I gave up playing the fool!"

But at the very time when the blacksmith was making up his mind to be resolute, some evil spirit set floating before him the laughing image of Oksana saying mockingly, "Get me the Czarina's slippers, blacksmith, and I will marry you!" Everything within him was stirred and he could think of nothing but Oksana.

The crowds of carol singers, the boys in one party and the girls in another, hurried from one street to the next. But the blacksmith went on and saw nothing, and took no part in the merrymaking which he had once loved more than anything.

Meanwhile the devil was making love in earnest at Solokha's: he kissed her hand with the same airs and graces as the assessor does the priest's daughter's, put his hand on his heart, sighed, and said bluntly that, if she would not consent to gratify his passion and re-ward his devotion in the usual way, he was ready for anything: would fling himself in the water and let his soul go straight to hell. Solokha was not so cruel; besides, the devil, as we know, was alone with her. She was fond of seeing a crowd hanging about her and was rarely without company. That evening, however, she was expecting to spend alone, because all the noteworthy inhabitants of the village had been invited to keep Christmas Eve at the sexton's. But it turned out otherwise: the devil had only just urged his suit, when suddenly they heard a knock and the voice of the resolute mayor. Solokha ran to open the door, while the nimble devil crept into a sack that was lying on the floor.

The mayor, after shaking the snow off his cap and drinking a glass of vodka from Solokha's hand, told her that he had not gone to the sexton's because it had begun to snow, and seeing a light in her hut, had dropped in, meaning to spend the evening with her.

The mayor had hardly had time to say this when they heard a knock at the door and the voice of the sexton: "Hide me somewhere," whispered the mayor. "I don't want to meet him now."

Solokha thought for some time where to hide so bulky a visitor; at last she selected the biggest coalsack. She shot the coal out into a barrel, and the brave mayor, mustaches, head, pelisse, and all, crept into the sack.

The sexton walked in, clearing his throat and rubbing his hands, and told her that no one had come to his party and that he was heartily glad of this opportunity to enjoy a visit to her and was not afraid of the snowstorm. Then he went closer to her and, with a cough and a smirk, touched her plump bare arm with his long fingers and said with an air expressive both of slyness and satisfaction: "And what have you here, magnificent Solokha?" and saying this he stepped back a little.

"What do you mean? My arm, Osip Nikiforovich!" answered Solokha.

"H'm! your arm! He-he-he!" cried the sexton, highly delighted with his opening. And he paced up and down the room.

Nikolai Gogol   Christmas Eve

"And what have you here, incomparable Solokha . . . ?" he said with the same air, going up to her again, lightly touching her neck and skipping back again in the same way.

"As though you don't see, Osip Nikiforovich!" answered Solokha; "my neck and my necklace on my neck."

"H'm! A necklace on your neck! He-he-he!" and the sexton walked again up and down the room, rubbing his hands.

"And what have you here, incomparable Solokha . . . ?" There's no telling what the sexton (a carnal-minded man) might have touched next with his long fingers, when suddenly they heard a knock at the door and the voice of the Cossack Chub.

"Oh dear, someone who's not wanted!" cried the sexton in alarm. "What now if I am caught here, a person of my position. . . ! It will come to Father Kondrat's ears. . . . "

But the sexton's apprehensions were really of a different nature; he was more afraid that his doings might come to the knowledge of his better half, whose terrible hand had already turned his thick mane into a very scanty one. "For God's sake, virtuous Solokha!" he said, trembling all over, "your loving-kindness, as it says in the Gospel of St. Luke, chapter thirt . . . thirt . . . What a knocking, aie, what a knocking! Ough, hide me somewhere!"

Solokha turned the coal out of another sack, and the sexton, whose proportions were not too ample, crept into it and settled at the very bottom, so that another half-sack of coal might have been put in on top of him.

"Good evening, Solokha!" said Chub, as he came into the hut. "Maybe you didn't expect me, eh? You didn't, did you? Perhaps I am in the way . . . ?" Chub went on with a good-humored and significant expression on his face, which betrayed that his slow-moving mind was at work and preparing to utter some sarcastic and amusing jest.

"Maybe you had some entertaining companion here ... ! Maybe you have someone in hiding already? Eh?" And enchanted by this observation of his, Chub laughed, inwardly triumphant at being the only man who enjoyed Solokha's favor. "Come, Solokha, let me have a drink of vodka now. I believe my throat's frozen stiff with this damned frost. God has sent us weather for Christmas Eve! How it has come on, do you hear, Solokha, how it has come

215

on . . . ? Ah, my hands are stiff, I can't unbutton my sheepskin! How the storm has come on . . ."

"Open the door!" a voice rang out in the street, accompanied by a thump on the door.

"Someone is knocking," said Chub, standing still.

"Open!" the shout rang out louder still.

"It's the blacksmith!" cried Chub, grabbing his pelisse. "Solokha, put me where you like; for nothing in the world will I show myself to that damned brute. May he have a pimple as big as a pile of hay under each of his eyes, the bastard!"

Solokha, herself alarmed, flew about like one distraught and, for-getting what she was doing, gestured to Chub to creep into the very sack in which the sexton was already sitting. The poor sexton dared not betray his pain by a cough or a groan when the heavy Cossack sat down almost on his head and put a frozen boot on each side of his face.

The blacksmith walked in, not saying a word nor removing his cap, and almost fell down on the bench. It could be seen that he was in a very bad humor.

At the very moment when Solokha was shutting the door after him, someone knocked at the door again. This was the Cossack Sverbiguz. He could not be hidden in the sack, because no sack big enough could be found anywhere. He was fatter than the mayor and taller than Chub's neighbor Panas. And so Solokha led him into the garden to hear from him there all that he had to tell her.

The blacksmith looked absent-mindedly at the corners of his hut, listening from time to time to the voices of the carol singers floating far away through the village. At last his eyes rested on the sacks. "Why are those sacks lying there? They ought to have been cleared away long ago. This foolish love has made me stupid. Tomorrow's Christmas and trash of all sorts is still lying about the hut. I'll carry them to the smithy!"

The blacksmith stooped down to the huge sacks, tied them up more tightly, and prepared to hoist them on his shoulders. But it was evident that his thoughts were straying, God knows where, or he would have heard how Chub gasped when the hair of his head was twisted in the string that tied the sack and the brave mayor began hiccupping quite distinctly.

Nikolai Gogol   Christmas Eve

"Can nothing drive that wretched Oksana out of my head?" the blacksmith was saying. "I don't want to think about her; but I keep thinking and thinking and, as luck will have it, of her and nothing else. How is it that thoughts creep into the mind against the will? The devil! The sacks seem to have grown heavier than they were! Something besides coal must have been put into them. I am a fool! I forget that now everything seems heavier to me. In the old days I could bend and unbend a copper coin or a horseshoe with one hand, and now I can't lift sacks of coal. I shall be blown over by the wind next . . . No!" he cried, pulling himself together after a pause, "I am not a weak woman! I won't let anyone make an ass of me! If there were ten such sacks, I would lift them all." And he briskly hoisted on his shoulders the sacks which two strong men could not have carried. "I'll take this one too," he went on, picking up the little one at the bottom of which the devil lay curled up. "I believe I put my tools in this one." Saying this he went out of the hut whistling the song: "I Can't Be Bothered with a Wife."

The singing, laughter, and shouts sounded louder and louder in the streets. The crowds of jostling people were reinforced by newcomers from neighboring villages. The boys were full of mischief and wild pranks. Often among the carols some gay song was heard which one of the young Cossacks had made up on the spot. All at once one of the crowd would sing out a New Year's song instead of a carol and bawl at the top of his voice:

Kind one, good one Give us a dumpling, A heap of kasha, And a ring of sausage!

A roar of laughter rewarded the wag. Little windows were thrown up and the withered hand of an old woman (the old women, together with the sedate fathers, were the only people left indoors) was thrust out with a sausage or a piece of pie.

The boys and the girls fought with one another in holding out their sacks and catching their booty. In one place the boys, coming together from all sides, surrounded a group of girls. There was loud noise and clamor; one flung a snowball, another pulled away a sack full of all sorts of good things. In another place, the girls caught a boy, gave him a kick, and sent him flying headlong with his sack into the snow. It seemed as though they were ready to make merry the whole night through. And, as though by design, the night was so splendidly warm. And the light of the moon seemed brighter still from the glitter of the snow.

The blacksmith stood still with his sacks. He thought he heard among the crowd of girls the voice and shrill laugh of

217

Oksana. Every vein in his body throbbed; flinging the sacks on the ground so that the sexton at the bottom groaned over the bruise he received, and the mayor gave a loud hiccup, he strolled with the little sack on his shoulders together with a group of boys after a crowd of girls, among whom he heard the voice of Oksana.

"Yes, it is she! She stands like a queen, her black eyes sparkling. A handsome boy is telling her something. It must be amusing, for she is laughing. But she is always laughing." As it were unconsciously, he could not say how, the blacksmith squeezed his way through the crowd and stood beside her.

"Oh, Vakula, you here! Good evening!" said the beauty, with a smile which almost drove Vakula mad. "Well, have you sung many carols? Oh, but what a little sack! And have you got the slippers that the Czarina wears? Get me the slippers and I will marry you . . . !" And laughing, she ran off with the other girls.

The blacksmith stood as though rooted to the spot. "No, I cannot bear it; it's too much for me . . ." he said at last. "But, my God, why is she so fiendishly beautiful? Her eyes, her words and every-thing, well, they scorch me, they fairly scorch me. . . . No, I can not control myself. It's time to put an end to it all. Damn my soul, I'll go and drown myself in the hole in the ice and it will all be over!"

Then with a resolute step he walked on, caught up with the group of girls, overtook Oksana, and said in a firm voice: "Farewell, Oksana! Find any lover you like, make a fool of whom you like; but me you will not see again in this world."

The beauty seemed amazed and would have said something, but with a wave of his hand the blacksmith ran away.

"Where are you off to, Vakula?" said the boys, seeing the black-smith running.

"Goodbye, friends!" the blacksmith shouted in answer. "Please God we shall meet again in the other world, but we shall not walk together again in this. Farewell! Do not remember evil of me! Tell Father Kondrat to sing a requiem mass for my sinful soul. Sinner that I am, for the sake of worldly things I did not finish painting the candles for the icons of the Martyr and the Virgin Mary. All the goods which will be found in my chest are for the Church. Fare-well!"

Saying this, the blacksmith started running again with the sack upon his back.

"He has gone crazy!" said the boys.

Nikolai Gogol   Christmas Eve

"A lost soul!" an old woman, who was passing, muttered devoutly. "I must go and tell them that the blacksmith has hanged himself!"

Meanwhile, after running through several streets, Vakula stopped to catch his breath. "Where am I running?" he thought, "as though everything were over already. I'll try one way more: I'll go to the Dnieper Cossack Puzaty Patsyuk; they say he knows all the devils and can do anything he likes. I'll go to him, for my soul is lost any-way!"

At that the devil, who had lain for a long while without moving, skipped for joy in the sack; but the blacksmith, thinking that he had somehow twitched the sack with his hand and caused the movement himself, gave the sack a punch with his big fist and, shaking it on his shoulders, set off to Puzaty Patsyuk.

This Puzaty Patsyuk certainly at one time had been a Dnieper Cossack; but no one knew whether he had been turned out of the camp or whether he had run away from Zaporozhye of his own accord.

For a long time, ten years or perhaps fifteen, he had been living in Dikanka. At first he had lived like a true Dnieper Cossack: he had done no work, slept three-quarters of the day, eaten as much as six hay cutters, and drunk almost a whole pailful at a time. He had somewhere to put it all, however, for though Patsyuk was not very tall he was fairly bulky horizontally. Moreover, the trousers he used to wear were so full that, however long a step he took, no trace of his leg was visible, and it seemed as though a wine distiller's ma-chine were moving down the street. Perhaps it was this that gave rise to his nickname, Puzaty. Before many weeks had passed after his coming to the village, everyone had found out that he was a wizard. If anyone were ill, he called in Patsyuk at once: Patsyuk had only to whisper a few words and it was as though the ailment had been lifted off by his hand. If it happened that a hungry gentleman was choked by a fishbone, Patsyuk could punch him so skillfully on the back that the bone went the proper way without causing any harm to the gentleman's throat. Of late years he was rarely seen anywhere. The reason for that was perhaps laziness, though possibly also the fact that it was every year becoming increasingly difficult for him to pass through a doorway. People had of late been obliged to go to him if they had need of him.

Not without some timidity, the blacksmith opened the door and saw Patsyuk sitting Turkish-fashion on the floor before a little tub on which stood a bowl of dumplings. This bowl stood as though purposely planned on a level with his mouth. Without moving a single finger, he bent his head a little toward the bowl and sipped the soup, from time to time catching the dumplings with his teeth.

"Well," thought Vakula to himself, "this fellow's even lazier than Chub: he does eat with a spoon, at least, while this fellow won't even lift his hand!"

Patsyuk must have been entirely engrossed in the dumplings, for he seemed to be quite unaware of the entrance of the blacksmith, who offered him a very low bow as soon as he stepped on the threshold.

"I have come to ask you a favor, Patsyuk!" said Vakula, bowing again.

Puzaty Patsyuk lifted his head and again began swallowing dumplings.

"They say that you—no offense meant . . ." the blacksmith said, taking heart, "I speak of this not by way of any insult to you—that you are a little akin to the devil."

When he had uttered these words, Vakula was alarmed, thinking that he had expressed himself too bluntly and had not sufficiently softened his language; and, expecting that Patsyuk would pick up the tub together with the bowl and fling them straight at his head, he turned aside a little and covered his face with his sleeve so that the hot dumpling soup might not spatter it. But Patsyuk looked up and again began swallowing the dumplings.

The blacksmith, reassured, made up his mind to go on. "I have come to you, Patsyuk. God give you everything, goods of all sorts in abundance and bread in proportion!" (The blacksmith would sometimes throw in a fashionable word: he had got into the way of it during his stay in Poltava when he was painting the fence for the officer.) "There is nothing but ruin before me, a sinner! Nothing in the world will help! What will be, will be. I have to ask help from the devil himself. Well, Patsyuk," the blacksmith said, trying to break Patsyuk's silence, "what am I to do?"

"If you need the devil, then go to the devil," answered Patsyuk, not lifting his eyes to him, but still chewing away at the dumplings.

"It is for that that I have come to you," answered the blacksmith, offering him another bow. "I suppose that nobody in the world but you knows the way to him!"

Patsyuk answered not a word, but ate up the remaining dumplings. "Do me a kindness, good man, do not refuse me!" persisted the blacksmith. "Whether it is pork or sausage or buckwheat flour or linen, say—millet or anything else in case of need . . . as is usual between good people . . . we will not grudge it. Tell me at least how, for instance, to get on the road to him."

"He need not go far who has the devil on his shoulders!" Patsyuk pronounced carelessly, without changing his position.

Vakula fastened his eyes upon him as though the interpretation of those words were written on his brow. "What does he mean?" his face asked dumbly, while his mouth stood half-open ready to swallow the first word like a dumpling.

But Patsyuk was still silent.

Then Vakula noticed that there were neither dumplings nor a tub before him; but two wooden bowls were standing on the floor instead—one was filled with turnovers, the other with some cream. His thoughts and his eyes unconsciously fastened on these dainties. "Let us see," he said to himself, "how Patsyuk will eat the turnovers. He certainly won't want to bend down to lap them up like the dumplings; besides he couldn't—he must first dip the turnovers in the cream."

He had hardly time to think this when Patsyuk opened his mouth, looked at the turnovers, and opened his mouth wider still. At that moment a turnover popped out of the bowl, splashed into the cream, turned over on the other side, leaped upward, and flew straight into his mouth. Patsyuk ate it and opened his mouth again, and another turnover went through the same performance. The only trouble he took was to munch it up and swallow it.

"What a miracle!" thought the blacksmith, his mouth dropping open with surprise, and at the same moment he was aware that a turnover was creeping toward him and was already smearing his mouth with cream. Pushing away the turnover and wiping his lips, the blacksmith began to reflect what marvels there are in the world and to what subtle devices the evil spirit may lead a man, saying to himself at the same time that no one but Patsyuk could help him.

"I'll bow to him once more; maybe he will explain properly. . . . He's a devil, though! Why, today is a fast day and he is eating turnovers with meat in them! What a fool I am, really. I am standing here and preparing to sin! Back . !" And the pious blacksmith ran headlong out of the hut.

But the devil, sitting in the sack and already gloating over his prey, could not endure letting such a glorious capture slip through his fingers. As soon as the blacksmith put down the sack the devil skipped out of it and straddled his neck.

A cold shudder ran over the blacksmith's skin; pale and scared, he did not know what to do; he was on the point of crossing himself. . . . But the devil, putting his snout down to Vakula's right ear, said: "It's me, your friend; I'll do anything for a friend and comrade! I'll give you as much money as you like," he squeaked into his left ear. "Oksana shall be yours this very day," he whispered, turning his snout again to the right ear. The blacksmith stood still, hesitating.

"Very well," he said at last; "for such a price I am ready to be yours!"

The devil clasped his hands in delight and began galloping up and down on the blacksmith's neck. "Now the blacksmith is done for!" he thought to himself: "now I'll pay you back, my sweet fellow, for all your paintings and false tales thrown up at the devils! What will my comrades say now when they learn that the most pious man of the whole village is in my hands!"

Here the devil laughed with joy, thinking how he would taunt all the long-tailed crew in hell, how furious the lame devil, who was considered the most resourceful among them, would be.

"Well, Vakula!" piped the devil, not dismounting from his neck, as though afraid he might escape, "you know nothing is done with-out a contract."

"I am ready!" said the blacksmith. "I have heard that among you contracts are signed with blood. Wait. I'll get a nail out of my pocket!"

And he put his hand behind him and caught the devil by the tail. "What a man you are for a joke!" cried the devil, laughing. "Come, let go, that's enough mischief!"

"Wait a minute, friend!" cried the blacksmith, "and what do you think of this?" As he said that he made the sign of the cross and the devil became as meek as a lamb. "Wait a minute," said the black-smith, pulling him by the tail to the ground: "I'll teach you to entice good men and honest Christians into sin."

Here the blacksmith leaped on the devil and lifted his hand to make the sign of the cross.

"Have mercy, Vakula!" the devil moaned piteously; "I will do anything you want, anything; only let me off with my life: do not lay the terrible cross upon me!"

"Ah, so that's your tone now, you damned German! Now I know what to do. Carry me at once on your back! Do you hear? And fly like a bird!"

"Where?" asked the miserable devil.

"To Petersburg, straight to the Czarina!" And the blacksmith almost fainted with terror as he felt himself soaring into the air.

Oksana stood for a long time pondering on the strange words of the blacksmith. Already an inner voice was telling her that she had treated him too cruelly. "What if he really does make up his mind to do something dreadful! I wouldn't be surprised! Perhaps his sorrow will make him fall in love with another girl, and in his anger he will begin calling her the greatest beauty in the village. But no, he loves me. I am so beautiful! He will not give me up for anything; he is playing, he is pretending. In ten minutes he will come back to look at me, for certain. I really was angry. I must, as though it were against my will, let him kiss me. Won't he be delighted!" And the frivolous beauty went back to jesting with her companions.

"Stop," said one of them, "the blacksmith has forgotten his sacks: look what fat sacks! He has made more by his carol singing than we have. I bet they must have put here at least a quarter of a sheep, and I am sure that there are no end of sausages and loaves in them. Wonderful! we shall have enough to feast on all Christmas week!"

"Are they the blacksmith's sacks?" asked Oksana. "We had better drag them to my hut and have a good look at what he has put in them."

All the girls laughingly approved of this proposal.

"But we can't lift them!" the whole group cried, trying to move the sacks.

"Wait a minute," said Oksana; "let us run for a sled and take them away on it!"

And the crowd of girls ran out to get a sled.

The captives were terribly bored with staying in the sacks, although the sexton had poked a fair-sized hole to peep through. If there had been no one about, he might have found a way to creep out; but to creep out of a sack in front of everybody, to be a laughingstock . . . that thought restrained him, and he made up his mind to wait, only uttering a slight groan under Chub's ill-mannered boots.

Chub himself was no less eager for freedom, feeling that there was something under him that was terribly uncomfortable to sit upon. But as soon as he heard his daughter's plan, he felt relieved and did not want to creep out, reflecting that it must be at least a hundred paces and perhaps two hundred to his hut; if he crept out, he would have to rearrange himself, button up his sheepskin, fasten his belt—such a lot of trouble! Besides, his winter cap had been left at Solokha's. Let the girls drag him in the sled.

But things turned out not at all as Chub was expecting. Just when the girls were running to fetch the sled, his lean neighbor, Panas, came out of the tavern, upset and ill-humored. The woman who kept the tavern could not be persuaded to serve him on credit. He thought to sit on in the tavern in the hope that some godly gentleman would come along and treat him; but as ill-luck would have it, all the gentlefolk were staying at home and like good Christians were eating rice and honey in the bosom of their families. Meditating on the degeneration of manners and the hard heart of the Jewess who kept the tavern, Panas made his way up to the sacks and stopped in amazement. "My word, what sacks somebody has flung down in the road!" he said, looking about him in all directions. "I'll bet there is pork in them. Some carol singer is in luck to get so many gifts of all sorts! What fat sacks! Suppose they are only stuffed full of buckwheat cake and biscuits, that's worth having; if there should be nothing but biscuits in them, that would be welcome, too; the Jewess would give me a dram of vodka for each cake. Let's make haste and get them away before anyone sees."

Here he flung on his shoulder the sack with Chub and the sexton in it, but felt it was too heavy. "No, it'll be too heavy for one to carry," he said; "and here by good luck comes the weaver Shapuvalenko. Good evening, Ostap!"

"Good evening!" said the weaver, stopping.

"Where are you going?"

"Oh, nowhere in particular."

"Help me carry these sacks, good man! Someone has been singing carols, and has dropped them in the middle of the road. We'll share the things."

"Sacks? sacks of what? White loaves or biscuits?"

"Oh, all sorts of things, I expect."

They hurriedly pulled some sticks out of the fence, laid the sack on them, and carried it on their shoulders.

"Where shall we take it? To the tavern?" the weaver asked on the way.

"That's just what I was thinking; but, you know, the damned Jewess won't trust us, she'll think we have stolen it somewhere; be-sides, I have only just come from the tavern. We'll take it to my hut. No one will hinder us there; the wife's not at home."

"Are you sure she is not at home?" the cautious weaver inquired.

"Thank God that I am not quite a fool yet," said Panas; "the devil would hardly take me where she is. I'm sure she will be trailing around with the other women till daybreak."

"Who is there?" shouted Panas' wife, opening the door of the hut as she heard the noise in the porch made by the two friends with the sack. Panas was dumbfounded.

"Well, that's it!" said the weaver, letting his hands fall.

Panas' wife was a treasure of a kind that is not uncommon in this world. Like her husband, she hardly ever stayed at home, but almost every day visited various cronies and well-to-do old women, flattered them, and ate with good appetite at their expense; she only quarreled with her husband in the mornings, as it was only then that she sometimes saw him. Their hut was twice as old as the district clerk's trousers; there was no straw in places on their thatched roof. Only the remnants of a fence could be seen, for everyone, as he went out of his house, thought it unnecessary to take a stick for the dogs, relying on passing by Panas' vegetable garden and pulling one out of his fence. The stove was not heated for three days at a time. Whatever the tender wife managed to beg from good Christians she hid as far as possible out of her husband's reach, and often robbed him of his gains if he had not had time to spend them on drink. In spite of his habitual imperturbability Panas did not like to give way to her, and consequently left his house every day with both eyes blackened, while his better half, sighing and groaning, waddled off to tell her old friends of her husband's unmannerliness and the blows she had to put up with from him.

Now you can imagine how disconcerted were the weaver and Panas by this unexpected apparition. Dropping the sack, they stood before it, and concealed it with the skirts of their coats, but it was already too late: Panas' wife, though she did not see well with her old eyes, had observed the sack.

"Well, that's good!" she said, with a face which betrayed the joy of a vulture. "That's good, that you have gained so much singing carols! That's how it always is with good Christians; but no, I'm sure you have stolen it somewhere. Show me your sack at once, do you hear, show me this very minute!"

"The bald devil may show you, but we won't," said Panas, assuming a dignified air.

"What's it to do with you?" said the weaver. "We've sung the carols, not you."

"Yes, you will show me, you wretched drunkard!" screamed the wife, striking her tall husband on the chin with her fist and forcing her way toward the sack. But the weaver and Panas manfully defended the sack and compelled her to beat a retreat. Before they recovered themselves the wife ran out again with a poker in her hands. She nimbly hit her husband a blow on the arms and the weaver one on his back and reached for the sack.

"Why did we let her pass?" said the weaver, regaining his senses. "Yes, we let her pass! Why did you let her pass?" said Panas coolly.

"Your poker is made of iron, it seems!" said the weaver after a brief silence, rubbing his back. "My wife bought one last year at the fair, gave twenty-five kopeks; that one's all right . . . it doesn't hurt . . ."

Meanwhile the triumphant wife, setting a lamp on the floor, untied the sack and peeped into it.

But her old eyes, which had so well described the sack, this time certainly deceived her.

"Oh, but there is a whole pig lying here!" she shrieked, clapping her hands in glee.

"A pig! Do you hear, a whole pig!" The weaver nudged Panas. "And it's all your fault."

"It can't be helped!" replied Panas, shrugging his shoulders.

"Can't be helped! Why are we standing still? Let us take away the sack! Here, come on! Go away, go away, it's our pig!" shouted the weaver, stepping forward.

"Move away, move away, you devilish woman! It's not your property!" said Panas, approaching.

His wife picked up the poker again, but at that moment Chub crawled out of the sack and stood in the middle of the room, stretching like a man who has just waked up from a long sleep.

Panas' wife shrieked, slapping her skirts, and they all stood with open mouths.

"Why did she say it was a pig, the ass! It's not a pig!" said Panas, staring open-eyed.

"God! What a man has been dropped into a sack!" said the weaver, staggering back in alarm. "You may say what you please, you can burst if you like, but the foul fiend has had a hand in it. Why, he would not go through a window!"

"It's Chub!" cried Panas, looking more closely.

"Why, who did you think it was?" said Chub, laughing. "Well, haven't I played you a fine trick? I'll bet you meant to eat me as pork! Wait a minute, I'll console you: there is something in the sack; if not a whole pig, it's certainly a little porker or some live beast. Something kept moving under me."

The weaver and Panas flew to the sack, the lady of the house clutched at the other side of it, and the battle would have been renewed had not the sexton, seeing that now he had no chance of concealment, scrambled out of the sack of his own accord.

The woman, astounded, let go of the leg by which she was beginning to drag the sexton out of the sack.

"Here's another of them!" cried the weaver in horror, "the devil knows what has happened to the world. . . . My head's going around. . . . Men are put into sacks instead of cakes or sausages!"

"It's the sexton!" said Chub, more surprised than any of them. "Well, then! You're a nice one, Solokha! To put one in a sack . . . I thought at the time her hut was very full of sacks. . . . Now I understand it all: she had a couple of men hidden in each sack. While I thought it was only me she . . . So now you know her!"

The girls were a little surprised on finding that one sack was missing.

"Well, there is nothing we can do, we must be content with this one," murmured Oksana.

The mayor made up his mind to keep quiet, reasoning that if he called out to them to untie the sack and let him out, the foolish girls would run away in all directions; they would think that the devil was in the sack—and he would be left in the street till next day. Meanwhile the girls, linking arms together, flew like a whirlwind with the sled over the crunching snow. Many of them sat on the sled for fun; others even clambered on top of the mayor. The mayor made up his mind to endure everything.

At last they arrived, threw open the door into the outer room of the hut, and dragged in the sack amid laughter.

"Let us see what is in it," they all cried, hastening to untie it.

At this point the hiccup which had tormented the mayor became so much worse that he began hiccupping and coughing loudly.

"Ah, there is someone in it!" they all shrieked, and rushed out of doors in horror.

"What the devil is it? Where are you tearing off to as though you were all possessed?" said Chub, walking in at the door.

"Oh, Daddy!" cried Oksana, "there is someone in the sack!"

"In the sack? Where did you get this sack?"

"The blacksmith threw it in the middle of the road," they all said at once.

"So that's it; didn't I say so?" Chub thought to himself. "What are you frightened at? Let us look. Come now, my man—I beg you won't be offended at our not addressing you by your proper name—crawl out of the sack!"

The mayor did crawl out.

"Oh!" shrieked the girls.

"So the mayor got into one, too," Chub thought to himself in bewilderment, scanning him from head to foot. "Well, I'll be damned!" He could say nothing more.

The mayor himself was no less confused and did not know how to begin. "I think it is a cold night," he said, addressing Chub.

"There is a bit of a frost," answered Chub. "Allow me to ask you what you rub your boots with, goose fat or tar?" He had not meant to say that; he had meant to ask: "How did you get into that sack, mayor?" and he did not himself understand how he came to say something utterly different.

"Tar is better," said the mayor. "Well, good night, Chub!" And pulling his winter cap down over his head, he walked out of the hut.

"Why was I such a fool as to ask him what he rubbed his boots with?" said Chub, looking toward the door by which the mayor had gone out.

"Well, Solokha is a fine one! To put a man like that in a sack . . . ! My word, she is a devil of a woman! While I, poor fool . . . But where is that damned sack?"

"I flung it in the corner, there is nothing more in it," said Oksana.

"I know all about that; nothing in it, indeed! Give it here; there is another one in it! Shake it well . . . What, nothing? My word, the cursed woman! And to look at her she is like a saint, as though she had never tasted anything but lenten fare . . . !"

But we will leave Chub to pour out his anger at leisure and will go back to the blacksmith, for it must be past eight o'clock.

At first it seemed dreadful to Vakula, particularly when he rose up from the earth to such a height that he could see nothing below, and flew like a fly so close under the moon that if he had not bent down he would have caught his cap in it. But in a little while he gained confidence and even began mocking the devil. (He was extremely amused by the way the devil sneezed and coughed when he took the little cyprus-wood cross off his neck and held it down to him. He purposely raised his hand to scratch his head, and the devil, thinking he was going to make the sign of the cross over him, flew along more swiftly than ever.) It was quite light at that height. The air was transparent, bathed in a light silvery mist. Everything was visible, and he could even see a sorcerer whisk by them like a hurricane, sitting in a pot, and the stars gathering together to play hide-and-seek, a whole swarm of spirits whirling away in a cloud, a devil dancing in the light of the moon and taking off his cap at the sight of the blacksmith galloping by, a broom flying back home, from which evidently a witch had just alighted at her destination. . . . And they met many other nasty things. They all stopped at the sight of the blacksmith to stare at him for a moment, and then whirled off and went on their way again. The blacksmith flew on till all at once Petersburg flashed before him, glittering with lights. (For a certain reason the city was illuminated that day.) The devil, flying over the city gate, turned into a horse and the blacksmith found himself mounted on a fiery steed in the middle of the street.

My goodness! the clatter, the uproar, the brilliant light; the walls rose up, four stories on each side; the thud of the horses' hoofs and the rumble of the wheels echoed and resounded from every quarter; houses seemed to pop up out of the ground at every step; the bridges trembled; carriages raced along; sled drivers and postilions shouted; the snow crunched under the thousand sleds flying from all parts; people passing along on foot huddled together, crowded under the houses which were studded with little lamps, and their immense shadows flitted over the walls with their heads reaching the roofs and the chimneys.

The blacksmith looked about him in amazement. It seemed to him as though all the houses had fixed their innumerable fiery eyes upon him, watching. Good Lord! he saw so many gentlemen in cloth fur-lined overcoats that he did not know whom to take off his cap to. "Good God, how many gentlemen are here!" thought the blacksmith. "I think everyone who comes along the street in a fur coat is the assessor and again the assessor! And those who are driving about in such wonderful chaises with glass windows, if they are not police captains they certainly must be commissars or perhaps something even more important." His words were cut short by a question from the devil:

"Am I to go straight to the Czarina?"

"No, I'm frightened," thought the blacksmith. "The Dnieper Cossacks, who marched in the autumn through Dikanka, are stationed here, where I don't know. They came from the camp with papers for the Czarina; anyway, I might ask their advice. Hey, Satan! creep into my pocket and take me to the Dnieper Cossacks."

And in one minute the devil became so thin and small that he had no difficulty creeping into the blacksmith's pocket. And before Vakula had time to look around he found himself in front of a big house, went up a staircase, hardly knowing what he was doing, opened a door, and drew back a little from the brilliant light on seeing the smartly furnished room; but he regained confidence a little when he recognized the Cossacks who had ridden through Dikanka and now, sitting on silk-covered sofas, their tar-smeared boots tucked under them, were smoking the strongest tobacco, usually called "root."

"Good day to you, gentlemen! God be with you, this is where we meet again," said the blacksmith, going up to them and tossing off a low bow.

"What man is that?" the one who was sitting just in front of the blacksmith asked another who was further away.

"You don't know me?" said the blacksmith. "It's me, Vakula the blacksmith! When you rode through Dikanka in the autumn you stayed nearly two days with me. God give you all health and long years! And I put a new iron hoop on the front wheel of your chaise!"

"Oh!" said the same Cossack, "it's that blacksmith who paints so well. Good day to you, neighbor! How has God brought you here?"

"Oh, I just wanted to have a look around. I was told . . . "

"Well, neighbor," said the Cossack, drawing himself up with dignity and wishing to show he could speak Russian too, "well, it's a big city."

The blacksmith, too, wanted to preserve his reputation and not to seem like a novice. Moreover, as we have had occasion to see before, he too could speak as if from a book.

"A considerable town!" he answered casually. "There is no denying the houses are very large, the pictures that are hanging up are uncommonly good. Many of the houses are painted exuberantly with letters in gold leaf. The configuration is superb, there is no other word for it!"

The Dnieper Cossacks, hearing the blacksmith express himself in such a manner, drew the most flattering conclusions in regard to him.

"We will have a little more talk with you, neighbor; now we are going at once to the Czarina."

"To the Czarina? Oh, be so kind, gentlemen, as to take me with you!"

"You?" a Cossack pronounced in the tone in which an old man speaks to his four-year-old charge when the latter asks to be seated on a real, big horse. "What would you do there? No, we can't do that. We are going to talk about our own affairs to the Czarina." And his face assumed an expression of great significance.

"Please take me!" the blacksmith persisted.

"Ask them to!" he whispered softly to the devil, banging on the pocket with his fist.

He had hardly said this, when another Cossack said: "Let's take him, friends!"

"Yes, let's take him!" others joined in.

"Put on the same clothing as we are wearing, then."

The blacksmith was hastily putting on a green coat when all at once the door opened and a man covered with gold braid said it was time to go.

Again the blacksmith was moved to wonder, as he was whisked along in an immense coach swaying on springs, as four-storied houses raced by him on both sides and the rumbling pavement seemed to be moving under the horses' hoofs.

"My goodness, how light it is!" thought the blacksmith to himself. "At home it is not so light as this in the daytime."

The coaches stopped in front of the palace. The Cossacks got out, went into a magnificent vestibule, and began ascending a brilliantly lighted staircase.

"What a staircase!" the blacksmith murmured to himself, "it's a pity to trample it with one's feet. What decorations! They say the stories are untrue! The devil they are! My goodness! what banisters, what workmanship! At least fifty rubles must have been spent on the iron alone!"

When they had mounted the stairs, the Cossacks walked through the first drawing room. The blacksmith followed them timidly, afraid of slipping on the parquet at every footstep. They walked through three drawing rooms, the blacksmith still overwhelmed with admiration. On entering the fourth, he could not help going up to a picture hanging on the wall. It was the Holy Virgin with the Child in her arms.

"What a picture! What a wonderful painting!" he thought. "It seems to be speaking! It seems to be alive! And the Holy Child! It's pressing its little hands together and laughing, poor thing! And the colors! My goodness, what colors! I think there is not a kopek-worth of ochre on it; it's all emerald green and crimson lake. And the blue simply glows! A fine piece of work! I'm sure the background was put in with the most expensive white lead. Wonderful as that painting is, though, this copper handle," he went on, going up to the door and fingering the lock, "is even more wonderful. Ah, what a fine finish! That's all done, I imagine, by German blacksmiths, and it must be terribly expensive."

Perhaps the blacksmith would have gone on reflecting for a long time, if a flunkey in livery had not nudged his arm and reminded him not to lag behind the others. The Cossacks passed through two more rooms and then stopped. They were told to wait in the third, in which there was a group of several generals in gold-braided uniforms. The Cossacks bowed in all directions and stood together.

A minute later, a rather thickset man of majestic stature, wearing the uniform of a Hetman and yellow boots, walked in, accompanied by a retinue. His hair was in disorder, he squinted a little, his face wore an expression of haughty dignity, and the habit of command could be seen in every movement. All the generals, who had been walking up and down rather superciliously in their gold uniforms, bustled about and seemed with low bows to be hanging on every word he uttered and even on his slightest gesture, so as to fly at once to carry out his wishes. But the Hetman did not even notice all that: he barely nodded to them and went up to the Cossacks.

The Cossacks all bowed low, to the ground.

"Are you all here?" he asked deliberately, speaking a little through his nose.

"All, little father!" answered the Cossacks, bowing again. "Don't forget to speak as I have told you!"

"No, little father, we will not forget."

"Is that the Czar?" asked the blacksmith of one of the Cossacks.

"Czar, indeed! It's Potiomkin himself," answered the other.

Voices were heard in the other room, and the blacksmith did not know which way to look for the number of ladies who walked in, wearing satin gowns with long trains, and courtiers in gold-laced coats with their hair tied in a tail at the back. He could see a blur of brilliance and nothing more.

The Cossacks all bowed down at once to the floor and cried out with one voice: "Have mercy, little mother, mercy!"

The blacksmith, too, though seeing nothing, stretched himself very zealously on the floor.

"Get up!" An imperious and at the same time pleasant voice sounded above them. Some of the courtiers bustled about and nudged the Cossacks.

"We will not get up, little mother! We will not get up! We will die, but we will not get up!" they shouted.

Potiomkin bit his lips. At last he went up himself and whispered sternly to one of the Cossacks. They rose to their feet.

Then the blacksmith, too, ventured to raise his head, and saw standing before him a short and, indeed, rather stout woman with blue eyes, and at the same time with that majestically smiling air which was so well able to subdue everything and could only belong to a queen.

"His Excellency has promised to make me acquainted today with my people whom I have not seen before," said the lady with the blue eyes, scrutinizing the men with curiosity.

"Are you well cared for here?" she went on, going nearer to them.

"Thank you, little mother! The provisions they give us are excellent, though the mutton here is not at all like what we have in Zaporozhye . . . What does our daily fare matter . . ?"

Potiomkin frowned, seeing that the Cossacks were saying some-thing quite different from what he had taught them . . .

One of them, drawing himself up with dignity, stepped forward:

"Be gracious, little mother! How have your faithful people angered you? Have we taken the hand of the vile Tartar? Have we come to agreement with the Turk? Have we been false to you in deed or in thought? How have we lost your favor? First we heard that you were commanding fortresses to be built everywhere against us; then we heard you mean to turn us into carbineers; now we hear of new oppressions. How are your Zaporozhye troops in fault? In having brought your army across the Perekop and helped your generals to slaughter the Tartars in the Crimea . . . ?"

Potiomkin casually rubbed with a little brush the diamonds with which his hands were studded and said nothing.

"What is it you want?" Catherine asked anxiously.

The Cossacks looked meaningly at one another.

"Now is the time! The Czarina asks what we want!" the blacksmith said to himself, and he suddenly flopped down on the floor.

"Your Imperial Majesty, do not command me to be punished! Show me mercy! Of what, be it said without offense to your Imperial Graciousness, are the little slippers made that are on your feet? I think there is no Swede nor a shoemaker in any kingdom in the world who can make them like that. Merciful heavens, if only my wife could wear such slippers!"

The Empress laughed. The courtiers laughed too. Potiomkin frowned and smiled at the same time. The Cossacks began nudging the blacksmith under the arm, wondering whether he had not gone out of his mind.

"Stand up!" the Empress said graciously. "If you wish to have slippers like these, it is very easy to arrange it. Bring him at once the very best slippers with gold on them! Indeed, this simple heartedness greatly pleases me! Here you have a subject worthy of your witty pen!" the Empress went on, turning to a gentleman with a full but rather pale face, who stood a little apart from the others and whose modest coat with big mother-of-pearl buttons on it showed that he was not one of the courtiers.

"You are too gracious, your Imperial Majesty. It needs a La Fontaine at least to do justice to it!" answered the man with the mother-of-pearl buttons, bowing.

"I tell you sincerely, I have not yet got over my delight at your Brigadier." You read so wonderfully well! I have heard, though," the Empress went on, turning again to the Cossacks, "that none of you are married in your camp."

"What next, little mother! Why, you know yourself, a man can not live without a wife," answered the same Cossack who had talked to the blacksmith, and the blacksmith wondered, hearing him address the Czarina, as though purposely, in coarse language, speaking like a peasant, as it is commonly called, though he could speak as if from a book.

"They are sly fellows!" he thought to himself. "I'll bet he does not do that for nothing."

"We are not monks," the Cossack went on, "but sinful folk. Ready like all honest Christians to fall into sin. There are among us many who have wives, but do not live with them in the camp. There are some who have wives in Poland; there are some who have wives in the Ukraine; there are some who have wives even in Turkey."

At that moment they brought the blacksmith the slippers.

"God, what fine embroidery!" he cried joyfully, taking the slippers. "Your Imperial Majesty! If the slippers on your feet are like this—and in them Your Honor, I expect, goes skating on the ice—what must the feet themselves be like! They must be made of pure sugar at least, I should think!"

The Empress, who had in fact very well-shaped and charming feet, could not help smiling at hearing such a compliment from the lips of a simple hearted blacksmith, who in his Dnieper Cossack uniform might be considered a handsome fellow in spite of his swarthy face.

Delighted with such gracious attention, the blacksmith would have liked to question the pretty Czarina thoroughly about everything: whether it was true that Czars eat nothing but honey, fat bacon, and such; but, feeling that the Cossacks were digging him in the ribs, he made up his mind to keep quiet. And when the Empress, turning to the older men, began questioning them about their manner of life and customs in the camp, he, stepping back, stooped down to his pocket, and said softly: "Get me away from here, quickly!" And at once he found himself outside the city gates.

"He is drowned! I swear he is drowned! May I never leave this spot if he is not drowned!" lisped the weaver's fat wife, standing with a group of Dikanka women in the middle of the street.

"Why, am I a liar, then? Have I stolen anyone's cow? Have I put the evil eye on someone, that I am not to be believed?" shouted a purple-nosed woman in a Cossack coat, waving her arms. "May I never want to drink water again if old Dame Pereperchikha didn't see with her own eyes the blacksmith hanging himself!"

"Has the blacksmith hanged himself? Well, "I never!" said the mayor, coming out of Chub's hut, and he stopped and pressed closer to the group.

"You had better say, may you never want to drink vodka, you old drunkard!" answered the weaver's wife. "He must be as crazy as you to hang himself! He drowned himself! He drowned himself in the hole in the ice! I know that as well as I know that you were in the tavern just now."

"You disgrace! See what she throws up at me!" the woman with the purple nose retorted wrathfully. "You had better hold your tongue, you wretch! Do you think I don't know that the sexton comes to see you every evening?"

The weaver's wife flared up.

"What about the sexton? Whom does he go to? What lies are you telling?"

"The sexton?" piped the sexton's wife, squeezing her way up to the combatants, in an old blue cotton coat lined with hareskin. "I'll let the sexton know! Who was it said the sexton?"

"Well, this is the lady the sexton visits!" said the woman with the purple nose, pointing to the weaver's wife.

"So it's you, you bitch!" said the sexton's wife, stepping up to the weaver's wife. "So it's you, is it, witch, who cast a spell over him and gave him foul poison to make him come to you!"

"Get behind me, Satan!" said the weaver's wife, staggering back. "Oh, you cursed witch, may you never live to see your children! Wretched creature! Tfoo!"

Here the sexton's wife spat straight into the other woman's face.

The weaver's wife tried to do the same, but spat instead on the unshaven chin of the mayor, who had come close to the combatants so that he might hear the quarrel better.

"Ah, nasty woman!" cried the mayor, wiping his face with the skirt of his coat and lifting his whip.

This gesture sent them all flying in different directions, cursing loudly.

"How disgusting!" repeated the mayor, still wiping his face. "So the blacksmith is drowned! My goodness! What a fine painter he was! What good knives and reaping hooks and plows he could forge! What a strong man he was! Yes," he went on musing; "there are not many fellows like that in our village. To be sure, I did notice while I was in that damned sack that the poor fellow was very much depressed. So that is the end of the blacksmith! He was and is not! And I was meaning to have my dapple mare shod . . . !" And filled with such Christian reflections, the mayor quietly made his way to his own hut.

Oksana was much troubled when the news reached her. She put little faith in the woman Pereperchikha's having seen it and in the women's talk; she knew that the blacksmith was too pious a man to bring himself to send his soul to perdition. But what if he really had gone away, intending never to return to the village? And, indeed, in any place it would be hard to find as fine a fellow as the black-smith. And how he had loved her! He had endured her whims longer than any one of them. . . . All night long the beauty turned over from her right side to her left and her left to her right, and could not fall asleep. Naked, she tossed sensuously in the darkness of her room. She reviled herself almost aloud; grew peaceful; made up her mind to think of nothing—and kept thinking all the time. She was in a perfect fever, and by the morning head over ears in love with the blacksmith.

Chub expressed neither pleasure nor sorrow at Vakula's fate. His thoughts were absorbed by one subject: he could not forget the treachery of Solokha and never stopped abusing her even in his sleep.

Morning came. Even before daybreak the church was full of people. Elderly women in white linen wimples, in white cloth tunics, crossed themselves piously at the church porch. Ladies in green and yellow blouses, some even in dark blue overdresses with gold streamers behind, stood in front of them. Girls who had a whole shopful of ribbons twined on their heads, and necklaces, crosses, and coins around their necks, tried to make their way closer to the icon-stand. But in front of all stood the gentlemen and humble peasants with mustaches, with forelocks, with thick necks and newly shaven chins, for the most part wearing hooded cloaks, below which peeped a white or sometimes a dark blue jacket. Wherever one looked every face had a festive air. The mayor was licking his lips in anticipation of the sausage with which he would break his fast; the girls were thinking how they would skate with the boys on the ice; the old women murmured prayers more zealously than ever. All over the church one could hear the Cossack Sverbiguz bowing to the ground. Only Oksana stood feeling unlike herself: she prayed without praying. So many different feelings, each more amazing, each more distressing than the other, crowded upon her heart that her face expressed nothing but overwhelming confusion; tears quivered in her eyes. The girls could not think why it was and did not suspect that the blacksmith was responsible. However, not only Oksana was concerned about the blacksmith. All the villagers observed that the holiday did not seem like a holiday, that something was lacking. To make things worse, the sexton was hoarse after his travels in the sack and he wheezed scarcely audibly; it is true that the chorister who was on a visit to the village sang the bass splendidly, but how much better it would have been if they had had the blacksmith too, who used always when they were singing Our Father or the Holy Cherubim to step up into the choir and from there sing it with the same chant with which it is sung in Poltava. Moreover, he alone performed the duty of a churchwarden. Matins were already over; after matins mass was over. . . . Where indeed could the blacksmith have vanished to?

It was still night as the devil flew even more swiftly back with the blacksmith, and in a flash Vakula found himself inside his own hut. At that moment the cock crowed.

"Where are you off to?" cried the blacksmith, catching the devil by his tail as he was about to run away. "Wait a moment, friend, that's not all: I haven't thanked you yet." Then, seizing a switch, he gave him three lashes, and the poor devil started running like a peasant who has just had a beating from the tax assessor. And so, instead of tricking, tempting, and fooling others, the enemy of mankind was fooled himself. After that Vakula went into the outer room, made himself a hole in the hay, and slept till dinner-time. When he woke up he was frightened at seeing that the sun was already high. "I've overslept myself and missed matins and mass!"

Then the worthy blacksmith was overwhelmed with distress, thinking that no doubt God, as a punishment for his sinful intention of damning his soul, had sent this heavy sleep, which had prevented him from even being in church on this solemn holiday. However, comforting himself with the thought that next week he would confess all this to the priest and that from that day he would begin making fifty genuflections a day for a whole year, he glanced into the hut; but there was no one there. Apparently Solokha had not yet returned.

Carefully he drew out from the breast of his coat the slippers and again marveled at the costly workmanship and at the wonderful adventure of the previous night. He washed and dressed himself in his best, put on the very clothes which he had got from the Dnieper Cossacks, took out of a chest a new cap of good astrakhan with a dark blue top not once worn since he had bought it while staying in Poltava; he also took out a new girdle of rainbow colors; he put all this together with a whip in a kerchief and set off straight to see Chub.

Chub opened his eyes wide when the blacksmith walked into his hut, and did not know what to wonder at most: the blacksmith's having risen from the dead, the blacksmith's having dared to come to see him, or the blacksmith's being dressed up as such a dandy, like a Dnieper Cossack. But he was even more astonished when Vakula untied the kerchief and laid before him a new cap and a girdle such as had never been seen in the village, and then fell down on his knees before him, and said in a tone of entreaty: "Have mercy, father! Be not angry! Here is a whip; beat me as much as your heart may desire. I give myself up, I repent of everything! Beat, but only be not angry. You were once a comrade of my father's, you ate bread and salt together and drank the cup of good-will."

It was not without secret satisfaction that Chub saw the blacksmith, who had never bowed to anyone in the village and who could twist five-kopek pieces and horseshoes in his hands like pan-cakes, lying now at his feet. In order to maintain his dignity still further, Chub took the whip and gave him three strokes on the back. "Well, that's enough; get up! Always obey the old! Let us forget everything that has passed between us. Come, tell me now what is it that you want?"

"Give me Oksana for my wife, father!"

Chub thought a little, looked at the cap and the girdle. The cap was delightful and the girdle, too, was not inferior to it; he thought of the treacherous Solokha and said resolutely: "Good! send the matchmakers!"

"Aie!" shrieked Oksana, as she crossed the threshold and saw the blacksmith, and she gazed at him with astonishment and delight.

"Look, what slippers I have brought you!" said Vakula, "they are the same as the Czarina wears!"

"No, no! I don't want slippers!" she said, waving her arms and keeping her eyes fixed upon him. "I am ready without slippers . . ." She blushed and could say no more.

The blacksmith went up to her and took her by the hand; the beauty looked down. Never before had she looked so exquisitely lovely. The enchanted blacksmith gently kissed her; her face flushed crimson and she was even lovelier.

The bishop of blessed memory was driving through Dikanka. He admired the site on which the village stands, and as he drove down the street stopped before a new hut.

"And whose is this hut so gaily painted?" asked his Reverence of a beautiful woman, who was standing near the door with a baby in her arms.

"The blacksmith Vakula's!" Oksana, for it was she, told him, bowing.

"Splendid! splendid work!" said his Reverence, examining the doors and windows. The windows were all outlined with a ring of red paint; everywhere on the doors there were Cossacks on horse-back with pipes in their teeth.

But his Reverence was even warmer in his praise of Vakula when he learned that by way of church penance he had painted free of charge the whole of the left choir in green with red flowers.

But that was not all. On the wall, to one side as you go in at the church, Vakula had painted the devil in hell—such a loathsome figure that everyone spat as he passed. And the women would take a child up to the picture, if it would go on crying in their arms, and would say: "There, look! What a kaka!" And the child, restraining its tears, would steal a glance at the picture and nestle closer to its mother.

Bobok

Fyodor Dostoevsky

Semyon Ardalyonovitch said to me all of a sudden the day before yesterday:

"Why, will you ever be sober, Ivan Ivanovitch? Tell me that, pray."

A strange requirement. I did not resent it, I am a timid man; but here they have actually made me out mad. An artist painted my portrait as it happened: "After all, you are a literary man," he said. I submitted, he exhibited it. I read: "Go and look at that morbid face suggesting insanity."

It may be so, but think of putting it so bluntly into print. In print everything ought to be decorous; there ought to be ideals, while instead of that . . .

Say it indirectly, at least; that's what you have style for. But no, he doesn't care to do it indirectly. Nowadays humour and a fine style have disappeared, and abuse is accepted as wit. I do not resent it: but God knows I am not enough of a literary man to go out of my mind. I have written a novel, it has not been published. I have written articles - they have been refused. Those articles I took about from one editor to another; everywhere they refused them: you have no salt they told me. "What sort of salt do you want?" I asked with a sneer. "Attic salt?"

They did not even understand, For the most part I translate from the French for the booksellers. I write advertisements for shopkeepers too: "Unique opportunity! Fine tea, from our own plantations . . ." I made a nice little sum over a panegyric on his deceased Excellency Pyotr Matveyitch. I compiled the "Art of pleasing the ladies", a commission from a bookseller. I have brought out some six little works of this kind in the course of my life. I am thinking of making a collection of the bons mobs of Voltaire, but am afraid it may seem a little flat to our people. Voltaire's no good now; nowadays we want a cudgel, not Voltaire. We knock each other's last teeth out nowadays. Well, so that's the whole extent of my literary activity. Though indeed I do send round letters to the editors gratis and fully signed. I give them all sorts of counsels and admonitions, criticize and point out the true path. The letter I sent last week to an editor's office was the fortieth I had sent in the last two years. I have wasted four roubles over stamps alone for them. My temper is at the bottom of it all.

I believe that the artist who painted me did so not for the sake of literature, but for the sake of two symmetrical warts on my forehead, a natural phenomenon, he would say. They have no ideas, so now they are out for phenomena. And didn't he succeed in getting my warts in his portrait - to the life. That is what they call realism.

And as to madness, a great many people were put down as mad among us last year. And in such language! "With such original talent . . . . and yet, after all, it appears". . . "however, one ought to have foreseen it long ago." That is rather artful; so that from the point of view of pure art one may really commend it. Well, but after all, these so-called madmen have turned out cleverer than ever. So it seems the critics can call them mad, but they cannot produce anyone better.

The wisest of all, in my opinion, is he who can, if only once a month, call himself a fool - a faculty unheard of nowadays. In old days, once a year at any rate a fool would recognize that he was a fool, but nowadays not a bit of it. And they have so muddled things up that there is no telling a fool from a wise man. They have done that on purpose.

I remember a witty Spaniard saying when, two hundred and fifty years ago, the French built their first madhouses: "They have shut up all their fools in a house apart, to make sure that they are wise men themselves." Just so: you don't show your own wisdom by shutting someone else in a madhouse. "K. has gone out of his mind, means that we are sane now." No, it doesn't mean that yet.

Fyodor Dostoevsky   Bobok

Hang it though, why am I maundering on? I go on grumbling and grumbling. Even my maidservant is sick of me. Yesterday a friend came to see me. "Your style is changing," he said; "it is choppy: you chop and chop - and then a parenthesis, then a parenthesis in the parenthesis, then you stick in something else in brackets, then you begin chopping and chopping again."

The friend is right. Something strange is happening to me. My character is changing and my head aches. I am beginning to see and hear strange things, not voices exactly, but as though someone beside me were muttering, "bobok, bobok, bobok!"

What's the meaning of this bobok? I must divert my mind.

I went out in search of diversion, I hit upon a funeral. A distant relation - a collegiate counselor, however. A widow and five daughters, all marriageable young ladies. What must it come to even to keep them in slippers. Their father managed it, but now there is only a little pension. They will have to eat humble pie. They have always received me ungraciously. And indeed I should not have gone to the funeral now had it not been for a peculiar circumstance. I followed the procession to the cemetery with the rest; they were stuck-up and held aloof from me. My uniform was certainly rather shabby. It's five-and-twenty years, I believe, since I was at the cemetery; what a wretched place!

To begin with the smell. There were fifteen hearses, with palls varying in expensiveness; there were actually two catafalques. One was a general's and one some lady's. There were many mourners, a great deal of feigned mourning and a great deal of open gaiety. The clergy have nothing to complain of; it brings them a good income. But the smell, the smell. I should not like to be one of the clergy here.

I kept glancing at the faces of the dead cautiously, distrusting my impressionability. Some had a mild expression, some looked unpleasant. As a rule the smiles were disagreeable, and in some cases very much so. I don't like them; they haunt one's dreams.

During the service I went out of the church into the air: it was a grey day, but dry. It was cold too, but then it was October. I walked about among the tombs. They are of different grades. The third grade cost thirty roubles; it's decent and not so very dear. The first two grades are tombs in the church and under the porch; they cost a pretty penny. On this occasion they were burying in tombs of the third grade six persons, among them the general and the lady.

I looked into the graves - and it was horrible: water and such water! Absolutely green, and . . . but there, why talk of it! The gravedigger was baling it out every minute. I went out while the service was going on and strolled outside the gates. Close by was an almshouse, and a little further off there was a restaurant. It was not a bad little restaurant: there was lunch and everything. There were lots of the mourners here. I noticed a great deal of gaiety and genuine heartiness. I had something to eat and drink.

Then I took part in the bearing of the coffin from the church to the grave. Why is it that corpses in their coffins are so heavy? They say it is due to some sort of inertia, that the body is no longer directed by its owner . . . or some nonsense of that sort, in opposition to the laws of mechanics and common sense. I don't like to hear people who have nothing but a general education venture to solve the problems that require special knowledge; and with us that's done continually. Civilians love to pass opinions about subjects that are the province of the soldier and even of the field-marshal; while men who have been educated as engineers prefer discussing philosophy and political economy.

I did not go to the requiem service. I have some pride, and if I am only received owing to some special necessity, why force myself on their dinners, even if it be a funeral dinner. The only thing I don't understand is why I stayed at the cemetery; I sat on a tombstone and sank into appropriate reflections.

I began with the Moscow exhibition and ended with reflecting upon astonishment in the abstract. My deductions about astonishment were these:

"To be surprised at everything is stupid of course, and to be astonished at nothing is a great deal more becoming and for some reason accepted as good form. But that is not really true. To my mind to be astonished at nothing is much more stupid than to be astonished at everything. And, moreover, to be astonished at nothing is almost the same as feeling respect for nothing. And indeed a stupid man is incapable of feeling respect."

"But what I desire most of all is to feel respect. I thirst to feel respect," one of my acquaintances said to me the other day.

He thirsts to feel respect! Goodness, I thought, what would happen to you if you dared to print that nowadays? At that point I sank into forgetfulness. I don't like reading the epitaphs of tombstones: they are everlastingly the same. An unfinished sandwich was lying on the tombstone near me; stupid and inappropriate. I threw it on the ground, as it was not bread but only a sandwich. Though I believe it is not a sin to throw bread on the earth, but only on the floor. I must look it up in Suvorin's calendar.

I suppose I sat there a long time-too long a time, in fact; I must have lain down on a long stone which was of the shape of a marble coffin. And how it happened I don't know, but I began to hear things of all sorts being said. At first I did not pay attention to it, but treated it with contempt. But the conversation went on. I heard muffled sounds as though the speakers' mouths were covered with a pillow, and at the same time they were distinct and very near. I came to myself, sat up and began listening attentively.

"Your Excellency, it's utterly impossible. You led hearts, I return your lead, and here you play the seven of diamonds. You ought to have given me a hint about diamonds."

"What, play by hard and fast rules? Where is the charm of that?"

"You must, your Excellency. One can't do anything without something to go upon. We must play with dummy, let one hand not be turned up."

"Well, you won't find a dummy here."

What conceited words! And it was queer and unexpected. One was such a ponderous, dignified voice, the other softly suave; I should not have believed it if I had not heard it myself. I had not been to the requiem dinner, I believe. And yet how could they be playing preference here and what general was this? That the sounds came from under the tombstones of that there could be no doubt. I bent down and read on the tomb:

"Here lies the body of Major-General Pervoyedov . . . a cavalier of such and such orders." Hm! "Passed away in August of this year . . . fifty-seven. . . . Rest, beloved ashes, till the joyful dawn!"

Hm, dash it, it really is a general! There was no monument on the grave from which the obsequious voice came, there was only a tombstone. He must have been a fresh arrival. From his voice he was a lower court councilor.

"Oh-ho-ho-ho!" I heard in a new voice a dozen yards from the general's resting-place, coming from quite a fresh grave. The voice belonged to a man and a plebeian, mawkish with its affectation of religious fervor. "Oh-ho-ho-ho!"

"Oh, here he is hiccupping again!" cried the haughty and disdainful voice of an irritated lady, apparently of the highest society. "It is an affliction to be by this shopkeeper!"

"I didn't hiccup; why, I've had nothing to eat. It's simply my nature. Really, madam, you don't seem able to get rid of your caprices here."

"Then why did you come and lie down here?"

"They put me here, my wife and little children put me here, I did not lie down here of myself. The mystery of death! And I would not have lain down beside you not for any money; I lie here as befitting my fortune, judging by the price. For we can always do that - pay for a tomb of the third grade."

"You made money, I suppose? You fleeced people?"

"Fleece you, indeed! We haven't seen the colour of your money since January. There's a little bill against you at the shop."

"Well, that's really stupid; to try and recover debts here is too stupid, to my thinking! Go to the surface. Ask my niece - she is my heiress."

"There's no asking anyone now, and no going anywhere. We have both reached our limit and, before the judgment-seat of God, are equal in our sins."

"In our sins," the lady mimicked him contemptuously. "Don't dare to speak to me."

"Oh-ho-ho-ho!"

"You see, the shopkeeper obeys the lady, your Excellency."

"Why shouldn't he?"

"Why, your Excellency, because, as we all know, things are different here."

"Different? How?"

"We are dead, so to speak, your Excellency."

"Oh, yes! But still . . ."

Well, this is an entertainment, it is a fine show, I must say! If it has come to this down here, what can one expect on the surface? But what a queer business! I went on listening, however, though with extreme indignation.

Fyodor Dostoevsky   **Bobok**

"Yes, I should like a taste of life! Yes, you know . . . I should like a taste of fife." I heard a new voice suddenly somewhere in the space between the general and the irritable lady.

"Do you hear, your Excellency, our friend is at the same game again. For three days at a time he says nothing, and then he bursts out with 'I should like a taste of life, yes, a taste of life!' And with such appetite, he-he!"

"And such frivolity."

"It gets hold of him, your Excellency, and do you know, he is growing sleepy, quite sleepy - he has been here since April; and then all of a sudden 'I should like a taste of life!'"

"It is rather dull, though," observed his Excellency.

"It is, your Excellency. Shall we tease Avdotya Ignatyevna again, he-he?"

"No, spare me, please. I can't endure that quarrelsome virago."

"And I can't endure either of you," cried the virago disdainfully. "You are both of you bores and can't tell me anything ideal. I know one little story about you, your Excellency - don't turn up your nose, please - how a manservant swept you out from under a married couple's bed one morning."

"Nasty woman," the general muttered through his teeth.

"Avdotya lgnatycvna, ma'am," the shopkeeper wailed suddenly again, "my dear lady, don't be angry, but tell me, am I going through the ordeal by torment now, or is it some- thing else?"

"Ah, he is at it again, as I expected! For there's a smell from him which means he is turning round!"

"I am not turning round, ma'am, and there's no particular smell from me, for I've kept my body whole as it should be, while you're regularly high. For the smell is really horrible even for a place like this. I don't speak of it, merely from politeness."

"Ah, you horrid, insulting wretch. He positively stinks and talks about me."

"Oh-ho-ho-ho! If only the time for my requiem would come quickly: I should hear their tearful voices over my head, my wife's lament and my children's soft weeping! . . ."

"Well, that's a thing to fret for! They'll stuff themselves with funeral rice and go home. . . . Oh, I wish somebody would wake up!"

249

"Avdotya Ignatyevna," said the insinuating government clerk, "wait a bit, the new arrivals will speak."

"And are there any young people among them?"

"Yes, there are, Avdotya lgnatyevna. There are some not more than lads."

"Oh, how welcome that would be!"

"Haven't they begun yet?" inquired his Excellency.

"Even those who came the day before yesterday haven't awakened yet, your Excellency. As you know, they sometimes don't speak for a week. It's a good job that today and yesterday and the day before they brought a whole lot. As it is, they are all last year's for seventy feet round."

"Yes, it will be interesting."

"Yes, your Excellency, they buried Tarasevitch, the privy councilor, today. I knew it from the voices. I know his nephew, he helped to lower the coffin just now."

"Hm, where is he, then?"

"Five steps from you, your Excellency, on the left. . . . Almost at your feet. You should make his acquaintance, your Excellency."

"Hm, no - it's not for me to make advances."

"Oh, he will begin of himself, your Excellency. He will be flattered. Leave it to me, your Excellency, and I . . ."

"Oh, oh! . . . What is happening to me?" croaked the frightened voice of a new arrival.

"A new arrival, your Excellency, a new arrival, thank God! And how quick he's been! Sometimes they don't say a word for a week."

"Oh, I believe it's a young man!" Avdotya Ignatyevna cried shrilly.

"I. . . I . . . it was a complication, and so sudden!" faltered the young man again. "Only the evening before, Schultz said to me, 'There's a complication,' and I died suddenly before morning. Oh! oh!"

"Well, there's no help for it, young man," the general observed graciously, evidently pleased at a new arrival. "You must be comforted. You are kindly welcome to our Vale of Jehoshaphat, so to call it. We are kind-hearted people, you will come to know us and appreciate us. Major-General Vassili Vassilitch Pervoyedov, at your service."

"Oh, no, no! Certainly not! I was at Schultz's; I had a complication, you know, at first it was my chest and a cough, and then I caught a cold: my lungs and influenza . . . and all of a sudden, quite unexpectedly . . . the worst of all was its being so unexpected."

"You say it began with the chest," the government clerk put in suavely, as though he wished to reassure the new arrival.

"Yes, my chest and catarrh and then no catarrh, but still the chest, and I couldn't breathe . . . and you know. . . "

"I know, I know. But if it was the chest you ought to have gone to Ecke and not to Schultz."

"You know, I kept meaning to go to Botkin's, and all at once . . ."

"Botkin is quite prohibitive," observed the general.

"Oh, no, he is not forbidding at all; I've heard he is so attentive and foretells everything beforehand."

"His Excellency was referring to his fees," the government clerk corrected him.

"Oh, not at all, he only asks three roubles, and he makes such an examination, and gives you a prescription . . . and I was very anxious to see him, for I have been told . . . Well, gentlemen, had I better go to Ecke or to Botkin?"

"What? To whom?" The general's corpse shook with agreeable laughter. The government clerk echoed it in falsetto.

"Dear boy, dear, delightful boy, how I love you!" Avdotya Ignatyevna squealed ecstatically. "I wish they had put some- one like you next to me."

No, that was too much! And these were the dead of our times! Still, I ought to listen to more and not be in too great a hurry to draw conclusions. That sniveling new arrival - I remember him just now in his coffin - had the expression of a frightened chicken, the most revolting expression in the world! However, let us wait and see.

But what happened next was such a Bedlam that I could not keep it all in my memory. For a great many woke up at once; an official - a civil councilor - woke up, and began discussing at once the project of a new sub-committee in a government department and of the probable transfer of various functionaries in connection with the sub-committee - which very greatly interested the general. I must confess I learnt a great deal that was new myself, so much so that I marveled at the channels by which one may sometimes in the metropolis learn government news. Then an engineer half woke up, but for a long time muttered absolute nonsense, so that our friends left off worrying him and let him lie till he was ready. At last the distinguished lady who had been buried in the morning under the catafalque showed symptoms of the reanimation of the tomb. Lebeziatnikov (for the obsequious lower court councilor whom I detested and who lay beside General Pervoyedov was called, it appears, Lebeziatnikov) became much excited, and surprised that they were all waking up so soon this time. I must own I was surprised too; though some of those who woke had been buried for three days, as, for instance, a very young girl of sixteen who kept giggling . . . giggling in a horrible and predatory way.

"Your Excellency, privy councilor Tarasevitch is waking!" Lebeziatnikov announced with extreme fussiness.

"Eh? What?" the privy councilor, waking up suddenly mumbled, with a lisp of disgust. There was a note of ill-humored peremptoriness in the sound of his voice.

I listened with curiosity - for during the last few days I had heard something about Tarasevitch – shocking and upsetting in the extreme.

"It's I, your Excellency, so far only I."

"What is your petition? What do you want?"

"Merely to inquire after your Excellency's health; in these unaccustomed surroundings everyone feels at first, as it were, oppressed. General Pervoyedov wishes to have the honour of making your Excellency's acquaintance, and hopes . . ."

"I've never heard of him."

"Surely, your Excellency! General Pervoyedov, Vassili Vassilitch . . ."

"Are you General Pervoyedov?"

"No, your Excellency, I am only the lower court councilor Lebeziatnikov, at your service, but General Pervoyedov. . ."

"Nonsense! And I beg you to leave me alone."

"Let him be." General Pervoyedov at last himself checked with dignity the disgusting officiousness of his sycophant in the grave.

"He is not fully awake, your Excellency, you must consider that; it's the novelty of it all. When he is fully awake he will take it differently."

"Let him be," repeated the general.

"Vassili Vassilitch! Hey, your Excellency!" a perfectly new voice shouted loudly and aggressively from close beside Avdotya lgnatyevna. It was a voice of gentlemanly insolence, with the languid pronunciation now fashionable and an arrogant drawl. "I've been watching you all for the last two hours. Do you remember me, Vassili Vassilitch? My name is Klinevitch, we met at the Volokonskys' where you, too, were received as a guest, I am sure I don't know why."

"What, Count Pyotr Petrovitch? . . .Can it be really you. . . and at such an early age? How sorry I am to hear it."

"Oh, I am sorry myself, though I really don't mind, and I want to amuse myself as far as I can everywhere. And I am not a count but a baron, only a baron. We are only a set of scurvy barons, risen from being flunkeys, but why I don't know and I don't care. I am only a scoundrel of the pseudo-aristocratic society, and I am regarded as 'a charming polisson'. My father is a wretched little general, and my mother was at one time received en haut lieu. With the help of the Jew Zifel I forged fifty thousand rouble notes last year and then I informed against him, while Julic Charpentier de Lusignan carried off the money to Bordeaux. And only fancy, I was engaged to be married - to a girl still at school, three months under sixteen, with a dowry of ninety thousand. Avdotya lgnatyevna, do you remember how you seduced me fifteen years ago when I was a boy of fourteen in the Corps des Pages?"

"Ah, that's you, you rascal! Well, you are a godsend, anyway, for here. . . ."

"You were mistaken in suspecting your neighbour, the business gentleman, of unpleasant fragrance. . . . I said nothing, but I laughed. The stench came from me: they had to bury me in a nailed-up coffin."

"Ugh, you horrid creature! Still, I am glad you are here; you can't imagine the lack of life and wit here."

"Quite so, quite so, and I intend to start here something original. Your Excellency - I don't mean you, Pervoyedov - your

Excellency the other one, Tarasevitch, the privy councilor! Answer! I am Klinevitch, who took you to Mlle. Furie in Lent, do you hear?"

"I do, Klinevitch, and I am delighted, and trust me .

"I wouldn't trust you with a halfpenny, and I don't care. I simply want to kiss you, dear old man, but luckily I can't. Do you know, gentlemen, what this grand-pere's little game was? He died three or four days ago, and would you believe it, he left a deficit of four hundred thousand government money from the fund for widows and orphans. He was the sole person in control of it for some reason, so that his accounts were not audited for the last eight years. I can fancy what long faces they all have now, and what they call him. It's a delectable thought, isn't it? I have been wondering for the last year how a wretched old man of seventy, gouty and rheumatic, succeeded in preserving the physical energy for his debaucheries - and now the riddle is solved! Those widows and orphans - the very thought of them must have egged him on! I knew about it long ago, I was the only one who did know; it was Julie told me, and as soon as I discovered it, I attacked him in a friendly way at once in Easter week: 'Give me twenty-five thousand, if you don't they'll look into your accounts to-morrow.' And just fancy, he had only thirteen thousand left then, so it seems it was very apropos his dying now. Grand-pere, grand-pere; do you hear?"

"Cher Khnevitch, I quite agree with you, and there was no need for you . . . to go into such details. Life is so full of suffering and torment and so little to make up for it . . . that I wanted at last to be at rest, and so far as I can see I hope to get all I can from here too."

"I bet that he has already sniffed Katiche Berestoy!"

"Who? What Katiche?" There was a rapacious quiver in the old man's voice.

"A-ah, what Katiche? Why, here on the left, five paces from me and ten from you. She has been here for five days, and if only you knew, grand-pere, what a little wretch she is! Of good family and breeding and a monster, a regular monster! I did not introduce her to anyone there, I was the only one who knew her. . . . Katiche, answer!"

"He-he-he!" the girl responded with a jangling laugh, in which there was a note of something as sharp as the prick of a needle. "He-he-he!"

"And a little blonde?" the grand-pere faltered, drawling out the syllables.

"He-he-he!"

"I . . . have long . . . I have long," the old man faltered breathlessly, "cherished the dream of a little fair thing of fifteen and just in such surroundings."

"Ach, the monster!" cried Avdotya Ignatyevna.

"Enough!" Klinevitch decided. "I see there is excellent material. We shall soon arrange things better. The great thing is to spend the rest of our time cheerfully; but what time? Hey, you, government clerk, Lebeziatnikov or whatever it is, I hear that's your name!"

"Semyon Yevseitch Lebeziatnikov, lower court councillor, at your service, very, very, very much delighted to meet you."

"I don't care whether you are delighted or not, but you seem to know everything here. Tell me first of all how it is we can talk? I've been wondering ever since yesterday. We are dead and yet we are talking and seem to be moving - and yet we are not talking and not moving. What jugglery is this?"

"If you want an explanation, baron, Platon Nikolaevitch could give you one better than I."

"What Platon Nikolaevitch is that? To the point. Don't beat about the bush."

"Platon Nikolaevitch is our home-grown philosopher, scientist and Master of Arts. He has brought out several philosophical works, but for the last three months he has been getting quite drowsy, and there is no stirring him up now. Once a week he mutters something utterly irrelevant."

"To the point, to the point!"

"He explains all this by the simplest fact, namely, that when we were living on the surface we mistakenly thought that death there was death. The body revives, as it were, here, the remains of life are concentrated, but only in consciousness. I don't know how to express it, but life goes on, as it were, by inertia. In his opinion everything is concentrated somewhere in consciousness and goes on for two or three months . . . sometimes even for half a year. . . . There is one here, for instance, who is almost completely decomposed, but once every six weeks he suddenly utters one word, quite senseless of course, about some bobok, 'Bobok,

bobok,' but you see that an imperceptible speck of life is still warm within him."

"It's rather stupid. Well, and how is it I have no sense of smell and yet I feel there's a stench?"

"That . . . he-he . . . Well, on that point our philosopher is a bit foggy. It's apropos of smell, he said, that the stench one perceives here is, so to speak, moral - he-he! It's the stench of the soul, he says, that in these two or three months it may have time to recover itself ... and this is, so to speak, the last mercy. . . . Only, I think, baron, that these are mystic ravings very excusable in his position . . ."

"Enough; all the rest of it, I am sure, is nonsense. The great thing is that we have two or three months more of life and then - bobok! I propose to spend these two months as agreeably as possible, and so to arrange everything on a new basis. Gentlemen! I propose to cast aside all shame."

"Ah, let us cast aside all shame, let us!" many voices could be heard saying; and strange to say, several new voices were audible, which must have belonged to others newly awakened. The engineer, now fully awake, boomed out his agreement with peculiar delight. The girl Katiche giggled gleefully.

"Oh, how I long to cast off all shame!" Avdotya lgnatyevna exclaimed rapturously.

"I say, if Avdotya lgnatyevna wants to cast off all shame. ."

"No, no, no, Klinevitch, I was ashamed up there all the same, but here I should like to cast off shame, I should like it awfully."

"I understand, Klinevitch," boomed the engineer, "that you want to rearrange life here on new and rational principles."

"Oh, I don't care a hang about that! For that we'll wait for Kudeyarov who was brought here yesterday. When he wakes he'll tell you all about it. He is such a personality, such a titanic personality! Tomorrow they'll bring along another natural scientist, I believe, an officer for certain, and three or four days later a journalist, and, I believe, his editor with him. But deuce take them all, there will be a little group of us anyway, and things will arrange themselves. Though meanwhile I don't want us to be telling lies. That's all I care about, for that is one thing that matters. One cannot exist on the surface without lying, for life and lying are synonymous, but here we will amuse ourselves by not lying. Hang it all, the grave has some value after all! We'll all tell our stories aloud, and we won't be ashamed of anything. First of all I'll tell you about myself. I am one of the predatory kind, you know. All that was bound and held in check by rotten cords up there on the surface. Away with cords and let us spend these two months in shameless truthfulness! Let us strip and be naked!"

"Let us be naked, let us be naked!" cried all the voices.

"I long to be naked, I long to be," Avdotya Ignatyevna shrilled.

"Ah . . . ah, I see we shall have fun here; I don't want Ecke after all."

"No, I tell you. Give me a taste of life!"

"He-he-he!" giggled Katiche.

"The great thing is that no one can interfere with us, and though I see Pervoyedov is in a temper, he can't reach me with his hand. Grand-pere, do you agree?"

"I fully agree, fully, and with the utmost satisfaction, but on condition that Katiche is the first to give us her biography."

"I protest! I protest with all my heart!" General Pervoyedov brought out firmly.

"Your Excellency!" the scoundrel Lebeziatnikov persuaded him in a murmur of fussy excitement, "your Excellency, it will be to our advantage to agree. Here, you see, there's this girl's . . . and all their little affairs."

"There's the girl, it's true, but . . ."

"It's to our advantage, your Excellency, upon my word it is! If only as an experiment, let us try it. . ."

"Even in the grave they won't let us rest in peace."

"In the first place, General, you were playing preference in the grave, and in the second we don't care a hang about you," drawled Klinevitch.

"Sir, I beg you not to forget yourself."

"What? Why, you can't get at me, and I can tease you from here as though you were Julie's lapdog. And another thing, gentlemen, how is he a general here? He was a general there, but here is mere refuse."

"No, not mere refuse. . . . Even here. . ."

"Here you will rot in the grave and six brass buttons will be all that will be left of you."

"Bravo, Klinevitch, ha-ha-ha!" roared voices.

"I have served my sovereign. . . . I have the sword . . ."

"Your sword is only fit to prick mice, and you never drew it even for that."

"That makes no difference; I formed a part of the whole."

"There are all sorts of parts in a whole."

"Bravo, Klinevitch, bravo! Ha-ha-ha!"

"I don't understand what the sword stands for," boomed the engineer.

"We shall run away from the Prussians like mice, they'll crush us to powder!" cried a voice in the distance that was unfamiliar to me, that was positively spluttering with glee.

"The sword, sir, is an honour," the general cried, but only I heard him. There arose a prolonged and furious roar, clamour, and hubbub, and only the hysterically impatient squeals of Avdotya Ignatyevna were audible.

"But do let us make haste! Ah, when are we going to begin to cast off all shame!"

"Oh-ho-ho! . . . The soul does in truth pass through torments!" exclaimed the voice of the plebeian, "and . . ."

And here I suddenly sneezed. It happened suddenly and unintentionally, but the effect was striking: all became as silent as one expects it to be in a churchyard, it all vanished like a dream. A real silence of the tomb set in. I don't believe they were ashamed on account of my presence: they had made up their minds to cast off all shame! I waited five minutes - not a word, not a sound. It cannot be supposed that they were afraid of my informing the police; for what could the police do to them? I must conclude that they had some secret unknown to the living, which they carefully concealed from every mortal.

"Well, my dears," I thought, "I shall visit you again." And with those words, I left the cemetery. No, that I cannot admit; no, I really cannot! The bobok case does not trouble me (so that is what the bobok signified!)

Depravity in such a place, depravity of the last aspirations, depravity of sodden and rotten corpses – and not even sparing the last moments of consciousness! Those moments have been granted, vouchsafed to them, and . . . and, worst of all, in such a place! No, that I cannot admit.

Fyodor Dostoevsky   Bobok

I shall go to other tombs, I shall listen everywhere. Certainly one ought to listen everywhere and not merely at one spot in order to form an idea. Perhaps one may come across something reassuring.

But I shall certainly go back to those. They promised their biographies and anecdotes of all sorts. Tfoo! But I shall go, I shall certainly go; it is a question of conscience!

I shall take it to the Citizen; the editor there has had his portrait exhibited too. Maybe he will print it.

Invoker of the Beast

Fyodor Sologub

I

It was quiet and tranquil, and neither joyous nor sad. There was an electric light in the room. The walls seemed impregnable. The window was overhung by heavy, dark-green draperies, even denser in tone than the green of the wall-paper. Both doors--the large one at the side, and the small one in the depth of the alcove that faced the window securely bolted. And there, behind them, reigned darkness and desolation in the broad corridor as well as in the spacious and cold reception-room, where melancholy plants yearned for their native soil.

Gurov was lying on the divan. A book was in his hands. He often paused in his reading. He meditated and mused during these pauses, and it was always about the same thing. Always about *them*.

They hovered near him. This he had noticed long ago. They were hiding. Their manner was importunate. They rustled very quietly. For a long time they remained invisible to the eye. But one day, when Gurov awoke rather tired, sad and pale, and languidly turned on the electric light to dissipate the greyish gloom of an early winter morning—he espied one of them suddenly.

Small, grey, shifty and nimble, *he* flashed by, and in the twinkling of an eye disappeared.

And thereafter, in the morning, or in the evening, Gurov grew used to seeing these small, shifty, house sprites run past him. This time he did not doubt that they would appear.

To begin with he felt a slight headache, afterwards a sudden flash of heat, then of cold. Then, out of the corner, there emerged the long, slender Fever with her ugly, yellow face and her bony dry hands; she lay down at this side, and embraced him, and fell to kissing him and to laughing. And these rapid kisses of the affectionate and cunning Fever, and these slow approaches of the slight headache were agreeable.

Feebleness spread itself over the whole, and lassitude also. This, too, was agreeable. It made him feel as though all the turmoil of life had receded into the distance. And people also became far away, unimportant, even unnecessary. He preferred to be with these quiet ones, these house sprites.

Gurov had not been out for some days. He had locked himself in at home. He did not permit any one to come to him. He was alone. He thought about them. He awaited them.

II

This tedious waiting was cut short in a strange and unexpected manner. He heard the slamming of a distant door, and presently he became aware of the sound of unhurried footfalls which came from the direction of the reception-room, just behind the door of his room. Someone was approaching with a sure and nimble step.

Gurov turned his head towards the door. A gust of cold entered the room. Before him stood a boy, most strange and wild in aspect. He was dressed in linen draperies, half-nude, barefoot, smooth-skinned, sun-tanned, with black tangled hair and dark, burning eyes. An amazingly perfect, handsome face; handsome to a degree which made, it terrible to gaze upon its beauty. And it portrayed neither good nor evil.

Gurov was not astonished. A masterful mood took hold of him. He could hear the house sprites scampering away to conceal themselves.

The boy began to speak.

"Aristomarchon! I Perhaps you have forgotten your promise? Is this the way of valiant men? You left me when I was in mortal danger, you had made a promise, which it is evident you did not mend to keep. I have sought for you such a long time! And here I cave found you, living at your ease, and in luxury."

Gurov fixed a perplexed gaze upon the half-nude, handsome lad; and turgid memories awoke in his soul. Something long since submerged arose in dim outlines and tormented his memory, which struggled to find a solution to the strange apparition; a solution, moreover, which seemed so near and so intimate.

And what of the invincibility of his walls? Something had happened round him, some mysterious transformation had taken place. But Gurov, engulfed in his vain exertions to recall something very near to him and yet slipping away in the tenacious embrace of ancient history, had not yet succeeded in grasping the nature of the change that he felt had taken place. He turned to the wonderful boy.

"Tell me, gracious boy, simply and clearly, without unnecessary reproaches, what had I promised you, and when had I left you in a time of mortal danger? I swear to you, by all the holies, that my conscience could never have permitted me such a mean action as you reproach me with."

The boy shook his head. In a sonorous voice, suggestive of the melodious outpouring of a stringed instrument, he said; "Aristamarchon, you always have been a man skillful with words, and not less skillful in matters requiring daring and prudence. If I have said that you left me in a moment of mortal danger I did not intend it as a reproach, and I do not understand why you speak of your conscience. Our projected affair was difficult and dangerous, but who can hear us now; before whom, with your craftily arranged words and your dissembling ignorance of what happened this morning at sunrise, can you deny that you had given me a promise?'

The electric light grew dim. The ceiling seemed to darken and to recede into height. There was a smell of grass; its forgotten name, once long ago, suggested something gentle and joyous. A breeze blew. Gurov raised himself, and asked: "What sort of an affair had we two contrived? Gracious boy, I deny nothing. Only I don't know what you are speaking of. I don't remember."

Gurov felt as though the boy were looking at him, yet not directly. He felt also vaguely conscious of another presence no less unfamiliar and alien than that of this curious stranger, and seemed to him that the unfamiliar form of this other presence coincided with his own form. An ancient soul, as it were, had taken possession of Gurov and enveloped him in the long-lost freshness of its vernal attributes.

It was growing darker, and there was increasing purity coolness in the air. There rose up in his soul the joy and ease of pristine existence. The stars glowed brilliantly in the dark sky. The boy spoke.

"We had undertaken to kill the Beast. I tell you this under multitudinous gaze of the all-seeing sky. Perhaps you were frightened. That's quite likely too! We had planned a great, terrible affair, that our names might be honored by future generations."

Soft, tranquil, and monotonous was the sound of a stream which purled its way in the nocturnal silence. The stream invisible, but its nearness was soothing and refreshing. They stood under the broad shelter of a tree and continued the conversation begun at some other time.

Gurov asked: "Why do you say that I had left you in a moment of mortal danger? Who am I that I should be frightened and run away?"

The boy burst into a laugh. His mirth had the sound of music, and as it passed into speech his voice still quavered with sweet, melodious laughter.

"Aristomarchon, how cleverly you feign to have forgotten all! I don't understand what makes you do this, and with such a mastery that you bring reproaches against yourself which I have not even dreamt of. You had left me in a moment of mortal danger because it had to be, and you could not have helped me otherwise than by forsaking me at the moment. You will surely not remain stubborn in your denial when I remind you of the words of the Oracle?"

Gurov suddenly remembered. A brilliant light, as it were, unexpectedly illumined the dark domain of things forgotten. And in wild ecstasy, in a loud and joyous voice, he exclaimed: "*One shall kill the Beast!*"

The boy laughed. And Aristomarchon asked : "Did you kill the beast, Timarides?"

"With what?" exclaimed Timarides. "However strong my hands are I was not one who could kill the Beast with a blow of the fist. We, Aristomarchon, had not been prudent and we were unarmed. We were playing in the sand by the stream. The Beast came upon us suddenly and he laid his paw upon me. It was for me to offer up my life as a sweet sacrifice to glory and to a noble cause; it was for you to execute our plan. And while he was tormenting my defenseless and unresisting body, you, fleet-footed Aristomarchon, could have run for your lance, and killed the now blood-intoxicated Beast. But the Beast did not accept my sacrifice. I lay under him, quiescent and still, gazing into his bloodshot eyes. He held his heavy paw on my shoulder, his breath came in hot, uneven gasps, and he sent out low snarls. Afterwards, he put out his huge, hot tongue and licked my face; then he left me."

"Where is he now?" asked Aristomarchon.

In a voice strangely tranquil and strangely sonorous in the quiet arrested stillness of the humid air, Timarides replied: "He followed me. I do not know how long I have been wandering until I found you. He followed me. I led him on by the smell of my blood. I do not know why he has not touched me until now. But here I have enticed him to you. You had better get the weapon which you had hidden so carefully and kill the Beast, while I in my turn will leave you in the moment of mortal danger, eye to eye with the enraged creature. Here's luck to you, Aristomarchon!"

As soon as he uttered these words Timarides started to run. For a short time his cloak was visible in the darkness, a Glimmering patch of white. And then he disappeared. In the same instant the air resounded with the savage bellowing of the Beast, and his ponderous tread became audible. Pushing aside the growth shrubs there emerged from the darkness the huge, monstrous head of the Beast, flashing a livid fire out of its two enormous, flaming eyes. And in the dark silence of nocturnal trees the towering ferocious shape of the Beast loomed ominously as it approached Aristomarchon.

Terror filled Aristomarchon's heart.

"Where is the lance?" was the thought that quickly flashed across his brain.

And in that instant, feeling the fresh night breeze on his face, Aristomarchon realized that he was running from the Beast. His ponderous springs and his spasmodic roars resounded closer and closer behind him. And as the Beast came up with him a loud cry rent the silence of the night. The cry came from Aristomarchon who, recalling then some ancient and terrible words, pronounced loudly the incantation of the walls.

And thus enchanted the walls erected themselves around him. . .

III

Enchanted, the walls stood firm and were lit up. A dreary light was cast upon them by the dismal electric lamp. Gurov was in his usual surroundings.

Again came the nimble Fever and kissed him with her yellow, dry lips, and caressed him with her dry, bony hands, which exhaled heat and cold. The same thin volume, with its white pages lay on the little table beside the divan where, as before, Gurov rested in the caressing embrace of the affectionate Fever, who showered upon him her rapid kisses. And again there stood beside him, laughing and rustling, the tiny house spites.

Gurov said loudly and indifferently: "The incantation of the walls!"

Then he paused. But in what consisted this incantation? He had forgotten the words. Or had they never existed at all?

The little, shifty, grey demons danced round the slender volume with its ghostly white pages, and kept on repeating with their rustling voices: "Our walls are strong. We are in the walls. Have nothing to fear from the outside."

In their midst stood one of them, a tiny object like themselves yet different from the rest. He was all black. His mantle fell from his shoulders in folds of smoke and flame. His eyes flashed like lightning. Terror and joy alternated quickly.

Gurov spoke: "Who are you?"

The black demon answered. "I am the Invoker of the Beast. In one of your long-past existences you left the lacerated body of Timarides on the banks of a forest stream. The Beast had satiated himself on the beautiful body of your friend; he had gorged him on the flesh that might have partaken of the fullness of earthly happiness; a creature of superhuman perfection had perished in order to gratify for a moment the appetite of the ravenous and ever insatiable Beast. And the blood, the wonderful blood, the sacred wine of happiness and joy, the wine of superhuman bliss-- what had been the fate of this wonderful blood? Alas I The thisty, ceaselessly thirsty Beast drank of it to gratify his momentary desire, and is thirsty anew. You had left the body of Timarides, mutilated by the Beast, on the banks of the forest stream; you forgot the promise you had given your valorous friend, and even the words of the ancient Oracle had not banished fear from your heart. And do you think that you are safe, that the Beast will not find you?'

There was austerity in the sound of his voice. While he was speaking the house sprites gradually ceased their dance; the little, grey house sprites stopped to listen to the Invoker of the Beast.

Gurov then said in reply: "I am not worried about the Beast! I have pronounced eternal enchantment upon my walls and the Beast shall never penetrate hither, into my enclosure."

The little grey ones were overjoyed, their voices tinkled with merriment and laughter; having gathered round, hand in hand, in a circle, they were on the point of bursting forth once more into dance, when the voice of the Invoker of the Beast rang out again, sharp and austere.

"But I am here. I am here because I have found you. I am here because the incantation of the walls is dead. I am here because Timarides is waiting and importuning me. Do you hear the gentle laugh of the brave, trusting lad? Do you hear the terrible bellowing of the Beast?"

From behind the wall, approaching nearer, could be heard the fearsome bellowing of the Beast.

"The Beast is bellowing behind the wall, the invincible wall!" exclaimed Gurov in terror. "My walls are enchanted for ever, and impregnable against foes."

Then spoke the black demon, and there was an imperious ring in his voice: 'I tell you, man, the incantation of the walls is dead. And if you think you can save yourself by pronouncing the incantation of the walls, why then don't you utter the words?"

A cold shiver passed down Gurov's spine. The incantation! He had forgotten the words of the ancient spell. And what mattered it? Was not the ancient incantation dead—dead?

Everything about him confirmed with irrefutable evidence the death of the ancient incantation of the walls—because the walls, and the light and the shade which fell upon them, seemed dead and wavering. The Invoker of the Beast spoke terrible words. And Gurov's mind was now in a whirl, now in pain, and the affectionate Fever did not cease to torment him with her passionate kisses. Terrible words resounded, almost deadening his senses--while the Invoker of the Beast grew larger and larger, and hot fumes breathed from him, and grim terror. His ejected fire, and when at last he grew so tall as to screen off the electric light, his black cloak suddenly fell from his shoulders. And Gurov recognized him--it was the boy Timarides.

"Will you kill the Beast?" asked Timarides in a sonorous voice. "I have enticed him, I have led him to you, I have destroyed the incantation of the walls. The cowardly gift of inimical gods, the incantation of the walls, had turned into naught my sacrifice, and had saved you from your action. But the ancient incantation of walls is dead—be quick, then, to take hold of your sword and kill the Beast. I have been a boy--I have become the Invoker of Beast. He had drunk of my blood, and now he thirsts anew; he had partaken also of my flesh, and he is hungry again, the insatiable, pitiless Beast. I have called him to you, and you, in fulfillment of your promise, may kill the Beast. Or die yourself."

He vanished. A terrible bellowing shook the walls. A gust of icy moisture blew across to Gurov.

The wall facing the spot where Gurov lay opened, and the huge, ferocious and monstrous Beast entered. Bellowing savagely, he approached Gurov and laid his ponderous paw upon his breast. Straight into his heart plunged the pitiless claws. A terrible pain shot through his whole body. Shifting his blood-red eyes the Beast inclined his head towards Gurov and, crumbling the bones of victim with his teeth, began to devour his yet-palpitating heart.

A Night In The Graveyard
Anton Chekhov

"Tell us a frightening story, Ivan Ivanitch!"

Ivan Ivanitch twirled his moustache, coughed, smacked his lips, pulled his chair nearer to the young ladies and began:

"My story starts as the best Russian stories generally do: I was, I confess, the worse for drink . . . I had seen in the New Year with an old friend and we'd slobbered about like nobody's business. In my defense I ought to say I didn't get drunk with any pleasure. To mark an occasion like that is quite absurd in my opinion, unworthy of reasonable men. The New Year like the Old is a mess, the only difference is that the Old was bad and the New is even worse . . . We should mark it not, I think, by merrymaking but by suffering, tears and plans for suicide. We should remember each New Year that death is nearer, hair sparser, wrinkles thicker, wife older, children bigger and money less . . .

"So I got drunk in grief . . . As I left my friend, the cathedral clock was striking two. The weather was foul: neither autumn nor winter, the devil himself couldn't tell the difference. It was so dark your eyes were blinkered: look where you will, there was nothing to see, as if you were inside a blacking box. Rain thrashed down and cold biting wind made horrible noises: whining, moaning, groaning, screeching as if a witch had taken over nature's orchestra. Slush slopped sadly under my feet and lanterns were as dim as weeping widows . . . Nature, it seemed, was sick. It was weather, in short, for ruffians and thieves but not for me, a modest drunken fellow. It plunged me into a melancholy mood.

" 'Life . . .' I mused, as I plashed through mud, '. . . is pale and empty vegetating . . . Illusion . . . Day after day, year after year . . . and you're still the same old brute . . . More years to come and still you're just Ivan Ivanitch, drinking, eating, sleeping ... And in the end they'll bury you, you dolt, eat funeral cakes at your expense and say: "A good fellow but a fool unfortunately, didn't leave much money." '

"I was going from Meschanska to Presnya . . . quite a distance for a decent drunk . . . Struggling on through dark, narrow streets, I didn't meet a living soul nor hear a sound of life. Afraid of mud getting into my galoshes, I walked first on the pavement but, for all my precautions, the mud got in and I moved to the road: less chance there of stumbling on stones or falling in the gutter. The way ahead was muffled in cold, thick fog: at first I passed some dimly burning lanterns but after a street or two even that comfort disappeared. I had to grope along . . . Peering into darkness and listening to moaning wind, I began to hurry . . . An inexplicable fear came over me . . . It turned to horror when I realized I'd made a mistake and lost my way . . .

"'Coachman!' I shouted.

"No answer came . . . So I decided to move straight ahead, willy-nilly, hoping that sooner or later I'd come to a main street where there'd be lights and coachmen. Without turning my head, afraid to glance aside, I began to run . . . Bitter wind blew against me and thick rain lashed into my eyes . . . At times I was running on the pavement, at others in the street. How I escaped a broken head after banging into so many pillars and lampposts I just can't understand."

Ivan Ivanitch drank a glass of vodka, twirled the other half of his moustache and went on:

"I don't remember how long I ran . . . All I recall is that in the end I stumbled and banged my head against a peculiar object of some sort ... I couldn't see it but groping at it I had the impression of something cold, wet and smoothly carved. . . . I sat on it and rested ... I don't want to try your patience so I'll only say that after a time, when I struck a match to light a cigarette, I saw that I was sitting on a gravestone . . . .

"The sight of that after nothing but mist, not a single human sound, made me shut my eyes and jump to my feet. . . . Moving some paces away, I blundered into something else . . . Imagine my horror! It was a wooden cross . . .

'My God,' I thought, 'I've blundered into a graveyard!' I covered my face with my hands and sank down on a grave-stone. 'Instead of going to Presnya I've come to Vaganki!'

"I'm not afraid of graveyards or the dead . . . I've no illusions and it's a long time since I took notice of an old wife's tale but there among the silent graves in the dark night and the moaning wind one somber thought after another came into my head, each worse than the last . . . I felt the hairs bristle on my crown and a coldness from within run over my back . . .

" 'It's not possible!' I consoled myself. 'This is an optical illusion, an hallucination . . . I'm imagining it all . . . under the influence of drink . . . Coward that I am!'

"But just then, as I tried to cheer myself, I heard quiet steps . . . Someone was walking slowly . . . But they were not human steps: they were too quiet, too slight . . .

"'A dead man . . .' I thought.

Soon this mysterious someone came up to me, touched my knee and sighed . . . Then I heard a wailing . . . It was ghastly, sepulchral, hideous to the spirit . . . If it's frightening for you to hear old women talk of the wailing dead, imagine my feelings as I listened to that sound. I was petrified with horror: not a trace of drunkenness was left . . . It seemed to me that if I opened my eyes and dared to peer into the fog I'd see a face of white and yellow bone, a ragged shroud . . .

" 'Oh God,' I prayed, 'if only it were morning!'

"But before morning I had to endure a horror that defies description. Sitting on a gravestone and listening to the wailing corpse, I heard other steps . . . Something or other was coming straight towards me with heavy, measured tread . . . When it reached me, this new ghost from the grave gave a sigh and a moment later a cold bony hand fell heavily on my shoulder . . . I lost consciousness."

Ivan Ivanitch drank a glass of vodka and spluttered. "Well?" asked the young ladies.

"I came to myself in a little square room with dawn's weak light glimmering through a tiny lattice window.

"'So the dead have dragged me to a crypt . . .' I thought. "Imagine, then, my joy to hear a human voice at the other side of a wall!

" 'Where'd you find him?' it asked gruffly.

" 'Near Belobricov's, monumental masons, your honor . . .' another gruff voice replied. 'Where they put their crosses and memorial stones. I saw him sitting there clutching a grave-stone with a whining dog beside him . . . He must have been drinking . . .'

"In the morning, when I woke up again, they sent me away . . ."

The Double

Fyodor Dostoevsky

CHAPTER I

It was a little before eight o'clock in the morning when Yakov Petrovitch Golyadkin, a titular councilor, woke up from a long sleep. He yawned, stretched, and at last opened his eyes completely. For two minutes, however, he lay in his bed without moving, as though he were not yet quite certain whether he were awake or still asleep, whether all that was going on around him were real and actual, or the continuation of his confused dreams. Very soon, however, Mr. Golyadkin's senses began more clearly and more distinctly to receive their habitual and everyday impressions. The dirty green, smoke-begrimed, dusty walls of his little room, with the mahogany chest of drawers and chairs, the table painted red, the sofa covered with American leather of a reddish colour with little green flowers on it, and the clothes taken off in haste overnight and flung in a crumpled heap on the sofa, looked at him familiarly. At last the damp autumn day, muggy and dirty, peeped into the room through the dingy window pane with such a hostile, sour grimace that Mr. Golyadkin could not possibly doubt that he was not in the land of Nod, but in the city of Petersburg, in his own flat on the fourth storey of a huge block of buildings in Shestilavotchny Street. When he had made this important discovery Mr. Golyadkin nervously closed his eyes, as though regretting his dream and wanting to go back to it for a moment. But a minute later he leapt out of bed at one bound, probably all at once grasping the idea about which his scattered and wandering thoughts had been revolving. From his bed he ran straight to a little round looking-glass that stood on his chest of drawers. Though the sleepy, short-sighted countenance and rather bald head reflected in the looking-glass were of such an insignificant type that at first sight they would certainly not have attracted particular attention in any one, yet the owner of the countenance was satisfied with all that he saw in the looking-glass. "What a thing it would be," said Mr. Golyadkin in an undertone, "what a thing it would be if I were not up to the mark today, if something were amiss, if some intrusive pimple had made its appearance, or anything else unpleasant had happened; so far, however, there's nothing wrong, so far everything's all right."

Greatly relieved that everything was all right, Mr. Golyadkin put the looking-glass back in its place and, although he had nothing on his feet and was still in the attire in which he was accustomed to go to bed, he ran to the little window and with great interest began looking for some-thing in the courtyard, upon which the windows of his flat looked out. Apparently what he was looking for in the yard quite satisfied him too; his face beamed with a self-satisfied smile. Then, after first peeping, however, behind the partition into his valet Petrushka's little room and making sure that Petrushka was not there, he went on tiptoe to the table, opened the drawer in it and, fumbling in the furthest corner of it, he took from under old yellow papers and all sorts of rubbish a shabby green pocket-book, opened it cautiously, and with care and relish peeped into the furthest and most hidden fold of it. Probably the roll of green, grey, blue, red and particoloured notes looked at Golyadkin, too, with approval: with a radiant face he laid the open pocketbook before him and rubbed his hands vigorously in token of the greatest satisfaction. Finally, he took it out—his comforting roll of notes—and, for the hundredth time since the previous day, counted them over, carefully smoothing out every note between his forefinger and his thumb.

"Seven hundred and fifty roubles in notes," he concluded at last, in a half-whisper. "Seven hundred and fifty roubles, a noteworthy sum! It's an agreeable sum," he went on, in a voice weak and trembling with gratification, as he pinched the roll with his fingers and smiled significantly; "it's a very agreeable sum! A sum agreeable to any one! I should like to see the man to whom that would be a trivial sum! There's no knowing what a man might not do with a sum like that. . . . What's the meaning of it, though?" thought Mr. Golyadkin; "where's Petrushka?" And still in the same attire he peeped behind the partition again. Again there was no sign of Petrushka; and the samovar standing on the floor was beside itself, fuming and raging in solitude, threatening every minute to boil over, hissing and lisping in its mysterious language, to Mr. Golyadkin something like, "Take me, good people, I'm boiling and perfectly ready."

"Damn the fellow," thought Mr. Golyadkin. "That lazy brute might really drive a man out of all patience; where's he dawdling now?"

In just indignation he went out into the hall, which consisted of a little corridor at the end of which was a door into the entry, and saw his servant surrounded by a good-sized group of lackeys of all sorts, a mixed rabble from outside as well as from the flats of the house. Petrushka was telling something, the others were listening. Apparently the subject of the conversation, or the conversation itself, did not please Mr. Golyadkin. He promptly called Petrushka and returned to his room, displeased and even upset. "That beast would sell a man for a halfpenny, and his master before any one," he thought to himself: "and he has sold me, he certainly has. I bet he has sold me for a farthing. Well?"

"They've brought the livery, sir."

"Put it on, and come here."

When he had put on his livery, Petrushka, with a stupid smile on his face, went in to his master. His costume was incredibly strange. He had on a much-worn green livery, with frayed gold braid on it, apparently made for a man a yard taller than Petrushka. In his hand he had a hat trimmed with the same gold braid and with a feather in it, and at his hip hung a footman's sword in a leather sheath. Finally, to complete the picture, Petrushka, who always liked to be in negligè, was barefooted. Mr. Golyadkin looked at Petrushka from all sides and was apparently satisfied. The livery had evidently been hired for some solemn occasion. It might be observed, too, that during his master's inspection Petrushka watched him with strange expectancy and with marked curiosity followed every movement he made, which extremely embarrassed Mr. Golyadkin.

"Well, and how about the carriage?"

"The carriage is here too."

"For the whole day?"

"For the whole day. Twenty-five roubles."

"And have the boots been sent?"

Stories That Scared Eeven Stalin

"Yes."

"Dolt! can't even say, `Yes, sir.' Bring them here."

Expressing his satisfaction that the boots fitted, Mr. Golyadkin asked for his tea, and for water to wash and shave. He shaved with great care and washed as scrupulously, hurriedly sipped his tea and proceeded to the principal final process of attiring himself: he put on an almost new pair of trousers; then a shirtfront with brass studs, and a very bright and agreeably flowered waistcoat; about his neck he tied a gay, parti-coloured cravat, and finally drew on his coat, which was also newish and carefully brushed. As he dressed, he more than once looked lovingly at his boots, lifted up first one leg and then the other, admired their shape, kept muttering something to himself, and from time to time made expressive grimaces. Mr. Golyadkin was, however, extremely absent-minded that morning, for he scarcely noticed the little smiles and grimaces made at his expense by Petrushka, who was helping him dress. At last, having arranged everything properly and having finished dressing, Mr. Golyadkin put his pocketbook in his pocket, took a final admiring look at Petrushka, who had put on his boots and was therefore also quite ready, and, noticing that everything was done and that there was nothing left to wait for, he ran hurriedly and fussily out on to the stairs, with a slight throbbing at his heart. The light-blue hired carriage with a crest on it rolled noisily up to the steps. Petrushka, winking to the driver and some of the gaping crowd, helped his master into the carriage; and, hardly able to suppress an idiotic laugh, shouted in an unnatural voice: "Off!" jumped up on the footboard, and the whole turnout, clattering and rumbling noisily, rolled into the Nevsky Prospect. As soon as the light-blue carriage dashed out of the gate, Mr. Golyadkin rubbed his hands convulsively and went off into a slow, noiseless chuckle, like a jubilant man who has succeeded in bringing off a splendid performance and is as pleased as Punch with the performance himself. Immediately after his access of gaiety, however, laugh-ter was replaced by a strange and anxious expression on the face of Mr. Golyadkin. Though the weather was damp and muggy, he let down both windows of the carriage and began carefully scrutinizing the passers-by to left and to right, at once assuming a decorous and sedate air when he thought any one was looking at him. At the turning from Liteyny Street into the Nevsky Prospect he was startled by a most unpleasant sensation and, frowning like some poor wretch whose corn has been accidentally trodden on, he huddled with almost panic-stricken haste into the darkest corner of his carriage.

He had seen two of his colleagues, two young clerks serving in the same government department. The young clerks were also, it seemed to Mr. Golyadkin, extremely amazed at meeting their colleague in such a way; one of them, in fact, pointed him out to the other. Mr. Golyadkin even fancied that the other had actually called his name, which, of course, was very unseemly in the street. Our hero concealed himself and did not respond. "The silly youngsters!" he began reflecting to him-self. "Why, what is there strange in it? A man in a carriage, a man needs to be in a carriage, and so he hires a carriage. They're simply noodles!, I know them—simply silly youngsters, who still need thrashing! They want to be paid a salary for playing pitch-farthing and dawdling about, that's all they're fit for. I'd let them all know, if only ..."

Mr. Golyadkin broke off suddenly, petrified. A smart pair of Kazan horses, very familiar to Mr. Golyadkin, in a fashionable droshky, drove rapidly by on the right side of his carriage. The gentleman sitting in the droshky, happening to catch a glimpse of Mr. Golyadkin, who was rather incautiously poking his head out of the carriage window, also appeared to be extremely astonished at the unexpected meeting and, bending out as far as he could, looked with the greatest curiosity and interest into the corner of the carriage in which our hero made haste to conceal himself. The gentleman in the droshky was Andrey Filippovitch, the head of the office in which Mr. Golyadkin served in the capacity of assistant to the chief clerk. Mr. Golyadkin, seeing that Andrey Filippovitch recognized him, that he was looking at him open-eyed and that it was impossible to hide, blushed up to his ears.

"Bow or not? Call back or not? Recognize him or not?" our hero wondered in indescribable anguish, "or pretend that I am not myself, but somebody else strikingly like me, and look as though nothing were the matter. Simply not I, not I-and that's all," said Mr. Golyadkin, taking off his hat to Andrey Filippovitch and keeping his eyes fixed upon him. "I'm ... I'm all right," he whispered with an effort; "I'm ... quite all right. It's not I, it's not I—and that is the fact of the matter."

Soon, however, the droshky passed the carriage, and the magnetism of his chief's eyes was at an end. Yet he went on blushing, smiling and muttering something to himself.. .

"I was a fool not to call back," he thought at last. 'I ought to have taken a bolder line and behaved with gentlemanly openness. I ought to have said `This is how it is, Andrey Filippovitch, I'm asked to the dinner too,' and that's all it is!"

Then, suddenly recalling how taken aback he had been, our hero flushed as hot as fire, frowned, and cast a terrible defiant glance at the front corner of the carriage, a glance calculated to reduce all his foes to ashes. At last, he was suddenly inspired to pull the cord attached to the driver's elbow, and stopped the carriage, telling him to drive back to Liteyny Street. The fact was, it was urgently necessary for Mr. Golyadkin, probably for the sake of his own peace of mind, to say something very interesting to his doctor, Krestyan Ivanovitch. And, though he had made Krestyan Ivanovitch's acquaintance quite recently, having, indeed, only paid him a single visit, and that one the previous week, to consult him about some symptom. But a doctor, as they say, is like a priest, and it would be stupid for him to keep out of sight, and, indeed, it was his duty to know his patients. "Will it be all right, though," our hero went on, getting out of the carriage at the door of a five-storey house in Liteyny Street, at which he had told the driver to stop the carriage: "Will it be all right? Will it be proper? Will it be appropriate? After all, though," he went on, thinking as he mounted the stairs out of breath and trying to suppress the beating of his heart, which had the habit of beating on all other people's staircases: "After all, it's on my own business and there's nothing reprehensible in it. . . . It would be stupid to keep out of sight. Why, of course, I shall behave as though I were quite all right, and have simply looked in as I passed. . . . He will see, that it's all just as it should be."

Reasoning like this, Mr. Golyadkin mounted to the second storey and stopped before flat number five, on which there was a handsome brass door-plate with the inscription

KRESTYAN IVANOVITCH RUTENSPITZ

Doctor of Medicine and Surgery

Stopping at the door, our hero made haste to assume an air of propriety, ease, and even of a certain affability, and prepared to pull the bell. As he was about to do so he promptly and rather appropriately reflected that it might be better to come tomorrow, and that it was not very pressing for the moment. But as he suddenly heard footsteps on the stairs, he immediately changed his mind again and at once rang Krestyan Ivanovitch's bell—with an air, moreover, of great determination.

CHAPTER II

The doctor of medicine and surgery, Krestyan Ivanovitch Rutenspitz, a very hale, though elderly man, with thick eyebrows and whiskers that were beginning to turn grey, eyes with an expressive gleam in them that looked capable of routing every disease, and, lastly, with orders of some distinction on his breast, was sitting in his consulting-room that morning in his comfortable armchair. He was drinking coffee, which his wife had brought him with her own hand, smoking a cigar and from time to time writing prescriptions for his patients. After prescribing a draught for an old man who was suffering from hemorrhoids and seeing the aged patient out by the side door, Krestyan Ivanovitch sat down to await the next visitor.

Mr. Golyadkin walked in.

Apparently Krestyan Ivanovitch did not in the least expect nor desire to see Mr. Golyadkin, for he was suddenly taken aback for a moment, and his countenance unconsciously assumed a strange and, one may almost say, a displeased expression. As Mr. Golyadkin almost always turned up inappropriately and was thrown into confusion whenever he approached any one about his own little affairs, on this occasion, too, he was desperately embarrassed. Having neglected to get ready his first sentence, which was invariably a stumbling-block for him on such occasions, he muttered something—apparently an apology—and, not knowing what to do next, took a chair and sat down, but, realizing that he had sat down without being asked to do so, he was immediately conscious of his lapse, and made haste to efface his offence against etiquette and good breeding by promptly getting up again from the seat he had taken uninvited. Then, on second thoughts, dimly perceiving that he had committed two stupid blunders at once, he immediately decided to commit a third—that is, tried to right himself, muttered some-thing, smiled, blushed, was overcome with embarrassment, sank into expressive silence, and finally sat down for good and did not get up again. Only, to protect himself from all contingencies, he looked at the doctor with that defiant glare which had an extraordinary power of.figuratively crushing Mr. Golyadkin's enemies and reducing them to ashes. This glance, moreover, expressed to the full Mr. Golyadkin's independence—that is, to speak plainly, the fact that Mr. Golyadkin was "all right," that he was "quite himself, like everybody else," and that there was "nothing wrong in his upper storey." Krestyan Ivanovitch coughed, cleared his throat, apparently in token of approval and assent to all this, and bent an inquisitorial interrogative gaze upon his visitor.

"I have come to trouble you a second time, Krestyan Ivanovitch," began Mr. Golyadkin, with a smile, "and now I venture to ask your indulgence a second time. . . ." He was obviously at a loss for words.

"H'm ... Yes!" pronounced Krestyan Ivanovitch, puffing out a spiral of smoke and putting down his cigar on the table, "but you must follow the treatment prescribed you; I explained to you that what would be beneficial to your health is a change of habits. . . . Entertainment, for instance, and, well, friends—you should visit your acquaintances, and not be hostile to the bottle; and likewise keep cheerful company."

Mr. Golyadkin, still smiling, hastened to observe that he thought he was like every one else, that he lived by himself, that he had entertainments like every one else . . . that, of course, he might go to the theatre, for he had the means like every one else, that he spent the day at the office and the evenings at home, that he was quite all right; he even observed, in passing, that he was, so far as he could see, as good as any one, that he lived at home, and, finally, that he had Petrushka. At this point Mr. Golyadkin hesitated.

"H'm! no, that is not the order of proceeding I want; and that is not at all what I would ask you. I am interested to know, in general, are you a great lover of cheerful company? Do you take advantages of festive occasions; and, well, do you lead a melancholy or cheerful manner of life?"

"Krestyan Ivanovitch, I . . ."

"H'm!-. . . I tell you," interrupted the doctor, "that you must have a radical change of life, must, in a certain sense, break in your character." (Krestyan Ivanovitch laid special stress on the word "break in," and paused for a moment with a very significant air.) "Must not shrink from gaiety, must visit entertainments and clubs, and in any case, be not hostile to the bottle. Sitting at home is not right for you . . . sitting at home is impossible for you."

"I like quiet, Krestyan Ivanovitch," said Mr. Golyadkin, with a significant look at the doctor and evidently seeking words to express his ideas more successfully: "In my flat there's only me and Petrushka. . . . I mean my man, Krestyan Ivanovitch. I mean to say, Krestyan Ivanovitch, that I go my way, my own way, Krestyan Ivanovitch. I keep myself to myself, and so far as I can see am not dependent on any one. I go out for walks, too, Krestyan Ivanovitch."

"What? Yes! well, nowadays there's nothing agreeable in walking: the climate's extremely bad."

"Quite so, Krestyan Ivanovitch. Though I'm a peaceable man, Krestyan Ivanovitch, as I've had the honour of explaining to you already, yet my way lies apart, Krestyan Ivanovitch. The ways of life are manifold. . . . I mean . . . I mean to say, Krestyan Ivanovitch. . . . Excuse me, Krestyan Ivanovitch, I've no great gift for eloquent speaking."

"H'm . . . you say . . ."

"I say, you must excuse me, Krestyan Ivanovitch, that as far as I can see I am no great hand at eloquence in speaking," Mr. Golyadkin articulated, stammering and hesitating, in a half-aggrieved voice. "In that respect, Krestyan Ivanovitch, I'm not quite like other people," he added, with a peculiar smile, "I can't talk much, and have never learnt to embellish my speech with literary graces. On the other hand; I act, Krestyan Ivanovitch; on the other hand, I act, Krestyan Ivanovitch."

"H'm . . . How's that . . . you act?" responded Krestyan Ivanovitch.

Then silence followed for half a minute. The doctor looked some-what strangely and mistrustfully at his visitor. Mr. Golyadkin, for his part, too, stole a rather mistrustful glance at the doctor.

"Krestyan Ivanovitch," he began, going on again in the same tone as before, somewhat irritated and puzzled by the doctor's extreme obstinacy: "I like tranquillity and not the noisy gaiety of the world. Among them, I mean, in the noisy world, Krestyan Ivanovitch, one must be able to polish the floor with one's boots . . ." (here Mr. Golyadkin made a slight scrape on the floor with his toe); "they expect it, and they expect puns too . . . one must know how to make a perfumed compliment . . . that's what they expect there. And I've not learnt to do it, Krestyan Ivanovitch, I've never learnt all those tricks, I've never had the time. I'm a simple person, and not ingenious, and I've no external polish. On that side I surrender, Krestyan Ivanovitch, I lay down my arms, speaking in that sense."

All this Mr. Golyadkin pronounced with an air which made it perfectly clear that our hero was far from regretting that he was laying down his arms in that sense and that he had not learnt these tricks; quite the contrary, indeed.-As Krestyan Ivanovitch listened to him, he looked down with a very unpleasant grimace on his face, seeming to have a presentiment of something. Mr. Golyadkin's tirade was followed by a rather long and significant silence.

"You have, I think, departed a little from the subject," Krestyan Ivanovitch said at last, in a low voice: "I confess I cannot altogether understand you."

"I'm not a great hand at eloquent speaking, Krestyan Ivanovitch; I've had the honour to inform you, Krestyan Ivanovitch, already," said Mr. Golyadkin, speaking this time in a sharp and resolute tone.

Hm! . . .

"Krestyan Ivanovitch!" began Mr. Golyadkin again in a low but more significant voice, in a somewhat solemn style and emphasizing every point: "Krestyan Ivanovitch, when I came in here I began with apologies. I repeat the same thing again, and again ask for your indulgence. There's no need for me to conceal it, Krestyan Ivanovitch. I'm an unimportant man, as you know; but, fortunately for me, I do not regret being an unimportant man. Quite the contrary, indeed, Krestyan Ivanovitch, and, to be perfectly frank, I'm proud that I'm not a great man but an unimportant man. I'm not one to intrigue and I'm proud of that too, I don't act on the sly, but openly, without cunning, and although I could do harm too, and a great deal of harm, indeed, and know to whom and how to do it, Krestyan Ivanovitch, yet I won't sully myself, and in that sense I wash my hands. In that sense, I say, I wash them, Krestyan Ivanovitch!" Mr. Golyadkin paused expressively for a moment; he spoke with mild fervour.

"I set to work, Krestyan Ivanovitch," our hero continued, "directly, openly, by no devious ways, for I disdain them, and leave them to others. I do not try to degrade those who are perhaps purer than you and I . . . that is, I mean, I and they, Krestyan Ivanovitch—I didn't mean you. I don't like insinuations; I've no taste for contemptible duplicity; I'm disgusted by slander and calumny. I only put on a mask at a masquerade, and don't wear one before people every day. I only ask you, Krestyan Ivanovitch, how you would revenge yourself upon your enemy, your most malignant enemy-the one you would consider such?" Mr. Golyadkin concluded with a challenging glance at Krestyan Ivanovitch.

Though Mr. Golyadkin pronounced this with the utmost distinctness and clearness, weighing his words with a self-confident air and reckoning on their probable effect, yet meanwhile he looked at Krestyan Ivanovitch with anxiety, with great anxiety, with extreme anxiety. Now he was all eyes: and timidly waited for the doctor's answer with irritable and agonized impatience. But to the perplexity and complete amazement of our hero, Krestyan Ivanovitch only muttered something to him-self; then he moved his armchair up to the table, and rather dryly though politely announced something to the effect that his time was precious, and that he did not quite understand; that he was ready, how-ever, to attend to him as far as he was able, but he would not go into anything further that did not concern him. At this point he took the pen, drew a piece of paper towards him, cut out of it the usual long strip, and announced that he would immediately prescribe what was necessary.

"No, it's not necessary, Krestyan Ivanovitch! No, that's not necessary at all!" said Mr. Golyadkin, getting up from his seat, and clutching Krestyan Ivanovitch's right hand. "That isn't what's wanted, Krestyan Ivanovitch."

And, while he said this, a queer change came over him. His grey eyes gleamed strangely; his lips began to quiver, all the muscles, all the features of his face began moving and working. He was trembling all over. After stopping the doctor's hand, Mr. Golyadkin followed his first movement by standing motionless, as though he had no confidence in him-self and were waiting for some inspiration for further action.

Then followed a rather strange scene.

Somewhat perplexed, Krestyan Ivanovitch seemed for a moment rooted to his chair and gazed open-eyed in bewilderment at Mr. Golyadkin, who looked at him in exactly the same way. At last Krestyan Ivanovitch stood up, gently holding the lining of Mr. Golyadkin's coat. For some seconds they both stood like that, motionless, with their eyes fixed on each other. Then, however, in an extraordinarily strange way came Mr. Golyadkin's second movement. His lips trembled, his chin began twitching, and our hero quite unexpectedly burst into tears. Sobbing, shaking his head and striking himself on the chest with his right hand, while with his left clutching the lining of the doctor's coat, he tried to say something and to make some explanation, but could not utter a word.

At last Krestyan Ivanovitch recovered from his amazement.

"Come, calm yourself!" he brought out at last, trying to make Mr. Golyadkin sit down in an armchair.

"I have enemies, Krestyan Ivanovitch, I have enemies; I have malignant enemies who have sworn to ruin me . . ." Mr. Golyadkin answered in a frightened whisper.

"Come, come, why enemies? you mustn't talk about enemies! You really mustn't. Sit down, sit down," Krestyan Ivanovitch went on, getting Mr. Golyadkin once for all into the armchair.

Mr. Golyadkin sat down at last, still keeping his eyes fixed on the doctor. With an extremely displeased air, Krestyan Ivanovitch strode from one end of the room to another. A long silence followed.

"I'm grateful to you, Krestyan Ivanovitch, I'm very grateful, and I'm very sensible of all you've done for me now. To my dying day I shall never forget your kindness, Krestyan Ivanovitch," said Mr. Golyadkin, getting up from his seat with an offended air.

"Come, give over! I tell you, give over!" Krestyan Ivanovitch responded rather sternly to Mr. Golyadkin's outburst, making him sit down again.

"Well, what's the matter? Tell me what is unpleasant," Krestyan Ivanovitch went on, "and what enemies are you talking about? What is wrong?"

"No, Krestyan Ivanovitch, we'd better leave that now," answered Mr. Golyadkin, casting down his eyes; "let us put all that aside for the time. . . . Till another time, Krestyan Ivanovitch, till a more convenient moment, when everything will be discovered and the mask falls off certain faces, and something comes to light. But, meanwhile, now, of course, after what has passed between us . . . you will agree yourself, Krestyan Ivanovitch. . . . Allow me to wish you good morning, Krestyan Ivanovitch," said Mr. Golyadkin, getting up gravely and resolutely and taking his hat.

"Oh, well . . . . as you like . . . h'm . . ." (A moment of silence followed.) "For my part, you know . . . whatever I can do . . . and I sincerely wish you well."

"I understand you, Krestyan Ivanovitch, I understand: I understand you perfectly now . . . In any case excuse me for having troubled you, Krestyan Ivanovitch."

"H'm, no, I didn't mean that. However, as you please; go on taking the medicines as before...

"I will go on with the medicines as you say, Krestyan Ivanovitch. I will go on with them, and I will get them at the same chemist's . . . To be a chemist nowadays, Krestyan Ivanovitch, is an important business. . . ." "How so? In what sense do you mean?"

"In a very ordinary sense, Krestyan Ivanovitch. I mean to say that nowadays that's the way of the world. . . ."

"H'm . . ."

"And that every silly youngster, not only a chemist's boy turns up his nose at respectable people."

"H'm. How do you understand that?"

"I'm speaking of a certain person, Krestyan Ivanovitch . . . of a common acquaintance of ours, Krestyan Ivanovitch, of Vladimir Semyonovitch. . . ."

"Ah!"

"Yes, Krestyan Ivanovitch: and I know certain people, Krestyan Ivanovitch, who don't quite keep to the general rule of telling the truth, sometimes."

"Ah! How so?"

"Why, yes, it is so: but that's neither here nor there: they sometimes manage to serve you up a fine egg in gravy."

"What? Serve up what?"

"An egg in gravy, Krestyan Ivanovitch. It's a Russian saying. They know how to congratulate some one at the right moment, for instance; there are people like that."

"Congratulate?"

"Yes, congratulate, Krestyan Ivanovitch, as some one I know very well did the other day!"

"Some one you know very well . . . Ah! how was that?" said Krestyan Ivanovitch, looking attentively at Mr. Golyadkin.

"Yes, some one I know very well indeed congratulated some one else I know very well—and, what's more, a comrade, a friend of his heart, on his promotion, on his receiving the rank of assessor. This was how it happened to come up: `I am exceedingly glad of the opportunity to offer you, Vladimir Semyonovitch, my congratulations, my sincere congratulations, on your receiving the rank of assessor. And I'm the more pleased, as all the world knows that there are old women nowadays who tell fortunes. . ."

At this point Mr. Golyadkin gave a sly nod, and screwing up his eyes, looked at Krestyan Ivanovitch. . . .

"H'm. So he said that. . . ."

"He did, Krestyan Ivanovitch, he said it and glanced at once at Andrey Filippovitch, the uncle of our Prince Charming, Vladimir Semyonovitch. But what is it to me, Krestyan Ivanovitch, that he has been made an assessor? What is it to me? And he wants to get married and the milk is scarcely dry on his lips, if I may be allowed the expression. And I said as much. Vladimir Semyonovitch, said I! I've said every-thing now; allow me to withdraw."

"H'm . . ."

"Yes, Krestyan Ivanovitch, allow me now, I say, to withdraw. But, to kill two birds with one stone, as I twitted our young gentleman with the old women, I turned to Klara Olsufyevna (it all happened the day before yesterday at Olsufy Ivanovitch's), and she had only just sung a song full of feeling, `You've sung songs full of feeling, madam,' said I, `but they've not been listened to with a pure heart.' And by that I hinted plainly, Krestyan Ivanovitch, hinted plainly, that they were not running after her now, but looking higher."

"Ah! And what did he say?"

"He swallowed the pill, Krestyan Ivanovitch, as the saying is."'
"H'm. . ."

"Yes, Krestyan Ivanovitch. To the old man himself, too, I said, `Olsufy Ivanovitch,' said I, 'I know how much I'm indebted to you, I appreciate to the full all the kindness you've showered upon me from my childhood up. But open your eyes, Olsufy Ivanovitch,' I said. `Look about you. I myself do things openly and aboveboard, Olsufy Ivanovitch..'"

"Oh, really!"

"Yes, Krestyan Ivanovitch. Really . . ."

"What did he say?"

"Yes, what, indeed, Krestyan Ivanovitch? He mumbled one thing and another, and `I know you,' and that `his Excellency was a benevolent man'—he rambled on. . . . But, there, you know! He's begun to be a bit shaky, as they say, with old age."

"Ah! so that's how it is now . . .

"Yes, Krestyan Ivanovitch. And that's how we all are! Poor old man! He looks towards the grave, breathes incense, as they say, while they concoct a piece of womanish gossip and he listens to it; without him they wouldn't . . ."

"Gossip, you say?"

"Yes, Krestyan Ivanovitch, they've concocted a womanish scandal. Our bear, too, had a finger in it, and his nephew, our Prince Charming. They've joined hands with the old women and, of course, they've concocted the affair. Would you believe it? They plotted the murder of some one! . . ."

"The murder of some one?"

"Yes, Krestyan Ivanovitch, the moral murder of some one. They spread about . . . I'm speaking of a man I know very well."

Krestyan Ivanovitch nodded.

"They spread rumours about him . . . I confess I'm ashamed to repeat them, Krestyan Ivanovitch."

"They spread a rumour that he had signed a promise to many though he was already engaged in another quarter . . . and would you believe it, Krestyan Ivanovitch, to whom?"

"Really?"

"To a cook, to a disreputable German woman from whom he used to get his dinners; instead of paying what he owed, he offered her his hand."

"Is that what they say?"

"Would you believe it, Krestyan Ivanovitch? A low German, a nasty, shameless German, Karolina Ivanovna, if you know . . ."

"I confess, for my part . . ."

"I understand you, Krestyan Ivanovitch, I understand, and for my part I feel it ..."

"Tell me, please, where are you living now?"

"Where am I living now, Krestyan Ivanovitch?"

"Yes . . . I want . . . I believe, you used to live . . ."

"Yes, Krestyan Ivanovitch, I did, I used to. To be sure I lived!" answered Mr. Golyadkin, accompanying his words with a little laugh, and somewhat disconcerting Krestyan Ivanovitch by his answer.

"No, you misunderstood me; I meant to say . . ."

"I, too, meant to say, Krestyan Ivanovitch, I meant it too," Mr. Golyadkin continued, laughing. "But I've kept you far too long, Krestyan Ivanovitch. I hope you will allow me now, to wish you good morning."

"H'm. . . ."

"Yes, Krestyan Ivanovitch, I understand you; I fully understand you now," said our hero, with a slight flourish before Krestyan Ivanovitch. "And so permit me to wish you good morning. . . ."

At this point our hero made a scrape with the toe of his boot and walked out of the room, leaving Krestyan Ivanovitch in the utmost amazement. As he went down the doctor's stairs he smiled and rubbed his hands gleefully. On the steps, breathing the fresh air and feeling himself at liberty, he was certainly prepared to admit that he was the happiest of mortals, and thereupon to go straight to his office—when suddenly his carriage rumbled up to the door: he glanced at it and remembered everything. Petrushka was already opening the carriage door. Mr. Golyadkin was completely overwhelmed by a strong and unpleasant sensation. He blushed, as it were, for a moment. Something seemed to stab him. He was just about to raise his foot to the carriage step when he suddenly turned round and looked towards Krestyan Ivanovitch's window. Yes, it was so! Krestyan Ivanovitch was standing at the window, was stroking his whiskers with his right hand and staring with some curiosity at the hero of our story.

"That doctor is silly," thought Mr. Golyadkin, huddling out of sight in the carriage; "extremely silly. He may treat his patients all right, but still . . . he's as stupid as a post."

Mr. Golyadkin sat down, Petrushka shouted "Off!" and the carriage rolled towards Nevsky Prospect again.

CHAPTER III

All that morning was spent by Mr. Golyadkin in a strange bustle of activity. On reaching the Nevsky Prospect our hero told the driver to stop at the bazaar. Skipping out of his carriage, he ran to the Arcade, accompanied by Petrushka, and went straight to a shop where gold and silver articles were for sale. One could see from his very air that he was overwhelmed with business and had a terrible amount to do. Arranging to purchase a complete dinner- and tea-service for fifteen hundred roubles and including in the bargain for that sum a cigar-case of ingenious form and a silver shaving-set, and finally, asking the price of some other articles, useful and agreeable in their own way, he ended by promising to come without fail next day, or to send for his purchases the same day. He took the number of the shop, and listening attentively to the shop-keeper, who was very pressing for a small deposit, said that he should have it all in good time. After which he took leave of the amazed shop-keeper and, followed by a regular flock of shopmen, walked along the Arcade, continually looking round at Petrushka and diligently seeking out fresh shops. On the way he dropped into a money-changer's and changed all his big notes into small ones, and though he lost on the exchange, his pocket-book was considerably fatter, which evidently afforded him extreme satisfaction. Finally, he stopped at a shop for ladies' dress materials. Here, too, after deciding to purchase goods for a considerable sum, Mr. Golyadkin promised to come again, took the number of the shop and, on being asked for a deposit, assured the shop-keeper that "he should have a deposit too, all in good time." Then he visited several other shops, making purchases in each of them, asked the price of various things, sometimes arguing a long time with the shopkeeper, going out of the shop and returning two or three times—in fact he displayed exceptional activity. From the Arcade our hero went to a well-known furniture shop, where he ordered furniture for six rooms; he admired a fashionable and very ingenious toilet table for ladies' use in the latest style, and, assuring the shopkeeper that he would certainly send for all these things, walked out of the shop, as usual promising a deposit. Then he went off somewhere else and ordered something more. In short, there seemed to be no end to the business he had to get through. At last, Mr. Golyadkin seemed to grow heartily sick of it all, and he began, goodness knows why, to be tormented by the stings of conscience. Nothing would have induced him now, for instance, to meet Andrey Filippovitch, or even Krestyan Ivanovitch.

At last, the town clock struck three. When Mr. Golyadkin finally took his seat in the carriage, of all the purchases he had made that morning he had, it appeared, in reality only got a pair of gloves and a bottle of scent, that cost a rouble and a half. As it was still rather early, he ordered his coachman to stop near a well-known restaurant in Nevsky Prospect which he only knew by reputation, got out of the carriage, and hurried in to have a light lunch, to rest and to wait for the hour fixed for the dinner.

Lunching as a man lunches who has the prospect before him of going out to a sumptuous dinner, that is, taking a snack of something in order to still the pangs, as they say, and drinking one small glass of vodka, Mr. Golyadkin established himself in an armchair and, modestly looking about him, peacefully settled down to an emaciated nationalist paper. After reading a couple of lines he stood up and looked in the looking-glass, set himself to rights and smoothed himself down; then he went to the window and looked to see whether his carriage was there . . . then he sat down again in his place and took up the paper. It was notice-able that our hero was in great excitement. Glancing at his watch and seeing that it was only a quarter past three and that he had consequently a good time to wait and, at the same time, opining that to sit like that was unsuitable, Mr. Golyadkin ordered chocolate, though he felt no particular inclination for it at the moment. Drinking the chocolate and noticing that the time had moved on a little, he went up to pay his bill.

He turned round and saw facing him two of his colleagues, the same two he had met that morning in Liteyny Street,—young men, very much his juniors both in age and in rank. Our hero's relations with them were neither one thing nor the other, neither particularly friendly nor openly hostile. Good manners were, of course, observed on both sides: there was no closer intimacy, nor could there be. The meeting at this moment was extremely distasteful to Mr. Golyadkin. He frowned a little, and was disconcerted for an instant.

"Yakov Petrovitch, Yakov Petrovitch!" chirped the two register clerks; "you here? what brings you? ..."

"Ah, it is you, gentlemen," Mr. Golyadkin interrupted hurriedly, somewhat embarrassed and scandalized by the amazement of the clerks and by the abruptness of their address, but feeling obliged, however, to appear jaunty and free and easy. "You've deserted, gentlemen, hehe—he. . . ." Then, to keep up his dignity and to condescend to the juveniles, with whom he never overstepped certain limits, he attempted to slap one of the youths on the shoulder; but this effort at good fellowship did not succeed and, instead of being a well-bred little jest, produced quite a different effect.

"Well, and our bear, is he still at the office?"

"Who's that, Yakov Petrovitch?"

"Why, the bear. Do you mean to say you don't know whose name that is? . . ." Mr. Golyadkin laughed and turned to the cashier to take his change.

"I mean Andrey Filippovitch, gentlemen," he went on, finishing with the cashier, and turning to the clerks this time with a very serious face. The two register clerks winked at one another.

"He's still at the office and asking for you, Yakov Petrovitch," answered one of them.

"At the office, eh! In that case, let him stay, gentlemen. And asking for me, eh?"

"He was asking for you, Yakov Petrovitch; but what's up with you, scented, pomaded, and such a swell? . . ."

"Nothing, gentlemen, nothing! that's enough," answered Mr. Golyadkin, looking away with a constrained smile. Seeing that Mr. Golyadkin was smiling, the clerks laughed aloud. Mr. Golyadkin was a little offended.

"I'll tell you as friends, gentlemen," our hero, said, after a brief silence, as though making up his mind (which, indeed, was the case) to reveal something to them. "You all know me, gentlemen, but hitherto you've known me only on one side. No one is to blame for that and I'm conscious that the fault has been partly my own."

Mr. Golyadkin pursed up his lips and looked significantly at the clerks. The clerks winked at one another again.

"Hitherto, gentlemen, you have not known me. To explain myself here and now would not be quite appropriate. I will only touch on it lightly in passing. There are people, gentlemen, who dislike round-about ways and only mask themselves at masquerades. There are people who do not see man's highest avocation in polishing the floor with their boots. There are people, gentlemen, who refuse to say that they are happy and enjoying a full life when, for instance, their trousers set properly. There are people, finally, who dislike dashing and whirling about for no object, fawning, and licking the dust, and above all, gentlemen, poking their noses where they are not wanted . . . I've told you almost everything, gentlemen; now allow me to withdraw. . . ."

Mr. Golyadkin paused. As the register clerks had now got all that they wanted, both of them with great incivility burst into shouts of laughter. Mr. Golyadkin flared up.

"Laugh away, gentlemen, laugh away for the time being! If you live long enough you will see," he said, with a feeling of offended dignity, taking his hat and retreating to the door.

"But I will say more, gentlemen," he added, turning for the last time to the register clerks, "I will say more—you are both here with me face to face. This, gentlemen, is my rule: if I fail I don't lose heart, if I succeed I persevere, and in any case I am never underhand. I'm not one to intrigue—and I'm proud of it. I've never prided myself on diplomacy. They say, too, gentlemen, that the bird flies itself to the hunter. It's true and I'm ready to admit it; but who's the hunter, and who's the bird in this case? That is still the question, gentlemen!"

Mr. Golyadkin subsided into eloquent silence, and, with a most significant air, that is, pursing up his lips and raising his eyebrows as high as possible, he bowed to the clerks and walked out, leaving them in the utmost amazement.

"What are your orders now?" Petrushka asked, rather gruffly; he was probably weary of hanging about in the cold. "What are your orders?" he asked Mr. Golyadkin, meeting the terrible, withering glance with which our hero had protected himself twice already that morning, and to which he had recourse now for the third time as he came down the steps.

"To Ismailovsky Bridge."

"To Ismailovsky Bridge! Off!"

"Their dinner will not begin till after four, or perhaps five o'clock," thought Mr. Golyadkin; "isn't it early now? However, I can go a little early; besides, it's only a family dinner. And so I can go sans facons, as they say among well-bred people. Why shouldn't I go sans facons? The bear told us, too, that it would all be san facons, and so I will be the same...."

Such were Mr. Golyadkin's reflections and meanwhile his excitement grew more and more acute. It could be seen that he was preparing himself for some great enterprise, to say nothing more; he muttered to himself, gesticulated with his right hand, continually looked out of his carriage window, so that, looking at Mr. Golyadkin, no one would have said that he was on his way to a good dinner, and only a simple dinner in his family circle—sans facons, as they say among well-bred people. Finally, just at Ismailovsky Bridge, Mr. Golyadkin pointed out a house; and the carriage rolled up noisily and stopped at the first entrance on the right. Noticing a feminine figure at the second storey window, Mr. Golyadkin kissed his hand to her. He had, however, not the slightest idea what he was doing, for he felt more dead than alive at the moment. He got out of the carriage pale, distracted; he mounted the steps, took off his hat, mechanically straightened himself, and though he felt a slight trembling in his knees, he went upstairs.

"Olsufy Ivanovitch?" he inquired of the man who opened the door.

"At home, sir; at least he's not at home, his honour's not at home."

"What? What do you mean, my good man? I—I've come to dinner, brother. Why, you know me?"

"To be sure I know you! I've orders not to admit you."

"You . . . you, brother . . . you must be making a mistake. It's I, my boy, I'm invited; I've come to dinner," Mr. Golyadkin announced, taking off his coat and displaying unmistakable intentions of going into the room.

"Allow me, sir, you can't, sir. I've orders not to admit you. I've orders to refuse you. That's how it is."

Mr. Golyadkin turned pale. At that very moment the door of the inner room opened and Gerasimitch, Olsufy Ivanovitch's old butler, came out.

"You see the gentleman wants to go in, Emelyan Gerasimitch, and I. ."

"And you're a fool, Alexeitch. Go inside and send the rascal Semyonitch here. It's impossible," he said politely but firmly, addressing Mr. Golyadkin. "It's quite impossible. His honour begs you to excuse him; he can't see you."

"He said he couldn't see me?" Mr. Golyadkin asked uncertainly. "Excuse me, Gerasimitch, why is it impossible?"

"It's quite impossible. I've informed your honour; they said `Ask him to excuse us.' They can't see you."

"Why not? How's that? Why."

"Allow me, allow me! . . ."

"How is it, though? It's out of the question! Announce me. . . . How is it? I've come to dinner. . . ."

"Excuse me, excuse me. . . ."

"Ah, well, that's a different matter, they asked to be excused: but, allow me, Gerasimitch; how is it, Gerasimitch?"

"Excuse me, excuse me!" replied Gerasimitch, very firmly putting away Mr. Golyadkin's hand and making way for two gentlemen who walked into the entry that very instant. The gentlemen in question were Andrey Filippovitch and his nephew, Vladimir Semyonovitch. Both of them looked with amazement at Mr. Golyadkin. Andrey Filippovitch seemed about to say something, but Mr. Golyadkin had by now made up his mind: he was by now walking out of Olsufy Ivanovitch's entry, blushing and smiling, with eyes cast down and a countenance of help-less bewilderment. "I will come afterwards, Gerasimitch; I will explain myself: I hope that all this will without delay be explained in due season. ."

"Yakov Petrovitch, Yakov Petrovitch . . ." He heard the voice of Andrey Filippovitch following him.

Mr. Golyadkin was by that time on the first landing. He turned quickly to Andrey Filippovitch.

"What do you desire, Andrey Filippovitch?" he said in a rather resolute voice.

"What's wrong with you, Yakov Petrovitch? In what way?"

"No matter, Andrey Filippovitch. I'm on my own account here. This is my private life, Andrey Filippovitch."

"What's that?"

"I say, Andrey Filippovitch, that this is my private life, and as for my being here, as far as I can see, there's nothing reprehensible to be found in it as regards my official relations."

"What! As regards your official . . . What's the matter with you, my good sir?"

"Nothing, Andrey Filippovitch, absolutely nothing; an impudent slut of a girl, and nothing more. . . ."

"What! What?" Andrey Filippovitch was stupefied with amazement. Mr. Golyadkin, who had up till then looked as though he would fly into Andrey Filippovitch's face, seeing that the head of his office was laughing a little, almost unconsciously took a step forward. Andrey Filippovitch jumped back. Mr. Golyadkin went up one step and then another. Andrey Filippovitch looked about him uneasily. Mr. Golyadkin mounted the stairs rapidly. Still more rapidly Andrey Filippovitch darted into the flat and slammed the door after him. Mr. Golyadkin was left alone. Everything grew dark before his eyes. He was utterly nonplussed, and stood now in a sort of senseless hesitation, as though recalling something extremely senseless, too, that had happened quite recently. "Ech, ech!" he muttered, smiling with constraint. Meanwhile, there came the sounds of steps and voices on the stairs, probably of other quests invited by Olsufy Ivanovitch. Mr. Golyadkin recovered himself to some extent; put up his raccoon collar, concealing himself behind it as far as possible, and began going downstairs with rapid little steps, tripping and stumbling in his haste. He felt overcome by a sort of weakness and numbness. His confusion was such that, when he came out on the steps, he did not even wait for his carriage but walked across the muddy court to it. When he reached his carriage and was about to get into it, Mr. Golyadkin inwardly uttered a desire to sink into the earth, or to hide in a mouse hole together with his carriage. It seemed to him that everything in Olsufy Ivanovitch's house was looking at him now out of every window. He knew that he would certainly die on the spot if he were to go back.

"What are you laughing at, blockhead?" he said in a rapid mutter to Petrushka, who was preparing to help him into the carriage.

"What should I laugh at? I'm not doing anything; where are we to drive now?"

"Go home, drive on. . . . "

"Home, off!" shouted Petrushka, climbing on to the footboard.

"What a crow's croak!" thought Mr. Golyadkin. Meanwhile, the carriage had driven a good distance from Ismailovsky Bridge. Suddenly our hero pulled the cord with all his might and shouted to the driver to turn back at once. The coachman turned his horses and within two minutes was driving into Olsufy Ivanovitch's yard again.

"Don't, don't, you fool, back!" shouted Mr. Golyadkin —and, as though he were expecting this order, the driver made no reply but, without stopping at the entrance, drove all round the courtyard and out into the street again.

Mr. Golyadkin did not drive home, but, after passing the Semyonovsky Bridge, told the driver to return to a side street and stop near a restaurant of rather modest appearance. Getting out of the carriage, our hero settled up with the driver and so got rid of his equipage at last. He told Petrushka to go home and await his return, while he went into the restaurant, took a private room and ordered dinner. He felt very ill and his brain was in the utmost confusion and chaos. For a long time he walked up and down the room in agitation; at last he sat down in a chair, propped his brow in his hands and began doing his very utmost to consider and settle something relating to his present position.

CHAPTER IV

That day the birthday of Klara Olsufyevna, the only daughter of the civil councilor, Berendyev, at one time Mr. Golyadkin's benefactor and patron, was being celebrated by a brilliant and sumptuous dinner-party, such as had not been seen for many a long day within the walls of the flats in the neighbourhood of Ismailovsky Bridge—a dinner more like some Balthazar's feast, with a suggestion of something Babylonian in its brilliant luxury and style, with Veuve-Clicquot champagne, with oysters and fruit from Eliseyev's and Milyutin's, with all sorts of fatted calves, and all grades of the government service. This festive day was to conclude with a brilliant ball, a small birthday ball, but yet brilliant in its taste, its distinction and its style. Of course, I am willing to admit that similar balls do happen sometimes, though rarely. Such balls, more like family rejoicings than balls, can only be given in such houses as that of the civil councilor, Berendyev. I will say more: I even doubt if such balls could be given in the houses of all civil councilors. Oh, if I were a poet! such as Homer or Pushkin, I mean, of course; with any lesser talent one would not venture—I should certainly have painted all that glorious day for you, oh, my readers, with a free brush and brilliant colours! Yes, I should begin my poem with my dinner, I should lay special stress on that striking and solemn moment when the first goblet was raised to the honour of the queen of the fete. I should describe to you the guests plunged in a reverent silence and expectation, as eloquent as the rhetoric of Demosthenes; I should describe for you, then,, how Audrey Filippovitch, having as the eldest of the guests some right to take precedence, adorned with his grey hairs and the orders that well befit grey hairs, got up from his seat and raised above his head the congratulatory glass of sparkling wine—brought from a distant kingdom to celebrate such occasions and more like heavenly nectar than plain wine. I would portray for you the guests and the happy parents raising their glasses, too, after Andrey Filippovitch, and fastening upon him eyes full of expectation. I would describe for you how the same Andrey Filippovitch, so often mentioned, after dropping a tear in the glass, delivered his congratulations and good wishes, proposed the toast and drank the health . . . but I confess, I freely confess, that I could not do justice to the solemn moment when the queen of the fete, Klara Olsufyevna, blushing like a rose in spring, with the glow of bliss and of modesty, was so overcome by her feelings that she sank into the arms of her tender mamma; how that tender mamma shed tears, and how the father, Olsufy Ivanovitch, a hale old man and a privy councilor, who had lost the use of his legs in his long years of service and been rewarded by destiny for his devotion with investments, a house, some small estates, and a beautiful daughter, sobbed like a little child and announced through his tears that his Excellency was a benevolent man. I could not, I positively could not, describe the enthusiasm that followed that moment in every heart, an enthusiasm clearly evinced in the conduct of a youthful register clerk (though at that moment he was more like a civil councilor than a register clerk), who was moved to tears, too, as he listened to Andrey Filippovitch. In his turn, too, Andrey Filippovitch was in that solemn moment quite unlike a collegiate councilor and the head of an office in the department—yes, he was some-thing else . . . what, exactly, I do not know, but not a collegiate councilor. He was more exalted! Finally . . . Oh, why do I not possess the secret of lofty, powerful language, of the sublime style, to describe these grand and edifying moments of human life, which seem created expressly to prove that virtue sometimes triumphs over ingratitude, free-thinking, vice and envy! I will say nothing, but in silence—which will be better than any eloquence—I will point to that fortunate youth, just entering on his twenty-sixth spring—to Vladimir Semyonovitch, Andrey Filippovitch's nephew, who in his turn now rose from his seat, who in his turn proposed a toast, and upon whom were fastened the tearful eyes of the parents, the proud eyes of Andrey Filippovitch, the modest eyes of the queen of the fete, the solemn eyes of the guests, and even the decorously envious eyes of some of the young man's youthful colleagues. I will say nothing of that, though I cannot refrain from observing that everything in that young man—who was, indeed, speaking in a complimentary sense, more like an elderly than a young man—everything, from his blooming cheeks to his assessorial rank seemed almost to proclaim aloud the lofty pinnacle a man can attain through morality and good principles! I will not describe how Anton Antonovitch Syetotchkin, a little old man as grey as a badger, the head clerk of a department, who was a colleague of Andrey Filippovitch's and had once been also of Olsufy Ivanovitch's, and was an old friend of the family and Klara Olsufyevna's godfather, in his turn proposed a toast, crowed like a cock, and cracked many little jokes; how by this extremely proper breach of propriety, if one may use such an expression, he made the whole company laugh till they cried, and how Klara Olsufyevna, at her parents' bidding, rewarded him for his jocularity and politeness with a kiss. I will only say that the guests, who must have felt like kinsfolk and brothers after such a dinner, at last rose from the table, and the elderly and more solid guests, after a brief interval spent in friendly conversation, interspersed with some candid, though, of course, very polite and proper observations, went decorously into the next room and, without losing valuable time, promptly divided them-selves up into parties and, full of the sense of their own dignity, installed themselves at tables covered with green baize. Meanwhile, the ladies established in the drawing-room suddenly became very affable and began talking about dress-materials. And the venerable host, who had lost the use of his legs in the service of loyalty and religion, and had been rewarded with all the blessings we have enumerated above, began walking about on crutches among his guests, supported by Vladimir Semyonovitch and Klara Olsufyevna, and he, too, suddenly becoming extremely affable, decided to improvise a modest little dance, regardless of expense; to that end a nimble youth (the one who was more like a civil councilor than a youth) was dispatched to fetch musicians, and musicians to the number of eleven arrived, and exactly at half-past eight struck up the inviting strains of a French quadrille, followed by various other dances. . . . It is needless to say that my pen is too weak, dull, and spiritless to describe the dance that owed its inspiration to the genial hospitality of the grey-headed host. And how, I ask, can the modest chronicler of Mr. Golyadkin's adventures, extremely interesting as they are in their own way, how can I depict the choice and rare mingling of beauty, brilliance, style, gaiety, polite solidity and solid politeness, sportiveness, joy, all the mirth and playfulness of these wives and daughters of petty officials, more like fairies than ladies—in a complimentary sense—with their lily shoulders and their rosy faces, their ethereal figures, their playfully agile homeopathic—to use the exalted language appropriate—little feet? How can I describe to you, finally, the gallant officials, their partners—gay and solid youths, steady, gleeful, decorously vague, smoking a pipe in the intervals between the dancing in a little green room apart, or not smoking a pipe in the intervals between the dances, every one of them with a highly respectable surname and rank in the service—all steeped in a sense of the elegant and a sense of their own dignity; almost all speaking French to their partners, or if Russian, using only the most well-bred expressions, compliments and profound observations, and only in the smoking-room permitting them-selves some genial lapses from this high tone, some phrases of cordial and friendly brevity, such, for instance, as: "'Pon my soul, Petka, you rake, you did kick off that polka in style," or, "I say, Vasya, you dog, you did give your partner a time of it." For all this, as I've already had the honour of explaining, oh, my readers! my pen fails me, and therefore I am dumb. Let us rather return to Mr. Golyadkin, the true and only hero of my very truthful tale.

The fact is that he found himself now in a very strange position, to say the least of it. He was here also, gentlemen—that is, not at the dance, but almost at the dance; he was "all right, though; he could take care of himself," yet at this moment he was a little astray; he was standing at that moment, strange to say—on the landing of the back stairs to Olsufy Ivanovitch's flat. But it was "all right" his standing there; he was "quite well." He was standing in a corner, huddled in a place which was not very warm, though it was dark, partly hidden by a huge cupboard and an old screen, in the midst of rubbish, litter, and odds and ends of all sorts, concealing himself for the time being and watching the course of proceedings as a disinterested spectator. He was only looking on now, gentlemen; he, too, gentlemen, might go in, of course . . . why should he not go in? He had only to take one step and he would go in, and would go in very adroitly. Just now, though he had been standing nearly three hours between the cupboard and the screen in the midst of the rubbish, litter, and odds and ends of all sorts, he was only quoting, in his own justification, a memorable phrase of the French minister, Villesle: "All things come in time to him who has the strength to wait." Mr. Golyadkin had read this sentence in some book on quite a different subject, but now very aptly recalled it. The phrase, to begin with, was exceedingly appropriate to his present position, and, indeed, why should it not occur to the mind of a man who had been waiting for almost three hours in the cold and the dark in expectation of a happy ending to his adventures. After quoting very appropriately the phrase of the French minister, Villesle, Mr. Golyadkin immediately thought of the Turkish Vizier, Martsimiris, as well as of the beautiful Margravine Luise, whose story he had read also in some book. Then it occurred to his mind that the Jesuits made it their rule that any means were justified if only the end were attained. Fortifying himself somewhat with this historical fact, Mr. Golyadkin said to himself, What were the Jesuits? The Jesuits were every one of them very great fools; that he was better than any of them; that if only the refreshment-room would be empty for one minute (the door of the refreshment-room opened straight into the passage to the back stairs, where Mr. Golyadkin was in hiding now), he would, in spite of all the Jesuits in the world, go straight in, first from the refreshment-room into the tea-room, then into the room where they were now playing cards, and then straight into the hall where they were now dancing the polka, and he would go in, he would certainly go in, in spite of anything he would go in—he would slip through—and that would be all, no one would notice him; and once there he would know what to do.

Well, so this is the position in which we find the hero of our perfectly true story, though, indeed, it is difficult to explain what was passing in him at that moment. The fact is that he had made his way to the back stairs and to the passage, on the ground that, as he said, "why shouldn't he? and everyone did go that way"; but he had not ventured to penetrate further, evidently he did not dare to do so . . . "not because there was anything he did not dare, but just because he did not care to, because he preferred to be in hiding"; so here he was, waiting now for a chance to slip in, and he had been waiting for it two hours and a half. "Why not wait? Villesle himself had waited. But what had Villesle to do with it?" thought Mr. Golyadkin: "How does Villesle come in? But how am I to . . . to go and walk in? . . . Ech, you dummy!" said Mr. Golyadkin, pinching his benumbed cheek with his benumbed fingers; "you silly fool, you silly old Golyadkin—silly fool of a surname! . . ."

But these compliments paid to himself were only by the way and without any apparent aim. Now he was on the point of pushing forward and slipping in; the refreshment-room was empty and no one was in sight. Mr. Golyadkin saw all this through the little window; in two steps he was at the door and had already opened it. "Should he go in or not? Come, should he or not? I'll go in . . . why not? to the bold all ways lie open!" Reassuring himself in this way, our hero suddenly and quite unexpectedly retreated behind the screen. "No," he thought. "Ah, now, somebody's coming in? Yes, they've come in; why did I dawdle when there were no people about? Even so, shall I go and slip in? ... No, how slip in when a man has such a temperament! Fie, what a low tendency! I'm as scared as a hen! Being scared is our special line, that's the fact of the matter! To be abject on every occasion is our line: no need to ask us about that. Just stand here like a post and that's all! At home I should be having a cup of tea now. . . . It would be pleasant, too, to have a cup of tea. If I come in later Petrushka'll grumble, maybe. Shall I go home?

Damnation take all this! I'll go and that 'll be the end of it!" Reflecting on his position in this way, Mr. Golyadkin dashed forward as though some one had touched a spring in him; in two steps he found himself in the refreshment-room, flung off his overcoat, took off his hat, hurriedly thrust these things into a corner, straightened himself and smoothed himself down; then . . . then he moved on to the tea-room, and from the tea-room darted into the next room, slipped almost unnoticed between the card-players, who were at the tip-top of excitement, then . . . Mr. Golyadkin forgot everything that was going on about him, and went straight as an arrow into the drawing-room.

As luck would have it they were not dancing. The ladies were promenading up and down the room in picturesque groups. The gentlemen were standing about in twos and threes or flitting about the room engaging partners. Mr. Golyadkin noticed nothing of this. He saw only Mara Olsufyevna, near her Andrey Filippovitch, then Vladimir Semyonovitch, two or three officers, and, finally, two or three other young men who were also very interesting and, as any one could see at once, were either very promising or had actually done something. . . . He saw some one else too. Or, rather, he saw nobody and looked at nobody ... but, moved by the same spring which had sent him dashing into the midst of a ball to which he had not been invited, he moved forward, and then forwarder and forwarder. On the way he jostled against a councilor and trod on his foot, and incidentally stepped on a very venerable old lady's dress and tore it a little, pushed against a servant with a tray and then ran against somebody else, and, not noticing all this, or rather noticing it but at the same time looking at no one, passing further and further forward, he suddenly found himself facing Klara Olsufyevna. There is no doubt whatever that he would, with the utmost delight, without winking an eyelid, have sunk through the earth at that moment; but what has once been done cannot be recalled . . . can never be recalled. What was he to do? "If I fail I don't lose heart, if I succeed I persevere." Mr. Golyadkin was, of course, not "one to intrigue," and "not accomplished in the art of polishing the floor with his boots." . . . And so, indeed, it proved. Besides, the Jesuits had some hand in it too . . . though Mr. Golyadkin had no thoughts to spare for them now! All the " moving, noisy, talking, laughing groups were suddenly hushed as though at a signal and, little by little, crowded round Mr. Golyadkin. He, however, seemed to hear nothing, to see nothing, he could not look . . . he could not possibly look at anything; he kept his eyes on the floor and so stood, giving himself his word of honour, in passing, to shoot himself one way or another that night. Making this vow, Mr.

Golyadkin inwardly said to himself, "Here goes!" and to his own great astonishment began unexpectedly to speak.

He began with congratulations and polite wishes. The congratulations went off well, but over the good wishes our hero stammered. He felt that if he stammered all would be lost at once. And so it turned out-he stammered and floundered . . . floundering, he blushed crimson; blushing, he was overcome with confusion. In his confusion he raised his eyes; raising his eyes he looked about him; looking about him—he almost swooned. . . . Every one stood still, every one was silent, every one was waiting; a little way off there was whispering; a little nearer there was laughter. Mr. Golyadkin fastened a humble, imploring look on Andrey Filippovitch. Andrey Filippovitch responded with such a look that if our hero had not been utterly crushed already he certainly would have been crushed a second time—that is, if that were possible. The silence lasted long.

"This is rather concerned with my domestic circumstances and my private life, Andrey Filippovitch," our hero, half-dead, articulated in a scarcely audible voice; "it is not an official incident, Andrey Filippovitch . . ."

"For shame, sir, for shame!" Andrey Filippovitch pronounced in a half whisper, with an indescribable air of indignation; he pronounced these words and, giving Klara Olsufyevna his arm, he turned away from Mr. Golyadkin.

"I've nothing to be ashamed of, Andrey Filippovitch," answered Mr. Golyadkin, also in a whisper, turning his miserable eyes about him, trying helplessly to discover in the amazed crowd something on which he could gain a footing and retrieve his social position.

"Why, it's all right, it's nothing, gentlemen! Why, what's the matter? Why, it might happen to any one," whispered Mr. Golyadkin, moving a little away and trying to escape from the crowd surrounding him.

They made way for him. Our hero passed through two rows of inquisitive and wondering spectators. Fate drew him on. He felt that himself, that fate was leading him on. He would have given a great deal, of course, for a chance to be back in the passage by the back stairs, without having committed a breach of propriety; but as that was utterly impossible he began trying to creep away into a corner and to stand there—modestly, decorously, apart, without interfering with any one, without attracting especial attention, but at the same time to win the favourable notice of his host and the company. At the same time Mr. Golyadkin felt as though the ground were giving way under him, as though he were staggering, falling. At last he made his way to a corner and stood in it, like an unconcerned, rather indifferent spectator, leaning his arms on the backs of two chairs, taking complete possession of them in that way, and trying, as far as he could, to glance confidently at Olsufy Ivanovitch's guests, grouped about him. Standing nearest him was an officer, a tall and handsome fellow, beside whom Golyadkin felt himself an insect.

"These two chairs, lieutenant, are intended, one for Klara Olsufyevna, and the other for Princess Tchevtchehanov; I'm taking care of them for them," said Mr. Golyadkin breathlessly, turning his imploring eyes on the officer. The lieutenant said nothing, but turned away with a murderous smile. Checked in this direction, our hero was about to try his luck in another quarter, and directly addressed an important councilor with a cross of great distinction on his breast. But the councilor looked him up and down with such a frigid stare that Mr. Golyadkin felt distinctly as though a whole bucketful of cold water had been thrown over him. He subsided into silence. He made up his mind that it was better to keep quiet, not to open his lips, and to show that he was "all right," that he was "like every one else," and that his position, as far as he could see, was quite a proper one. With this object he riveted his gaze on the lining of his coat, then raised his eyes and fixed them upon a very respectable-looking gentleman. "That gentleman has a wig on," thought Mr. Golyadkin; "and if he takes off that wig he will be bald, his head will be as bare as the palm of my hand." Having made this important discovery, Mr. Golyadkin thought of the Arab Emirs, whose heads are left bare and shaven if they take off the green turbans they wear as a sign of their descent from the prophet Mahomet. Then, probably from some special connection of ideas with the Turks, he thought of Turkish slippers and at once, apropos of that, recalled the fact that Andrey Filippovitch was wearing boots, and that his boots were more like slippers than boots. It was evident that Mr. Golyadkin had become to some extent reconciled to his position. "What if that chandelier," flashed through Mr. Golyadkin's mind, "were to come down from the ceiling and fall upon the company. I should rush at once to save Klara Olsufyevna. `Save her!' I should cry. `Don't be alarmed, madam, it's of no consequence, I will rescue you, I.' Then . ." At that moment Mr. Golyadkin looked about in search of Klara Olsufyevna, and saw Gerasimitch, Olsufy Ivanovitch's old butler. Gerasimitch, with a most anxious and solemnly official air, was making straight for him. Mr. Golyadkin started and frowned from an unaccountable but most disagreeable sensation; he looked about him mechanically; it occurred to his mind if only he could somehow creep off somewhere, unobserved, on the sly—simply disappear, that is, behave as though he had done nothing at all, as though the matter did not concern him in the least! . . . But before our hero could make up his mind to do anything Gerasimitch was standing before him.

"Do you see, Gerasimitch," said our hero, with a little smile, addressing Gerasimitch; "you go and tell them—do you see the candle there in the chandelier, Gerasimitch —it will be falling down directly: so, you know, you must tell them to see it; it really will fall down, Gerasimitch. . . ."

"The candle? No, the candle's standing straight; but somebody is asking for you, sir."

"Who is asking for me, Gerasimitch?"

"I really can't say, sir, who it is. A man with a message. 'Is Yakov Petrovitch Golyadkin here?' says he. 'Then call him out,' says he, 'on very urgent and important business . . .' you see."

"No, Gerasimitch, you are making a mistake; in that you are making a mistake, Gerasimitch."

"I doubt it, sir."

"No, Gerasimitch, it isn't doubtful; there's nothing doubtful about it, Gerasimitch. Nobody's asking for me, but I'm quite at home here—that is, in my right place, Gerasimitch."

Mr. Golyadkin took breath and looked about him. Yes! Every one in the room, all had their eyes fixed upon him, and were listening in a sort of solemn expectation. The men had crowded a little nearer and were all attention. A little further away the ladies were whispering together. The master of the house made his appearance at no great distance from Mr. Golyadkin, and though it was impossible to detect from his expression that he, too, was taking a close and direct interest in Mr. Golyadkin's position, for everything was being done with delicacy, yet, nevertheless, it all made our hero feel that the decisive moment had come for him. Mr. Golyadkin saw clearly that the time had come for a bold stroke, the chance of putting his enemies to shame. Mr. Golyadkin was in great agitation. He was aware of a sort of inspiration and, in a quivering and impressive voice, he began again, addressing the waiting butler.

"No, my dear fellow, no one's calling for me. You are mistaken. I will say more: you were mistaken this morning, too, when you assured me. . . . dared to assure me, I say" (he raised his voice), "that Olsufy Ivanovitch, who had been my benefactor as long as I can remember and has, in a sense, been a father to me, was shutting his door upon me at the moment of solemn family rejoicing for his paternal heart." (Mr. Golyadkin looked about him complacently, but with deep feeling. A tear glittered on his eyelash.) "I repeat, my friend," our hero concluded, "you were mistaken, you were cruelly and unpardonably mistaken. . . .

The moment was a solemn one. Mr. Golyadkin felt that the effect was quite certain. He stood with modestly downcast eyes, expecting Olsufy Ivanovitch to embrace him. Excitement and perplexity were apparent in the guests, even the inflexible and terrible Gerasimitch faltered over the words "I doubt it . . ." when suddenly the ruthless orchestra, apropos of nothing, struck up a polka. All was lost; all was scattered to the winds. Mr. Golyadkin started; Gerasimitch stepped back; every-thing in the room began undulating like the sea; and Vladimir Semyonovitch led the dance with Klara Olsufyevna, while the handsome lieutenant followed with Princess Tchevtchehanov. Onlookers, curious and delighted, squeezed in to watch them dancing the polka—an interesting, fashionable new dance which every one was crazy over. Mr. Golyadkin was, for the time, forgotten. But suddenly all were thrown, into excitement, confusion and bustle; the music ceased . . . a strange incident had occurred. Tired out with the dance, and almost breathless with fatigue, Klara Olsufyevna, with glowing cheeks and heaving bosom, sank into an armchair, completely exhausted. . . . All hearts turned to the fascinating creature, all vied with one another in complimenting her and thanking her for the pleasure conferred on them,—all at once there stood before her Mr. Golyadkin. He was pale, extremely perturbed; he, too, seemed completely exhausted, he could scarcely move. He was smiling for some reason, he stretched out his hand imploringly. Klara Olsufyevna was so taken aback that she had not time to withdraw hers and mechanically got up at his invitation. Mr. Golyadkin lurched forward, first once, then a second time, then lifted his leg, then made a scrape, then gave a sort of stamp, then stumbled . . . he, too, wanted to dance with Klara Olsufyevna. Klara Olsufyevna uttered a shriek; every one rushed to release her hand from Mr. Golyadkin's, and in a moment our hero was carried almost ten paces away by the rush of the crowd. A circle formed round him too. Two old ladies, whom he had almost knocked down in his retreat, raised a great shrieking and outcry. The confusion was awful; all were asking questions, every one was shouting, every one was finding fault. The orchestra was silent. Our hero whirled round in his circle and mechanically, with a semblance of a smile, muttered something to himself, such as, "Why not?" and "that the polka, so far, at least, as he could see, was a new and very interesting dance, invented for the diversion of the ladies . . . but that since things had taken this turn, he was ready to consent." But Mr. Golyadkin's consent no one apparently thought of asking. Our hero was suddenly aware that some one's hand was laid on his arm, that another hand was pressed against his back, that he was with peculiar solicitude being guided in a certain direction. At last he noticed that he was going straight to the door. Mr. Golyadkin wanted to say something, to do something. . . . But no, he no longer wanted to do anything. He only mechanically kept laughing in answer. At last he was aware that they were putting on his greatcoat, that his hat was thrust over his eyes; finally he felt that he was in the entry on the stairs in the dark and cold. At last he stumbled, he felt that he was falling down a precipice; he tried to cry out—and suddenly found himself in the courtyard. The air blew fresh on him, he stood still for a minute; at that very instant, the strains reached him of the orchestra striking up again. Mr. Golyadkin suddenly recalled it all; it seemed to him that all his flagging energies came back to him again. He had been standing as though riveted to the spot, but now he started off and rushed away headlong, anywhere, into the air, into freedom, wherever chance might take him.

CHAPTER V

It was striking midnight from all the clock towers in Petersburg when Mr. Golyadkin, beside himself, ran out on the Fontanka Quay, close to the Ismailovsky Bridge, fleeing from his foes, from persecution, from a hailstorm of nips and pinches aimed at him, from the shrieks of excited old ladies, from the Ohs and Ahs of women and from the murderous eyes of Andrey Filippovitch. Mr. Golyadkin was killed—killed entirely, in the full sense of the word, and if he still preserved the power of running, it was simply through some sort of miracle, a miracle in which at last he refused himself to believe. It was an awful November night—wet, foggy, rainy, snowy, teeming with colds in the head, fevers, swollen faces, quinseys, inflammations of all kinds and descriptions—teeming, in fact, with all the gifts of a Petersburg November. The wind howled in the deserted streets, lifting up the black water of the canal above the rings on the bank, and irritably brushing against the lean lamp-posts which chimed in with its howling in a thin, shrill creak, keeping up the endless squeaky, jangling concert with which every inhabitant of Petersburg is so familiar. Snow and rain were falling both at once. Lashed by the wind, the streams of rainwater spurted almost horizontally, as though from a fireman's hose, pricking and stinging the face of the luckless Mr. Golyadkin like a thousand pins and needles. In the stillness of the night, broken only by the distant rumbling of carriages, the howl of the wind and the creaking of the lamp-posts, there was the dismal sound of the splash and gurgle of water, rushing from every roof, every porch, every pipe and every cornice, on to the granite of the pavement. There was not a soul, near or far, and, indeed, it seemed there could not be at such an hour and in such weather. And so only Mr. Golyadkin, alone with his despair, was fleeing in terror along the pavement of Fontanka, with his usual rapid little step, in haste to get home as soon as possible to his flat on the fourth storey in Shestilavotchny Street.

Though the snow, the rain, and all the nameless horrors of a raging snowstorm and fog, under a Petersburg November sky, were attacking Mr. Golyadkin, already shattered by misfortunes, were showing him no mercy, giving him no rest, drenching him to the bone, glueing up his eyelids, blowing right through him from all sides, baffling and perplexing him—though all this was hurled upon Mr. Golyadkin at once, as though conspiring and combining with all his enemies to make a grand day, evening, and night for him, in spite of all this Mr. Golyadkin was almost insensible to this final proof of the persecution of destiny: so violent had been the shock and the impression made upon him a few minutes before at the civil councilor Berendyev's! If any disinterested spectator could have glanced casually at Mr. Golyadkin's painful progress, he would instantly have grasped the awful horror of his pitiful plight and would certainly have said that Mr. Golyadkin looked as though he wanted to hide from himself, as though he were trying to run away from himself! Yes! It was really so. One may say more: Mr. Golyadkin did not want only to run away from himself, but to be obliterated, to cease to be, to return to dust. At the moment he took in nothing surrounding him, understood nothing of what was going on about him, and looked as though the miseries of the stormy night, of the long tramp, the rain, the snow, the wind, all the cruelty of the weather, did not exist for him. The golosh slipping off the boot on Mr. Golyadkin's right foot was left behind in the snow and slush on the pavement of Fontanka, and Mr. Golyadkin did not think of turning back to get it, did not, in fact, notice that he had lost it. He was so perplexed. that, in spite of everything surrounding him, he stood several times stockstill in the middle of the pavement, completely possessed by the thought of-his recent horrible humiliation; at that instant he was dying, disappearing; then he suddenly set off again like mad and ran and ran without looking back, as though he were pursued, as though he were fleeing from some still more awful calamity.... The position was truly awful!... At last Mr. Golyadkin halted in exhaustion, leaned on the railing in the attitude of a man whose nose has suddenly begun to bleed, and began looking intently at the black and troubled waters of the canal. There is no knowing what length of time he spent like this. All that is known is that at that instant Mr. Golyadkin reached such a pitch of despair, was so harassed, so tortured, so exhausted, and so weakened in what feeble faculties were left him that he forgot everything, forgot the Ismailovsky Bridge, forgot Shestilavotchny Street, forgot his present plight.... After all, what did it matter to him? The thing was done. The decision was affirmed and ratified; what could he do? All at once ... all at once he started and involuntarily skipped a couple of paces aside. With unaccountable uneasiness he began gazing about him; but no one was there, nothing special had happened, and yet ... and yet he fancied that just now, that very minute, some one was standing near him, beside him, also leaning on the railing, and—marvelous to relate!—had even said something to him, said something quickly, abruptly, not quite intelligibly, but something quite private, something concerning himself.

"Why, was it my fancy?" said Mr. Golyadkin, looking round once more. "But where am I standing? ... Ech, ech," he thought finally, shaking his head, though he began gazing with an uneasy, miserable feeling into the damp, murky distance, straining his sight and doing his utmost to pierce with his shortsighted eyes the wet darkness that stretched all round him. There was nothing new, however, nothing special caught the eye of Mr. Golyadkin. Everything seemed to be all right, as it should be, that is, the snow was falling more violently, more thickly and in larger flakes, nothing could be seen twenty paces away, the lamp-posts creaked more shrilly than ever and the wind seemed to intone its melancholy song even more tearfully, more piteously, like an importunate beggar whining for a copper to get a crust of bread. At the same time a new sensation took possession of Mr. Golyadkin's whole being: agony upon agony, terror upon terror ... a feverish tremor ran through his veins. The moment was insufferably unpleasant! "Well, it's no matter," he said, to encourage himself. "Well, no matter; perhaps it's no matter at all, and there's no stain on any one's honour. Perhaps it's as it should be," he went on, without understanding what he was saying. "Perhaps it will all be for the best in the end, and there will be nothing to complain of, and every one will be justified."

Talking like this and comforting himself with words, Mr. Golyadkin shook himself a little, shook off the snow which had drifted in thick layers on his hat, his collar, his overcoat, his tie, his boots and everything; but his strange feeling, his strange, obscure misery he could not get rid of, could not shake off. Somewhere in the distance there was the boom of a cannon shot. "Ach, what weather!" thought our hero. "Tchoo! isn't there going to be a flood? It seems as though the water has risen so violently."

Mr. Golyadkin had hardly said or thought this when he saw a person coming towards him, belated, no doubt, like him, through some accident. An unimportant, casual incident, one might suppose, but for some unknown reason Mr. Golyadkin was troubled, even scared, and rather flurried. It was not that he was exactly afraid of some ill-intentioned man, but just that "perhaps . . . after all, who knows, this belated individual," flashed through Mr. Golyadkin's mind, "maybe he's that very thing, maybe he's the very principal thing in it, and isn't here for nothing, but is here with an object, crossing my path and provoking me." Possibly, however, he did not think this precisely, but only had a passing feeling of something like it—and very unpleasant. There was no time, however, for thinking and feeling. The stranger was already within two paces. Mr. Golyadkin, as he invariably did, hastened to assume a quite peculiar air, an air that expressed clearly that he, Golyadkin, kept himself to himself, that he was "all right," that the road was wide enough for all, and that he, Golyadkin, was not interfering with any one. Suddenly he stopped short as though petrified, as though struck by lightning, acid quickly turned round after the figure which had only just passed him—turned as though some one had given him a tug from behind, as though the wind had turned him like a weather-cock. The passer-by vanished quickly in the snowstorm. He, too, walked quickly; he was dressed like Mr. Golyadkin and, like him, too, wrapped up from head to foot, and he, too, tripped and trotted along the pavement of Fontanka with rapid little steps that suggested that he was a little scared.

"What—what is it?" whispered Mr. Golyadkin, smiling mistrustfully, though he trembled all over. An icy shiver ran down his back. Mean-while, the stranger had vanished completely; there was no sound of his step, while Mr. Golyadkin still stood and gazed after him. At last, how-ever, he gradually came to himself.

"Why, what's the meaning of it?" he thought with vexation. "Why, have I really gone out of my mind, or what?" He turned and went on his way, making his footsteps more rapid and frequent, and doing his best not to think of anything at all. He even closed his eyes at last with the same object. Suddenly, through the howling of the wind and the uproar of the storm, the sound of steps very close at hand reached his ears again. He started and opened his eyes. Again a rapidly approaching figure stood out black before him, some twenty paces away. This little figure was hastening, tripping along, hurrying nervously; the distance between them grew rapidly less. Mr. Golyadkin could by now get a full view of this second belated companion. He looked full at him and cried out with amazement and horror; his legs gave way under him. It was the same individual who had passed him ten minutes before, and who now quite unexpectedly turned up facing him again. But this was not the only marvel that struck Mr. Golyadkin. He was so amazed that he stood still, cried out, tried to say something, and rushed to overtake the stranger, even shouted something to him, probably anxious to stop him as quickly as possible. The stranger did, in fact, stop ten paces from Mr. Golyadkin, so that the light from the lamp-post that stood near fell full upon his whole figure—stood still, turned to Mr. Golyadkin, and with impatient and anxious face waited to hear what he would say.

"Excuse me, possibly I'm mistaken," our hero brought out in a quavering voice.

The stranger in silence, and with an air of annoyance, turned and rapidly went on his way, as though in haste to make up for the two seconds he had wasted on Mr. Golyadkin. As for the latter, he was quivering in every nerve, his knees shook and gave way under him, and with a moan he squatted on a stone at the edge of the pavement. There really was reason, however, for his being so overwhelmed. The fact is that this stranger seemed to him now somehow familiar. That would have been nothing, though. But he recognized, almost certainly recognized this man. He had often seen him, that man, had seen him some time, and very lately too; where could it have been? Surely not yesterday? But, again, that was not the chief thing that Mr. Golyadkin had often seen him before; there was hardly anything special about the man; the man at first sight would not have aroused any special attention. He was just a man like any one else, a gentleman like all other gentlemen, of course, and perhaps he had some good qualities and very valuable ones too—in fact, he was a man who was quite himself. Mr. Golyadkin cherished no sort of hatred or enmity, not even the slightest hostility towards this man—quite the contrary, it would seem, indeed—and yet (and this was the real point) he would not for any treasure on earth have been willing to meet that man, and especially to meet him as he had done now, for instance. We may say more: Mr. Golyadkin knew that man perfectly well: he even knew what he was called, what his name was; and yet nothing would have induced him, and again, for no treasure on earth would he have consented to name him, to consent to acknowledge that he was called so-and-so, that his father's name was this and his surname was that. Whether Mr. Golyadkin's stupefaction lasted a short time or a long time, whether he was sitting for a long time on the stone of the pavement I cannot say; but, recovering himself a little at last, he suddenly fell to running, without looking round, as fast as his legs could carry him; his mind was preoccupied, twice he stumbled and almost fell—and through this circumstance his other boot was also bereaved of its golosh. At last Mr. Golyadkin slackened his pace a little to get breath, looked hurriedly round and saw that he had already, with-out being aware of it, run right across Fontanka, had crossed the Anitchkov Bridge, had passed part of the Nevsky Prospect and was now standing at the turning into Liteyny Street. Mr. Golyadkin turned into Liteyny Street. His position at that instant was like that of a man standing at the edge of a fearful precipice, while the earth is bursting open under him, is already shaking, moving, rocking for the last time, falling, drawing him into the abyss, and yet the luckless wretch has not the strength, nor the resolution, to leap back, to avert his eyes from the yawning gulf below; the abyss draws him and at last he leaps into it of himself, himself hastening the moment of his destruction. Mr. Golyadkin knew, felt and was firmly convinced that some other evil would certainly befall him on the way, that some unpleasantness would overtake him, that he would, for instance, meet his stranger once more: but—strange to say, he positively desired this meeting, considered it inevitable, and all he asked was that it might all be quickly over, that he should be relieved from his position in one way or, another, but as soon as possible. And meanwhile he ran on and on, as though moved by some external force, for he felt a weakness and numbness in his whole being: he could not think of anything, though his thoughts caught at everything like brambles. A little lost dog, soaked and shivering, attached itself to Mr. Golyadkin, and ran beside him, scurrying along with tail and ears drooping, looking at him from time to time with timid comprehension. Some remote, long-forgotten idea—some memory of something that had happened long ago—came back into his mind now, kept knocking at his brain as with a hammer, vexing him and refusing to be shaken off.

"Ech, that horrid little cur!" whispered Mr. Golyadkin, not under-standing himself.

At last he saw his stranger at the turning into Italyansky Street. But this time the stranger was not coming to meet him, but was going in the same direction as he was, and he, too, was running, a few steps in front. At last they turned into Shestilavotchny Street.

Mr. Golyadkin caught his breath. The stranger stopped exactly before the house in which Mr. Golyadkin lodged. He heard a ring at the bell and almost at the same time the grating of the iron bolt. The gate opened, the stranger stooped, darted in and disappeared. Almost at the same instant Mr. Golyadkin reached the spot and like an arrow flew in at the gate. Heedless of the grumbling porter, he ran, gasping for breath, into the yard, and immediately saw his interesting companion, whom he had lost sight of for a moment.

The stranger darted towards the staircase which led to Mr. Golyadkin's flat. Mr. Golyadkin rushed after him. The stairs were dark, damp and dirty. At every turning there were heaped-up masses of refuse from the flats, so that any unaccustomed stranger who found himself on the stairs in the dark was forced to travel to and fro for half an hour in danger of breaking his legs, cursing the stairs as well as the friends who lived in such an inconvenient place. But Mr. Golyadkin's companion seemed as though familiar with it, as though at home; he ran up lightly, without difficulty, showing a, perfect knowledge of his surroundings.. Mr. Golyadkin had almost caught him up; in fact, once or twice the stranger's coat flicked him on the nose. His heart stood still. The stranger stopped before the door of Mr. Golyadkin's flat, knocked on it, and (which would, however, have surprised Mr. Golyadkin at any other time) Petrushka, as though he had been sitting up in expectation, opened the door at once and, with a candle in his hand, followed the stranger as the latter went in. The hero of our story dashed into his lodging beside himself; without taking off his hat or coat he crossed the little passage and stood still in the doorway of his room, as though thunderstruck. All his presentiments had come true. All that he had dreaded and surmised was coming to pass in reality. His breath failed him, his head was in a whirl. The stranger, also in his coat and hat, was sitting before him on his bed, and with a faint smile, screwing up his eyes, nodded to him in a friendly way.

Mr. Golyadkin wanted to scream, but could not—to protest in some way, but his strength failed him. His hair stood on end, and he almost fell down with horror. And, indeed, there was good reason. He recognized his nocturnal visitor. The nocturnal visitor was no other than himself—Mr. Golyadkin himself, another Mr. Golyadkin, but absolutely the same as himself—in fact, what is called a double in every respect. . . .

CHAPTER VI

AT eight o'clock next morning Mr. Golyadkin woke up in his bed. At once all the extraordinary incidents of the previous day and the wild, incredible night, with all its almost impossible adventures, presented themselves to his imagination and memory with terrifying vividness. Such intense, diabolical malice on the part of his enemies, and, above all, the final proof of that malice, froze Mr. Golyadkin's heart. But at the same time it was all so strange, incomprehensible, wild, it seemed so impossible, that it was really hard to credit himself that it was all an incredible delusion, a passing aberration of the fancy, a darkening of the mind, if he had not fortunately known by bitter experience to what lengths spite will sometimes carry any one, what a pitch of ferocity an enemy may reach when he is bent on revenging his honour and prestige. Besides, Mr. Golyadkin's exhausted limbs, his heavy head, his aching back, and the malignant cold in his head bore vivid witness to the probability of his expedition of the previous night and upheld the reality of it, and to some extent of all that had happened during that expedition. And, indeed, Mr. Golyadkin had known long, long before that something was being got up among them, that there was some one else with them. But after all, thinking it over thoroughly, he made up his mind to keep quiet, to submit and not to protest for the time.

"They are simply plotting to frighten me, perhaps, and when they see that I don't mind, that I make no protest, but keep perfectly quiet and put up with it meekly, they'll give it up, they'll give it up of themselves, give it up of their own accord."

Such, then, were the thoughts in the mind of Mr. Golyadkin as, stretching in his bed, hying to rest his exhausted limbs, he waited for Petrushka to come into his room as usual. . . . He waited for a full quarter of an hour. He heard the lazy scamp fiddling about with the samovar behind the screen, and yet he could not bring himself to call him. We may say more: Mr. Golyadkin was a little afraid of confronting Petrushka.

"Why, goodness knows," he thought, "goodness knows how that rascal looks at it all. He keeps on saying nothing, but he has his own ideas."

At last the door creaked and Petrushka came in with a tray in his hands. Mr. Golyadkin stole a timid glance at him, impatiently waiting to see what would happen, waiting to see whether he would not say something about a certain circumstance. But Petrushka said nothing; he was, on the contrary, more silent, more glum and ill-humoured than usual; he looked askance from under his brows at everything; altogether it was evident that he was very much put out about something; he did not even once glance at his master, which, by the way, rather piqued the latter. Setting all he had brought on the table, he turned and went out of the room without a word.

"He knows, he knows, he knows all about it, the scoundrel!" Mr. Golyadkin grumbled to himself as he took his tea. Yet our hero did not address a single question to his servant, though Petrushka came into his room several times afterwards on various errands. Mr. Golyadkin was in great trepidation of spirit. He dreaded going to the office. He had a strong presentiment that there he would find something that would not be "just so."

"You may be sure," he thought, "that as soon as you go you will light upon something! Isn't it better to endure in patience? Isn't it better to wait a bit now? Let them do what they like there; but I'd better stay here a bit today, recover my strength, get better, and think over the whole affair more thoroughly, then afterwards I could seize the right moment, fall upon them like snow from the sky, and get off scot free myself."

Reasoning like this, Mr. Golyadkin smoked pipe after pipe; time was flying. It was already nearly half-past nine.

"Why, it's half-past nine already," thought Mr. Golyadkin; "it's late for me to make my appearance. Besides, I'm ill, of course I'm ill, I'm certainly ill; who denies it? What's the matter with me? If they send to make inquiries, let the executive clerk come; and, indeed, what is the matter with me really? My back aches, I have a cough, and a cold in my head; and, in fact, it's out of the question for me to go out, utterly out of the question in such weather. I might be taken ill and, very likely, die; nowadays especially the death-rate is so high. . .

With such reasoning Mr. Golyadkin succeeded at last in setting his conscience at rest, and defended himself against the reprimands he expected from Andrey Filippovitch for neglect of his duty. As a rule in such cases our hero was particularly fond of justifying himself in his own eyes with all sorts of irrefutable arguments, and so completely setting his conscience at rest. And so now, having completely soothed his conscience, he took up his pipe, filled it, and had no sooner settled down comfortably to smoke, when he jumped up quickly from the sofa, flung away the pipe, briskly washed, shaved, and brushed his hair, got into his uniform and so on, snatched up some papers, and flew off to the office.

Mr. Golyadkin went into his department timidly, in quivering expectation of something unpleasant—an expectation which was none the less disagreeable for being vague and unconscious; he sat timidly down in his invariable place next the head clerk, Anton Antonovitch Syetotchkin. Without looking at anything or allowing his attention to be distracted, he plunged into the contents of the papers that lay before him. He made up his mind and vowed to himself to avoid, as far as possible, anything provocative, anything that might compromise him, such as indiscreet questions, jests, or unseemly allusions to any incidents of the previous evening; he made up his mind also to abstain from the usual interchange of civilities with his colleagues, such as inquiries after health and such like. But evidently it was impossible, out of the question, to keep to this. Anxiety and uneasiness in regard to anything near him that was annoying always worried him far more than the annoyance itself. And that was why, in spite of his inward vows to refrain from entering into anything, whatever happened, and to keep aloof from everything, Mr. Golyadkin from time to time, on the sly, very, very quietly, raised his head and stealthily looked about him to right and to left, peeped at the countenances of his colleagues, and tried to gather whether there were not something new and particular in them referring to himself and with sinister motives concealed from him. He assumed that there must be a connection between all that had happened yesterday and all that surrounded him now. At last, in his misery, he began to long for something—goodness knows what—to happen to put an end to it—even some calamity—he did not care. At this point destiny caught Mr. Golyadkin: he had hardly felt this desire when his doubts were solved in the strangest and most unexpected manner.

The door leading from the next room suddenly gave a soft and timid creak, as though to indicate that the person about to enter was a very unimportant one, and a figure, very familiar to Mr. Golyadkin, stood shyly before the very table at which our hero was seated. The latter did not raise his head—no, he only stole a glance at him, the tiniest glance; but he knew all, he understood all, to every detail. He grew hot with shame, and buried his devoted head in his papers with precisely the same object with which the ostrich, pursued by hunters, hides his head in the burning sand. The new arrival bowed to Andrey Filippovitch, and thereupon he heard a voice speaking in the regulation tone of con-descending politeness with which all persons in authority address their subordinates in public offices.

"Take a seat here," said Andrey Filippovitch, motioning the new-comer to Anton Antonovitch's table. "Here, opposite Mr. Golyadkin, and we'll soon give you something to do."

Andrey Filippovitch ended by making a rapid gesture that decorously admonished the newcomer of his duty, and then he immediately became engrossed in the study of the papers that lay in a heap before him.

Mr. Golyadkin lifted his eyes at last, and that he did not fall into a swoon was simply because he had foreseen it all from the first, that he had been forewarned from the first, guessing in his soul who the stranger was. Mr. Golyadkin's first movement was to look quickly about him, to see whether there were any whispering, any office joke being cracked on the subject, whether any one's face was agape with wonder, whether, indeed, some one had not fallen under the table from terror. But to his intense astonishment there was no sign of anything of the sort. The behaviour of his colleagues and companions surprised him. It seemed contrary to the dictates of common sense. Mr. Golyadkin was positively scared at this extraordinary reticence. The fact spoke for itself; it was a strange, horrible, uncanny thing. It was enough to rouse any one. All this, of course, only passed rapidly through Mr. Golyadkin's mind. He felt as though he were burning in a slow fire. And, indeed, there was enough to make him. The figure that was sitting opposite Mr. Golyadkin now was his terror, was his shame, was his nightmare of the evening before; in short, was Mr. Golyadkin himself, not the Mr. Golyadkin who was sitting now in his chair with his mouth wide open and his pen petrified in his hand, not the one who acted as assistant to his chief, not the one who liked to efface himself and slink away in the crowd, not the one whose deportment plainly said, "Don't touch me and I won't touch you," or, "Don't interfere with me, you see I'm not touching you"; no, this was another Mr. Golyadkin, quite different, yet, at the same time, exactly like the first—the same height, the same figure, the same clothes, the same baldness; in fact, nothing, absolutely nothing, was lacking to complete the likeness, so that if one were to set them side by side, nobody, absolutely nobody, could have undertaken to distinguish which was the real Golyadkin and which was the counterfeit, which was the old one and which was the new one, which was the original and which was the copy.

Our hero was—if the comparison can be made—in the position of a man upon whom some practical joker has stealthily, by way of jest, turned a burning-glass.

"What does it mean? Is it a dream?" he wondered. "Is it reality or the continuation of what happened yesterday? And besides, by what right is this all being done? Who sanctioned such a clerk, who authorized this? Am I asleep, am I in a waking dream?"

Mr. Golyadkin tried pinching himself, even tried to screw up his courage to pinch some one else. . . . No, it was not a dream, and that was all about it. Mr. Golyadkin felt that the sweat was trickling down him in big drops; he felt that what was happening to him was something incredible, unheard of, and for that very reason was, to complete his misery, utterly unseemly, for Mr. Golyadkin realized and felt how disadvantageous it was to be the first example of such a burlesque adventure. He even began to doubt his own existence, and though he was pre-pared for anything and had been longing for his doubts to be settled in any way whatever, yet the actual reality was startling in its unexpectedness. His misery was poignant and overwhelming. At times he lost all power of thought and memory. Coming to himself after such a moment, he noticed that he was mechanically and unconsciously moving the pen over the paper. Mistrustful of himself, he began going over what he had written—and could make nothing of it. At last the other Mr. Golyadkin, who had been sitting discreetly and decorously at the table, got up and disappeared through the door into the other room. Mr. Golyadkin looked round—everything was quiet; he heard nothing but the scratching of pens, the rustle of turning over pages, and conversation in the corners furthest from Andrey Filippovitch's seat. Mr. Golyadkin looked at Anton Antonovitch, and as, in all probability, our hem's countenance fully reflected his real condition and harmonized with the whole position, and was consequently, from one point of view, very remarkable, good-natured Anton Antonovitch, laying aside his pen, inquired after his health with marked sympathy.

"I'm very well, thank God, Anton Antonovitch," said Mr. Golyadkin, stammering. "I am perfectly well, Anton Antonovitch. I am all right now, Anton Antonovitch," he added uncertainly, not yet fully trusting Anton Antonovitch, whose name he had mentioned so often.

"I fancied you were not quite well: though that's not to be wondered at; no, indeed! Nowadays especially there's such a lot of illness going about. Do you know . . ."

"Yes, Anton Antonovitch, I know there is such a lot of illness . . . I did not mean that, Anton Antonovitch," Mr. Golyadkin went on, looking intently at Anton Antonovitch. "You see, Anton Antonovitch, I don't even know how you, that is, I mean to say, how to approach this matter, Anton Antonovitch. . . ."

"How so? I really . . . do you know . . . I must confess I don't quite understand; you must . . . you must explain, you know, in what way you are in difficulties," said Anton Antonovitch, beginning to be in difficulties himself, seeing that there were actually tears in Mr. Golyadkin's eyes.

"Really, Anton Antonovitch . . . I . . . here . . . there's a clerk here, -Anton Antonovitch . . ."

"Well! I don't understand now."

"I mean to say, Anton Antonovitch, there's a new clerk here."

"Yes, there is; a namesake of yours."

"What?" cried Mr. Golyadkin.

"I say a namesake of yours; his name's Golyadkin too. Isn't he a brother of yours?"

"No, Anton Antonovitch, I . . ."

"H'm! you don't say so! Why, I thought he must be a relation of yours. Do you know, there's a sort of family likeness."

Mr. Golyadkin was petrified with astonishment, and for the moment he could not speak. To treat so lightly such a horrible, unheard-of thing, a thing undeniably rare and curious in its way, a thing which would have amazed even an unconcerned spectator, to talk of a family resemblance when he could see himself as in a looking-glass!

"Do you know, Yakov Petrovitch, what I advise you to do?" Anton Antonovitch went on. "Go and consult a doctor. Do you know, you look somehow quite unwell. Your eyes look peculiar . . . you know, there's a peculiar expression in them."

"No, Anton Antonovitch, I feel, of course . . . that is, I keep wanting to ask about this clerk."

"Well?"

"That is, have not you noticed, Anton Antonovitch, something peculiar about him, something very marked?"

"That is. . . ?"

"That is, I mean, Anton Antonovitch, a striking likeness with some-body, for instance; with me, for instance? You spoke just now, you see, Anton Antonovitch, of a family likeness. You let slip the remark. . . . You know there really are sometimes twins exactly alike, like two drops of water, so that they can't be told apart. Well, it's that that I mean."

"To be sure," said Anton Antonovitch, after a moment's thought, speaking as though he were struck by the fact for the first time; "yes, indeed! You are right, there is a striking likeness, and you are quite right in what you say. You really might be mistaken for one another," he went on, opening his eyes wider and wider; "and, do you know, Yakov Petrovitch, it's positively a marvellous likeness, fantastic, in fact, as the saying is; that is, just as you . . Have you observed, Yakov Petrovitch? I wanted to ask you to explain it; yes, I must confess I didn't take particular notice at first. It's wonderful, it's really wonderful! And, you know, you are not a native of these parts, are you, Yakov Petrovitch?"

"No."

"He is not from these parts, you know, either. Perhaps he comes from the same part of the country as you do. Where, may I make bold to inquire, did your mother live for the most part?"

"You said . . you say, Anton Antonovitch, that he is not a native of these parts?"

"No, he is not. And, indeed, how strange it is!" continued the talkative Anton Antonovitch, for whom it was a genuine treat to gossip. "It may well arouse curiosity; and yet, you know, you might often pass him by, brush against him, without noticing anything. But you mustn't be upset about it. It's a thing that does happen. Do you know, the same thing, I must tell you, happened to my aunt on my mother's side; she saw her own double before her death . . ."

"No, I—excuse my interrupting you, Anton Antonovitch—I wanted to find out, Anton Antonovitch, how that clerk . . . that is, on what footing is he here?"

"In place of Semyon Ivanovitch, to fill the vacancy left by his death; .the post was vacant, so he was appointed. Do you know, I'm told poor dear Semyon Ivanovitch left three children, all tiny dots. The widow fell at the feet of his Excellency. They do say she's hiding something; she's got a bit of money, but she's hiding it."

"No, Anton Antonovitch, I was still referring to that circumstance."

"You mean . . . ? To be sure! but why are you so interested in that? I tell you not to upset yourself. All this is temporary to some extent. Why, after all, you know, you have nothing to do with it. So it has been ordained by God Almighty, it's His will, and it is sinful repining. His wisdom is apparent in it. And as far as I can make out, Yakov Petrovitch, you are not to blame in any way. There are all sorts of strange things in the world! Mother Nature is liberal with her gifts, and you are not called upon to answer for it, you won't be responsible. Here, for instance, you have heard, I expect, of those—what's their name?—oh, the Siamese twins who are joined together at the back, live and eat and sleep together. I'm told they get a lot of money."

"Allow me, Anton Antonovitch . . ."

"I understand, I understand! Yes! But what of it? It's no matter, I tell you, as far as I can see there's nothing for you to upset yourself about. After all, he's a clerk—as a clerk he seems to be a capable man. He says his name is Golyadkin, that he's not a native of this district, and that he's a titular councilor. He had a personal interview with his Excellency."

"And how did his Excellency . . . ?"

"It was all right; I am told he gave a satisfactory account of himself, gave his reasons, said, 'It's like this, your Excellency,' and that he was 'without means and anxious to enter the service, and would be particularly flattered to be serving under his Excellency . . . all that was proper, you know; he expressed himself neatly. He must be a sensible man. But of course he came with a recommendation; he couldn't have got in without that. . . ."

"Oh, from whom ... that is, I mean, who is it has had a hand in this shameful business?"

"Yes, a good recommendation, I'm told; his Excellency, I'm told, laughed with Andrey Filippovitch."

"Laughed with Andrey Filippovitch?"

"Yes, he only just smiled and said that it was all right, and that he had nothing against it, so long as he did his duty. . . ."

"Well, and what more? You relieve me to some extent, Anton Antonovitch; go on, I entreat you."

"Excuse me, I must tell you again. . . . Well, then, come, it's nothing, it's a very simple matter; you mustn't upset yourself, I tell you, and there's nothing suspicious about it. ."

"No. I . . . that is, Anton Antonovitch, I want to ask you, didn't his Excellency say anything more . . . about me, for instance?"

"Well! To be sure! No, nothing of the sort; you can set your mind quite at rest. You know it is, of course, a rather striking circumstance, and at first . . . why, here, I, for instance, I scarcely noticed it. I really don't know why I didn't notice it till you mentioned it. But you can set your mind at rest entirely. He said nothing particular, absolutely nothing," added good-natured Anton Antonovitch, getting up from his chair.

"So then, Anton Antonovitch, I . . ."

"Oh, you must excuse me. Here I've been gossiping about these trivial matters, and I've business that is important and urgent. I must inquire about it."

"Anton Antonovitch!" Andrey Filippovitch's voice sounded, summoning him politely, "his Excellency has been asking for you."

"This minute, I'm coming this minute, Andrey Filippovitch." And Anton Antonovitch, taking a pile of papers, flew off first to Andrey Filippovitch and then into his Excellency's room.

"Then what is the meaning of it?" thought Mr. Golyadkin. "Is there some sort of game going on? So the wind's in that quarter now. . . . That's just as well; so things have taken a much pleasanter turn," our hero said to himself, rubbing his hands, and so delighted that he scarcely knew where he was. "So our position is an ordinary thing. So it turns out to be all nonsense, it comes to nothing at all. No one has done any-thing really, and they are not budging, the rascals, they are sitting busy over their work; that's splendid, splendid! I like the good-natured fellow, I've always liked him, and I'm always ready to respect him . . . though it must be said one doesn't know what to think; this Anton Antonovitch . . . I'm afraid to trust him; his hair's very grey, and he's so old he's getting shaky. It's an immense and glorious thing that his Excellency said nothing, and let it pass! It's a good thing! I approve! Only why does Andrey Filippovitch interfere with his grins? What's he got to do with it? The old rogue. Always on my track, always, like a black cat, on the watch to run across a man's path, always thwarting and annoying a man, always annoying and thwarting a man. . . ."

Mr. Golyadkin looked around him again, and again his hopes revived. Yet he felt that he was troubled by one remote idea, an unpleasant idea. It even occurred to him that he might try somehow to make up to the clerks, to be the first in the field even (perhaps when leaving the office or going up to them as though about his work), to drop a hint in the course of conversation, saying, "This is how it is, what a striking likeness, gentlemen, a strange circumstance, a burlesque farce!"—that is, treat it all lightly, and in this way sound the depth of the danger. "Devils breed in still waters," our hero concluded inwardly.

Mr. Golyadkin, however, only contemplated this; he thought better of it in time. He realized that this would be going too far. "That's your temperament," he said to himself, tapping-himself lightly on the fore-head; "as soon as you gain anything you are delighted! You're a simple soul! No, you and I had better be patient, Yakov Petrovitch; let us wait and be patient!"

Nevertheless, as we have mentioned already, Mr. Golyadkin was buoyed up with the most confident hopes, feeling as though he had risen from the dead.

"No matter," he thought, "it's as though a hundred tons had been lifted off my chest! Here is a circumstance, to be sure! The box has been opened by lifting the lid. Krylov is right, a clever chap, a rogue, that Krylov, and a great fable-writer! And as for him, let him work in the office, and good luck to him so long as he doesn't meddle or interfere with anyone; let him work in the office—I consent and approve!"

Meanwhile the hours were passing, flying by, and before he noticed the time it struck four. The office was closed. Andrey Filippovitch took his hat, and all followed his example in due course. Mr. Golyadkin dawdled a little on purpose, long enough to be the last to go out when all the others had gone their several ways. Going out from the street he felt as though he were in Paradise, so that he even felt inclined to go a longer way round, and to walk along the Nevsky Prospect.

"To be sure this is destiny," thought our hero, "this unexpected turn in affairs. And the weather's more cheerful, and the frost and the little sledges. And the frost suits the Russian, the Russian gets on capitally with the frost. I like the Russian.

Fyodor Dostoevsky   The Double

And the dear little snow, and the first few flakes in autumn; the sportsman would say, 'It would be nice to go shooting hares in the first snow.' Well, there, it doesn't matter."

This was how Mr. Golyadkin's enthusiasm found expression. Yet something was fretting in his brain, not exactly melancholy, but at times he had such a gnawing at his heart that he did not know how to find relief.

"Let us wait for the day, though, and then we shall rejoice. And, after all, you know, what does it matter? Come, let us think it over, let us look at it. Come, let us consider it, my young friend, let us consider it. Why, a man's exactly like you in the first place, absolutely the same. Well, what is there in that? If there is such a man, why should I weep over it? What is it to me? I stand aside, I whistle to myself, and that's all! That's what I laid myself open to, and that's all about it! Let him work in the office! Well, it's strange and marvellous, they say, that the Siamese twins ... But why bring in the Siamese twins? They are twins, of course, but even great men, you know, sometimes look queer creatures. In fact, we know from history that the famous Suvorov used to crow like a cock. . . . But there, he did all that with political motives; and he was a great general . . . but what are generals, after all? But I keep myself to myself, that's all, and I don't care about any one else, and, secure in my innocence, I scorn my enemies. I am not one to intrigue, and I'm proud of it. Genuine, straightforward, neat and nice, meek and mild."

All at once Mr. Golyadkin broke off, his tongue failed him and he began trembling like a leaf; he even closed his eyes for a minute. Hoping, however, that the object of his terror was only an illusion, he opened his eyes at last and stole a timid glance to the right. No, it was not an illusion! . . . His acquaintance of that morning was tripping along by his side, smiling, peeping into his face, and apparently seeking an opportunity to begin a conversation with him. The conversation was not begun, however. They both walked like this for about fifty paces. All Mr. Golyadkin's efforts were concentrated on muffling himself up, hiding himself in his coat and pulling his hat down as far as possible over his eyes. To complete his mortification, his companion's coat and hat looked as though they had been taken off Mr. Golyadkin himself.

"Sir," our hero articulated at last, trying to speak almost in a whisper, and not looking at his companion, "we are going different ways, I believe. . . . I am convinced of it, in fact," he said, after a brief pause. "I am convinced, indeed, that you quite understand me," he added, rather severely, in conclusion.

"I could have wished . . ." his companion pronounced at last, "I could have wished . . . no doubt you will be magnanimous and pardon me . . . I don't know to whom to address myself here . . . my circumstances . . . I trust you will pardon my intrusiveness. I fancied, indeed, that, moved by compassion, you showed some interest in me this morning. On my side, I felt drawn to you from the first moment. I . . ."

At this point Mr. Golyadkin inwardly wished that his companion might sink into the earth. "If I might venture to hope that you would accord me an indulgent hearing, Yakov Petrovitch . . ."

"We—here, we—we . . . you had better come home with me," answered Mr. Golyadkin. "We will cross now to the other side of the Nevsky Prospect, it will be more convenient for us there, and then by the little back street . . . we'd better go by the back street."

"Very well, by all means let us go by the back street," our hero's meek companion responded timidly, suggesting by the tone of his reply that it was not for him to choose, and that in his position he was quite prepared to accept the back street. As for Mr. Golyadkin, he was utterly unable to grasp what was happening to him. He could not believe in himself. He could not get over his amazement.

CHAPTER VII

He recovered himself a little on the staircase as he went up to his flat.

"Oh, I'm a sheep's head," he railed at himself inwardly. "Where am I taking him? I am thrusting my head into the noose. What will Petrushka think, seeing us together? What will the scoundrel dare to imagine now? He's suspicious. . . ."

But it was too late to regret it. Mr. Golyadkin knocked at the door; it was opened, and Petrushka began taking off the visitor's coat as well as his master's. Mr. Golyadkin looked askance, just stealing a glance at Petrushka, trying to read his countenance and divine what he was thinking. But to his intense astonishment he saw that his servant showed no trace of surprise, but seemed, on the contrary, to be expecting something of the sort. Of course he did look morose, as it was; he kept his eyes turned away and looked as though he would like to fall upon somebody.

"Hasn't somebody bewitched them all today?" thought our hero. "Some devil must have got round them. There certainly must be something peculiar in the whole lot of them today. Damn it all, what a worry it is!"

Such were Mr. Golyadkin's thoughts and reflections as he led his visitor into his room and politely asked him to sit down. The visitor appeared to be greatly embarrassed, he was very shy, and humbly watched every movement his host made, caught his glance, and seemed trying to divine his thoughts from them. There was a down-trodden, crushed, scared look about all his gestures, so that—if the comparison may be allowed—he was at that moment rather like the man who, having lost his clothes, is dressed up in somebody else's: the sleeves work up to the elbows, the waist is almost up to his neck, and he keeps every minute pulling down the short waistcoat; he wriggles side-ways and turns away, tries to hide himself, or peeps into every face, and listens whether people are talking of his position, laughing at him or putting him to shame—and he is crimson with shame and overwhelmed with confusion and wounded vanity. . . . Mr. Golyadkin put down his hat in the window, and carelessly sent it flying to the floor. The visitor darted at once to pick it up, brushed off the dust, and carefully put it back, while he laid his own on the floor near a chair, on the edge of which he meekly seated himself. This little circumstance did something to open Mr. Golyadkin's eyes; he realized that the man was in great straits, and so did not put himself out for his visitor as he had done at first, very properly leaving all that to the man himself. The visitor, for his part, did nothing either; whether he was shy, a little ashamed, or from politeness was waiting for his host to begin is not certain and would be difficult to determine. At that moment Petrushka came in; he stood still in the doorway, and fixed his eyes in the direction furthest from where the visitor and his master were seated.

"Shall I bring in dinner for two?" he said carelessly, in a husky voice.

"I—I don't know . . . you . . . yes, bring dinner for two, my boy."

Petrushka went out. Mr. Golyadkin glanced at his visitor. The latter crimsoned to his ears. Mr. Golyadkin was a kindhearted man, and so in the kindness of his heart he at once elaborated a theory.

"The fellow's hard up," he thought. "Yes, and in his situation only one day. Most likely he's suffered in his time. Maybe his good clothes are all that he has, and nothing to get him a dinner. Ah, poor fellow, how crushed he seems! But no matter; in a way it's better so. . . . Excuse me," began Mr. Golyadkin, "allow me to ask what I may call you."

"I . . . I . . . I'm Yakov Petrovitch," his visitor almost whispered, as though conscience-stricken and ashamed, as though apologizing for being called Yakov Petrovitch too.

"Yakov Petrovitch!" repeated our hero, unable to conceal his confusion.

"Yes, just so. . . . The same name as yours," responded the meek visitor, venturing to smile and speak a little jocosely. But at once he drew back, assuming a very serious air, though a little disconcerted, noticing that his host was in no joking mood.

" You . . . allow me to ask you, to what am I indebted for the honour . . . ?"

"Knowing your generosity and your benevolence," interposed the visitor in a rapid but timid voice, half rising from his seat, "I have ventured to appeal to you and to beg for your . . . acquaintance and protection . . ." he concluded, choosing his phrases with difficulty and trying to select words not too flattering or servile, that he might not compromise his dignity and not so bold as to suggest an unseemly equality. In fact, one may say the visitor behaved like a gentlemanly beggar with a darned waistcoat, with an honourable passport in his pocket, who has not yet learnt by practice to hold out his hand properly for alms.

"You perplex me," answered Mr. Golyadkin, gazing round at himself, his walls and his visitor. "In what could I . . . that is, I mean, in what way could I be of service to you?"

"I felt drawn to you, Yakov Petrovitch, at first sight, and, graciously forgive me, I built my hopes on you—I made bold to build my hopes on you, Yakov Petrovitch. I . . . I'm in a desperate plight here, Yakov Petrovitch; I'm poor, I've had a great deal of trouble, Yakov Petrovitch, and have only recently come here. Learning that you, with your innate goodness and excellence of heart, are of the same name . . ."

Mr. Golyadkin frowned.

"Of the same name as myself and a native of the same district, I made up my mind to appeal to you, and to make known to you my difficult position."

"Very good, very good; I really don't know what to say," Mr. Golyadkin responded in an embarrassed voice. "We'll have a talk after dinner. . . ."

The visitor bowed; dinner was brought in. Petrushka laid the table, and Mr. Golyadkin and his visitor proceeded to partake of it. The dinner did not last long, for they were both in a hurry, the host because he felt ill at ease, and was, besides, ashamed that the dinner was a poor one—he was partly ashamed because he wanted to give the visitor a good meal, and partly because he wanted to show him he did not live like a beggar. The visitor, on his side too, was in terrible confusion and extremely embarrassed. When he had finished the piece of bread he had taken, he was afraid to put out his hand to take another piece, was ashamed to help himself to the best morsels, and was continually assuring his host that he, was not at all hungry, that the dinner was excellent, that he was absolutely satisfied with it, and should not forget it to his dying day. When the meal was over Mr. Golyadkin lighted his pipe, and offered a second, which was brought in, to the visitor. They sat facing each other, and the visitor began telling his adventures.

Mr. Golyadkin junior's story lasted for three or four hours. His history was, however, composed of the most trivial and wretched, if one may say so, incidents. It dealt with details of service in some court of law in the provinces, of prosecutors and presidents, of some department intrigues, of the depravity of some registration clerks, of an inspector, of the sudden appointment of a new chief in the department, of how the second Mr. Golyadkin had suffered, quite without any fault on his part; of his aged aunt, Pelagea Semyonovna; of how, through various intrigues on the part of his enemies, he had lost his situation, and had come to Petersburg on foot; of the harassing and wretched time he had spent here in Petersburg, how for a long time he had tried in vain to get a job, had spent all his money, had nothing left, had been living almost in the street, lived on a crust of bread and washed it down with his tears, slept on the bare floor, and finally how some good Christian had exerted himself on his behalf, had given him an introduction, and had nobly got him into a new berth. Mr. Golyadkin's visitor shed tears as he told his story, and wiped his eyes with a blue-check handkerchief that looked like oilcloth. He ended by making a clean breast of it to Mr. Golyadkin, and confessing that he was not only for the time without means of subsistence and money for a decent lodging, but had not even the wherewithal to fit himself out properly, so that he had not, he said in conclusion, been able to get together enough for a pair of wretched boots, and that he had had to hire a uniform for the time.

Mr. Golyadkin was melted; he was genuinely touched. Even though his visitor's story was the paltriest story, every word of it was like heavenly manna to his heart. The fact was that Mr. Golyadkin was beginning to forget his last misgivings, to surrender his soul to freedom and rejoicing, and at last mentally dubbed himself a fool. It was all so natural! And what a thing to break his heart over, what a thing to be so distressed about! To be sure there was, there really was, one ticklish circumstance— but, after all, it was not a misfortune; it could be no disgrace to a man, it could not cast a slur on his honour or ruin his career, if he were innocent, since nature herself was mixed up in it. Moreover, the visitor begged for protection, wept, railed at destiny, seemed such an artless, pitiful, insignificant person, with no craft or malice about him, and he seemed now to be ashamed himself, though ,perhaps on different grounds, of the strange resemblance of his countenance with that of Mr. Golyadkin's. His behaviour was absolutely unimpeachable; his one desire was to please his host, and he looked as a man looks who feels conscience-stricken and to blame in regard to some one else. If any doubtful point were touched upon, for instance, the visitor at once agreed with Mr. Golyadkin's opinion. If by mistake he advanced an opinion in opposition to Mr. Golyadkin's, and afterwards noticed that he had made a slip, he immediately corrected his mistake, explained himself and made it clear that he meant the same thing as his host, that he thought as he did and took the same view of everything as he did. In fact, the visitor made every possible effort to "make up to" Mr. Golyadkin, so that the latter made up his mind at last that his visitor must be a very amiable person in every way. Meanwhile, tea was brought in; it was nearly nine o'clock. Mr. Golyadkin felt in a very good-humour, grew lively and skittish, let himself go a little, and finally plunged into a most animated and interesting conversation with his visitor. In his festive moments Mr. Golyadkin was fond of telling interesting anecdotes. So now he told the visitor a great deal about Petersburg, about its entertainments and attractions, about the theatre, the clubs, about Brulov's picture, and about the two Englishmen who came from England to Petersburg on purpose to look at the iron railing of the Summer Garden, and returned at once when they had seen it; about the office; about Olsufy Ivanovitch and Andrey Filippovitch; about the way that Russia was progressing, was hour by hour progressing towards a state of perfection, so that

"Art and letters flourish here today";

about an anecdote he had lately read in the Northern Bee concerning a boa-constrictor in India of immense strength; about Baron Brambeus, and so on. In short, Mr. Golyadkin was quite happy, first, because his mind was at rest, secondly, because, so far from being afraid of his enemies, he was quite prepared now to challenge them all to mortal combat; thirdly, because he was now in the role of patron and was doing a good deed. Yet he was conscious at the bottom of his heart that he was not perfectly happy, that there was still a hidden worm gnawing at his heart, though it was only a tiny one. He was extremely worried by the thought of the previous evening at Olsufy Ivanovitch's. He would have given a great deal now for nothing to have happened of what took place then.

"It's no matter, though!" our hero decided at last, and he firmly resolved in his heart to behave well in future and never to be guilty of such pranks again. As Mr. Golyadkin was now completely worked up, and had suddenly become almost blissful, the fancy took him to have a jovial time. Rum was brought in by Petrushka, and punch was pre-pared. The visitor and his host drained a glass each, and then a second. The visitor appeared even more amiable than before, and gave more than one proof of his frankness and charming character; he entered keenly into Mr. Golyadkin's joy, seemed only to rejoice in his rejoicing, and to look upon him as his one and only benefactor. Taking up a pen and a sheet of paper, he asked Mr. Golyadkin not to look at what he was going to write, but afterwards showed his host what he had written. It turned out to be a verse of four lines, written with a good deal of feeling, in excellent language and handwriting, and evidently was the composition of the amiable visitor himself. The lines were as follows;

"If thou forget me,
I shall not forget thee;
Though all things may be,
Do not thou forget me."

With tears in his eyes Mr. Golyadkin embraced his companion, and, completely overcome by his feelings, he began to initiate his friend into some of his own secrets and private affairs, Andrey Filippovitch and Klara Olsufyevna being prominent in his remarks.

"Well, you may be sure we shall get on together, Yakov Petrovitch," said our hero to his visitor. "You and I will take to each other like fish to the water, Yakov Petrovitch; we shall be like brothers; we'll be cunning, my dear fellow, we'll work together; we'll get up an intrigue, too, to pay them out. To pay them out we'll get up an intrigue too. And don't you trust any of them. I know you, Yakov Petrovitch, and I understand your character; you'll tell them everything straight out, you know, you're a guileless soul! You must hold aloof from them all, my boy."

His companion entirely agreed with him, thanked Mr. Golyadkin, and he, too, grew tearful at last.

"Do you know, Yasha," Mr. Golyadkin went on in a shaking voice, weak with emotion, "you must stay with me for a time, or stay with me for-ever. We shall get on together. What do you say, brother, eh? And don't you worry or repine because there's such a strange circumstance about us now; it's a sin to repine, brother; it's nature! And Mother Nature is liberal with her gifts, so there, brother Yasha! It's from love for you that I speak, from brotherly love. But we'll be cunning, Yasha; we'll lay a mine, too, and we'll make them laugh the other side of their mouths."

They reached their third and fourth glasses of punch at last, and then Mr. Golyadkin began to be aware of two sensations: the one that he was extraordinarily happy, and the other that he could not stand upon his legs. The guest was, of course, invited to stay the night. A bed was somehow made up on two chairs: Mr. Golyadkin junior declared that under a friend's roof the bare floor would be a soft bed, that for his part he could sleep anywhere, humbly and gratefully; that he was in paradise now, that he had been through a great deal of trouble and grief in his time; he had seen ups and downs, had all sorts of things to put up with, and—who could tell what the future would be?—maybe he would have still more to put up with. Mr. Golyadkin senior protested against this, and began to maintain that one must put one's faith in God. His guest entirely agreed, observing that there was, of course, no one like God. At this point Mr. Golyadkin senior observed that in certain respects the Turks were right in calling upon God even in their sleep. Then, though disagreeing with certain learned professors in the slanders they had promulgated against the Turkish prophet Mahomet and recognizing him as a great politician in his own line, Mr. Golyadkin passed to a very interesting description of an Algerian barber's shop which he had read in a book of miscellanies. The friends laughed heartily at the simplicity of the Turks, but paid due tribute to their fanaticism, which they ascribed to opium. . . . At last the guest began undressing, and thinking in the kindness of his heart that very likely he hadn't even a decent shirt, Mr. Golyadkin went behind the screen to avoid embarrassing a man who had suffered enough, and partly to reassure himself as far as possible about Petrushka, to sound him, to cheer him up if he could, to be kind to the fellow so that every one might be happy and that everything might be pleasant all round. It must be remarked that Petrushka still rather bothered Mr. Golyadkin.

"You go to bed now, Pyotr," Mr. Golyadkin said blandly, going into his servant's domain; "you go to bed now and wake me up at eight o'clock. Do you understand, Petrushka?"

Mr. Golyadkin spoke with exceptional softness and friendliness. But Petrushka remained mute. He was busy making his bed, and did not even turn round to face his master, which he ought to have done out of simple respect.

"Did you hear what I said, Pyotr?" Mr. Golyadkin went on. "You go to bed now and wake me tomorrow at eight o'clock; do you under-stand?"

"Why, I know that; what's the use of telling me?" Petrushka grumbled to himself.

"Well, that's right, Petrushka; I only mentioned it that you might be happy and at rest. Now we are all happy, so I want you, too, to be happy and satisfied. And now I wish you good-night. Sleep, Petrushka, sleep; we all have to work. . . . Don't think anything amiss, my man . . ." Mr. Golyadkin began, but stopped short. "Isn't this too much?" he thought. "Haven't I gone too far? That's how it always is; I always overdo things."

Our hero felt much dissatisfied with himself as he left Petrushka. He was, besides, rather wounded by Petrushka's grumpiness and rudeness. "One jests with the rascal, his master does him too much honour, and the rascal does not feel it," thought Mr. Golyadkin. "But there, that's the nasty way of all that sort of people!"

Somewhat shaken, he went back to his room, and, seeing that his guest had settled himself for the night, he sat down on the edge of his bed for a minute.

"Come, you must own, Yasha," he began to whisper, wagging his head, "you're a rascal, you know; what a way you've treated me! You see, you've got my name, do you know that?" he went on, jesting in a rather familiar way with his visitor. At last, saying a friendly good-night to him, Mr. Golyadkin began preparing for the night. The visitor meanwhile began snoring. Mr. Golyadkin in his turn got into bed, laughing and whispering to himself: "You are drunk today, my dear fellow, Yakov Petrovitch, you rascal, you old Golyadkin—what a surname to have! Why, what are you so pleased about? You'll be crying tomorrow, you know, you sniveller; what am Ito do with you?"

At this point a rather strange sensation pervaded Mr. Golyadkin's whole being, something like doubt or remorse.

"I've been over-excited and let myself go," he thought; "now I've a noise in my head and I'm drunk; I couldn't restrain myself, ass that I am! and I've been babbling bushels of nonsense, and, like a rascal, I was planning to be so sly. Of course, to forgive and forget injuries is the height of virtue; but it's a bad thing, nevertheless! Yes, that's so!"

At this point Mr. Golyadkin got up, took a candle and went on tiptoe to look once more at his sleeping guest. He stood over him for a long time, meditating deeply.

"An unpleasant picture! A burlesque, a regular burlesque, and that's the fact of the matter!"

At last Mr. Golyadkin settled down finally. There was a humming, a buzzing, a ringing in his head. He grew more and more drowsy . . . tried to think about something, to remember something very interesting, to decide something very important, some delicate question—but could not. Sleep descended upon his devoted head, and he slept as people generally do sleep who are not used to drinking and have consumed five glasses of punch at some festive gathering.

CHAPTER VIII

Mr. Golyadkin woke up next morning at eight o'clock as usual; as soon as he was awake he recalled all the adventures of the previous evening—and frowned as he recalled them. "Ugh, I did play the fool last night!" he thought, sitting up and glancing at his visitor's bed. But what was his amazement when he saw in the room no trace, not only of his visitor, but even of the bed on which his visitor had slept!

"What does it mean?" Mr. Golyadkin almost shrieked. "What can it be? What does this new circumstance portend?"

While Mr. Golyadkin was gazing in open-mouthed bewilderment at the empty spot, the door creaked and Petrushka came in with the tea-tray.

"Where, where?" our hero said in a voice hardly audible, pointing to the place which had been occupied by his visitor the night before.

At first Petrushka made no answer and did not look at his master, but fixed his eyes upon the corner to the right till Mr. Golyadkin felt compelled to look into that corner too. After a brief silence, however, Petrushka in a rude and husky voice answered that his master was not at home.

"You idiot; why I'm your master, Petrushka!" said Mr. Golyadkin in a breaking voice, looking open-eyed at his servant.

Petrushka made no reply, but he gave Mr. Golyadkin such a look that the latter crimsoned to his ears—looked at him with an insulting reproachfulness almost equivalent to open abuse. Mr. Golyadkin was utterly flabbergasted, as the saying is. At last Petrushka explained that the other one had gone away an hour and a half ago, and would not wait. His answer, of course, sounded truthful and probable; it was evident that Petrushka was not lying; that his insulting look and the phrase the other one employed by him were only the result of the disgusting circumstance with which he was already familiar, but still he understood, though dimly, that something was wrong, and that destiny had some other surprise, not altogether a pleasant one, in store for him.

"All right, we shall see," he thought to himself. "We shall see in due time; we'll get to the bottom of all this. . . . Oh, Lord, have mercy upon us!" he moaned in conclusion, in quite a different voice. "And why did I invite him, to what end did I do all that?

Why, I am thrusting my head into their thievish noose myself; I am tying the noose with my own hands. Ach, you fool, you fool! You can't resist babbling like some silly boy, some chancery clerk, some wretched creature of no class at all, some rag, some rotten dishcloth; you're a gossip, an old woman! . . . Oh, all ye saints! And he wrote verses, the rogue, and expressed his love for me! How could .. . How can I show him the door in a polite way if he turns up again, the rogue? Of course, there are all sorts of ways and means. I can say this is how it is, my salary being so limited. . . . Or scare him off in some way saying that, taking this and that into consideration, I am forced to make clear . . . that he would have to pay an equal share of the cost of board and lodging, and pay the money in advance. H'm! No, damn it all, no! That would be degrading to me. It's not quite delicate! Couldn't I do something like this: suggest to Petrushka that he should annoy him in some way, should be disrespectful, be rude, and get rid of him in that way. Set them at each other in some way. . . . No, damn it all, no! It's dangerous and again, if one looks at it from that point of view—it's not the right thing at all! Not the right thing at all! but there, even if he doesn't come, it will be a bad look-out, too! I babbled to him last night! . . . Ach, it's a bad look-out, a bad look-out! Ach, we're in a bad way! Oh, I'm a cursed fool, a cursed fool! You can't train yourself to behave as you ought, you can't conduct yourself reasonably. Well, what if he comes, and refuses. And God grant he may come! I should be very glad if he did come. . . ."

Such were Mr. Golyadkin's reflections as he swallowed his tea and glanced continually at the clock on the wall.

"It's a quarter to nine; it's time to go. And something will happen! What will there be there? I should like to know what exactly lies hidden in this—that is, the object, the aim, and the various intrigues. It would be a good thing to find out what all these people are plotting, and what will be their first step. . . ."

Mr. Golyadkin could endure it no longer. He threw down his unfinished pipe, dressed and set off for the office, anxious to ward off the danger if possible and to reassure himself about everything by his presence in person. There was danger: he knew himself that there was danger.

"We . . . will get to the bottom of it," said Mr. Golyadkin, taking off his coat and goloshes in the entry. "We'll go into all these matters immediately."

Making up his mind to act in this way, our hero put himself to rights, assumed a correct and official air, and was just about to pass into the adjoining room, when suddenly, in the very doorway, he jostled against his acquaintance of the day before, his friend and companion. Mr. Golyadkin junior seemed not to notice Mr. Golyadkin senior, though they met almost nose to nose. Mr. Golyadkin junior seemed to be busy, to be hastening somewhere, was breathless; he had such an official, such a business-like air that it seemed as though any one could read in his face: 'Entrusted with a special commission.' . . .

"Oh, it's you, Yakov Petrovitch!" said our hero, clutching the hand of his last night's visitor.

"Presently, presently, excuse me, tell me about it afterwards," cried Mr. Golyadkin junior, dashing on.

"But, excuse me; I believe, Yakov Petrovitch, you wanted."
"What is it? Make haste and explain."

At this point his visitor of the previous night halted as though reluctantly and against his will, and put his ear almost to Mr. Golyadkin's nose.

"I must tell you, Yakov Petrovitch, that I am surprised at your behaviour . . . behaviour which seemingly I could not have expected at all."

"There's a proper form for everything. Go to his Excellency's secretary and then appeal in the proper way to the directors of the office. Have you got your petition?"

"You . . . I really don't know, Yakov Petrovitch! You simply amaze me, Yakov Petrovitch! You certainly don't recognize me or, with your characteristic gaiety, you are joking."

"Oh, it's you," said Mr. Golyadkin junior, seeming only now to recognize Mr. Golyadkin senior. "So it's you? Well, have you had a good night?"

Then, smiling a little—a formal and conventional smile, by no means the sort of smile that was befitting (for, after all, he owed a debt of gratitude to Mr. Golyadkin senior)—smiling this formal and conventional smile, Mr. Golyadkin junior added that he was very glad Mr. Golyadkin senior had had a good night; then he made a slight bow and shuffling a little with his feet, looked to the right, and to the left, then dropped his eyes to the floor, made for the side door and muttering in a hurried whisper that he had a special commission, dashed into the next room. He vanished like an apparition.

"Well, this is queer!" muttered our hero, petrified for a moment; "this is queer! This is a strange circumstance."

At this point Mr. Golyadkin felt as though he had pins and needles all over him.

"However," he went on to himself, as he made his way to his department, "however, I spoke long ago of such a circumstance: I had a pre-sentiment long ago that he had a special commission. Why, I said yesterday that the man must certainly be employed on some special commission."

"Have you finished copying out the document you had yesterday, Yakov Petrovitch," Anton Antonovitch Syetotchkin asked Mr. Golyadkin, when the latter was seated beside him. "Have you got it here?"

"Yes," murmured Mr. Golyadkin, looking at the head clerk with a rather helpless glance.

"That's right! I mention it because Andrey Filippovitch has asked for it twice. I'll be bound his Excellency wants it. . . ."

"Yes, it's finished. . . ."

"Well, that's all right then."

"I believe, Anton Antonovitch, I have always performed my duties properly. I'm always scrupulous over the work entrusted to me by my superiors, and I attend to it conscientiously."

"Yes. Why, what do you mean by that?"

"I mean nothing, Anton Antonovitch. I only want to explain, Anton Antonovitch, that I . . that is, I meant to express that spite and malice sometimes spare no person whatever in their search for their daily and revolting food. . ."

"Excuse me, I don't quite understand you. What person are you alluding to?"

"I only meant to say, Anton Antonovitch, that I'm seeking the straight path and I scorn going to work in a roundabout way. That I am not one to intrigue, and that, if I may be allowed to say so, I may very justly be proud of it. . . ."

"Yes. That's quite so, and to the best of my comprehension I thoroughly endorse your remarks; but allow me to tell you, Yakov Petrovitch, that personalities are not quite permissible in good society, that I, for instance, am ready to put up with anything behind my back—for every one's abused behind his back—but to my face, if you please, my good sir, I don't allow any one to be impudent. I've grown grey in the government service, sir, and I don't allow any one to be impudent to me in my old age. . . ."

"No, Anton Antonovitch . . . you see, Anton Antonovitch . . . you haven't quite caught my meaning. To be sure, Anton Antonovitch, I for my part could only think it an honour. . ."

"Well, then, I ask your pardon too. We've been brought up in the old school. And it's too late for us to learn your newfangled ways. I believe we've had understanding enough for the service of our country up to now. As you are aware, sir, I have an order of merit for twenty-five years' irreproachable service. . . ."

"I feel it, Anton Antonovitch, on my side, too, I quite feel all that. But 3 didn't mean that, I am speaking of a mask, Anton Antonovitch. . . ." "A mask?"

"Again you . . . I am apprehensive that you are taking this, too, in a wrong sense, that is the sense of my remarks, as you say yourself, Anton Antonovitch. I am simply enunciating a theory, that is, I am advancing 'the idea, Anton Antonovitch, that persons who wear a mask have become far from uncommon, and that nowadays it is hard to recognize the man beneath the mask. . . ."

"Well, do you know, it's not altogether so hard. Sometimes it's fairly easy. Sometimes one need not go far to look for it."

"No, you know, Anton Antonovitch, I say, I say of myself, that I, for instance, do not put on a mask except when there is need of it; that is simply at carnival time or at some festive gathering, speaking in the literal sense; but that I do not wear a mask before people in daily life, speaking in another less obvious sense. That's what I meant to say, Anton Antonovitch."

"Oh, well, but we must drop all this, for now I've no time to spare," said Anton Antonovitch, getting up from his seat and collecting some papers in order to report upon them to his Excellency. "Your business, as I imagine, will be explained in due course without delay. You will see for yourself whom you should censure and whom you should blame, and thereupon I humbly beg you to spare me from further private explanations and arguments which interfere with my work. . . ."

"No, Anton Antonovitch," Mr. Golyadkin, turning a little pale, began to the retreating figure of Anton Antonovitch; "I had no thought of the kind."

"What does it mean?" our hero went on to himself, when he was left alone; "what quarter is the wind in now, and what is one to make of this new turn?"

At the very time when our bewildered and half-crushed hero was setting himself to solve this new question, there was a sound of movement and bustle in the next room, the door opened and Andrey Filippovitch, who had been on some business in his Excellency's study, appeared breathless in the doorway, and called to Mr. Golyadkin. Knowing what was wanted and anxious not to keep Andrey Filippovitch waiting, Mr. Golyadkin leapt up from his seat, and as was fitting immediately bustled for all he was worth getting the manuscript that was required finally neat and ready and preparing to follow the manuscript and Andrey Filippovitch into his Excellency's study. Suddenly, almost slipping under the arm of Audrey Filippovitch, who was standing right in the doorway, Mr. Golyadkin junior darted into the room in breathless haste and bustle, with a solemn and resolutely official air; he bounded straight up to Mr. Golyadkin senior, who was expecting nothing less than such a visitation.

"The papers, Yakov Petrovitch, the papers . . . his Excellency has been pleased to ask for them; have you got them ready?" Mr. Golyadkin senior's friend whispered in a hurried undertone. "Andrey Filippovitch is waiting for you."

"I know he is waiting without your telling me," said Mr. Golyadkin senior, also in a hurried whisper.

"No, Yakov Petrovitch, I did not mean that; I did not mean that at all, Yakov Petrovitch, not that at all; I sympathize with you, Yakov Petrovitch, and am moved by genuine interest."

"Which I most humbly beg you to spare me. Allow me, allow me . . "You'll put it in an envelope, of course, Yakov Petrovitch, and you'll put a mark in the third page; allow me, Yakov Petrovitch. . . . "You allow me, if you please. . . . "

"But, I say, there's a blot here, Yakov Petrovitch; did you know there was a blot here? . . . "

At this point Andrey Filippovitch called Yakov Petrovitch a second time.

"One moment, Andrey Filippovitch, I'm only just . . . Do you under-stand Russian, sir?"

"It would be best to take it out with a penknife, Yakov Petrovitch. You had better rely upon me; you had better not touch it yourself, Yakov Petrovitch, rely upon me—I'll do it with a penknife. . . ."

Andrey Filippovitch called Mr. Golyadkin a third time.

"But, allow me, where's the blot? I don't think there's a blot at all."

"It's a huge blot. Here it is! Here, allow me, I saw it here . . you just let me, Yakov Petrovitch, I'll just touch it with the penknife, I'll scratch it out with the penknife from true-hearted sympathy. There, like this; see, it's done."

At this point, and quite unexpectedly, Mr. Golyadkin junior over-powered Mr. Golyadkin senior in the momentary struggle that had arisen between them, and so, entirely against the latter's will, suddenly, without rhyme or reason, took possession of the document required by the authorities, and instead of scratching it out with the penknife in true-hearted sympathy as he had perfidiously promised Mr. Golyadkin senior, hurriedly rolled it up, put it under his arm, in two bounds was beside Andrey Filippovitch, who noticed none of his manoeuvres, and flew with the latter into the Director's room. Mr. Golyadkin remained as though riveted to the spot, holding the penknife in his hand and apparently on the point of scratching something out with it.

Our hero could not yet grasp his new position. He could not at once recover himself. He felt the blow, but thought that it was somehow all right. In terrible, indescribable misery he tore himself at last from his seat, rushed straight to the Director's room, imploring heaven on the way that it might somehow all be arranged satisfactorily and so would be all right. . . . In the furthermost room, which adjoined the Director's private room, he ran straight upon Andrey Filippovitch in company with his namesake. Both of them were coming back; Mr. Golyadkin moved aside. Andrey Filippovitch was talking with a good-humoured smile, Mr. Golyadkin senior's namesake was smiling, too, fawning upon Andrey Filippovitch and tripping about at a respectful distance from him, and was whispering something in his ear with a delighted air, to which Andrey Filippovitch assented with a gracious nod. In a flash our hero grasped the whole position. The fact was that the work had surpassed his Excellency's expectations (as he learnt afterwards) and was finished punctually by the time it was needed. His Excellency was extremely pleased with it. It was even said that his Excellency had said "Thank you" to Mr. Golyadkin junior, had thanked him warmly, had said that he would remember it on occasion and would never forget it. . . . Of course, the first thing Mr. Golyadkin did was to protest, to protest with the utmost vigour of which he was capable. Pale as death, and hardly knowing what he was doing, he rushed up to Andrey Filippovitch. But the latter, hearing that Mr. Golyadkin's business was a private matter, refused to listen, observing firmly that he had not a minute to spare even for his own affairs.

The curtness of his tone and his refusal struck Mr. Golyadkin.

"I had better, perhaps, try in another quarter. . . . I had better appeal to Anton Antonovitch."

But to his disappointment Anton Antonovitch was not available either: he, too, was busy over something somewhere!

"Ah, it was not without design that he asked me to spare him explanation and discussion!" thought our hero. "This was what the old rogue had in his mind! In that case I shall simply make bold to approach his Excellency."

Still pale and feeling that his brain was in a complete ferment, greatly perplexed as to what he ought to decide to do, Mr. Golyadkin sat down on the edge of the chair. "It would have been a great deal better if it had all been just nothing," he kept incessantly thinking to himself. "Indeed, such a mysterious business was utterly improbable. In the first place, it was nonsense, and secondly it could not happen. Most likely it was imagination, or something else happened, and not what really did happen; or perhaps I went myself . . . and somehow mistook myself for some one else . . . . in short, it's an utterly impossible thing."

Mr. Golyadkin had no sooner made up his mind that it was an utterly impossible thing than Mr. Golyadkin junior flew into the room with papers in both hands as well as under his arm. Saying two or three words about business to Andrey Filippovitch as he passed, exchanging remarks with one, polite greetings with another, and familiarities with a third, Mr. Golyadkin junior, having apparently no time to waste, seemed on the point of leaving the room, but luckily for Mr. Golyadkin senior he stopped near the door to say a few words as he passed two or three clerks who were at work there. Mr. Golyadkin senior rushed straight at him. As soon as Mr. Golyadkin junior saw Mr. Golyadkin senior's movement he began immediately, with great uneasiness, looking about him to make his escape. But our hero already held his last night's guest by the sleeve. The clerks surrounding the two titular councilors stepped back and waited with curiosity to see what would happen. The senior titular councilor realized that public opinion was not on his side, he realized that they were intriguing against him: which made it all the more necessary to hold his own now. The moment was a decisive one.

"Well!" said Mr. Golyadkin junior, looking rather impatiently at Mr. Golyadkin senior.

The latter could hardly breathe.

"I don't know," he began, "in what way to make plain to you the strangeness of your behaviour, sir."

"Well. Go on." At this point Mr. Golyadkin junior turned round and winked to the clerks standing round, as though to give them to under-stand that a comedy was beginning.

"The impudence and shamelessness of your manners with me, sir, in the present case, unmasks your true character ... better than any words of mine could do. Don't rely on your trickery: it is worthless. . . ."

"Come, Yakov Petrovitch, tell me now, how did you spend the night?" answered Mr. Golyadkin junior, looking Mr. Golyadkin senior straight in the eye.

"You forget yourself, sir," Said the titular councilor, completely flabbergasted, hardly able to feel the floor under his feet. "I trust that you will take a different tone. . . ."

"My darling!" exclaimed Mr. Golyadkin junior, making a rather unseemly grimace at Mr. Golyadkin senior, and suddenly, quite unexpectedly, under the pretence of caressing him, he pinched his chubby cheek with two fingers.

Our hero grew as hot as fire. . . . As soon as Mr. Golyadkin junior noticed that his opponent, quivering in every limb, speechless with rage, as-red as a lobster, and exasperated beyond all endurance, might actually be driven to attack him, he promptly and in the most shame-less way hastened to be beforehand with his victim. Patting him two or three times on the cheek, tickling him two or three times, playing with him for a few seconds in this way while his victim stood rigid and beside himself with fury to the no little diversion of the young men standing round, Mr. Golyadkin junior ended with a most revolting shamelessness by giving Mr. Golyadkin senior a poke in his rather prominent stomach, and with a most venomous and suggestive smile said to him: "You're mischievous, brother Yakov, you are mischievous! We'll be sly, you and I, Yakov Petrovitch, we'll be sly."

Then, and before our hero could gradually come to himself after the last attack, Mr. Golyadkin junior (with a little smile beforehand to the spectators standing round) suddenly assumed a most businesslike, busy and official air, dropped his eyes to the floor and, drawing himself in, shrinking together, and pronouncing rapidly "on a special commission" he cut a caper with his short leg, and darted away into the next room. Our hero could not believe his eyes and was still unable to pull himself together. . . .

At last he roused himself. Recognizing in a flash that he was ruined, in a sense annihilated, that he had disgraced himself and sullied his reputation, that he had been turned into ridicule and treated with con-tempt in the presence of spectators, that he had been treacherously insulted, by one whom he had looked on only the day before as his greatest and most trustworthy friend, that he had been put to utter con-fusion, Mr. Golyadkin senior rushed in pursuit of his enemy. At the moment he would not even think of the witnesses of his ignominy.

"They're all in a conspiracy together," he said to himself; "they stand by each other and set each other on to attack me." After taking a dozen steps, however, our hero perceived clearly that all pursuit would be vain and useless, and so he turned back. "You won't get away," he thought, "you will get caught one day; the wolf will have to pay for the sheep's tears."

With ferocious composure and the most resolute determination Mr. Golyadkin went up to his chair and sat down upon it. "You won't escape," he said again.

Now it was not a question of passive resistance: there was determination and pugnacity in the air, and any one who had seen how Mr. Golyadkin at that moment, flushed and scarcely able to restrain his excitement, stabbed his pen into the inkstand and with what fury he began scribbling on the paper, could be certain beforehand that the matter would not pass off like this, and could not end in a simple, womanish way. In the depth of his soul he formed a resolution, and in the depth of his heart swore to carry it out. To tell the truth he still did not quite know how to act, or rather did not know at all, but never mind, that did not matter!

"Imposture and shamelessness do not pay nowadays, sir. Imposture and shamelessness, sir, lead to no good, but lead to the halter. Grishka Otrepyov was the only one, sir, who gained by imposture, deceiving the blind people and even that not for long."

In spite of this last circumstance Mr. Golyadkin proposed to wait till such time as the mask should fall from certain persons and something should be made manifest. For this it was necessary, in the first place, that office hours should be over as soon as possible, and till then our hero proposed to take no step. Then, when office hours were over, he would take one step. He knew then how he must act after taking that step, how to arrange his whole plan of action, to abase the horn of arrogance and crush the snake gnawing the dust in contemptible impotence. To allow himself to be treated like a rag used for wiping dirty boots, Mr. Golyadkin could not. He could not consent to that, especially in the present case. Had it not been for that last insult, our hero might have, perhaps, brought himself to control his anger; he might, perhaps, have been silent, have submitted and not have protested too obstinately; he would just have disputed a little, have made a slight complaint, have proved that he was in the right, then he would have given way a little, then, perhaps, he would have given way a little more, then he would have come round altogether, then, especially when the opposing party solemnly admitted that he was right, perhaps, he would have overlooked it completely, would even have been a little touched, there might even, perhaps—who could tell—spring up a new, close, warm friendship, on an even broader basis than the friendship of last night, so that this friendship might, in the end, completely eclipse the unpleasantness of the rather unseemly resemblance of the two individuals, so that both the titular councilors might be highly delighted, and might go on living till they were a hundred, and so on. To tell the whole truth, Mr. Golyadkin began to regret a little that he had stood up for himself and his rights, and had at once come in for unpleasantness in consequence.

"Should he give in," thought Mr. Golyadkin, "say he was joking, I would forgive him. I would forgive him even more if he would acknowledge it aloud. But I won't let myself be treated like a rag. And I have not allowed even persons very different from him to treat me so, still less will I permit a depraved person to attempt it. I am not a rag. I am not a rag, sir!"

In short, our hero made up his mind; "You're in fault yourself, sir!" he thought. He made up his mind to protest, and to protest with all his might to the very last. That was the sort of man he was! He could not consent to allow himself to be insulted, still less to allow himself to be treated as a rag, and, above all, to allow a thoroughly vicious man to treat him so. No quarrelling, however, no quarrelling! Possibly if some one wanted, if some one, for instance, actually insisted on turning Mr. Golyadkin into a rag, he might have done so, might have done so with-out opposition or punishment (Mr. Golyadkin was himself conscious of this at times), and he would have been a rag and not

Golyadkin—yes, a nasty, filthy rag; but that rag would not have been a simple rag, it would have been a rag possessed of dignity, it would have been a rag possessed of feelings and sentiments, even though dignity was defenceless and feelings could not assert themselves, and lay hidden deep down in the filthy folds of the rag, still the feelings were there. . .

The hours dragged on incredibly slowly; at last it struck four. Soon after, all got up and, following the head of the department, moved each on his homeward way. Mr. Golyadkin mingled with the crowd; he kept a vigilant look out, and did not lose sight of the man he wanted. At last our hero saw that his friend ran up to the office attendants who handed the clerks their overcoats, and hung about near them waiting for his in his usual nasty way. The minute was a decisive one. Mr. Golyadkin forced his way somehow through the crowd and, anxious not to be left behind, he, too, began fussing about his overcoat. But Mr. Golyadkin's friend and companion was given his overcoat first because on this occasion, too, he had succeeded, as he always did, in making up to them, whispering something to them, cringing upon them and getting round them.

After putting on his overcoat, Mr. Golyadkin junior glanced ironically at Mr. Golyadkin senior, acting in this way openly and defiantly, looked about him with his characteristic insolence, finally he tripped to and fro among the other clerks—no doubt in order to leave a good impression on them—said a word to one, whispered something to another, respectfully accosted a third, directed a smile at a fourth, gave his hand to a fifth, and gaily darted downstairs. Mr. Golyadkin senior flew after him, and to his inexpressible delight overtook him on the last step, and seized him by the collar of his overcoat. It seemed as though Mr. Golyadkin junior was a little disconcerted, and he looked about him with a helpless air.

"What do you mean by this?" he whispered to Mr. Golyadkin at last, in a weak voice.

"Sir, if you are a gentleman, I trust that you remember our friendly relations yesterday," said our hero.

"Ah, yes! Well? Did you sleep well?"

Fury rendered Mr. Golyadkin senior speechless for a moment.

"I slept well, sir . . . but allow me to tell you, sir, that you are playing a very complicated game. . . ."

"Who says so? My enemies say that," answered abruptly the man who called himself Mr. Golyadkin, and saying this, he unexpectedly freed himself from the feeble hand of the real Mr. Golyadkin. As soon as he was free he rushed away from the stairs, looked around him, saw a cab, ran up to it, got in, and in one moment vanished from Mr. Golyadkin senior's sight. The despairing titular councilor, abandoned by all, gazed about him, but there was no other cab. He tried to run, but his legs gave way under him. With a look of open-mouthed astonishment on his countenance, feeling crushed and shriveled up, he leaned helplessly against a lamp post, and remained so for some minutes in the middle of the pavement. It seemed as though all were over for Mr. Golyadkin.

CHAPTER IX

Everything, apparently, and even nature itself, seemed up in arms against Mr. Golyadkin; but he was still on his legs and unconquered; he felt that he was unconquered. He was ready to struggle. He rubbed his hands, with such feeling and such energy when he recovered from his first amazement that it could be deduced from his very air that he would not give in. Yet the danger was imminent; it was evident; Mr. Golyadkin felt it; but how to grapple with it, with this danger?—that was the question. The thought even flashed through Mr. Golyadkin's mind for a moment, "After all, why not leave it so, simply give it up? Why, what is it? Why, it's nothing. I'll keep apart as though it were not I," thought Mr. Golyadkin. "I'll let it all pass; it's not I, and that's all about it; he's separate too, maybe he'll give it up too; he'll hang about, the rascal, he'll hang about. He'll come back and give it up again. That's how it will be! I'll take it meekly. And, indeed, where is the danger? Come, what danger is there? I should like any one to tell me where the danger lies in this business. It is a trivial affair. An everyday affair. . . ."

At this point Mr. Golyadkin's tongue failed; the words died away on his lips; he even swore at himself for this thought; he convicted himself on the spot of abjectness, of cowardice for having this thought; things were no forwarder, however. He felt that to make up his mind to some course of action was absolutely necessary for him at the moment; he even felt that he would have given a great deal to any one who could have told him what he must decide to do. Yes, but how could he guess what? Though, indeed, he had no time to guess. In any case, that he might lose no time he took a cab and dashed home.

"Well? What are you feeling now?" he wondered; "what are you graciously pleased to be thinking of, Yakov Petrovitch? What are you doing? What are you doing now, you rogue, you rascal? You've brought yourself to this plight, and now you are weeping and whimpering!"

So Mr. Golyadkin taunted himself as he jolted along in the vehicle. To taunt himself and so to irritate his wounds was, at this time, a great satisfaction to Mr. Golyadkin, almost a voluptuous enjoyment.

"Well," he thought, "if some magician were to turn up now, or if it could come to pass in some official way and I were told: 'Give a finger of your right hand, Golyadkin—and it's a bargain with you; there shall not be the other Golyadkin, and you will be happy, only you won't have your finger'—yes, I would sacrifice my finger, I would certainly sacrifice it, I would sacrifice it without winking. . . . The devil take it all!" the despairing titular councilor cried at last. "Why, what is it all for? Well, it all had to be; yes, it absolutely had to; yes, just this had to be, as though nothing else were possible! And it was all right at first. Every one was pleased and happy. But there, it had to be! There's nothing to be gained by talking, though; you must act."

And so, almost resolved upon some action, Mr. Golyadkin reached home, and without a moment's delay snatched up his pipe and, sucking at it with all his might and puffing out clouds of smoke to right and to left, he began pacing up and down the room in a state of violent excitement. Meanwhile, Petrushka began laying the table. At last Mr. Golyadkin made up his mind completely, flung aside his pipe, put on his overcoat, said he would not dine at home and ran out of the flat. Petrushka, panting, overtook him on the stairs, bringing the hat he had forgotten. Mr. Golyadkin took his hat, wanted to say something incidentally to justify himself in Petrushka's eyes that the latter might not think anything particular, such as, "What a queer circumstance! here he forgot his hat—and so on," but as Petrushka walked away at once and would not even look at him, Mr. Golyadkin put on his hat without further explanation, ran downstairs, and repeating to himself that perhaps everything might be for the best, and that affairs would somehow be arranged, though he was conscious among other things of a cold chill right down to his heels, he went out into the street, took a cab and hastened to Andrey Filippovitch's.

"Would it not be better tomorrow, though?" thought Mr. Golyadkin, as he took hold of the bell-rope of Audrey Filippovitch's flat. "And, besides, what can I say in particular? There is nothing particular in it. It's such a wretched affair, yes, it really is wretched, paltry, yes, that is, almost a paltry affair . . . yes, that's what it all is, the incident. . . ." Suddenly Mr. Golyadkin pulled at the bell; the bell rang; footsteps were heard within. . . . Mr. Golyadkin cursed himself on the spot for his hastiness and audacity. His recent unpleasant experiences, which he had almost forgotten over his work, and his encounter with Andrey Filippovitch immediately came back into his mind. But by now it was too late to run away: the door opened. Luckily for Mr. Golyadkin he was informed that Andrey Filippovitch had not returned from the office and had not dined at home.

"I know where he dines: he dines near the Ismailovsky Bridge," thought our hero; and he was immensely relieved. To the footman's inquiry what message he would leave, he said: "It's all right, my good man, I'll look in later," and he even ran downstairs with a certain cheerful briskness. Going out into the street, he decided to dismiss the cab and paid the driver. When the man asked for something extra, saying he had been waiting in the street and had not spared his horse for his honour, he gave him five kopecks extra, and even willingly; and then walked on.

"It really is such a thing," thought Mr. Golyadkin, "that it cannot be left like that; though, if one looks at it that way, looks at it sensibly, why am I hurrying about here, in reality? Well, yes, though, I will go on discussing why I should take a lot of trouble; why I should rush about, exert myself, worry myself and wear myself out. To begin with, the thing's done and there's no recalling it . . . of course, there's no recalling it! Let us put it like this: a man turns up with a satisfactory reference, said to be a capable clerk, of good conduct, only he is a poor man and has suffered many reverses—all sorts of ups and downs—well, poverty is not a crime: so I must stand aside. Why, what nonsense it is! Well, he came; he is so made, the man is so made by nature itself that he is as like another man as though they were two drops of water, as though he were a perfect copy of another man; how could they refuse to take him into the department on that account? If it is fate, if it is only fate, if it is only blind chance that is to blame—is he to be treated like a rag, is he to be refused a job in the office? . . . Why, what would become of justice after that? He is a poor man, hopeless, downcast; it makes one's heart ache: compassion bids one care for him! Yes! There's no denying, there would be a fine set of head officials, if they took the same view as a reprobate like me! What an addlepate I am! I have foolishness enough for a dozen! Yes, yes! They did right, and many thanks to them for being good to a poor, luckless fellow. . . . Why, let us imagine for a moment that we are twins, that we had been born twin brothers, and nothing else—there it is! Well, what of it? Why, nothing! All the clerks can get used to it. . . . And an outsider, coming into our office, would certainly find nothing unseemly or offensive in the circumstance. In fact, there is really some-thing touching in it; to think that the divine Providence created two men exactly alike, and the heads of the department, seeing the divine handiwork, provided for two twins. It would, of course," Mr. Golyadkin went on, drawing a breath and dropping his voice, "it would, of course . . . it would, of course, have been better if there had been . . if there had been nothing of this touching kindness, and if there had been no twins either. . . . The devil take it all! And what need was there for it? And what was the particular necessity that admitted of no delay! My goodness! The devil has made a mess of it! Besides, he has such a character, too, he's of such a playful, horrid disposition —he's such a scoundrel, he's such a nimble fellow! He's such a toady! Such a lick-spittle! He's such a Golyadkin! I daresay he will misconduct himself; yes, he'll disgrace my name, the blackguard! And now I have to look after him and wait upon him! What an infliction! But, after all, what of it? It doesn't matter. Granted, he's a scoundrel, well, let him be a scoundrel, but to make up for it, the other one's honest; so he will be a scoundrel and I'll be honest, and they'll say that this Golyadkin's a rascal, don't take any notice of him, and don't mix him up with the other; but the other one's honest, virtuous, mild, free from malice, always to be relied upon in the service, and worthy of promotion; that's how it is, very good . . but what if . . . what if they get us mixed up! . . . He is equal to anything! Ah, Lord, have mercy upon us!... He will counterfeit a man, he will counterfeit him, the rascal—he will change one man for another as though he were a rag, and not reflect that a man is not a rag. Ach, mercy on us! Ough, what a calamity! . . ."

Reflecting and lamenting in this way, Mr. Golyadkin ran on, regard-less of where he was going. He came to his senses in Nevsky Prospect, only owing to the chance that he ran so neatly full-tilt into a passer-by that he saw stars in his eyes. Mr. Golyadkin muttered his excuses with-out raising his head, and it was only after the passer-by, muttering some-thing far from flattering, had walked a considerable distance away, that he raised his nose and looked about to see where he was and how he had got there. Noticing when he did so that he was close to the restaurant in which he had sat for a while before the dinner-party at Olsufy Ivanovitch's, our hero was suddenly conscious of a pinching and nipping sensation in his stomach; he remembered that he had not dined; he had no prospect of a dinner-party anywhere. And so, without losing precious time, he ran upstairs into the restaurant to have a snack of something as quickly as possible, and to avoid delay by making all the haste he could. And though everything in the restaurant was rather dear, that little circumstance did not on this occasion make Mr. Golyadkin pause, and, indeed, he had no time to pause over such a trifle. In the brightly lighted room the customers were standing in rather a crowd round the counter, upon which lay heaps of all sorts of such edibles as are eaten by well-bred persons at lunch. The waiter scarcely had time to fill glasses, to serve, to take money and give change. Mr. Golyadkin waited for his turn and modestly stretched out his hand for a savoury patty. Retreating into a corner, turning his back on the company and eating with appetite, he went back to the attendant, put down his plate and, knowing the price, took out a ten-kopeck piece and laid the coin on the counter, catching the waiter's eye as though to say, "Look, here's the money, one pie," and so on.

"One rouble ten kopecks is your bill," the waiter filtered through his teeth.

Mr. Golyadkin was a good deal surprised.

"You are speaking to me? . . . I . . . I took one pie, I believe."
"You've had eleven," the man retorted confidently.

"You . . . so it seems to me ... I believe, you're mistaken. . . . I really took only one pie, I think."

"I counted them; you took eleven. Since you've had them you must pay for them; we don't give anything away for nothing."

Mr. Golyadkin was petrified. "What sorcery is this, what is happening to me?" he wondered. Meanwhile, the man waited for Mr. Golyadkin to make up his mind; people crowded round Mr. Golyadkin; he was already feeling in his pocket for a silver rouble, to pay the full amount at once, to avoid further trouble. "Well, if it was eleven, it was eleven," he thought, turning as red as a lobster. "Why, what does it matter if eleven pies have been eaten? Why, a man's hungry, so he eats eleven pies; well, let him eat, and may it do him good; and there's nothing to wonder at in that, and there's nothing to laugh at. . ."

At that moment something seemed to stab Mr. Golyadkin. He raised his eyes and—at once he guessed the riddle. He knew what the sorcery was. All his difficulties were solved. . .

In the doorway of the next room, almost directly behind the waiter and facing Mr. Golyadkin, in the doorway which, till that moment, our hero had taken for a looking-glass, a man was standing—he was standing, Mr. Golyadkin was standing—not the original Mr. Golyadkin, the hero of our story, but the other Mr. Golyadkin, the new Mr. Golyadkin. The second Mr. Golyadkin was apparently in excellent spirits. He smiled to Mr. Golyadkin the first, nodded to him, winked, shuffled his feet a little, and looked as though in another minute he would vanish, would disappear into the next room, and then go out, maybe, by a back way out; and there it would be, and all pursuit would be in vain. In his hand he had the last morsel of the tenth pie, and before Mr. Golyadkin's very eyes he popped it into his mouth and smacked his lips.

"He has impersonated me, the scoundrel!" thought Mr. Golyadkin, flushing hot with shame. "He is not ashamed of the publicity of it! Do they see him? I fancy no one notices him. . . ."

Mr. Golyadkin threw down his rouble as though it burnt his fingers, and without noticing the waiter's insolently significant grin, a smile of triumph and serene power, he extricated himself from the crowd, and rushed away without looking round. "We must be thankful that at least he has not completely compromised any one!" thought Mr. Golyadkin senior. "We must be thankful to him, the brigand, and to fate, that everything was satisfactorily settled. The waiter was rude, that was all. But, after all, he was in the right. One rouble and ten kopecks were owing: so he was in the right. `We don't give things away for nothing,' he said! Though he might have been more polite, the rascal . . ."

All this Mr. Golyadkin said to himself as he went downstairs to the entrance, but on the last step he stopped suddenly, as though he had been shot, and suddenly flushed till the tears came into his eyes at the insult to his dignity. After standing stockstill for half a minute, he stamped his foot resolutely, at one bound leapt from the step into the street and, without looking round, rushed breathless and unconscious of fatigue back home to his flat in Shestilavotchny Street. When he got home, without changing his coat, though it was his habit to change into an old coat at home, without even stopping to take his pipe, he sat down on the sofa, drew the inkstand towards him, took up a pen, got a sheet of notepaper, and with a hand that trembled from inward excitement, began scribbling the following epistle

"Dear Sir Yakov Petrovitch!

"I should not take up my pen if my circumstances, and your own action, sir, had not compelled me to that step. Believe me that nothing but necessity would have induced me to enter upon such a discussion with you; and therefore, first of all, I beg you, sir, to look upon this step of mine not as a premeditated design to insult you, but as the inevitable consequence of the circumstance that is a bond between us now."

("I think that's all right, proper, courteous, though not lacking in force and firmness. . . . I don't think there is anything for him to take offence at. Besides, I'm fully within my rights," thought Mr. Golyadkin, reading over what he had written.)

"Your strange and sudden appearance, sir, on a stormy night, after the coarse and unseemly behaviour of my enemies to me, for whom I feel too much contempt even to mention their names, was the starting-point of all the misunderstanding existing between us at the present time. Your obstinate desire to persist in your course of action, sir, and forcibly to enter the circle of my existence and all my relations in practical life, transgresses every limit imposed by the merest politeness and every rule of civilized society. I imagine there is no need, sir, for me to refer to the seizure by you of my papers, and particularly to your taking away my good name, in order to gain the favour of my superiors—favour you have not deserved. There is no need to refer here either to your intentional and insulting refusal of the necessary explanation in regard to us. Finally, to omit nothing, I will not allude here to your last strange, one may even say, your incomprehensible behaviour to me in the coffee-house. I am far from lamenting over the needless—for me—loss of a rouble; but I cannot help expressing my indignation at the recollection of your public outrage upon me, to the detriment of my honour, and what is more, in the presence of several persons of good breeding, though not belonging to my circle of acquaintance."

("Am I not going too far?" thought Mr. Golyadkin. "Isn't it too much; won't it be too insulting—that taunt about good breeding, for instance? . . . But there, it doesn't matter! I must show him the resoluteness of my character. I might, however, to soften him, flatter him, and butter him up at the end. But there, we shall see.")

"But I should not weary you with my letter, sir, if I were not firmly convinced that the nobility of your sentiments and your open, candid character would suggest to you yourself a means for retrieving all laps-es and returning everything to its original position.

"With full confidence I venture to rest assured that you will not take my letter in a sense derogatory to yourself, and at the same time that you will not refuse to explain yourself expressly on this occasion by letter, sending the same by my man.

"In expectation of your reply, I have the honour, dear sir, to remain,

> "Your humble servant,
>
> "Y. GOLYADKIN."

"Well, that is quite all right. The thing's done, it has come to letter-writing. But who is to blame for that? He is to blame himself: by his own action he reduces a man to the necessity of resorting to epistolary composition. And I am within my rights. . . ."

Reading over his letter for the last time, Mr. Golyadkin folded it up, sealed it and called Petrushka. Petrushka came in looking, as usual, sleepy and cross about something.

"You will take this letter, my boy . . . do you understand?" Petrushka did not speak.

"You will take it to the department; there you must find the secretary on duty, Vahramyev. He is the one on duty today. Do you understand that?"

"I understand."

"'I understand'! He can't even say, 'I understand, sir!' You must ask for the secretary, Vahramyev, and tell him that your master desired you to send his regards, and humbly requests him to refer to the address book of our office and find out where the titular councilor, Golyadkin, is living?"

Petrushka remained mute, and, as Mr. Golyadkin fancied, smiled.

"Well, so you see, Pyotr, you have to ask him for the address, and find out where the new clerk, Golyadkin, lives."

"Yes,"

"You must ask for the address and then take this letter there. Do you understand?"

"I understand."

"If there . . . where you have to take the letter, that gentleman to whom you have to give the letter, that Golyadkin . . . What are you laughing at, you blockhead?"

"What is there to laugh at? What is it to me! I wasn't doing anything, -sir. It's not for the likes of us to laugh. . . ."

"Oh, well . . . if that gentleman should ask, 'How is your master, how is he'; if he . . . well, if he should ask you anything—you hold your tongue, and answer, 'My master is all right, and begs you for an answer to his letter.' Do you understand?"

"Yes, sir."

"Well, then, say, 'My master is all right and quite well,' say, 'and is just getting ready to pay a call: and he asks you,' say, 'for an answer in writing.' Do you understand?"

"Yes."

"Well, go along, then.

"Why, what a bother I have with this blockhead too! He's laughing, and there's nothing to be done. What's he laughing at? I've lived to see trouble. Here I've lived like this to see trouble. Though perhaps it may all turn out for the best. . . . That rascal will be loitering about for the next two hours now, I expect; he'll go off somewhere else. . . . There's no sending him anywhere. What a misery it is! . . . What misery has come upon me!"

Feeling his troubles to the full, our hero made up his mind to remain passive for two hours till Petrushka returned. For an hour of the time he walked about the room, smoked, then put aside his pipe and sat down to a book, then he lay down on the sofa, then took up his pipe again, then again began running about the room. He tried to think things over but was absolutely unable to think about anything. At last the agony of remaining passive reached the climax and Mr. Golyadkin made up his mind to take a step. "Petrushka will come in another hour," he thought. "I can give the key to the porter, and I myself can, so to speak . . . I can investigate the matter: I shall investigate the matter in my own way."

Without loss of time, in haste to investigate the matter, Mr. Golyadkin took his hat, went out of the room, locked up his flat, went in to the porter, gave him the key, together with ten kopecks—Mr. Golyadkin had become extraordinarily freehanded of late—and rushed off. Mr. Golyadkin went first on foot to the Ismailovsky Bridge. It took him half an hour to get there. When he reached the goal of his journey he went straight into the yard of the house so familiar to him, and glanced up at the windows of the civil councilor Berendyev's flat. Except for three windows hung with red curtains all the rest was dark.

"Olsufy Ivanovitch has no visitors today," thought Mr. Golyadkin; "they must all be staying at home today."

After standing for some time in the yard, our hero tried to decide on some course of action. But he was apparently not destined to reach a decision. Mr. Golyadkin changed his mind, and with a wave of his hand went back into the street.

"No, there's no need for me to go today. What could I do here? . . . No, I'd better, so to speak . . . I'll investigate the matter personally."

Coming to this conclusion, Mr. Golyadkin rushed off to his office. He had a long way to go. It was horribly muddy, besides, and the wet snow lay about in thick drifts. But it seemed as though difficulty did not exist for our hero at the moment. He was drenched through, it is true, and he was a good deal spattered with mud.

"But that's no matter, so long as the object is obtained."

And Mr. Golyadkin certainly was nearing his goal. The dark mass of the huge government building stood up black before his eyes.

"Stay," he thought; "where am I going, and what am I going to do here? Suppose I do find out where he lives? Meanwhile, Petrushka will certainly have come back and brought me the answer. I am only wasting my precious time, I am simply wasting my time. Though shouldn't I, perhaps, go in and see Vahramyev? But, no, I'll go later. . . . Ech! There was no need to have gone out at all. But, there, it's my temperament! I've a knack of always seizing a chance of rushing ahead of things, whether there is a need to or not. . . . H'm! . . . what time is it? It must be nine by now. Petrushka might come and not find me at home. It was pure folly on my part to go out . . . Ech, it is really a nuisance!"

Sincerely acknowledging that he had been guilty of an act of folly, our hero ran back to Shestilavotchny Street. He arrived there, weary and exhausted. From the porter he learned that Petrushka had not dreamed of turning up yet.

"To be sure! I foresaw it would be so," thought our hero; "and mean-while it's nine o'clock. Ech, he's such a good-for-nothing chap! He's always drinking somewhere! Mercy on us! What a day has fallen to my miserable lot!"

Reflecting in this way, Mr. Golyadkin unlocked his flat, got a light, took off his outdoor things, lighted his pipe and, tired, worn-out, exhausted and hungry, lay down on the sofa and waited for Petrushka. The candle burnt dimly; the light flickered on the wall. . . . Mr. Golyadkin gazed and gazed, and thought and thought, and fell asleep at last, worn out.

It was late when he woke up. The candle had almost burnt down, was smoking and on the point of going out. Mr. Golyadkin jumped up, shook himself, and remembered it all, absolutely all. Behind the screen he heard Petrushka snoring lustily. Mr. Golyadkin rushed to the window—not a light anywhere. He opened the movable pane—all was still; the city was asleep as though it were dead: so it must have been two or three o'clock; so it proved to be, indeed; the clock behind the partition made an effort and struck two. Mr. Golyadkin rushed behind the partition.

He succeeded, somehow, though only after great exertions, in rousing Petrushka, and making him sit up in his bed. At that moment the candle went out completely. About ten minutes passed before Mr. Golyadkin succeeded in finding another candle and lighting it. In the interval Petrushka had fallen asleep again.

"You scoundrel, you worthless fellow!" said Mr. Golyadkin, shaking him up again. "Will you get up, will you wake?" After half an hour of effort Mr. Golyadkin succeeded, however, in rousing his servant thoroughly, and dragging him out from behind the partition. Only then, our hero remarked the fact that Petrushka was what is called dead-drunk and could hardly stand on his legs.

"You good-for-nothing fellow!" cried Mr. Golyadkin; "you ruffian! You'll be the death of me! Good heavens! whatever has he done with the letter? Ach, my God! where is it? . . . And why did I write it? As though there were any need for me to have written it! I went scribbling away out of pride, like a noodle! I've got myself into this fix out of pride! That is what dignity does for you, you rascal, that is dignity! . . . Come, what have you done with the letter, you ruffian? To whom did you give it?"

"I didn't give any one any letter; and I never had any letter . . . so there!"

Mr. Golyadkin wrung his hands in despair.

"Listen, Pyotr . . . listen to me, listen to me. . . ."

"I am listening. . . ."

"Where have you been?—answer . . ."

"Where have I been. . . . I've been to see good people! What is it to me!"

"Oh, Lord, have mercy on us! Where did you go, to begin with? Did you go to the department? . . . Listen, Pyotr, perhaps you're drunk?"

"Me drunk! If I should be struck on the spot this minute, not a drop, not a drop—so there. . ."

"No, no, it's no matter your being drunk. . . . I only asked; it's all right your being drunk; I don't mind, Petrushka, I don't mind. . . . Perhaps it's only that you have forgotten, but you'll remember it all. Come, try to remember—have you been to that clerk's, to Vahramyev's; have you been to him or not?"

"I have not been, and there's no such clerk. Not if I were this minute . . ."

"No, no, Pyotr! No, Petrushka, you know I don't mind. Why, you see I don't mind. . . . Come, what happened? To be sure, it's cold and damp in the street, and so a man has a drop, and it's no matter. I am not angry. I've been drinking myself today, my boy. . . . Come, think and try and remember, did you go to Vahramyev?"

"Well, then, now, this is how it was, it's the truth—I did go, if this very minute . . ."

"Come, that is right, Petrushka, that is quite right that you've been. You see I'm not angry... Come, come," our hero went on, coaxing his servant more and more, patting him on the shoulder and smiling to him, "come, you had a little nip, you scoundrel. . . . You had twopenn'orth of something, I suppose? You're a sly rogue! Well, that's no matter; come, you see that I'm not angry. . . . I'm not angry, my boy, I'm not angry. . . ."

"No, I'm not a sly rogue, say what you like. . . . I only went to see some good friends. I'm not a rogue, and I never have been a rogue. . . ."

"Oh, no, no, Petrushka; listen, Petrushka, you know I'm not scolding when I called you a rogue. I said that in fun, I said it in a good sense. You see, Petrushka, it is sometimes a compliment to a man when you call him a rogue, a cunning fellow, that he's a sharp chap and would not let any one take him in. Some men like it. . . . Come, come, it doesn't matter! Come, tell me, Petrushka, without keeping anything back, openly, as to a friend . . . did you go to Vahramyev's, and did he give you the address?"

"He did give me the address, he did give me the address too. He's a nice gentleman! 'Your master,' says he, 'is a nice man,' says he, 'very nice man;' says he, 'I send my regards,' says he, 'to your master, thank him and say that I like him,' says he—'how I do respect your master,' says he. 'Because,' says he, 'your master, Petrushka,' says he, 'is a good man, and you,' says he, 'Petrushka, are a good man too. . . .'"

"Ah, mercy on us! But the address, the address! You Judas!" The last word Mr. Golyadkin uttered almost in a whisper.

"And the address . . . he did give the address too."

"He did? Well, where does Golyadkin, the clerk Golyadkin, the titular councilor, live?"

"'Why,' says he, 'Golyadkin will be now at Shestilavotchny Street. When you get into Shestilavotchny Street take the stairs on the right and it's the fourth floor. And there,' says he, 'you'll find Golyadkin'"

"You scoundrel!" our hero cried, out of patience at last. "You're a ruffian! Why, that's my address; why, you are talking about me. But there's another Golyadkin; I'm talking of the other one, you scoundrel!"

"Well, that's as you please! What is it to me? Have it your own way. . . ."

"And the letter, the letter? . . .

"What letter? There wasn't any letter, and I didn't see any letter." "But what have you done with it, you rascal?"

"I delivered the letter, I delivered it. He sent his regards. 'Thank you,' says he, 'your master's a nice man,' says he. 'Give my regards,' says he, 'to your master. . . .

"But who said that? Was it Golyadkin said it?"

Petrushka said nothing for a moment, and then, with a broad grin, he stared straight into his master's face. . . ."

"Listen, you scoundrel!" began Mr. Golyadkin, breathless, beside himself with fury; "listen, you rascal, what have you done to me? Tell me what you've done to me! You've destroyed me, you villain, you've cut the head off my shoulders, you, Judas!"

"Well, have it your own way! I don't care," said Petrushka in a resolute voice, retreating behind the screen.

"Come here, come here, you ruffian. . . ."

"I'm not coming to you now, I'm not coming at all. What do I care, I'm going to good folks. . . . Good folks live honestly, good folks live without falsity, and they never have doubles. . . ."

Mr. Golyadkin's hands and feet went icy cold, his breath failed him. . . .

"Yes," Petrushka went on, "they never have doubles. God doesn't afflict honest folk. . . ."

"You worthless fellow, you are drunk! Go to sleep now, you ruffian! And tomorrow you'll catch it," Mr. Golyadkin added in a voice hardly audible. As for Petrushka, he muttered something more; then he could be heard getting into bed, making the bed creak. After a prolonged yawn, he stretched; and at last began snoring, and slept the sleep of the just, as they say. Mr. Golyadkin was more dead than alive. Petrushka's behaviour, his very strange hints, which were yet so remote that it was useless to be angry at them, especially as they were uttered by a drunken man, and, in short, the sinister turn taken by the affair altogether, all this shook Mr. Golyadkin to the depths of his being.

"And what possessed me to go for him in the middle of the night?" said our hero, trembling all over from a sickly sensation. "What the devil made me have anything to do with a drunken man! What could I expect from a drunken man? Whatever he says is a lie. But what was he hinting at, the ruffian? Lord, have mercy on us! And why did I write all that letter? I'm my own enemy, I'm my own murderer! As if I couldn't hold my tongue? I had to go scribbling nonsense! And what now! You are going to ruin, you are like an old rag, and yet you worry about your pride; you say, 'my honour is wounded,' you must stick up for your honour! My own murderer, that is what I am!"

Thus spoke Mr. Golyadkin and hardly dared to stir for terror. At last his eyes fastened upon an object which excited his interest to the utmost. In tenor lest the object that caught his attention should prove to be an illusion, a deception of his fancy, he stretched out his hand to it with hope, with dread, with indescribable curiosity. . . . No, it was not a deception! Not a delusion! It was a letter, really a letter, undoubtedly a letter, and addressed to him. Mr. Golyadkin took the letter from the table. His heart beat terribly.

"No doubt that scoundrel brought it," he thought, "put it there, and then forgot it; no doubt that is how it happened: no doubt that is just how it happened. . . ."

The letter was from Vahramyev, a young fellow-clerk who had once been his friend. "I had a presentiment of this, though," thought our hero, "and I had a presentiment of all that there will be in the letter. . . ."

The letter was as follows--

"Dear Sir Yakov Petrovitch!

"Your servant is drunk, and there is no getting any sense out of him. For that reason I prefer to reply by letter. I hasten to inform you that the commission you've entrusted to me—that is, to deliver a letter to a certain person you know, I agree to carry out carefully and exactly. That person, who is very well known to you and who has taken the place of a friend to me, whose name I will refrain from mentioning (because I do not wish unnecessarily to blacken the reputation of a perfectly innocent man), lodges with us at Karolina Ivanovna's, in the room in which, when you were among us, the infantry officer from Tambov used to be. That person, however, is always to be found in the company of honest and true-hearted persons, which is more than one can say for some people. I intend from this day to break off all connection with you; it's impossible for us to remain on friendly terms and to keep up the appearance of comradeship congruous with them. And, therefore, I beg you, my dear sir, immediately on the receipt of this candid letter from me, to send me the two roubles you owe me for the razor of foreign make which I sold you seven months ago, if you will kindly remember, when you were still living with us in the lodgings of Karolina Ivanovna, alady whom I respect from the bottom of my heart. I am acting in this way because you, from the accounts I hear from sensible persons, have lost your dignity and reputation and have become a source of danger to the morals of the innocent and uncontaminated. For some persons are not straightforward, their words are full of falsity and their show of good intentions is suspicious. People can always be found capable of insulting Karolina Ivanovna, who is always irreproachable in her conduct, and an honest woman, and, what's more, a maiden lady, though no longer young—though, on the other hand, of a good foreign family—and this fact I've been asked to mention in this letter by several persons, and I speak also for myself. In any case you will learn all in due time, if you haven't learnt it yet, though you've made yourself notorious from one end of the town to the other, according to the accounts I hear from sensible people, and consequently might well have received intelligence relating to you, my dear sir, in many places. In conclusion, I beg to inform you, my dear sir, that a certain person you know, whose name I will not mention here, for certain honourable reasons, is highly respected by right-thinking people, and is, moreover, of lively and agreeable disposition, and is equally successful in the service and in the society of persons of common sense, is true in word and in friendship, and does not insult behind their back those with whom he is on friendly terms to their face.

"In any case, I remain

"Your obedient servant,

"N. VAHRAMYEV."

"P.S. You had better dismiss your man: he is a drunkard and probably gives you a great deal of trouble; you had better engage Yevstafy, who used to be in service here, and is now out of a place. Your present servant is not only a drunkard, but, what's more, he's a thief, for only last week he sold a pound of lump sugar to Karolina Ivanovna at less than cost price, which, in my opinion, he could not have done otherwise than by robbing you in a very sly way, little by little, at different times. I write this to you for your own good, although some people can do nothing but insult and deceive everybody, especially persons of honesty and good nature; what is more, they slander them behind their back and misrepresent them, simply from envy, and because they can't call themselves the same.

V.

After reading Vahramyev's letter our hero remained for a long time sitting motionless on his sofa. A new light seemed breaking through the obscure and baffling fog which had surrounded him for the last two days. Our hero seemed to reach a partial understanding. . . . He tried to get up from the sofa to take a turn about the room, to rouse himself, to collect his scattered ideas, to fix them upon a certain subject and then to set himself to rights a little, to think over his position thoroughly. But as soon as he tried to stand up he fell back again at once, weak and helpless. "Yes, of course, I had a presentiment of all that; how he writes though, and what is the real meaning of his words. Supposing I do understand the meaning; but what is it leading to? He should have said straight out: this and that is wanted, and I would have done it. Things have taken such a turn, things have come to such an unpleasant pass! Oh, if only tomorrow would make haste and come, and I could make haste and get to work! I know now what to do. I shall say this and that, I shall agree with his arguments, I won't sell my honour, but maybe; but he, that person we know of, that disagreeable person, how does he come to be mixed up in it? And why has he turned up here? Oh, if tomorrow would make haste and come! They'll slander me before then, they are intriguing, they are working to spite me! The great thing is not to lose time, and now, for instance, to write a letter, and to say this and that and that I agree to this and that. And as soon as it is daylight tomorrow send it off, before he can do anything .. and so checkmate them, get in before them, the darlings. . . . They will ruin me by their slanders, and that's the fact of the matter!"

Mr. Golyadkin drew the paper to him, took up a pen and wrote the following missive in answer to the secretary's letter

"Dear Sir Nestor Ignatyevitch!

"With amazement mingled with heartfelt distress I have perused your insulting letter to me, for I see clearly that you are referring to me when you speak of certain discreditable persons and false friends. I see with genuine sorrow how rapidly the calumny has spread and how deeply it has taken root, to the detriment of my prosperity, my honour and my good name. And this is the more distressing and mortifying that even honest people of a genuinely noble way of thinking and, what is even more important, of straightforward and open dispositions, abandon the interests of honourable men and with all the qualities of their hearts attach themselves to the pernicious corruption, which in our difficult and immoral age has unhappily increased and multiplied so greatly and so disloyally. In conclusion, I will say that the debt of two roubles of which you remind me I regard as a sacred duty to return to you in its entirety.

"As for your hints concerning a certain person of the female sex, concerning the intentions, calculations and various designs of that person, I can only tell you, sir, that I have but a very dim and obscure understanding of those insinuations. Permit me, sir, to preserve my honourable way of thinking and my good name undefiled, in any case. I am ready to stoop to an explanation in person, preferring a personal interview to a written explanation as more secure, and I am, moreover, ready to enter into conciliatory proposals on mutual terms, of course. To that end I beg you, my dear sir, to convey to that person my readiness for a personal arrangement and, what is more, to beg her to fix the time and place of the interview. It grieved me, sir, to read your hints of my having insulted you, having been treacherous to our original friendship and having spoken ill of you. I ascribe this misunderstanding to the abominable calumny, envy and ill-will of those whom I may justly stigmatize as my bitterest foes. But I suppose they do not know that innocence is strong through its very innocence, that the shamelessness, the insolence and the revolting familiarity of some persons, sooner or later gains the stigma of universal contempt; and that such persons come to ruin through nothing but their own worthlessness and the corruption of their own hearts. In conclusion, I beg you, sir, to convey to those persons that their strange pretensions and their dishonourable and fantastic desire to squeeze others out of the position which those others occupy, by their very existence in this world, and to take their place, are deserving of contempt, amazement, compassion and, what is more, the madhouse; moreover, such efforts are severely prohibited by law, which in my opinion is perfectly just, for every one ought to be satisfied with his own position. Every one has his fixed position, and if this is a joke it is a joke in very bad taste. I will say more: it is utterly immoral, for, I make bold to assure you, sir, my own views which I have expounded above, in regard to keeping one's own place, are purely moral.

"In any case I have the honour to remain,

"Your humble servant,

"Y. GOLYADKIN."

CHAPTER X

Altogether, we may say, the adventures of the previous day had thoroughly unnerved Mr. Golyadkin. Our hero passed a very bad night; that is, he did not get thoroughly off to sleep for five minutes: as though some practical joker had scattered bristles in his bed. He spent the whole night in a sort of half-sleeping state, tossing from side to side, from right to left, moaning and groaning, dozing off for a moment, waking up again a minute later, and all was accompanied by a strange misery, vague memories, hideous visions—in fact, everything disagreeable that can be imagined. . . .

At one moment the figure of Andrey Filippovitch appeared before him in a strange, mysterious half-light. It was a frigid, wrathful figure, with a cold, harsh eye and with stiffly polite words of blame on its lips . . . and as soon as Mr. Golyadkin began going up to Andrey Filippovitch to defend himself in some way and to prove to him that he was not at all such as his enemies represented him, that he was like this and like that, that he even possessed innate virtues of his own, superior to the average—at once a person only too well known for his discreditable behaviour appeared on the scene, and by some most revolting means instantly frustrated poor Mr. Golyadkin's efforts, on the spot, almost before the latter's eyes, blackened his reputation, trampled his dignity in the mud, and then immediately took possession of his place in the service and in society.

At another time Mr. Golyadkin's head felt sore from some sort of slight blow of late conferred and humbly accepted, received either in the course of daily life or somehow in the performance of his duty, against which blow it was difficult to protest. . . . And while Mr. Golyadkin was racking his brains over the question why it was so difficult to protest even against such a blow, this idea of a blow gradually melted away into a different form—into the form of some familiar, trifling, or rather important piece of nastiness which he had seen, heard, or even himself committed—and frequently committed, indeed, and not on nasty grounds, not from any nasty impulse, even, but just because it happened—sometimes, for instance, out of delicacy, another time owing to his absolute defenselessness—in fact, because . . . because, in fact, Mr. Golyadkin knew perfectly well because of what! At this point Mr. Golyadkin blushed in his sleep, and, smothering his blushes, muttered to himself that in this case he ought to be able to show the strength of his character, he ought to be able to show in this case the remarkable strength of his character, and then wound up by asking himself, "What, after all, is strength of character? Why understand it now? . . ."

But what irritated and enraged Mr. Golyadkin most of all was that invariably, at such a moment, a person well known for his undignified burlesque behaviour turned up uninvited, and, regardless of the fact that the matter was apparently settled, he, too, would begin muttering, with an unseemly little smile "What's the use of strength of character! How could you and I, Yakov Petrovitch, have strength of character? . . ."

Then Mr. Golyadkin would dream that he was in the company of a number of persons distinguished for their wit and good breeding; that he, Mr. Golyadkin, too, was conspicuous for his wit and politeness, that everybody liked him, even some of his enemies who were present began to like him, which was very agreeable to Mr. Golyadkin; that every one gave him precedence, and that at last Mr. Golyadkin himself, with gratification, overheard the host, drawing one of the guests aside, speak in his, Mr. Golyadkin's, praise . . . and all of a sudden, apropos of nothing, there appeared again a person, notorious for his treachery and brutal impulses, in the form of Mr. Golyadkin junior, and on the spot, at once, by his very appearance on the scene, Mr. Golyadkin junior destroyed the whole triumph and glory of Mr. Golyadkin senior, eclipsed Mr.

Golyadkin senior, trampled him in the mud, and, at last, proved clearly that Golyadkin senior—that is, the genuine one—was not the genuine one at all but the sham, and that he, Golyadkin junior, was the real one; that, in fact, Mr. Golyadkin senior was not at all what he appeared to be, but something very disgraceful, and that consequently he had no right to mix in the society of honourable and well-bred people. And all this was done so quickly that Mr. Golyadkin had not time to open his mouth before all of them were subjugated, body and soul, by the wicked, sham Mr. Golyadkin, and with profound contempt rejected him, the real and innocent Mr. Golyadkin. There was not one person left whose opinion the infamous Mr. Golyadkin would not have changed round. There was not left one person, even the most insignificant of the company, to whom the false and worthless Mr. Golyadkin would not make up in his blandest manner, upon whom he would not fawn in his own way, before whom he would not burn sweet and agreeable incense, so that the flattered person simply sniffed and sneezed till the tears came; in token of the intensest pleasure. And the worst of it was that all this was done in a flash: the swiftness of movement of the false and worthless Mr. Golyadkin was marvellous! He scarcely had time, for instance, to make up to one person and win his good graces—and before one could wink an eye he was at another. He stealthily fawns on another, drops a smile of benevolence, twirls on his short, round, though rather wooden-looking leg, and already he's at a third, and is cringing upon a third, he's making up to him in a friendly way; before one has time to open one's mouth, before one has time to feel surprised he's at a fourth, at the same maneuvers with him—it was horrible: sorcery and nothing else! And every one was pleased with him and everybody liked him, and every one was exalting him, and all were proclaiming in chorus that his politeness and sarcastic wit were infinitely superior to the politeness and sarcastic wit of the real Mr. Golyadkin and putting the real and innocent Mr. Golyadkin to shame thereby and rejecting the veritable Mr. Golyadkin, and shoving and pushing out the loyal Mr. Golyadkin, and showering blows on the man so well known for his love towards his fellow creatures! . . .

In misery, in terror and in fury, the cruelly treated Mr. Golyadkin ran out into the street and began trying to take a cab in order to drive straight to his Excellency's, or, at any rate, to Audrey Filippovitch's, but—horror! The cabman absolutely refused to take Mr. Golyadkin, saying, "We can-not drive two gentlemen exactly alike, sir; a good man tries to live honestly, your honour, and never has a double." Overcome with shame, the unimpeachable, honest Mr. Golyadkin looked round and did, in fact, assure himself with his own eyes that the cabman and Petrushka, who had joined them, were all quite right, for the depraved Mr. Golyadkin was actually on the spot, beside him, close at hand, and with his characteristic nastiness was again, at this critical moment, certainly preparing to do something very unseemly, and quite out of keeping with that gentlemanliness of character which is usually acquired by good breeding—that gentlemanliness of which the loathsome Mr. Golyadkin the second was always boasting on every opportunity. Beside himself with shame and despair, the utterly ruined though perfectly just Mr. Golyadkin dashed headlong away, wherever fate might lead him; but with every step he took, with every thud of his foot on the granite of the pavement, there leapt up as though out of the earth a Mr. Golyadkin precisely the same, perfectly alike, and of a revolting depravity of heart. And all these precisely similar Golyadkins set to running after one another as soon as they appeared, and stretched in a long chain like a file of geese, hobbling after the real Mr. Golyadkin, so there was nowhere to escape from these duplicates—so that Mr. Golyadkin, who was in every way deserving of compassion, was breathless with terror; so that at last a terrible multitude of duplicates had sprung into being; so that the whole town was obstructed at last by duplicate Golyadkins, and the police officer, seeing such a breach of decorum, was obliged to seize all these duplicates by the collar and to put them into the watch-house, which happened to be beside him. . . . Numb and chill with horror, our hero woke up, and numb and chill with horror felt that his waking state was hardly more cheerful. . . . It was oppressive and harrowing. . . . He was overcome by such anguish that it seemed as though someone were gnawing at his heart.

At last Mr. Golyadkin could endure it no longer. "This shall not be!" he cried, resolutely sitting up in bed, and after this exclamation he felt fully awake.

It seemed as though it were rather late in the day. It was unusually light in the room. The sunshine filtered through the frozen panes and flooded the room with light, which surprised Mr. Golyadkin not a little and, so far as Mr. Golyadkin could remember, at least, there had scarcely ever be en such exceptions in the course of the heavenly luminary before. Our hero had hardly time to wonder at this when he heard the clock buzzing behind the partition as though it was just on the point of striking. "Now," thought Mr. Golyadkin, and he prepared to listen with painful suspense. . :

But to complete Mr. Golyadkin's astonishment, the clock whirred and only struck once.

"What does this mean?" cried our hero, finally leaping out of bed. And, unable to believe his ears, he rushed behind the screen just as he was. It actually was one o'clock. Mr. Golyadkin glanced at Petrushka's bed; but the room did not even smell of Petrushka: his bed had long been made and left, his boots were nowhere to be seen either—an unmistakab le sign that Petrushka was not in the house. Mr. Golyadkin rushed to the door: the door was locked. "But where is he, where is Petrushka?" he went on in a whisper, conscious of intense excitement and feeling a perceptible tremor run all over him . . . Suddenly a thought floated into his mind . . . Mr. Golyadkin rushed to the table, looked all over it, felt all round—yes, it was true, his letter of the night before to Vahramyev was not there. Petrushka was nowhere behind the screen either, the clock had just struck one, and some new points were evident to him in Vahramyev's letter, points that were obscure at first sight though now they were fully explained. Petrushka had evidently been bribed at last! "Yes, yes, that was so!"

"So this was how the chief plot was hatched!" cried Mr. Golyadkin, slapping himself on the forehead, opening his eyes wider and wider; "so in that filthy German woman's den the whole power of evil lies hidden now! So she was only making a strategic diversion in directing me to the Ismailovsky Bridge--she was putting me off the scent, confusing me (the worthless witch), and in that way laying her mines! Yes, that is so! If one only looks at the thing from that point of view, all of this is bound to be so, and the scoundrel's appearance on the scene is fully explained: it's all part and parcel of the same thing. They've kept him in reserve a long while, they had him in readiness for the evil day. This is how it has all turned out! This is what it has come to. But there, never mind. No time has been lost so far."

At this point Mr. Golyadkin recollected with horror that it was past one in the afternoon. "What if they have succeeded by now? . . ." He uttered a moan. . . . "But, no, they are lying, they've not had time—we shall see. . .

He dressed after a fashion, seized paper and a pen, and scribbled the following missive

"Dear Sir Yakov Petrovitch!

"Either you or I, but both together is out of the question! And so I must inform you that your strange, absurd, and at the same time impossible desire to appear to be my twin and give yourself out as such serves no other purpose than to bring about your complete disgrace and discomfiture. And so I beg you, for the sake of your own advantage, to step aside and make way for really honourable men of loyal aims. In the opposite case I am ready to determine upon extreme measures. I lay down my pen and await . . . However, I remain ready to oblige or to meet you with pistols.

Our hero rubbed his hands energetically when he had finished the letter. Then, pulling on his greatcoat and putting on his hat, he unlocked his flat with a spare key and set off for the department. He reached the office but could not make up his mind to go in—it was by now too late. It was half-past two by Mr. Golyadkin's watch. All at once a circumstance of apparently little importance settled some doubts in Mr. Golyadkin's mind: a flushed and breathless figure suddenly made its appearance from behind the screen of the department building and with a stealthy movement like a rat he darted up the steps and into the entry. It was a copying clerk called Ostafyev, a man Mr. Golyadkin knew very well, who was rather useful and ready to do anything for a trifle. Knowing Ostafyev's weak spot and surmising that after his brief, unavoidable absence he would probably be greedier than ever for tips, our hero made up his mind not to be sparing of them, and immediately darted up the steps, and then into the entry after him, called to him and, with a mysterious air, drew him aside into a convenient comer behind a huge iron stove. And having led him there, our hero began questioning him.

"Well, my dear fellow, how are things going in there . . . you under-stand me? . . ."

"Yes, your. honour, I wish you good health, your honour."

"All right, my good man, all right; but I'll reward you, my good fellow. Well, you see, how are things?"

"What is your honour asking?" At this point Ostafyev held his hand as though by accident before his open mouth.

"You see, my dear fellow, this is how it is . . . but don't you imagine . . . Come, is Andrey Filippovitch here? . . ."

"Yes, he is here."

"And are the clerks here?"

"Yes, sir, they are here as usual."

"And his Excellency too?"

"And his Excellency too." Here the man held his hand before his open mouth again, and looked rather curiously and strangely at Mr. Golyadkin, so at least our hero fancied.

"And there's nothing special there, my good man?"

"No, sir, certainly not, sir."

"So there's nothing concerning me, my friend. Is there nothing going on there—that is, nothing more than . . . eh? nothing more, you understand, my friend?"

"No, sir, I've heard nothing so far, sir." Again the man put his hand before his mouth and again looked rather strangely at Mr. Golyadkin. The fact was, Mr. Golyadkin was trying to read Ostafyev's countenance, trying to discover whether there was not something hidden in it. And, in fact, he did look as though he were hiding something: Ostafyev seemed to grow colder and more churlish, and did not enter into Mr. Golyadkin's interests with the same sympathy as at the beginning of the conversation. "He is to some extent justified," thought Mr. Golyadkin. "After all, what am I to him? Perhaps he has already been bribed by the other side, and that's why he has just been absent. But, here, I'll try him. . . ." Mr. Golyadkin realized that the moment for kopecks had arrived.

"Here, my dear fellow . . ."

"I'm feelingly grateful for your honour's kindness."

"I'll give you more than that."

"Yes, your honour."

"I'll give you some more directly, and when the business is over I'll give you as much again. Do you understand?"

The clerk did not speak. He stood at attention and stared fixedly at Mr. Golyadkin.

"Come, tell me now: have you heard nothing about me? . ."

"I think, so far, I have not . . . so to say . . . nothing so far." Ostafyev, like Mr. Golyadkin, spoke deliberately and preserved a mysterious air, moving his eyebrows a little, looking at the ground, trying to fall into the suitable tone, and, in fact, doing his very utmost to earn what had been promised him, for what he had received already he reckoned as already earned.

"And you know nothing?"

"So far, nothing, sir."

"Listen . . . you know . . . maybe you will know . . ."

"Later on, of course, maybe I shall know."

"It's a poor look out," thought our hero. "Listen: here's something more, my dear fellow."

"I am truly grateful to your honour."

"Was Vahramyev here yesterday? . . ."

"Yes, sir."

"And . . . somebody else? . . . Was he? . . . Try and remember, brother." The man ransacked his memory for a moment, and could think of nothing appropriate.

"No, sir, there wasn't anybody else."

"H'm!" a silence followed.

"Listen, brother, here's some more; tell me all, every detail."

"Yes, sir," Ostafyev had by now become as soft as silk; which was just what Mr. Golyadkin needed.

"Explain to me now, my good man, what footing is he on?"

"All right, sir, a good one, sir," answered the man, gazing open-eyed at Mr. Golyadkin.

"How do you mean, all right?"

"Well, it's just like that, sir." Here Ostafyev twitched his eyebrows significantly. But he was utterly nonplussed and didn't know what more to say.

"It's a poor look out," thought Mr Golyadkin.

"And hasn't anything more happened . . . in there . . . about Vahramyev?"

"But everything is just as usual."

"Think a little."

"There is, they say . . ."

"Come, what?"

Ostafyev put his hand in front of his mouth.

"Wasn't there a letter . . . from here . . . to me?"

"Mihyeev the attendant went to Vahramyev's lodging, to their German landlady, so I'll go and ask him, if you like."

"Do me the favour, brother, for goodness' sake! . . . I only mean . . . you mustn't imagine anything, brother, I only mean . . . Yes, you question him, brother, find out whether they are not getting up something concerning me. Find out how he is acting. That is what I want; that is what you must find out, my dear fellow, and then I'll reward you, my good man. . . ."

"I will, your honour, and Ivan Semyonovitch sat in your place to-day, sir.

"Ivan Semyonovitch? Oh! Really, you don't say so."

"Andrey Filippovitch told him to sit there."

"Re-al-ly! How did that happen? You must find out, brother; for God's sake find out, brother; find it all out—and I'll reward you, my dear fellow; that's what I want to know . . . and don't you imagine any-thing, brother. . . ."

"Just so, sir, just so; I'll go at once. And aren't you going in to-day, sir?"

"No, my friend; I only looked round, I only looked round, you know. I only came to have a look round, my friend, and I'll reward you after-wards, my friend."

"Yes, sir." The man ran rapidly and eagerly up the. stairs and Mr. Golyadkin was left alone.

"It's a poor look out!" he thought. "Ech, it's a bad business, a bad business! Ech! things are in a bad way with us now! What does it all mean? What did that drunkard's insinuations mean, for instance, and whose trickery was it? Ah! I know now whose it was. And what a thing this is. No doubt they found out and made him sit there. . . . But, after all, did they sit him there? It was Andrey Filippovitch sat him there, he sat Ivan Semyonovitch there himself; why did he make him sit there and with what object? Probably they found out. . . . That is Vahramyev's work—that is, not Vahramyev, he is as stupid as an ashen post, Vahramyev is, and they are all at work on his behalf, and they egged that scoundrel on to come here for the same purpose, and the German woman brought up her grievance, the one-eyed hussy. I always suspected that this intrigue was not without an object and that in all this old-womanish gossip there must be something, and I said as much to Krestyan Ivanovitch, telling him they'd sworn to cut a man's throat—in a moral sense, of course—and they pounced upon Karolina Ivanovna. Yes, there are master hands at work in this, one can see! Yes, sir, there are master hands at work here, and not Vahramyev's. I've said already that Vahramyev is stupid, but .. . I know who it is behind it all, it's that rascal, that impostor! It's only that he relies upon, which is partly proved by his successes in the best society. And it would certainly be desirable to know on what footing he stands now. What is he now among them? Only, why have they taken Ivan Semyonovitch? What the devil do they want with Ivan Semyonovitch? Could not they have found any one else? Though it would come to the same thing whoever it had been, and the only thing I know is that I have suspected Ivan Semyonovitch for a long time past. I noticed long ago what a nasty, horrid old man he was—they say he lends money and takes interest like any Jew. To be sure, the bear's the leading spirit in the whole affair. One can detect the bear in the whole affair. It began in "this way. It began at the lsmailovsky Bridge; that's how it began . . ."

At this point Mr. Golyadkin frowned, as though he had taken a bite out of a lemon, probably remembering something very unpleasant.

"But, there, it doesn't matter," he thought. "I keep harping on my own troubles. What will Ostafyev find out? Most likely he is staying on or has been delayed somehow. It is a good thing, in a sense, that I am intriguing like this, and am laying mines on my side too. I've only to give Ostafyev ten kopecks and he's . . . so to speak, on my side. Only the point is, is he really on my side? Perhaps they've got him on their side too. and they are carrying on an intrigue by means of him on their side too. He looks a ruffian, the rascal, a regular ruffian; he's hiding something, the rogue. `No, nothing,' says he, `and I am deeply grateful to your honour,' says he. You ruffian, you!"

He heard a noise . . Mr. Golyadkin shrank up and skipped behind the stove. Some one came down stairs and went out into the street. "Who could that be going away now?" our hero thought to himself. A minute later footsteps were audible again. . . . At this point Mr. Golyadkin could not resist poking the very tip of his nose out beyond his corner—he poked it out and instantly withdrew it again, as though some ; one had pricked it with a pin. This time some one he knew well was coming—that is the scoundrel, the intriguer and the reprobate—he was approaching with his usual mean, tripping little step, prancing and shuffling with his feet as though he were going to kick some one.

"The rascal," said our hero to himself.

Mr. Golyadkin could not, however, help observing that the rascal had under his arm a huge green portfolio belonging to his Excellency.

"He's on a special commission again," thought Mr. Golyadkin, flushing crimson and shrinking into himself more than ever from vexation.

As soon as Mr. Golyadkin junior had slipped past Mr. Golyadkin senior without observing him in the least, footsteps were heard for the third time, and this time Mr. Golyadkin guessed that these were Ostafyev's. It was, in fact, the sleek figure of a copying clerk, Pisarenko by name. This surprised Mr. Golyadkin. Why had he mixed up other people in their secret? Our hero wondered. What barbarians! Nothing is sacred to them! "Well, my friend?" he brought out, addressing Pisarenko: "who sent you, my friend? . . ."

"I've come about your business. There's no news so far from any one. But should there be any we'll let you know."

"And Ostafyev?" "It was quite impossible for him to come, your honour. His Excellency has walked through the room twice, and I've no time to stay."

"Thank you, my good man, thank you . . . only, tell me . . ."

"Upon my word, sir, I can't stay. . . . They are asking for us every minute . . . but if your honour will stay here, we'll let you know if any-thing happens concerning your little affair."

"No, my friend, you just tell me . . ."

"Excuse me, I've no time to stay, sir," said Pisarenko, tearing himself away from Mr. Golyadkin, who had clutched him by the lapel of his coat. "I really can't. If your honour will stay here we'll let you know."

"In a minute, my good man, in a minute! In a minute, my good fellow! I tell you what, here's a letter; and I'll reward you, my good man."

"Yes, sir."

"Try and give it to Mr. Golyadkin my dear fellow."

"Golyadkin?"

"Yes, my man, to Mr. Golyadkin."

"Very good, sir; as soon as I get off I'll take it, and you stay here, meanwhile; no one will see you here. . . ."

"No, my good man, don't imagine . . . I'm not standing here to avoid being seen. But I'm not going to stay here now, my friend. . . . I'll be close here in the side street. There's a coffee-house near here; so I'll wait there, and if anything happens, you let me know about anything, you understand?"

"Very good, sir. Only let me go; I understand."

"And I'll reward you," Mr. Golyadkin called after Pisarenko, when he had at last released him. . . .

"The rogue seemed to be getting rather rude," our hero reflected as he stealthily emerged from behind the stove. "There's some other dodge here. That's clear. . . . At first it was one thing and another . . . he really was in a hurry, though; perhaps there's a great deal to do in the office. And his Excellency had been through the room twice. . . . How did that happen? . . . Ough! never mind! It may mean nothing, perhaps; but now we shall see. . . ."

At this point Mr. Golyadkin was about to open the door, intending to go out into the street, when suddenly, at that very instant, his Excellency's carriage dashed up to the door. Before Mr. Golyadkin had time to recover from the shock, the door of the carriage was opened from within and a gentleman jumped out. This gentleman was no other than Mr. Golyadkin junior, who had only gone out ten minutes before. Mr. Golyadkin senior remembered that the Director's flat was only a couple of paces away.

"He has been out on a special commission," our hero thought to himself.

Meanwhile, Mr. Golyadkin junior took out of the carriage a thick green portfolio and other papers. Finally, giving some orders to the coachman, he opened the door, almost ran up against Mr. Golyadkin senior, purposely avoided noticing him, acting in this way expressly to annoy him, and mounted the office staircase at a rapid canter.

"It's a bad look out," thought Mr. Golyadkin. "This, is what it has come to now! Oh, good Lord! Look at him."

For half a minute our hero remained motionless. At last he made up his mind. Without pausing to think, though he was aware of a violent palpitation of the heart and a tremor in all his limbs, he ran up the stairs after his enemy.

"Here goes; what does it matter to me? I have nothing to do with the case," he thought, taking off his hat, his greatcoat and his goloshes in the entry.

When Mr. Golyadkin walked into his office, it was already getting dusk. Neither Andrey Filippovitch nor Anton Antonovitch were in the room. Both of them were in the Director's room, handing in reports. The Director, so it was rumoured, was in haste to report to a still higher Excellency. In consequence of this, and also because twilight was coming on, and the office hours were almost over, several of the clerks, especially the younger ones, were, at the moment when our hero entered, enjoying a period of inactivity; gathered together in groups, they were talking, arguing, and laughing, and some of the most youthful—that is, belonging to the lowest grades in the service, had got up a game of pitch-farthing in a corner, by a window. Knowing what was proper, and feeling at the moment a special need to conciliate and get on with them, Mr. Golyadkin immediately approached those with whom he used to get on best, in order to wish them good day, and so on. But his colleagues answered his greetings rather strangely. He was unpleasantly impressed by a certain coldness, even curtness, one might almost say severity in their manner. No one shook hands with him. Some simply said, "Good day" and walked away; others barely nodded; one simply turned away and pretended not to notice him; at last some of them —and what mortified Mr. Golyadkin most of all, some of the youngsters of the lowest grades, mere lads who, as Mr. Golyadkin justly observed about them, were capable of nothing but hanging about and playing pitch-farthing at every opportunity—little by little collected round Mr. Golyadkin, formed a group round him and almost barred his way. They all looked at him with a sort of insulting curiosity.

It was a bad sign. Mr. Golyadkin felt this, and very judiciously decided not to notice it. Suddenly a quite unexpected-event completely finished him off, as they say, and utterly crushed him.

At the moment most trying to Mr. Golyadkin senior, suddenly, as though by design, there appeared in the group of fellow clerks surrounding him the figure of Mr. Golyadkin junior, gay as ever, smiling a little smile as ever, nimble, too, as ever; in short, mischievous, skip-ping and tripping, chuckling and fawning, with sprightly tongue and sprightly toe, as always, precisely as he had been the day before at a very unpleasant moment for Mr. Golyadkin senior, for instance.

Grinning, tripping and turning with a smile that seemed to say "good evening," to every one, he squeezed his way into the group of clerks, shaking hands with one, slapping another on the shoulder, putting his arm round another, explaining to a fourth how he had come to be employed by his Excellency, where he had been, what he had done, what he had brought with him; to the fifth, probably his most intimate friend, he gave a resounding kiss—in fact, everything happened as it had in Mr. Golyadkin's dream. When he had skipped about to his heart's content, polished them all off in his usual way, disposed them all in his favour, whether he needed them or not, when he had lavished his blandishments to the delectation of all the clerks, Mr. Golyadkin junior suddenly, and most likely by mistake, for he had not yet had time to notice his senior, held out his hand to Mr. Golyadkin senior also. Probably also by mistake—though he had had time to observe the dishonourable Mr. Golyadkin junior thoroughly, our hero at once eagerly seized the hand so unexpectedly held out to him and pressed it in the warmest and friendliest way, pressed it with a strange, quite unexpected, inner feeling, with a tearful emotion. Whether our hero was misled by the first movement of his worthless foe, or was taken unawares, or, without recognizing it, felt at the bottom of his heart how defenseless he was—it is difficult to say. The fact remains that Mr. Golyadkin senior, apparently knowing what he was doing, of his own free will, before witnesses, solemnly shook hands with him whom he called his mortal foe. But what was the amazement, the stupefaction and fury, what was the horror and the shame of Mr. Golyadkin senior, when his enemy and mortal foe, the dishonourable Mr. Golyadkin junior, noticing the mistake of that persecuted, innocent, perfidiously deceived man, without a trace of shame, of feeling, of compassion or of conscience, pulled his hand away with insufferable rudeness and insolence. What was worse, he shook the hand as though it had been polluted with something horrid; what is more, he spat aside with disgust, accompanying this with a most insulting gesture; worse still, he drew out his handkerchief and, in the most unseemly way, wiped all the fingers that had rested for one moment in the hand of Mr. Golyadkin senior. While he did this Mr. Golyadkin junior looked about him in his characteristic horrid way, took care that every one should see what he was doing, glanced into people's eyes and evidently tried to insinuate to every one everything that was most unpleasant in regard to Mr. Golyadkin senior. Mr. Golyadkin junior's revolting behaviour seemed to arouse general indignation among the clerks that surrounded them; even the frivolous youngsters showed their displeasure. A murmur of protest rose on all sides. Mr. Golyadkin could not but discern the general feeling; but suddenly—an appropriate witticism that bubbled from the lips of Mr. Golyadkin junior shattered, annihilated our hero's last hopes, and inclined the balance again in favour of his deadly and undeserving foe.

"He's our Russian Faublas, gentlemen; allow me to introduce the youthful Faublas," piped Mr. Golyadkin junior, with his characteristic insolence, pirouetting and threading his way among the clerks, and directing their attention to the petrified though genuine Mr. Golyadkin. "Let us kiss each other; darling," he went on with insufferable familiarity, addressing the man he had so treacherously insulted. Mr. Golyadkin junior's unworthy jest seemed to touch a responsive chord, for it contained an artful allusion to an incident with which all were apparently familiar. Our hero was painfully conscious of the hand of his enemies. But he had made up his mind by now. With glowing eyes, with pale face, with a fixed smile he tore himself somehow out of the crowd and with uneven, hurried steps made straight for his Excellency's private room. In the room next to the last he was met by Andrey Filippovitch, who had only just come out from seeing his Excellency, and although there were present in this room at the moment a good number of persons of whom Mr. Golyadkin knew nothing, yet our hero did not care to take such a fact into consideration. Boldly, resolutely, directly, almost wondering at himself and inwardly admiring his own courage, without loss of time he accosted Andrey Filippovitch, who was a good deal surprised by this unexpected attack.

"Ah! . . . What is it . . . what do you want?" asked the head of the division, not hearing Mr. Golyadkin's hesitating words.

"Andrey Filippovitch, may . . . might I, Andrey Filippovitch, may I have a conversation with his Excellency at once and in private?" our hero said resolutely and distinctly, fixing the most determined glance on Andrey Filippovitch.

"What next! of course not." Andrey Filippovitch scanned Mr. Golyadkin from head to foot.

"I say all this, Andrey Filippovitch, because I am surprised that no one here unmasks the impostor and scoundrel."

"Wha-a-at!"

"Scoundrel, Andrey Filippovitch!"

"Of whom are you pleased to speak in those terms?"

"Of a certain person, Andrey Filippovitch; I'm alluding, Andrey Filippovitch, to a certain person; I have the right . . . I imagine, Andrey Filippovitch, that the authorities would surely encourage such action," added Mr. Golyadkin, evidently hardly knowing what he was saying. "Andrey Filippovitch . . . but no doubt you see yourself, Andrey Filippovitch, that this honourable action is a mark of my loyalty in every way—of my looking upon my superior as a father, Andrey Filippovitch; I as much as to say look upon my benevolent superior as a father and blindly trust my fate to him. It's as much as to say . . . you see . . ." At this point Mr. Golyadkin's voice trembled and two tears ran down his eyelashes.

As Andrey Filippovitch listened to Mr. Golyadkin he was so astonished that he could not help stepping back a couple of paces. Then he looked about him uneasily . . . It is difficult to say how the matter would have ended. But suddenly the door of his Excellency's room was opened, and he himself came out, accompanied by several officials. All the persons in his room following in a string. His Excellency called Andrey Filippovitch and walked beside him, beginning to discuss some business details.

When all had set off and gone out of the room, Mr. Golyadkin woke up. Growing calmer, he took refuge under the wing of Anton Antonovitch, who came last in the procession and who, Mr. Golyadkin fancied, looked stern and anxious. "I've been talking nonsense, I've been making a mess of it again, but there, never mind," he thought.

"I hope, at least, that you, Anton Antonovitch, will consent to listen to me and to enter into my position," he said quietly, in a voice that still trembled a little. "Rejected by all, I appeal to you. I am still at a loss to understand what Andrey Filippovitch's words mean, Anton Antonovitch. Explain them to me if you can. . . ."

"Everything will be explained in due time," Anton Antonovitch replied sternly and emphatically, and as Mr. Golyadkin fancied with an air that gave him plainly to understand that Anton Antonovitch did not wish to continue the conversation. "You will soon know all about it. You will be officially informed about every thing today."

"What do you mean by officially informed, Anton Antonovitch? Why officially?" our hero asked timidly.

"It is not for you and me to discuss what our superiors decide upon, Yakov Petrovitch."

"Why our superiors, Anton Antonovitch?" said our hero, still more intimidated; "why our superiors? I don't see what reason there is to trouble our superiors in the matter, Anton Antonovitch . . . Perhaps you mean to say something about yesterday's doings, Anton Antonovitch?"

"Oh no, nothing to do with yesterday; there's something else amiss with you."

"What is there amiss, Anton Antonovitch? I believe, Anton Antonovitch, that I have done nothing amiss."

"Why, you were meaning to be sly with some one," Anton Antonovitch cut in sharply, completely flabbergasting Mr. Golyadkin.

Mr. Golyadkin started, and turned as white as a pocket-handkerchief.

"Of course, Anton Antonovitch," he said, in a voice hardly audible, "if one listens to the voice of calumny and hears one's enemies' tales, without heeding what the other side has to say in its defence, then, of course . . . then, of course, Anton Antonovitch, one must suffer innocently and for nothing."

"To be sure; but your unseemly conduct, in injuring the reputation of a virtuous young lady belonging to that benevolent, highly distinguished and well-known family who had befriended you. . .

"What conduct do you mean, Anton Antonovitch?"

"What I say. Do you know anything about your praiseworthy conduct in regard to that other young lady who, though poor, is of honourable foreign extraction?"

"Allow me, Anton Antonovitch . . . if you would kindly listen to me, Anton Antonovitch . . ."

"And your treacherous behaviour and slander of another person, your charging another person with your own sins. Ah, what do you call that?"

"I did not send him away, Anton Antonovitch," said our hero, with a tremor; "and I've never instructed Petrushka, my man, to do anything of the sort . . . He has eaten my bread, Anton Antonovitch, he has taken advantage of my hospitality," our hero added expressively and with deep emotion, so much so that his chin twitched a little and tears were ready to start again.

"That is only your talk, that he has eaten your bread," answered Anton Antonovitch, somewhat offended, and there was a perfidious note in his voice which sent a pang to Mr. Golyadkin's heart.

"Allow me most humbly to ask you again, Anton Antonovitch, is his Excellency aware of all this business?"

"Upon my word, you must let me go now, though. I've no time for

you now. . . . You'll know everything you need to know to-day." "Allow me, for God's sake, one minute, Anton Antonovitch." "Tell me afterwards . . ."

"No, Anton Antonovitch; I . . . you see, Anton Antonovitch . . . only listen . . . I am not one for freethinking, Anton Antonovitch; I shun free-thinking; I am quite ready for my part . . . and, indeed, I've given up that idea. . . ."

"Very good, very good. I've heard that already."

"No, you have not heard it, Anton Antonovitch. It is something else, Anton Antonovitch; it's a good thing, really, a good thing and pleasant to hear. . . . As I've explained to you, Anton Antonovitch, I admit that idea, that divine Providence has created two men exactly alike, and that a benevolent government, seeing the hand of Providence, provided a berth for two twins. That is a good thing, Anton Antonovitch. You see that it is a very good thing, Anton Antonovitch, and that I am very far from freethinking. I look upon my benevolent government as a father; I say `yes,' by all means; you are benevolent authorities, and you, of course. . . . A young man must be in the service. . . . Stand up for me, Anton Antonovitch, take my part, Anton Antonovitch. . . . I am all right . . . Anton Antonovitch, for God's sake, one little word more . . . Anton Antonovitch. . . ."

But by now Anton Antonovitch was far away from Mr. Golyadkin. . . . Our hero was so bewildered and overcome by all that had happened and all that he had heard that he did not know where he was standing, what he had heard, what he had done, what was being done to him, and what was going to be done to him.

With imploring eyes he sought for Anton Antonovitch in the crowd of clerks, that he might justify himself further in his eyes and say some-thing to him extremely high toned and very agreeable, and creditable to himself. . . . By degrees, however, a new light began to break upon our hero's bewildered mind, a new and awful light that revealed at once a whole perspective of hitherto unknown and utterly unsuspected circumstances. . . . At that moment somebody gave our bewildered hero a poke in the ribs. He looked around. Pisarenko was standing before him.

"A letter, your honour."

"Ah, you've been out already, then, my good man?"

"No, it was brought at ten o'clock this morning. Sergey Mihyeev, the attendant, brought it from Mr. Vahramyev's lodging."

"Very good, very good, and I'll reward you now, my dear fellow."

Saying this, Mr. Golyadkin thrust the letter in the side pocket of his uniform and buttoned up every button of it; then he looked round him, and to his surprise, found that he was by now in the hall of the department, in a group of clerks crowding at the outer door, for office hours were over. Mr. Golyadkin had not only failed till that moment to observe this circumstance, but had no notion how he suddenly came to be wearing his greatcoat and goloshes and to be holding his hat in his hand, All the clerks were standing motionless, in reverential expectation. The fact was that his Excellency was standing at the bottom of the stairs waiting for his carriage, which was for some reason late in arriving, and was carrying on a very interesting conversation with Andrey

Filippovitch and two councilors. At a little distance from Andrey Filippovitch stood Anton Antonovitch and several other clerks, who were all smiles, seeing that his Excellency was graciously making a joke. The clerks who were crowded at the top of the stairs were smiling too, in expectation of his Excellency's laughing again. The only one who was not smiling was Fedosyevitch, the corpulent hall-porter, who stood stiffly at attention, holding the handle of the door, waiting impatiently for the daily gratification that fell to his share—that is, the task of flinging one half of the door wide open with a swing of his arm, and then, with a low bow, reverentially making way for his Excellency to pass. But the one who seemed to be more delighted than any and to feel the most satisfaction of all was the worthless and ungentlemanly enemy of Mr. Golyadkin. At that instant he positively forgot all the clerks, and even gave up tripping and pirouetting in his usual odious way; he even for-got to make up to anybody. He was all eyes and ears, he even doubled himself up strangely, no doubt in the strained effort to hear, and never took his eyes off his Excellency, and only from time to time his arms, legs and head twitched with faintly perceptible tremors that betrayed the secret emotions of his soul.

"Ah, isn't he in a state!" thought our hero; "he looks like a favourite, the rascal! I should like to know how it is that he deceives society of every class. He has neither brains nor character, neither education nor feeling; he's a lucky rogue! Mercy on us! How can a man, when you think of it, come and make friends with every one so quickly! And he'll get on, I swear the fellow will get on, the rogue will make his way—he's a lucky rascal! I should like to know, too, what he keeps whispering to every one—what plots he is hatching with all these people, and what secrets they are talking about? Lord, have mercy on us! If only I could . . . get on with them a little too . . . say this and that and the other. Hadn't I better ask him . . . tell him I won't do it again; say I'm in fault, and a young man must serve nowadays, your Excellency'? I am not in the least abashed by my obscure position—so there! I am not going to protest in any way, either; I shall bear it all with meekness and patience, so there! Is that the way to behave? . . . Though you'll never see through him, though, the rascal; you can't reach him with anything you say; you can't hammer reason into his head. . . . We'll make an effort, though. I may happen to hit on a good moment, so I'll make an effort. . . ."

Feeling in his uneasiness, his misery and his bewilderment that he couldn't leave things like this, that the critical moment had come, that he must explain himself to some one, our hero began to move a little towards the place where his worthless and undeserving enemy stood: but at that very moment his Excellency's long-expected carriage rolled up into the entrance, Fedosyevitch flung open the door and, bending double, let his Excellency pass out. All the waiting clerks streamed out towards the door, and for a moment separated Mr. Golyadkin senior from Mr. Golyadkin junior.

"You shan't get away!" said our hero, forcing his way through the crowd while he kept his eyes fixed on the man he wanted. At last the crowd dispersed. Our hero felt he was free and flew in pursuit of his enemy.

CHAPTER XI

Mr. Golyadkin's breath failed him; he flew as though on wings after his rapidly retreating enemy. He was conscious of immense energy. Yet in spite of this terrible energy he might confidently have said that at that moment a humble gnat—had a gnat been able to exist in Petersburg at that time of the year—could very easily have knocked him down. He felt, too, that he was utterly weak again, that he was carried along by a peculiar outside force, that it was not he himself who was running, but, on the contrary, that his legs were giving way under him, and refused to obey him. This all might turn out for the best, however.

"Whether it is for the best or not for the best," thought Mr. Golyadkin, almost breathless from running so quickly, "but that the game is lost there cannot be the slightest doubt now; that I am utterly done for is certain, definite, signed and ratified."

In spite of all this our hero felt as though he had risen from the dead, as though he had withstood a battalion, as though he had won a victory when he succeeded in clutching the overcoat of his enemy, who had already raised one foot to get into the cab he had engaged.

"My dear sir! My dear sir!" he shouted to the infamous Mr. Golyadkin junior, holding him by the button. "My dear sir, I hope that you . . ."

"No, please do not hope for anything," Mr. Golyadkin's heartless enemy answered evasively, standing with one foot on the step of the cab and vainly waving the other leg in the air, in his efforts to get in, trying to preserve his equilibrium, and at the same time trying with all his might to wrench his coat away from Mr.

Golyadkin senior, while the latter held on to it with all the strength that had been vouchsafed to him by nature.

"Yakov Petrovitch, only ten minutes . . ."

"Excuse me, I've no time . . ."

"You must admit, Yakov Petrovitch . . . please, Yakov Petrovitch. . . . For God's sake, Yakov Petrovitch . . . let us have it out—in a straight-forward way . . . one little second, Yakov Petrovitch . . ."

"My dear fellow, I can't stay," answered Mr. Golyadkin's dishonourable enemy, with uncivil familiarity, disguised as good-natured heartiness; "another time, believe me, with my whole soul and all my heart; but now I really can't . . ."

"Scoundrel!" thought our hero. "Yakov Petrovitch," he cried miserably. "I have never been your enemy. Spiteful people have described me unjustly. . . . I am ready, on my side . . . Yakov Petrovitch, shall we go in here together, at once, Yakov Petrovitch? And with all my heart, as you have so justly expressed it just now, and in straightforward, honourable language, as you have expressed it just now—here into this coffee-house; there the facts will explain themselves: they will really, Yakov Petrovitch. Then everything will certainly explain itself. . ."

"Into the coffee-house? Very good. I am not against it. Let us go into the coffee-house on one condition only, my dear, on one condition—that these things shall be cleared up. We will have it all out, darling," said Mr. Golyadkin junior, getting out of the cab and shamelessly slap-ping our hero on the shoulder; "You friend of my heart, for your sake, Yakov Petrovitch, I am ready to go by the back street (as you were pleased to observe so aptly on one occasion, Yakov Petrovitch). Why, what a rogue he is! Upon my word, he does just what he likes with one!"

Mr. Golyadkin's false friend went on, fawning upon him and cajoling him with a little smile. The coffee-house which the two Mr. Golyadkins entered stood some distance away from the main street and was at the moment quite empty. A rather stout German woman made her appearance behind the counter. Mr. Golyadkin and his unworthy enemy went into the second room, where a puffy-looking boy with a closely shaven head was busy with a bundle of chips at the stove, trying to revive the smoldering fire. At Mr. Golyadkin junior's request chocolate was served.

"And a sweet little lady-tart," said Mr. Golyadkin junior, with a sly wink at Mr. Golyadkin senior.

Our hero blushed and was silent.

"Oh, yes, I forgot, I beg your pardon. I know your taste. We are sweet on charming little Germans, sir; you and I are sweet on charming and agreeable little Germans, aren't we, you upright soul? We take their lodgings, we seduce their morals, they win our hearts with their beer-soup and their milksoup, and we give them notes of different sorts, that's what we do, you Faublas, you deceiver!" All this Mr. Golyadkin junior said, making an unworthy though villainously artful allusion to a certain personage of the female sex, while he fawned upon our hero, smiled at him with an amiable air, with a deceitful show of being delighted with him and pleased to have met him. Seeing that Mr. Golyadkin senior was by no means so stupid and deficient in breeding and the manners of good society as to believe in him, the infamous man resolved to change his tactics and to make a more open attack upon him. After uttering his disgusting speech, the false Mr. Golyadkin ended by slapping the real and substantial Mr. Golyadkin on the shoulder, with a revolting effrontery and familiarity. Not content with that, he began playing pranks utterly unfit for well-bred society; he took it into his head to repeat his old, nauseous trick—that is, regardless of the resistance and faint cries of the indignant Mr. Golyadkin senior, he pinched the latter on the cheek. At the spectacle of such depravity our hero boiled within, but was silent . . only for the time, however.

"That is the talk of my enemies," he answered at last, in a trembling voice, prudently restraining himself. At the same time our hero looked round uneasily towards the door. The fact was that Mr. Golyadkin junior seemed in excellent spirits, and ready for all sorts of little jokes, unseemly in a public place, and, speaking generally, not permissible by the laws of good manners, especially in well-bred society.

"Oh, well, in that case, as you please," Mr. Golyadkin junior gravely responded to our hero's thought, setting down upon the table the empty cup which he had gulped down with unseemly greed. "Well, there's no need for me to stay long with you, however. . . . Well, how are you getting on now, Yakov Petrovitch?"

"There's only one thing I can tell you, Yakov Petrovitch," our hero answered, with sangfroid and dignity; "I've never been your enemy."

"H'm. . . . Oh, what about Petrushka? Petrushka is his name, I fancy? Yes, it is Petrushka! Well, how is he? Well? The same as ever?"

"He's the same as ever, too, Yakov Petrovitch," answered Mr. Golyadkin senior, somewhat amazed. "I don't know, Yakov Petrovitch . . . from my standpoint . . . from a candid, honourable standpoint, Yakov Petrovitch, you must admit, Yakov Petrovitch. . . ."

"Yes, but you know yourself, Yakov Petrovitch," Mr. Golyadkin junior answered in a soft and expressive voice, so posing falsely as a sorrowful man overcome with remorse and deserving compassion. "You know yourself we live in difficult times. . . . I appeal to you, Yakov Petrovitch; you are an intelligent man and your reflections are just," Mr. Golyadkin junior said in conclusion, flattering Mr. Golyadkin senior in an abject way. "Life is not a game, you know yourself, Yakov Petrovitch," Mr. Golyadkin junior added, with vast significance, assuming the character of a clever and learned man, who is capable of passing judgments on lofty subjects.

"For my part, Yakov Petrovitch," our hero answered warmly, "for my part, scorning to be roundabout and speaking boldly and openly, using straightforward, honourable language and putting the whole matter on an honourable basis, I tell you I can openly and honourably assert, Yakov Petrovitch, that I am absolutely pure, and that, you know it yourself, Yakov Petrovitch, the error is mutual—it may all be the world's judgment, the opinion of the slavish crowd. . . . I speak openly, Yakov Petrovitch, everything is possible. I will say, too, Yakov Petrovitch, if you judge it in this way, if you look at the matter from a lofty, noble point of view, then I will boldly say, without false shame I will say, Yakov Petrovitch, it will positively be a pleasure to me to discover that I have been in error, it will positively be a pleasure to me to recognize it. You know yourself you are an intelligent man and, what is more, you are a gentleman. Without shame, without false shame, I am ready to recognize it," he wound up with dignity and nobility.

"It is the decree of destiny, Yakov Petrovitch . . . but let us drop all this," said Mr. Golyadkin junior. "Let us rather use the brief moment of our meeting for a more pleasant and profitable conversation, as is only suitable between two colleagues in the service. . . . Really, I have not succeeded in saying two words to you all this time. . . . I am not to blame for that, Yakov Petrovitch. . . ."

"Nor I," answered our hero warmly, "nor I, either! My heart tells me, Yakov Petrovitch, that I'm not to blame in all this matter. Let us blame fate for all this, Yakov Petrovitch," added Mr. Golyadkin senior, in a quick, conciliatory tone of voice. His voice began little by little to soft-en and to quaver.

"Well! How are you in health?" said the sinner in a sweet voice.

"I have a little cough," answered our hero, even more sweetly.

"Take care of yourself. There is so much illness going about, you may easily get quinsy; for my part I confess I've begun to wrap myself up in flannel."

"One may, indeed, Yakov Petrovitch, very easily get quinsy," our hero pronounced after a brief silence; "Yakov Petrovitch, I see that I have made a mistake, I remember with softened feelings those happy moments which we were so fortunate as to spend together, under my poor, though I venture to say, hospitable roof . . ."

"In your letter, however, you wrote something very different," said Mr. Golyadkin junior reproachfully, speaking on this occasion—though only on this occasion—quite justly.

"Yakov Petrovitch, I was in error'. . . . I see clearly now that I was in error in my unhappy letter too. Yakov Petrovitch, I am ashamed to look at you, Yakov Petrovitch, you wouldn't believe. . . . Give me that letter that I may tear it to pieces before your eyes, Yakov Petrovitch, and if that is utterly impossible I entreat you to read it the other way before—precisely the other way before—that is, expressly with a friendly intention, giving the opposite sense to the whole letter. I was in error. Forgive me, Yakov Petrovitch, I was quite . . . I was grievously in error, Yakov Petrovitch."

"You say so?" Mr. Golyadkin's perfidious friend inquired, rather casually and indifferently.

"I say that I was quite in error, Yakov Petrovitch, and that for my part, quite without false shame, I am . . ."

"Ah, well, that's all right! That's a nice thing your being in error," answered Mr. Golyadkin junior.

"I even had an idea, Yakov Petrovitch," our candid hero answered in a gentlemanly way, completely failing to observe the horrible perfidy of his deceitful enemy; "I even had an idea that here were two people created exactly alike. . . ."

"Ah, is that your idea?"

At this point the notoriously worthless Mr. Golyadkin took up his hat. Still failing to observe his treachery, Mr. Golyadkin senior, too, got up and with a noble, simple-hearted smile to his false friend, tried in his innocence to be friendly to him, to encourage him, and in that way to form a new friendship with him.

"Goody-bye, your Excellency," Mr. Golyadkin junior called out suddenly. Our hero started, noticing in his enemy's face something positively Bacchanalian, and, solely to get rid of him, put two fingers into the unprincipled man's outstretched hand; but then . . . then his enemy's shamelessness passed all bounds. Seizing the two fingers of Mr. Golyadkin's hand and at first pressing them, the worthless fellow on the spot, before Mr. Golyadkin's eyes, had the effrontery to repeat the shameful joke of the morning. The limit of human patience was exhausted.

He had just hidden in his pocket the handkerchief with which he had wiped his fingers when Mr.Golyadkin senior recovered from the shock and dashed after him into the next room, into which his irreconcilable foe had in his usual hasty way hastened to decamp. As though perfectly innocent, he was standing at the counter eating pies, and with perfect composure, like a virtuous man, was making polite remarks to the German woman behind the counter.

"I can't go into it before ladies," thought our hero, and he, too, went up to the counter, so agitated that he hardly knew what he was doing.

"The tart is certainly not bad! What do you think?" Mr. Golyadkin junior began upon his unseemly sallies again, reckoning, no doubt, upon Mr. Golyadkin's infinite patience. The stout German, for her part, looked at both her visitors with pewtery, vacant-looking eyes, smiling affably and evidently not understanding Russian. Our hero flushed red as fire at the words of the unabashed Mr. Golyadkin junior, and, unable to control himself, rushed at him with the evident intention of tearing him to pieces and finishing off completely, but Mr. Golyadkin junior, in his usual mean way, was already far off; he took flight, he was already on the steps. It need hardly be said that, after the first moment of stupefaction with which Mr. Golyadkin senior was naturally overcome, he recovered himself and went at full speed after his insulting enemy, who had already got into a cab, whose driver was obviously in collusion with him. But at that very instant the stout German, seeing both her customers make off, shrieked and rang her bell with all her might. Our hero was on the point of flight, but he turned back, and, without asking for change, flung her money for himself and for the shameless man who had left without paying, and although thus delayed he succeeded in catching up his enemy. Hanging on to the side of the cab with all the force bestowed on him by nature, our hero was carried for some time along the street, clambering upon the vehicle, while Mr. Golyadkin junior did his utmost to dislodge him. Meanwhile the cab-man, with whip, with reins, with kicks and with shouts urged on his exhausted nag, who quite unexpectedly dropped into a gallop, biting at the bit, and kicking with his hind legs in a horrid way. At last our hero succeeded in climbing into the cab, facing his enemy and with his back to the driver, his knees touching the knees and his right hand clutching the very shabby fur collar of his depraved and exasperated foe.

The enemies were borne along for some time in silence. Our hero could scarcely breathe. It was a bad road and he was jolted at every step and in peril of breaking his neck. Moreover, his exasperated foe still refused to acknowledge himself vanquished and was trying to shove him off into the mud. To complete the unpleasantness of his position the weather was detestable. The snow was falling in heavy flakes and doing its utmost to creep under the unfastened overcoat of the genuine Mr. Golyadkin. It was foggy and nothing could be seen. It was difficult to tell through what street and in what direction they were being taken. . . . It seemed to Mr. Golyadkin that what was happening to him was somehow familiar. One instant he tried to remember whether he had had a presentiment of it the day before, in a dream, for instance. . . .

At last his wretchedness reached the utmost pitch of agony. Leaning upon his merciless opponent, he was beginning to cry out. But his cries died away upon his lips. . . There was a moment when Mr. Golyadkin forgot everything, and made up his mind that all this was of no consequence and that it was all nothing, that it was happening in some inexplicable manner, and that, therefore, to protest was effort thrown away. . . . But suddenly and almost at the same instant that our hero was drawing this conclusion, an unexpected jolt gave quite a new turn to the affair.

Mr. Golyadkin fell off the cab like a sack of flour and rolled on the ground, quite correctly recognizing, at the moment of his fall, that his excitement had been very inappropriate. Jumping up at last, he saw that they had arrived somewhere; the cab was standing in the middle of some courtyard, and from the first glance our hero noticed that it was the courtyard of the house in which was Olsufy Ivanovitch's flat. At the same instant he noticed that his enemy was mounting the steps, probably on his way to Olsufy Ivanovitch's. In indescribable misery he was about to pursue his enemy, but, fortunately for himself, prudently thought better of it. Not forgetting to pay the cabman, Mr. Golyadkin ran with all his might along the street, regardless of where he was going. The snow was falling heavily as before; as before it was muggy, wet, and dark. Our hero did not walk, but flew, coming into collision with every one on the way—men, women and children, and himself rebounding from every one—men, women and children. About him and after him he heard frightened voices, squeals, screams. . . . But Mr. Golyadkin seemed unconscious and would pay no heed to anything. . . . He came to himself, however, on Semyonovsky Bridge, and then only through succeeding in tripping against and upsetting two peasant women and the wares they were selling, and tumbling over them.

"That's no matter," thought Mr. Golyadkin, "that can easily be set right," and he felt in his pocket at once, intending to make up for the cakes, apples, nuts and various trifles he had scattered, with a rouble. Suddenly a new light dawned upon Mr. Golyadkin; in his pocket he felt the letter given him in the morning by the clerk. Remembering that there was a tavern he knew close by, he ran to it without a moment's delay, settled himself at a little table lighted up by a tallow candle, and, .taking no notice of anything, regardless of the waiter who came to ask for his orders, broke the seal and began reading the following letter, which completely astounded him-

"You noble man, who are suffering for my sake, and will be dear to my heart for ever!

"I am suffering, I am perishing—save me! The slanderer, the intriguer, notorious for the immorality of his tendencies, has entangled me in his snares and I am undone! I am lost! But he is abhorrent to me, while you! . . . They have separated us, they have intercepted my letters to you—and all this has been the work of the vicious man who has taken advantage of his one good quality—his likeness to you. A man can always be plain in appearance, yet fascinate by his intelligence, his strong feelings and his agreeable manners. . . I am ruined! I am being married against my will, and the chief part in this intrigue is taken by my parent, benefactor and civil councilor, Olsufy Ivanovitch, no doubt desirous of securing me a place and relations in well-bred society. . .But I have made up my mind and I protest by all the powers bestowed on me by nature. Be waiting for me with a carriage at nine o'clock this evening at the window of Olsufy Ivanovitch's flat. We are having another ball and a handsome lieutenant is coming. I will come out and we will fly. Moreover, there are other government offices in which one can be of service to one's country. In any case, remember, my friend, that innocence is strong in its very innocence. Farewell. Wait with the carriage at the entrance. I shall throw myself into the protection of your arms at two o'clock in the night.

"Yours till death,

"KLARA OLSUFYEVNA."

Fyodor Dostoevsky   The Double

After reading the letter our hero remained for some minutes as though petrified. In terrible anxiety, in terrible agitation, white as a sheet, with the letter in his hand, he walked several times up and down the room; to complete the unpleasantness of his position, though our hero failed to observe it, he was at that moment the object of the exclusive attention of every one in the room. Probably the disorder of his attire, his unrestrained excitement, his walking, or rather running about the room, his gesticulating with both hands, perhaps some enigmatic words unconsciously addressed to the air, probably all this prejudiced 'Mr. Golyadkin in the opinion of the customers, and even the waiter began to look at him suspiciously. Coming to himself, Mr. Golyadkin noticed that he was standing in the middle of the room and was in an almost unseemly, discourteous manner staring at an old man of very respectable appearance who, having dined and said grace before the ikon, had sat down again and fixed his eyes upon Mr. Golyadkin. Our hero looked vaguely about him and noticed that every one, actually every one, was looking at him with a hostile and suspicious air. All at once a retired military man in a red collar asked loudly for the Police News. Mr. Golyadkin started and turned crimson: he happened to look down and saw that he was in such disorderly attire as he would not have worn even at home, much less in a public place. His boots, his trousers and the whole of his left side were covered with mud; the trouser-strap was torn off his right foot, and his coat was even torn in many places. In extreme misery our hero went up to the table at which he had read the letter, and saw that the attendant was coming up to him with a strange and impudently peremptory expression of face. Utterly disconcerted and crestfallen, our hero began to look about the table at which he was now standing. On the table stood a dirty plate, left there from some-body's dinner, a soiled table-napkin and a knife, fork and spoon that had just been used. "Who has been having dinner?" thought our hero. "Can it have been I? Anything is possible! I must have had dinner without noticing it; what am I to do?"

Raising his eyes, Mr. Golyadkin again saw beside him the waiter who was about to address him. "How much is my bill, my lad?" our hero inquired, in a trembling voice.

A loud laugh sounded round Mr. Golyadkin, the waiter himself grinned. Mr. Golyadkin realized that he had blundered again, and had done something dreadfully stupid. He was overcome by confusion, and to avoid standing there with nothing to do he put his hand in his pocket to get out his handkerchief; but to the indescribable amazement of himself and all surrounding him, he pulled out instead of his handkerchief the bottle of medicine which Krestyan Ivanovitch had prescribed for him four days earlier. "Get the medicine at the same chemist's," floated through Mr. Golyadkin's brain. . . .

Suddenly he started and almost cried out in horror. A new light dawned. . . . The dark reddish and repulsive liquid had a sinister gleam to Mr. Golyadkin's eyes. . . . The bottle dropped from his hands and was instantly smashed. Our hero cried out and stepped back a pace to avoid the spilled medicine . . . he was trembling in every limb, and drops of sweat came out on to his brow and temples. "So my life is in danger!" Meantime there was a stir, a commotion in the room; every one surrounded Mr. Golyadkin, every one talked to Mr. Golyadkin, some even caught hold of Mr. Golyadkin. But our hero was dumb and motionless, seeing nothing, hearing nothing, feeling nothing. . . . At last, as though tearing himself from the place, he rushed out of the tavern, pushing away all and each who tried to detain him; almost unconscious, he got into the first cab that passed him and drove to his flat.

In the entry of his flat he met Mihyeev, an attendant from the office, with an official envelope in his hand.

"I know, my good man, I know all about it," our exhausted hero answered, in a weak, miserable voice; "it's official . . ."

The envelope did, in fact, contain instructions to Mr. Golyadkin, signed by Andrey Filippovitch, to give up the business in his hands to Ivan Semyonovitch. Taking the envelope and giving ten kopecks to the man, Mr. Golyadkin went into his flat and saw that Petrushka was collecting all his odds and ends, all his things into a heap, evidently intending to abandon Mr. Golyadkin and move to the flat of Karolina Ivanovna, who had enticed him to take the place of Yevstafy.

CHAPTER XII

Petrushka came in swaggering, with a strangely casual manner and an air of vulgar triumph on his face. It was evident that he had some idea in his head, that he felt thoroughly within his rights, and he looked like an unconcerned spectator—that is, as though he were anybody's servant rather than Mr. Golyadkin's.

"I say, you know, my good lad," our hero began breathlessly, "what time is it?"

Without speaking, Petrushka went behind his partition, then returned, and in a rather independent tone announced that it was nearly half-past seven.

"Well, that's all right, my lad, that's all right. Come, you see, my boy . . . allow me to tell you, my good lad, that everything, I fancy, is at an end between us."

Petrushka said nothing.

"Well, now as everything is over between us, tell me openly, as a friend, where you have been."

"Where I've been? To see good people, sir."

"I know, my good lad, I know. I have always been satisfied with you, and I give you a character. . . . Well, what are you doing with them now?"

"Why, sir! You know yourself. We all know a decent man won't teach you any harm."

"I know, my dear fellow, I know. Nowadays good people are rare, my lad; prize them, my friend. Well, how are they?"

"To be sure, they . . . Only I can't serve you any longer, sir; as your honour must know."

"I know, my dear fellow, I know your zeal and devotion; I have seen it all, my lad, I've noticed it. I respect you, my friend. I respect a good and honest man, even though he's a lackey."

"Why, yes, to be sure! The likes of us, of course, as you know yourself, are as good as anybody. That's so. We all know, sir, there's no getting on without a good man."

"Very well, very well, my boy, I feel it. . . . Come, here's your money and here's your character. Now we'll kiss and say goodbye, brother. . . . Come, now, my lad, I'll ask one service of you, one last service," said Mr. Golyadkin, in a solemn voice. "You see, my dear boy, all sorts of things happen. Sorrow is concealed in gilded palaces, and there's no escaping it. You know, my boy, I've always been kind to you, my boy."

Petrushka remained mute.

"I believe I've always been kind to you, my dear fellow. . . . Come, how much linen have we now, my dear boy?"

"Well, it's all there. Linen shirts six, three pairs of socks; four shirt-fronts; flannel vests; of underlinen two sets. You know all that yourself. I've got nothing of yours, sir. . . . I look after my master's belongings, sir. I am like that, sir . . . we all know . . . and I've . . . never been guilty of anything of the sort, sir, you know yourself, sir . . ."

"I trust you, my lad, I trust you. I didn't mean that, my friend, I didn't mean that, you know, my lad; I tell you what."

"To be sure, sir, we know that already. Why, when I used to be in service at General Stolbnyakov's . . . I lost the place through the family's going away to Saratov . . . they've an estate there . . ."

"No; I didn't mean that, my lad, I didn't mean that; don't think any-thing of the sort, my dear fellow . . .

"To be sure. It's easy, as you know yourself, sir, to take away the character of folks like us. And I've always given satisfaction—ministers, generals, senators, counts—I've served them all. I've been at Prince Svintchatkin's, at Colonel Pereborkin's, at General Nedobarov'sthey've gone away too, they've gone to their property. As we all know . . ."

"Yes, my lad, very good, my lad, very good. And now I'm going away, my friend. . . . A different path lies before each man, no one can tell what road he may have to take. Come, my lad, put out my clothes now, lay out my uniform too . . . and my other trousers, my sheets, quilts and pillows . . .

"Am I to pack them all in the bag?"

"Yes, my lad, yes; the bag, please. Who knows what may happen to us. Come, my dear boy, you can go and find a carriage . . ." "A carriage? . . ."

"Yes, my lad, a carriage; a roomy one, and take it by the hour. And ,don't you imagine anything . . ."

"And are you meaning to go far away, sir?"

"I don't know, my lad, I don't know that either. I think you had better pack my feather bed too. What do you think, my lad? I am relying on you, my dear fellow . . ."

"Is your honour setting off at once?"

"Yes, my friend, yes! Circumstances have turned out so . . . so it is, my dear fellow, so it is . . ."

"To be sure, sir; when we were in the regiment the same thing happened to the lieutenant; they eloped from a country gentleman's . . ." "Eloped? . . . How! My dear fellow!"

"Yes, sir, eloped, and they were married in another house. Everything was got ready beforehand. There was a hue and cry after them; the late prince took their part, and so it was all settled . . ."

"They were married, but . . . how is it, my dear fellow. . . . How did you come to know, my boy?"

"Why, to be sure! The earth is full of rumours, sir. We know, sir, we've all . . . to be sure, there's no one without sin. Only I'll tell you now, sir, let me speak plainly and vulgarly, sir; since it has come to this, I must tell you, sir; you have an enemy—you've a rival, sir, a powerful rival, so there . . ."

"I know, my dear fellow, I know; you know yourself, my dear fellow. . . . So, you see, I'm relying upon you. What are we to do now, my friend! How do you advise me?"

"Well, sir, if you are in that way now, if you've come, so to say, to such a pass, sir, you'll have to make some purchases, sir—say some sheets, pillows, another feather bed, a double one, a good quilt—here at the neighbours' downstairs—she's a shopkeeper, sir—she has a good fox-fur cloak, so you might look at it and buy it, you might have a look at it at once. You'll need it now, sir; it's a good cloak, sir, satin-lined with fox. . ."

"Very good, my lad, very good, I agree; I rely upon you, I rely upon you entirely; a cloak by all means, if necessary. . . . Only make haste, make haste! For God's sake make haste! I'll buy the cloak—only please make haste! It will soon be eight o'clock. Make haste for God's sake, my dear lad! Hurry up, my lad. . ."

Petrushka ran to gather together a bundle of linen, pillows, quilt, sheets, and all sorts of odds and ends, tied them up and rushed head-long out of the room. Meanwhile, Mr. Golyadkin seized the letter once more, but he could not read it. Clutching his devoted head, he leaned against the wall in a state of stupefaction. He could not think of anything, he could do nothing either, and could not even tell what was happening to him. At last, seeing that time was passing and neither Petrushka nor the fur cloak had made their appearance, Mr. Golyadkin made up his mind to go himself. Opening the door into the entry, he heard below noise, talk, disputing, scuffling. . . . Several of the women of the neighbouring flats were shouting, talking and protesting about something—Mr. Golyadkin knew what. Petrushka's voice was heard: then there was a sound of footsteps.

"My goodness! They'll bring all the world in here," moaned Mr. Golyadkin, wringing his hands in despair and rushing back into his room. Running back into his room, he fell almost senseless on the sofa with his face in the pillow. After lying a minute in this way, he jumped up and, without waiting for Petrushka, he put on his goloshes, his hat and his greatcoat, snatched up his papers and ran headlong downstairs.

"Nothing is wanted, nothing, my dear fellow! I will manage myself—everything myself. I don't need you for the time, and meantime, things may take a better turn, perhaps," Mr. Golyadkin muttered to Petrushka, meeting him on the stairs; then he ran out into the yard, away from the house. There was a faintness at his heart, he had not yet made up his mind what was his position, what he was to do, how he was to act in the present critical position.

"Yes, how am I to act? Lord, have mercy on me! And that all this should happen!" he cried out at last in despair, tottering along the street at random; "that all this must needs happen! Why, but for this, but for just this, everything would have been put right; at one stroke, at one skilful, vigorous, firm stroke it would have been set right. I would have my finger cut off to have it set right! And I know, indeed, how it would have been settled. This is how it would have been managed: I'd have gone on the spot . . . said how it was . . . `with your permission, sir, I'm neither here nor there in it . . . things aren't done like that,' I would say, `my dear sir, things aren't done like that, there's no accepting an impostor in our office; an impostor . . . my dear sir, is a man . . . who is worth-less and of no service to his country. Do you understand that? Do you understand that, my dear sir,' I should say! That's how it would be. . . . But no . . . after all, things are not like that . . . not a bit like that. . . , I am talking nonsense, like a fool! A suicidal fool! It's not like that at all, you suicidal fool. . . . This is how things are done, though, you profligate man! . . . Well, what am I to do with myself now? Well, what am I going to do with myself now. What am I fit for now? Come, what are you fit for now, for instance, you, Golyadkin, you, you worthless fellow! Well, what now? I must get a carriage; `hire a carriage and bring it here,' says she, 'we shall get our feet wet without a carriage,' says she. . . . And who could ever have thought it! Fie, fie, my young lady! Fie, fie, a young lady of virtuous behaviour! Well, well, the girl we all thought so much of! You've distinguished yourself, madam, there's no doubt of that! you've distinguished yourself! . . . And it all comes from immoral education. And now that I've looked into it and seen through it all I see that it is due to nothing else but immorality. Instead of looking after her as a child . . . and the rod at times . . . they stuff her with sweets and dainties, and the old man is always doting over her:

saying 'my dear, my love, my beauty,' saying, 'we'll marry you to a count!' . . . And now she has come forward herself and shown her cards, as though to say that's her little game! Instead of keeping her at home as a child, they sent her to a boarding-school, to a French madame, an emigree, a Madame Falbalas or something, and she learned all sorts of things at that Madame Falbalas', and this is how it always turns out. 'Come,' says she, 'and be happy! Be in a carriage,' she says, 'at such a time, under the windows, and sing a sentimental serenade in the Spanish style; I await you and I know you love me, and we will fly together and live in a hut.' But the fact is it's impossible; since it has come to that, madam, it's impossible, it is against the law to abduct an innocent, respectable girl from her parents' roof without their sanction! And, if you come to that, why, what for and what need is there to do it? Come, she should marry a suitable person, the man marked out by destiny, and that would be the end of it. But I'm in the government service, I might lose my berth through it: I might be arrested for it, madam! I tell you that! If you did not know it. It's that German woman's doing. She's at the bottom of it all, the witch; she cooked the whole kettle of fish. For they've slandered a man, for they've invented a bit of womanish gossip about him, a regular performance by the advice of Andrey Filippovitch, that's what it came from. Otherwise how could Petrushka be mixed up in it? What has he to do with it? What need for that rogue to be in it? No, I cannot, madam, I cannot possibly, not on any account. . . . No, madam, this time you must really excuse me. It's all your doing, madam, it's not all the German's doing, it's not the witch's doing at all, but simply yours. For the witch is a good woman, for the witch is not to blame in any way; it's your fault, madam; it's you who are to blame, let me tell you! I shall be charged with a crime through you, madam. . . . A man might be ruined . . . a man might lose sight of himself, and not be able to restrain himself—a wedding, indeed! And how is it all going to end? And how will it all be arranged? I would give a great deal to know all that! . . ."

So our hero reflected in his despair. Coming to himself suddenly, he observed that he was standing somewhere in Liteyny Street. The weather was awful: it was a thaw; snow and rain were falling—just as at that memorable time when at the dread hour of midnight all Mr. Golyadkin's troubles had begun. "This is a nice night for a journey!" thought Mr. Golyadkin, looking at the weather; "it's death all round. . . . Good Lord! Where am I to find a carriage, for instance? I believe there's something black there at the corner. We'll see, we'll investigate. . . . Lord, have mercy on us!" our hero went on, bending his weak and tottering steps in the direction in which he saw something that looked like a cab.

"No, I know what I'll do; I'll go straight and fall on my knees, if I can, and humbly beg, saying 'I put my fate in your hands, in the hands of my superiors'; saying, 'Your Excellency, be a protector and a benefactor'; and then I'll say this and that, and explain how it is and that it is an unlawful act; 'Do not destroy me, I look upon you as my father, do not abandon me . . . save my dignity, my honour, my name, my reputation . . . and save me from a miscreant, a vicious man. . . . He's another person, your Excellency, and I'm another person too; he's apart and I am myself by myself too; I am really myself by myself, your Excellency; really myself by myself,' that's what I shall say. 'I cannot be like him. Change him, dismiss him, give orders for him to be changed and a god-less, licentious impersonation to be suppressed . . . that it may not be an example to others, your Excellency. I look upon you as a father'; those in authority over us, our benefactors and protectors, are bound, of course, to encourage such impulses. . . . There's something chivalrous about it: I shall say, 'I look upon you, my benefactor and superior, as a father, and trust my fate to you, and I will not say anything against it; I put myself in your hands, and retire from the affair myself' . . . that's what I would say."

"Well, my man, are you a cabman?"

"Yes. . ."

"I want a cab for the evening . . ."

"And does your honour want to go far?"

"For the evening, for the evening; wherever I have to go, my man, wherever I have to go."

"Does your honour want to drive out of town?"

"Yes, my friend, out of town, perhaps. I don't quite know myself yet, I can't tell you for certain, my man. Maybe you see it will all be settled for the best. We all know, my friend . . ."

"Yes, sir, of course we all know. Please God it may."

"Yes, my friend, yes; thank you, my dear fellow; come, what's your fare, my good man? . . ."

"Do you want to set off at once?"

"Yes, at once, that is, no, you must wait at a certain place. . . . A little while, not long, you'll have to wait . . ."

"Well, if you hire me for the whole time, I couldn't ask less than six roubles for weather like this . . ."

"Oh, very well, my friend; and I thank you, my dear fellow. So, come, you can take me now, my good man."

"Get in; allow me, I'll put it straight a bit—now will your honour get in. Where shall I drive?"

"To the Ismailovsky Bridge, my friend."

The driver plumped down on the box, with difficulty roused his pair of lean nags from the trough of hay, and was setting off for Ismailovsky Bridge. But suddenly Mr. Golyadkin pulled the cord, stopped the cab, and besought him in an imploring voice not to drive to Ismailovsky Bridge, but to turn back to another street. The driver turned into another street, and ten minutes later Mr. Golyadkin's newly hired equipage was standing before the house in which his Excellency had a flat. Mr. Golyadkin got out of the carriage, begged the driver to be sure to wait and with a sinking heart ran upstairs to the third storey and pulled the bell; the door was opened and our hero found himself in the entry of his Excellency's flat.

"Is his Excellency graciously pleased to be at home?" said Mr. Golyadkin, addressing the man who opened the door.

"What do you want?" asked the servant, scrutinizing Mr. Golyadkin from head to foot.

"I, my friend . . I am Golyadkin, the titular councilor, Golyadkin. . . . T o say . . . something or other . . . to explain."

"You must wait; you cannot . . ."

"My friend, I cannot wait; my business is important, it's business that admits of no delay . . ."

"But from whom have you come? Have you brought papers? . .
"No, my friend, I am on my own account. Announce me, my friend, say something or other, explain. I'll reward you, my good man . . ."

"I cannot. His Excellency is not at home, he has visitors. Come at ten o'clock in the morning . . ."

"Take in my name, my good man, I can't wait—it is impossible. . . . You'll have to answer for it, my good man."

"Why, go and announce him! What's the matter with you; want to save your shoe leather?" said another lackey, who was lolling on the bench and had not uttered a word till then.

"Shoe leather! I was told not to show any one up, you know; their time is the morning."

"Announce him, have you lost your tongue?"

"I'll announce him all right—I've not lost my tongue. It's not my orders; I've told you, it's not my orders. Walk inside."

Mr. Golyadkin went into the outermost room; there was a clock on the table. He glanced at it: it was half-past eight. His heart ached within him. Already he wanted to turn back, but at that very moment the footman standing at the door of the next room had already boomed out Mr. Golyadkin's name.

"Oh what lungs." Thought our hero in indescribable misery. "Why, you ought to have said: `he has come most humbly and meekly to make an explanation . . . something . . . be graciously pleased to see him.' . . . Now the whole business is ruined; all my hopes are scattered to the winds. But . . . however . . . never mind. . . ."

There was no time to think, moreover. The lackey, returning, said, "Please walk in," and led Mr. Golyadkin into the study.

When our hero went in, he felt as though he were blinded, for he could see nothing at all. . . . But three or four figures seemed flitting before his eyes: "Oh, yes, they are the visitors," flashed through Mr. Golyadkin's mind. At last our hero could distinguish clearly the star on the black coat of his Excellency, then by degrees advanced to seeing the black coat and at last gained the power of complete vision. . . .

"What is it?" said a familiar voice above Mr. Golyadkin.

"The titular councilor, Golyadkin, your Excellency."

"Well?"

"I have come to make an explanation . . ."

"How? . . . What?"

"Why, yes. This is how it is. I've come for an explanation, your Excellency . . ."

"But you . . . but who are you? . . ."

"M—m—m—mist—er Golyadkin, your Excellency, a titular councilor."

"Well, what is it you want?"

"Why, this is how it is, I look upon you as a father; I retire . . . defend me from my enemy! . . ."

"What's this? . . ."

"We all know . . ."

"What do we all know?"

Mr. Golyadkin was silent: his chin began twitching a little. "Well?"

"I thought it was chivalrous, your Excellency. . . . 'There's something chivalrous in it,' I said, 'and I look upon my superior as a father' . . . this is what I thought; 'protect me, I tear . . . earfully . . . b . . . beg and that such imp . . . impulses ought . . . to . . . be encouraged . . .'"

His Excellency turned away, our hero for some minutes could distinguish nothing. There was a weight on his chest. His breathing was labored; he did not know where he was standing. . . . He felt ashamed and sad. God knows what followed. . . . Recovering himself, our hero noticed that his Excellency was talking with his guests, and seemed to be briskly and emphatically discussing something with them. One of the visitors Mr. Golyadkin recognized at once. This was Audrey Filippovitch; he knew no one else; yet there was another person that seemed familiar—a tall, thick-set figure, middle-aged, possessed of very thick eyebrows and whiskers and a significant sharp expression. On his chest was an order and in his mouth a cigar. This gentleman was smoking and nodding significantly without taking the cigar out of his mouth, glancing from time to time at Mr. Golyadkin. Mr. Golyadkin felt awkward; he turned away his eyes and immediately saw another very strange visitor. Through a door which our hero had taken for a looking-glass, just as he had done once before—he made his appearance—we know who: a very intimate friend and acquaintance of Mr. Golyadkin's. Mr. Golyadkin junior had actually been till then in a little room close by, hurriedly writing something; now, apparently, he was needed—and he came in with papers under his arm, went up to his Excellency, and while Waiting for exclusive attention to be paid him succeeded very adroitly in putting his spoke into the talk and consultation, taking his place a little behind Audrey Filippovitch's back and partly screening him from the gentleman smoking the cigar. Apparently Mr. Golyadkin junior took an extreme interest in the conversation, to which he was listening now in a gentlemanly way, nodding his head, fidgeting with his feet, smiling, continually looking at his Excellency—as it were beseeching him with his eyes to let him put his word in.

"The scoundrel," thought Mr. Golyadkin, and involuntarily he took a step forward. At this moment his Excellency turned round, and came rather hesitatingly towards Mr. Golyadkin.

"Well, that's all right, that's all right; well, run along, now. I'll look into your case, and give orders for you to be taken. . ."

At this point his Excellency glanced at the gentleman with the thick whiskers. The latter nodded in assent.

Mr. Golyadkin felt and distinctly understood that they were taking him for something different and not looking at him in the proper light at all.

"In one way or another I must explain myself," he thought; "I must say, 'This is how it is, your Excellency."

At this point in his perplexity he dropped his eyes to the floor and to his great astonishment he saw a good-sized patch of something white on his Excellency's boots.

"Can there be a hole in them?" thought Mr. Golyadkin. Mr. Golyadkin was, however, soon convinced that his Excellency's boots were-not split, but were only shining brilliantly—a phenomenon fully explained by the fact that they were patent leather and highly polished.

"It is what they call blick," thought our hero; "the term is used particularly in artists' studios; in other places such a reflected light is called a rib of light."

At this point Mr. Golyadkin raised his eyes and saw that the time had come to speak, for things might easily end badly.

Our hero took a step forward.

"I say this is how it is, your Excellency," he said, "and there's no accepting impostors nowadays."

His Excellency made no answer, but rang the bell violently. Our hero took another step forward.

"He is a vile, vicious man, your Excellency," said our hero, beside himself and faint with terror, though he still pointed boldly and resolutely at his unworthy twin, who was fidgeting about near his Excellency. "I say this is how it is, and I am alluding to a well-known person."

There was a general sensation at Mr. Golyadkin's words. Audrey Filippovitch and the gentleman with the cigar nodded their heads; his Excellency impatiently tugged at the bell to summon the servants. At this point Mr. Golyadkin junior came forward in his turn.

"Your Excellency," he said, "I humbly beg permission to speak." There was something very resolute in Mr. Golyadkin junior's voice; everything showed that he felt himself completely in the right.

"Allow me to ask you," he began again, anticipating his Excellency's reply in his eagerness, and this time addressing Mr. Golyadkin; "allow me to ask you, in whose presence you are making this explanation? Before whom are you standing, in whose room are you? . . ."

Mr. Golyadkin junior was in a state of extraordinary excitement, flushed and glowing with wrath and indignation; there were positively tears in his eyes.

A lackey, appearing in the doorway, roared at the top of his voice the name of some new arrivals, the Bassavryukovs.

"A good aristocratic name, hailing from Little Russia," thought Mr. Golyadkin, and at that moment he felt some one lay a very friendly hand on his back, then a second hand was laid on his back. Mr. Golyadkin's infamous twin was tripping about in front leading the way; and our hero saw clearly that he was being led to the big doors of the room.

"Just as it was at Olsufy Ivanovitch's," he thought, and he found himself in the hall. Looking round, he saw beside him two of his Excellency's lackeys and his twin.

"The greatcoat, the greatcoat, the greatcoat, the greatcoat, my friend! The greatcoat of my best friend!" whispered the depraved man, snatching the coat from one of the servants, and by way of a nasty and ungentlemanly joke flinging it straight at Mr. Golyadkin's head. Extricating himself from under his coat, Mr. Golyadkin distinctly heard the two lackeys snigger. But without listening to anything, or paying attention to it, he went out of the hall and found himself on the lighted stairs, Mr. Golyadkin junior following him.

"Good-bye, your Excellency!" he shouted after Mr. Golyadkin senior.

"Scoundrel!" our hero exclaimed, beside himself.

'Well, scoundrel, then . . ."

"Depraved man! . . ."

"Well, depraved man, then . . ." answered Mr. Golyadkin's unworthy enemy, and with his characteristic baseness he looked down from the top of the stairs straight into Mr. Golyadkin's face as though begging him to go on. Our hero spat with indignation and ran out of the front door; he was so shattered, so crushed, that he had no recollection of how he got into the cab or who helped him in. Coming to himself, he found that he was being driven to Fontanka. "To Ismailovsky Bridge, then," thought Mr. Golyadkin. At this point Mr. Golyadkin tried to think of something else, but could not; there was something so terrible that he could not explain it. . . . "Well, never mind," our hero concluded, and he drove to Ismailovsky Bridge.

CHAPTER XIII

It seemed as though the weather meant to change for the better. The snow, which had till then been coming down in regular clouds, began growing less and less and at last almost ceased. The sky became visible and here and there tiny stars sparkled in it. It was only wet, muddy, damp and stifling, especially for Mr. Golyadkin, who could hardly breathe as it was. His greatcoat, soaked and heavy with wet, sent a sort of unpleasant warm dampness all through him and weighed down his exhausted legs. A feverish shiver sent sharp, shooting pains all over him; he was in a painful cold sweat of exhaustion, so much so that Mr. Golyadkin even forgot to repeat at every suitable occasion with his characteristic firmness and resolution his favourite phrase that "it all, maybe, most likely, indeed, might turn out for the best." "But all this does not matter for the time," our hero repeated, still staunch and not downhearted, wiping from his face the cold drops that streamed in all directions from the brim of his round hat, which was so soaked that it could hold no more water. Adding that all this was nothing so far, our hero tried to sit on a rather thick clump of wood, which was lying near a heap of logs in Olsufy Ivanovitch's yard. Of course, it was no good thinking of Spanish serenades or silken ladders, but it was. quite necessary to think of a modest corner, snug and private, if not altogether warm. He felt greatly tempted, we may mention in passing, by that corner in the back entry of Olsufy Ivanovitch's flat in which he had once, almost at the beginning of this true story, stood for two hours between a cupboard and an old screen among all sorts of domestic odds and ends and useless litter. The fact is that Mr. Golyadkin had been standing waiting for two whole hours on this occasion in Olsufy Ivanovitch's yard. But in regard to that modest and snug little corner there were certain drawbacks which had not existed before. The first drawback was the fact that it was probably now a marked place and that certain pre-cautionary measures had been taken in regard to it since the scandal at Olsufy Ivanovitch's last ball. Secondly, he had to wait for a signal from Klara Olsufyevna, for there was bound to be some such signal, it was always a feature in such cases and, "it didn't begin with us and it won't end with us."

At this point Mr. Golyadkin very appropriately remembered a novel he had read long ago in which the heroine, in precisely similar circumstances, signaled to Alfred by tying a pink ribbon to her window. But now, at night, in the climate of Petersburg, famous for its dampness and unreliability, a pink ribbon was hardly appropriate and, in fact, was utterly out of the question.

"No, it's not a matter of silk ladders," thought our hero, "and I had better stay here quietly and comfortably. . . . I had better stand here."

And he selected a place in the yard exactly opposite the window, near a stack of firewood. Of course, many persons, grooms and coachmen, were continually crossing the yard, and there was, besides, the rumbling of wheels and the snorting of horses and so on; yet it was a convenient place, whether he was observed or not; but now, anyway, there was the advantage of being to some extent in shadow, and no one could see Mr. Golyadkin while he himself could see everything.

The windows were brightly lit up, there was some sort of ceremonious party at Olsufy Ivanovitch's. But he could hear no music as yet.

"So it's not a ball, but a party of some other sort," thought our hero, somewhat aghast. "Is it today?" floated the doubt through him. "Have I made a mistake in the date? Perhaps; anything is possible. . . . Yes, to be sure, anything is possible. . . . Perhaps she wrote a letter to me yesterday, and it didn't reach me, and perhaps it did not reach me because Petrushka put his spoke in, the rascal! Or it was tomorrow in the letter, that is, that I . . . should do everything tomorrow, that is—wait with a carriage. . . ."

At this point our hero turned cold all over and felt in his pocket for the letter, to make sure. But to his surprise the letter was not in his pocket.

"How's this?" muttered Mr. Golyadkin, more dead than alive. "Where did I leave it? Then I must have lost it. That is the last straw!" he moaned at last. "Oh, if it falls into evil hands! Perhaps it has already. Good Lord! What may it not lead to! It may lead to something such that . . . Ach, my miserable fate!" At this point Mr. Golyadkin began trembling like a leaf at the thought that perhaps his vicious twin had thrown the greatcoat at him with the object of stealing the letter of which he had somehow got an inkling from Mr. Golyadkin's enemies.

"What's more, he's stealing it," thought our hero, "as evidence . . . but why evidence! . . ."

After the first shock of horror, the blood rushed to Mr. Golyadkin's head. Moaning and gnashing his teeth, he clutched his burning head, sank back on his block of wood and relapsed into brooding. . . . But he could form no coherent thoughts. Figures kept flitting through his brain, incidents came back to his memory, now vaguely, now distinctly, the tunes of some foolish songs kept ringing in his ears. . . . He was in great distress, unnatural distress!

"My God, my God!" our hero thought, recovering himself a little, and suppressing a muffled sob, "give me fortitude in the immensity of my afflictions! That I am done for, utterly destroyed—of that there can be no doubt, and that's all in the natural order of things, since it cannot be otherwise. To begin with, I've lost my berth, I've certainly lost it, I must have lost it. . . . Well, supposing things are set right somehow. Sup-posing I have money enough to begin with: I must have another lodging, furniture of some sort. . . . In the first place, I shan't have Petrushka. I can get on without the rascal . . . somehow, with help from the people of the house; well, that will be all right! I can go in and out when I like, and Petrushka won't grumble at my coming in late—yes, that is so; that's why it's-a good thing to have the people in the house. . . . Well, supposing that's all right; but all that's nothing to do with it, all that's nothing to do with it."

At this point the thought of the real position again dawned upon Mr. Golyadkin's memory. He looked round.

"Oh, Lord, have mercy on me, have mercy on me! What am I talking about?" he thought, growing utterly desperate and clutching his burning head in his hands. . . .

"Won't you soon be going, sir?" a voice pronounced above Mr. Golyadkin. Our hero started; before him stood his cabman, who was also drenched through and shivering; growing impatient, and having nothing to do, he had thought fit to take a look at Mr. Golyadkin behind the woodstack.

"I am all right, my friend. . . . I am coming soon, soon, very soon; you wait. . . ."

The cabman walked away, grumbling to himself. "What is he grumbling about?" Mr. Golyadkin wondered through his tears.

"Why, I have hired him for the evening, why, I'm . . . within my rights now . . . that's so! I've hired him for the evening, and that's the end of it. If one stands still, it's just the same. That's for me to decide. I am free to drive on or not to drive on. And my staying here by the woodstack has nothing to do with the case . . . and don't dare to say anything; think, the gentle-man wants to stand behind the woodstack, and so he's standing behind it . . . and he is not disgracing any one's honour! That's the fact of the matter.

"I tell you what it is, madam, if you care to know. Nowadays, madam, nobody lives in a hut, or anything of that sort. No, indeed. And in our industrial age there's no getting on without morality, a fact of which you are a fatal example, madam. . . . You say we must get a job as a register clerk and live in a hut on the sea-shore. In the first place, madam, there are no register clerks on the sea-shore, and in the second place we can't get a job as a register clerk. For supposing, for example, I send in a petition, present myself—saying a register clerk's place or something of the sort . . . and defend me from my enemy . . . they'll tell you, madam, they'll say, to be sure . . . we've lots of register clerks, and here you are not at Madame Falbalas', where you learnt the rules of good behaviour of which you are such a fatal example. Good behaviour, madam, means staying at home, honouring your father and not thinking about suitors prematurely. Suitors will come in good time, madam, that's so! Of course, you are bound to have some accomplishments, such as playing the piano sometimes, speaking French, history, geography, scripture and arithmetic, that's the truth of it! And that's all you need. Cooking, too, cooking certainly forms part of the education of a well-behaved girl! But as it is, in the first place, my fine lady, they won't let you go, they'll raise a hue and cry after you, and then they'll lock you up in a nunnery. How will it be then, madam? What will you have me do then? Would you have me, madam, follow the example of some stupid novels, and melt into tears on a neighboring hillock, gazing at the cold walls of your prison house, and finally die, following the example of some wretched German poets and novelists. Is that it, madam? But, to begin with, allow me to tell you, as a friend, that things are not done like that, and in the second place I would have given you and your parents, too, a good thrashing for letting you read French books; for French books teach you no good. There's a poison in them . . . a pernicious poison, madam! Or do you imagine, allow me to ask you, or do you imagine that we shall elope with impunity, or something of that sort . . . that we shall have a hut on the shore of the sea and so on; and that we shall begin billing and cooing and talking about our feelings, and that so we shall spend our lives in happiness and content; and then there would be little ones-so then we shall . . . shall go to our father, the civil concilor, Olsufy Ivanovitch, and say 'we've got a little one, and so, on this propitious occasion remove your curse, and bless the couple.' No, madam, I tell you again, that's not the way to do things, and for the first thing there'll be no billing and cooing and please don't reckon on it. Nowadays, madam, the husband is the master and a good, well brought-up wife should try and please him in every way. And endearments, madam, are not in favour, nowadays, in our industrial age; the day of Jean Jacques Rousseau is over. The husband comes home, for instance, hungry from the office, and asks, 'Isn't there something to eat, my love, a drop of vodka to drink, a bit of salt fish to eat?' So then, madam, you must have the vodka and the herring ready. Your husband will eat it with relish, and he won't so much as look at you, he'll only say 'Run into the kitchen, kitten,' he'll say, 'and look after the dinner,' and at most, once a week, he'll kiss you, even then rather indifferently. . . . That's how it will be with us, my young lady! Yes, even then indifferently. . . . That's how it will be, if one considers it, if it has come to one's looking at the thing in that way. . . . And how do I come in? Why have you mixed me up in your caprices? 'The noble man who is suffering for your sake and will be dear to your heart for ever,' and so on. But in the first place, madam, I am not suited to you, you know yourself, I'm not a great hand at compliments, I'm not fond of uttering perfumed trifles for the ladies. I'm not fond of lady-killers, and I must own I've never been a beauty to look at. You won't find any swagger or false shame in me, and I tell you so now in all sincerity. This is the fact of the matter: we can boast of nothing but a straightforward, open character and common sense; we have nothing to do with intrigues. I am not one to intrigue, I say so and I'm proud of it—that's the fact of the matter! . . . I wear no mask among straightforward people, and to tell you the whole truth . . ."

Suddenly Mr. Golyadkin started. The red and perfectly sopping beard of the cabman appeared round the woodstack again. . . .

"I am coming directly, my friend. I'm coming at once, you know," Mr. Golyadkin responded in a trembling and failing voice.

The cabman scratched his head, then stroked his beard, and moved a step forward . . . stood still and looked suspiciously at Mr. Golyadkin.

"I am coming directly, my friend; you see, my friend . . . I just a little, you see, only a second! . . . more . . . here, you see, my friend. . . ."

"Aren't you coming at all?" the cabman asked at last, definitely coming up to Mr. Golyadkin.

"No, my friend, I'm coming directly. I am waiting, you see, my friend. . . ."

"So I see. . . ."

"You see, my friend, I . . . What part of the country do you come from, my friend?"

"We are under a master . . ."

"And have you a good master? . . ."

"All right. . . ."

"Yes, my friend; you stay here, my friend, you see . . . Have you been in Petersburg long, my friend?"

"It's a year since I came. . . ."

"And are you getting on all right, my friend?"

"Middling."

"To be sure, my friend, to be sure. You must thank Providence, my friend. You must look out for straightforward people. Straightforward people are none too common nowadays, my friend; he would give you washing, food, and drink, my good fellow, a good man would. But sometimes you see tears shed for the sake of gold, my friend . . . you see a lamentable example; that's the fact of the matter, my friend. ."

The cabman seemed to feel sorry for Mr. Golyadkin. "Well, your honour, I'll wait. Will your honour be waiting long?"

"No, my friend, no; I . . . you know . . . I won't wait any longer, my good man. . . . What do you think, my friend? I rely upon you. I won't stay any longer."

"Aren't you going at all?"

"No, my friend, no; I'll reward you, my friend . . . that's the fact of the matter. How much ought I to give you, my dear fellow?"

"What you hired me for, please, sir. I've been waiting here a long time; don't be hard on a man, sir."

"Well, here, my good man, here."

At this point Mr. Golyadkin gave six whole roubles to the cabman, and made up his mind in earnest to waste no more time, that is, to clear off straight away, especially as the cabman was dismissed and everything was over, and so it was useless to wait longer. He rushed out of the yard, went out of the gate, turned to the left and without looking round took to his heels, breathless and rejoicing. "Perhaps it will all be for the best," he thought, "and perhaps in this way I've run away from trouble." Mr. Golyadkin suddenly became all at once lighthearted. "Oh, if only it could turn out for the best!" thought our hero, though he put little faith in his own words. "I know what I'll do . . ." he thought. "No, I know, I'd better try the other tack. . . . Or wouldn't it be better to do this? . . ." In this way, hesitating and seeking for the solution of his doubts, our hero ran to Semyonovsky Bridge; but while running to Semyonovsky Bridge he very rationally and conclusively decided to return.

"It will be better so," he thought. "I had better try the other tack, that is . . . I will just go—I'll look on simply as an outsider, and that will be the end of it; I am simply an onlooker, an outsider—and nothing more, whatever happens—it's not my fault, that's the fact of the matter! That's how it shall be now."

Deciding to return, our hero actually did return, the more readily because with this happy thought he conceived of himself now as quite an outsider.

"It's the best thing; one's not responsible for anything, and one will see all that's necessary . . . that's the fact of the matter!"

It was a safe plan and that settled it. Reassured, he crept back under the peaceful shelter of his soothing and protecting woodstack, and began gazing intently at the window. This time he was not destined to gaze and wait for long. Suddenly a strange commotion became apparent at all the windows. Figures appeared, curtains were drawn back, whole groups of people were crowding to the windows at Olsufy Ivanovitch's flat. All were peeping out looking for something in the yard. From the security of his woodstack, our hero, too, began with curiosity watching the general commotion, and with interest craned forward to right and to left so far as he could within the shadow of the woodstack. Suddenly he started, held his breath and almost sat down with horror. It seemed to him—in short, he realized, that they were looking for nothing and for nobody but him, Mr. Golyadkin! Every one was looking in his direction. It was impossible to escape; they saw him. . . . In a flutter, Mr. Golyadkin huddled as closely as he could to the woodstack, and only then noticed that the treacherous shadow had betrayed him, that it did not cover him completely. Our hero would have been delighted at that moment to creep into a mouse-hole in the woodstack, and there meekly to remain, if only it had been possible.

But it was absolutely impossible. In his agony he began at last staring openly and boldly at the windows, it was the best thing to do. . . . And suddenly he glowed with shame. He had been fully discovered, every one was staring at him at once, they were all waving their hands, all were nodding their heads at him, all were calling to him; then several windows creaked as they opened, several voices shouted something to him at once. . . .

"I wonder why they don't whip these naughty girls as children," our hero muttered to himself, losing his head completely. Suddenly there ran down the steps he (we know who), without his hat or greatcoat, breathless, rubbing his hands, wriggling, capering, perfidiously displaying intense joy at seeing Mr. Golyadkin.

"Yakov Petrovitch," whispered this individual, so notorious for his worthlessness, "Yakov Petrovitch, are you here? You'll catch cold. It's chilly here, Yakov Petrovitch. Come indoors."

"Yakov Petrovitch! No, I'm all right, Yakov Petrovitch," our hero muttered in a submissive voice.

"No, this won't do, Yakov Petrovitch, I beg you, I humbly beg you to wait with us. 'Make him welcome and bring him in,' they say, 'Yakov Petrovitch..'"

"No, Yakov Petrovitch, you see, I'd better. . . . I had better go home, Yakov Petrovitch . . ." said our hero, burning at a slow fire and freezing at the same time with shame and terror.

"No—no—no—no!" whispered the loathsome person. "No—no no, on no account! Come along," he said resolutely, and he dragged Mr. Golyadkin senior to the steps. Mr. Golyadkin senior did not at all want to go, but as every one was looking at them, it would have been stupid to struggle and resist; so our hero went—though, indeed, one cannot say that he went, because he did not know in the least what was being done with him. Though, after all, it made no difference!

Before our hero had time to recover himself and come to his senses, he found himself in the drawing-room. He was pale, disheveled, harassed; with lusterless eyes he scanned the crowd—horror! The drawing-room, all the rooms—were full to overflowing. There were masses of people, a whole galaxy of ladies; and all were crowding round Mr. Golyadkin, all were pressing towards Mr. Golyadkin, all were squeezing Mr. Golyadkin and he perceived clearly that they were all forcing him in one direction.

"Not towards the door," was the thought that floated through Mr. Golyadkin's mind.

They were, in fact, forcing him not towards the door but Olsufy Ivanovitch's easy chair. On one side of the armchair stood Klara Olsufyevna, pale, languid, melancholy, but gorgeously dressed. Mr. Golyadkin was particularly struck by a little white flower which rested on her superb hair. On the other side of the armchair stood Vladimir Semyonovitch, clad in black, with his new order in his buttonhole. Mr. Golyadkin was led in, as we have described above, straight up to Olsufy Ivanovitch—on one side of him Mr. Golyadkin junior, who had assumed an air of great decorum and propriety, to the immense relief of our hero, while on the other side was Andrey Filippovitch, with a very solemn expression on his face.

"What can it mean?" Mr. Golyadkin wondered.

When he saw that he was being led to Olsufy Ivanovitch, an idea struck him like a flash of lightning. The thought of the intercepted letter darted through his brain. In great agony our hero stood before Olsufy Ivanovitch's chair.

"What will he say now?" he wondered to himself. "Of course, it will be. all aboveboard now, that is, straightforward and, one may say, honourable; I shall say this is how it is, and so on."

But what our hero apparently feared did not happen. Olsufy Ivanovitch received Mr. Golyadkin very warmly, and though he did not hold out his hand to him, yet as he gazed at our hero, he shook his grey and venerable head—shook it with an air of solemn melancholy and yet of goodwill. So, at least, it seemed to Mr. Golyadkin. He even fancied that a tear glittered in Olsufy Ivanovitch's lusterless eyes; he raised his eyes and saw that there seemed to be tears, too, on the eyelashes of Klara Olsufyevna, who was standing by—that there seemed to be some-thing of the same sort even in the eyes of Vladimir Semyonovitch—that the unruffled and composed dignity of Andrey Filippovitch had the same significance as the general tearful sympathy—that even the young man who was so much like a civil councilor, seizing the opportunity, was sobbing bitterly. . . . Though perhaps this was only all Mr. Golyadkin's fancy, because he was so much moved himself, and distinctly felt the hot tears running down his cold cheeks. . . .

Feeling reconciled with mankind and his destiny, and filled with love at the moment, not only for Olsufy Ivanovitch, not only for the whole party collected there, but even for his noxious twin (who seemed now to be by no means noxious, and not even to be his twin at all, but a person very agreeable in himself and in no way connected with him), our hero, in a voice broken with sobs, tried to express his feelings to Olsufy Ivanovitch, but was too much overcome by all that he had gone through, and could not utter a word; he could only, with an expressive gesture, point meekly to his heart . . .

At last, probably to spare the feelings of the old man, Andrey Filippovitch led Mr. Golyadkin a little away, though he seemed to leave him free to do as he liked. Smiling, muttering something to himself, somewhat bewildered, yet almost completely reconciled with fate and his fellow creatures, our hero began to make his way through the crowd of guests. Every one made way for him, every one looked at him with strange curiosity and with mysterious, unaccountable sympathy. Our hero went into another room; he met with the same attention everywhere; he was vaguely conscious of the whole crowd closely following him, noting every step he took, talking in undertones among themselves of something very interesting, shaking their heads, arguing and discussing in whispers. Mr. Golyadkin wanted very much to know what they were discussing in whispers. Looking round, he saw near him Mr. Golyadkin junior. Feeling an overwhelming impulse to seize his hand and draw him aside, Mr. Golyadkin begged the other Yakov Petrovitch most particularly to cooperate with him in all his future undertakings, and not to abandon him at a critical moment. Mr. Golyadkin junior nodded his head gravely and warmly pressed the hand of Mr. Golyadkin senior. Our hero's heart was quivering with the intensity of his emotion. He was gasping for breath, however; he felt so oppressed—so oppressed; he felt that all those eyes fastened upon him were oppressing and dominating him. . . . Mr. Golyadkin caught a glimpse of the councilor who wore a wig. The latter was looking at him with a stern, searching eye, not in the least softened by the general sympathy. . . .

Our hero made up his mind to go straight up to him in order to smile at him and have an immediate explanation, but this somehow did not come off. For one instant Mr. Golyadkin became almost unconscious, almost lost all memory, all feeling.

When he came to himself again he noticed that he was the centre of a large ring formed by the rest of the party round him. Suddenly Mr. Golyadkin's name was called from the other room; the shout was at once taken up by the whole crowd. All was noise and excitement, all rushed to the door of the first room, almost carrying our hero along with them. In the crush the hard-hearted councilor in the wig was side by side with Mr. Golyadkin, and, taking our hero by the hand, he made him sit down beside him opposite Olsufy Ivanovitch, at some distance from the latter, however. Every one in the room sat down; the guests were arranged in rows round Mr. Golyadkin and Olsufy Ivanovitch.

Everything was hushed; every one preserved a solemn silence; every one was watching Olsufy Ivanovitch, evidently expecting something out of the ordinary. Mr. Golyadkin noticed that beside Olsufy Ivanovitch's chair and directly facing the councilor sat Mr. Golyadkin junior, with Andrey Filippovitch. The silence was prolonged; they were. evidently expecting something.

"Just as it is in a family when some one is setting off on a far journey. We've only to stand up and pray now," thought our hero.

Suddenly there was a general stir which interrupted Mr. Golyadkin's reflections. Something they had long been waiting for happened.

"He is coming, he is coming!" passed from one to another in the crowd.

"Who is it that is coming?" floated through Mr. Golyadkin's mind, and he shuddered at a strange sensation. "High time too!" said the councilor, looking . intently at Andrey Filippovitch. Andrey Filippovitch, for his part, glanced at Olsufy Ivanovitch. Olsufy Ivanovitch gravely and solemnly nodded his head.

"Let us stand up," said the councillor, and he made Mr. Golyadkin get up. All rose to their feet. Then the councillor took Mr. Golyadkin senior by the hand, and Andrey Filippovitch took Mr. Golyadkin junior, and in this way these two precisely similar persons were conducted through the expectant crowd surrounding them. Our hero looked about him in perplexity; but he was at once checked and his attention was called to Mr. Golyadkin junior, who was holding out his hand to him.

"They want to reconcile us," thought our hero, and with emotion he held out his hand to Mr. Golyadkin junior; and then— then bent his head forward towards him. The other Mr. Golyadkin did the same. . . .

At this point it seemed to Mr. Golyadkin senior that his perfidious friend was smiling, that he gave a sly, hurried wink to the crowd of onlookers, and that there was something sinister in the face of the worthless Mr. Golyadkin junior, that he even made a grimace at the moment of his Judas kiss. . . .

There was a ringing in Mr. Golyadkin's ears, and a darkness before his eyes; it seemed to him that an infinite multitude, an unending series of precisely similar Golyadkins were noisily bursting in at every door of the room; but it was too late . . . the resounding, treacherous kiss was over, and . .

Then quite an unexpected event occurred. . . . The door opened noisily, and in the doorway stood a man, the very sight of whom sent a chill to Mr. Golyadkin's heart. He stood rooted to the spot. A cry of horror died away in his choking throat. Yet Mr. Golyadkin knew it all beforehand, and had had a presentiment of something of the sort for a long time. The new arrival went up to Mr. Golyadkin gravely and solemnly. Mr. Golyadkin knew this personage very well. He had seen him before, had seen him very often, had seen him that day. . . . This personage was a tall, thick-set man in a black dress-coat with a good-sized cross on his breast, and was possessed of thick, very black whiskers; nothing was lacking but the cigar in the mouth to complete the picture. Yet this person's eyes, as we have mentioned already, sent a chill to the heart of Mr. Golyadkin. With a grave and solemn air this terrible man approached the pitiable hero of our story. . . . Our hero held out his hand to him; the stranger took his hand and drew him along with him. . . . With a crushed and desperate air our hero looked about him.

"It's . . . it's Krestyan Ivanovitch Rutenspitz, doctor of medicine and surgery; your old acquaintance, Yakov Petrovitch!" a detestable voice whispered in Mr. Golyadkin's ear. He looked round: it was Mr. Golyadkin's twin, so revolting in the despicable meanness of his soul. A malicious, indecent joy shone in his countenance; he was rubbing his hands with rapture, he was turning his head from side to side in ecstasy, he was fawning round every one in delight and seemed ready to dance with glee. At last he pranced forward, took a candle from one of the servants and walked in front, showing the way to Mr. Golyadkin and Krestyan Ivanovitch. Mr. Golyadkin heard the whole party in the drawing-room rush out after him, crowding and squeezing one another, and all beginning to repeat after Mr. Golyadkin himself, "It is all right, don't be afraid, Yakov Petrovitch; this is your old friend and acquaintance, you know, Krestyan Ivanovitch Rutenspitz. . . ."

At last they came out on the brightly lighted stairs; there was a crowd of people on the stairs too. The front door was thrown open noisily, and Mr. Golyadkin found himself on the steps, together with Krestyan Ivanovitch. At the entrance stood a carriage with four horses that were snorting with impatience. The malignant Mr. Golyadkin junior in three bounds flew down the stairs and opened the carriage door him-self. Krestyan Ivanovitch, with an impressive gesture, asked Mr. Golyadkin to get in. There was no need of the impressive gesture, however; there were plenty of people to help him in. . . . Faint with horror, Mr. Golyadkin looked back. The whole of the brightly lighted staircase was crowded with people; inquisitive eyes were looking at him from all sides; Olsufy Ivanovitch himself was sitting in his easy chair on the top landing, and watching all that took place with deep interest. Every one was waiting. A murmur of impatience passed through the crowd when Mr. Golyadkin looked back.

"I hope I have done nothing . . . nothing reprehensible . . . or that can call for severity . . . and general attention in regard to my official relations," our hero brought out in desperation. A clamor of talk rose all round him, all were shaking their heads, tears started from Mr. Golyadkin's eyes.

"In that case I'm ready. . . . I have full confidence . . . and I entrust my fate to Krestyan Ivanovitch. . . ."

No sooner had Mr. Golyadkin declared that he entrusted his fate to Krestyan Ivanovitch than a dreadful, deafening shout of joy came from all surrounding him and was repeated in a sinister echo through the whole of the waiting crowd. Then Krestyan Ivanovitch on one side and Andrey Filippovitch on the other helped Mr. Golyadkin into the carriage; his double, in his usual nasty way, was helping to get him in from behind. The unhappy Mr. Golyadkin senior took his last look on all and everything, and, shivering like a kitten that has been drenched with cold water—if the comparison may be permitted—got into the carriage. Krestyan Ivanovitch followed him in immediately. The carriage door slammed. There was a swish of the whip on the horses' backs . . . the horses started off. . . . The crowd dashed after Mr. Golyadkin. The shrill, furious shouts of his enemies pursued him by way of good wishes for his journey. For some time several persons were still running by the carriage that bore away Mr. Golyadkin; but by degrees they were left behind, till at last they had all disappeared. Mr. Golyadkin's unworthy twin kept up longer than any one. With his hands in the trouser pockets of his green uniform he ran on with a satisfied air, skipping first to one and then to the other side of the carriage, sometimes catching hold of the window-frame and hanging on by it, poking his head in at the window, and throwing farewell kisses to Mr. Golyadkin. But he began to get tired, he was less and less often to be seen, and at last vanished altogether. There was a dull ache in Mr. Golyadkin's heart; a hot rush of blood set Mr. Golyadkin's head throbbing; he felt stifled; he longed to unbutton himself—to bare his breast, to cover it with snow and pour cold water on it. He sank at last into forgetfulness. . . .

When he came to himself, he saw that the horses were taking him along an unfamiliar road. There were dark patches of copse on each side of it; it was desolate and deserted. Suddenly he almost swooned; two fiery eyes were staring at him in the darkness, and those two eyes were glittering with malignant, hellish glee. "That's not Krestyan Ivanovitch! Who is it? Or is it he? It is. It is Krestyan Ivanovitch, but not the old Krestyan Ivanovitch, it's another Krestyan Ivanovitch! It's a terrible Krestyan Ivanovitch! . . ."

"Krestyan Ivanovitch, I . . . I believe . . . I'm all right, Krestyan Ivanovitch," our hero was beginning timidly in a trembling voice, hoping by his meekness and submission to soften the terrible Krestyan Ivanovitch a little.

"You get free quarters, wood, with light, and service, the which you deserve not," Krestyan Ivanovitch's answer rang out, stem and terrible as a judge's sentence.

Our hero shrieked and clutched his head in his hands. Alas! For a long while he had been haunted by a presentiment of this.

www.ingramcontent.com/pod-product-compliance
Lightning Source LLC
LaVergne TN
LVHW010146070526
838199LV00062B/4273